MANDASUE HELLER

Broke

HODDER

First published in 2013 by Hodder & Stoughton
An Hachette UK company

First published in paperback in 2013 by Hodder & Stoughton

4

A CIP catalogue record for this title is available
from the British Library

ISBN 978 0 340 96014 1

Typeset in Plantin Light by
Palimpsest Book Production Ltd, Falkirk, Stirlingshire

Printed and bound by Clays Ltd, St Ives plc

Hodder & Stoughton policy is to use papers that are natural,
renewable and recyclable products and made from wood
grown in sustainable forests. The logging and manufacturing
processes are expected to conform to the environmental
regulations of the country of origin.

Hodder & Stoughton Ltd
338 Euston Road
London NW1 3BH.

www.hodder.co.uk

Broke

About the author

Mandasue Heller was born in Cheshire and moved to Manchester in 1982. There, she found the inspiration for her novels: she spent ten years living in the infamous Hulme Crescents and has sung in cabaret and rock groups, seventies soul cover bands and blues jam bands. She still lives in the Manchester area with her musician partner.

For Win; my mum, Jean; my children, Michael, Andrew, Azzura (& Michael); and my gorgeous grandchildren, Marissa, Lariah and Antonio. Also, Ava, Amber, Martin, Jade, Reece, Kyro and Diaz, Nats and Dan, Auntie Doreen, Pete, Lorna, Cliff, Chris and Glen. And not forgetting the rest of my family, past and present, here and abroad. I love you all.

ACKNOWLEDGEMENTS

As I write the acknowledgements for this, my twelfth book, I'm finding it harder and harder to include everybody who has helped, or has meant something to me, without actually naming them all. So if you don't see your name here, please don't think that I don't appreciate everything you have done, because I do.

Much love, as always, to Win's mum and dad, his fantastic kids, his sisters, nieces, nephew, aunts and uncles.

Love also to great friends The Duchess, Liz Paton and Norman Brown. Also to Betty (and Ronnie) Schwartz, Wayne Brookes and Martina Cole, for being there from the start and helping to make my journey a smooth one.

The usual gratitude to my editor, Carolyn Caughey, for the unwavering faith, support and advice you've given me. Also, Emma, Lucy, Auriol, Emilie, Francine – and the rest of the brilliant Hodder team. And not forgetting Phil Pelham, who has spent many an hour driving me and Win around without ever once complaining.

Massive thanks to Jeffery Deaver for taking the time to read my last book – and being generous enough to give me such a wonderful review.

Immeasurable thanks to Cat Ledger – for everything.
And thanks also to Nick Austin.

I can't leave out the fantastic buyers from Waterstone's, W.H. Smith, Asda, etc, who have supported me so fantastically. And a huge thank-you to you, the readers, for making this worthwhile.

And, lastly, a special thank-you to Jac and Brian Capron, and the rest of my FB&T friends, for the amazing support you have shown me over this last year. You guys rock!

'For, when debts are payable, right or wrong, a short-term loan is as bad as a long . . .

So why in heaven (before we are there) should we give our hearts to a dog to tear?'

Rudyard Kipling

PROLOGUE

PROLOGUE

Lacklustre strands of tinsel lined the community centre walls, and silver balloons etched with *Mr & Mrs Taylor* bobbed limply against the ceiling above the heads of the drunken reception guests.

The DJ, 'Cheap 'n' Cheerful Chas', had been hired from an ad in the newsagent's window, and so far he'd lived up to his name in the worst possible way by spinning the biggest load of shite the guests had ever heard. But booze had a way of turning tripe into treasure, so it hadn't taken long for the mutterings of discontent to change to whoops of delight. The *Shoop Shoop Song* had brought every female in the room to her feet, and then it was down onto their boat-rowing bottoms for *Oops, Upside Your Head*, followed by the cheesiest fool-maker of them all: *The Birdie Song*.

Halfway through her fourth Vodka WKD, Amy, the bride, was having the time of her life. Everything had gone perfectly to plan, and she felt like the queen of the ball in her hired Cinderella dress, with her blonde hair coiled up and held in place by a pearl tiara. When her all-time favourite, Whitney's *Saving All My Love*, came on, she raised her bottle into the air and sang along with her friends at the top of her voice. But just as they reached the chorus, something popped down below, and a puddle seeped out around her white satin shoes.

'Christ, I hope that's booze, not piss?' her friend teased, pointing at it.

'No, I think her waters have broke,' said another girl.

'They can't have.' Amy stared down in dismay. 'I'm not due for another three weeks. Mum! *Muuum!*'

Sonia Clark was standing by the wall chatting to an elderly aunt. Glancing round when she heard her daughter's panicked voice, she noticed the girls huddled together on the dance floor and rushed over.

'Oh, bloody hell,' she squawked when she saw what was happening. 'I *told* you not to overdo it. And you're not supposed to be drinking, neither!' She snatched the bottle out of Amy's hand.

'I've only had one,' Amy lied, clutching at her stomach as a sharp pain ripped through her. 'I don't feel well.'

'What's wrong?' Jane Taylor, the groom's mum, asked, wandering over. 'She's not gone and started, has she?'

'Nothing for you to worry about,' Sonia said frostily. 'She's *my* daughter, I'll look after her.' She turned back to Amy now and, seeing the pain on her face, said, 'Right, we need to get you to hospital. Just let me find your dad.'

'Isn't that him over there?' Jane pointed towards the front of the stage where a group of Amy's scantily clad school friends were sexy-dancing around a fat middle-aged man.

Furious, Sonia shoved Jane aside and yelled, 'John Clark! Get your arse over here before I crack you one!'

'I think I'm gonna puke,' Amy moaned.

'Not here, you don't!' hissed Sonia. 'They're already going to make us pay extra to clean up the mess you've just made. And pick your dress up before it gets ruined and they keep me deposit for that, an' all.'

'Mum, stop it!' Amy complained when Sonia started yanking her skirt up. 'You're making a show of me.'

'What's up?' John Clark ambled over, wiping his sweaty brow on his sodden shirt sleeve.

'She's started.' Sonia scowled. 'Go and fetch the car – you'll have to drive her to A and E.'

'I'm not going with him, he's pissed,' Amy protested. Then, doubling over at yet another pain, she sobbed, 'Where's Mark? I want Mark.'

'Where is he?' Sonia asked Jane. Getting a shrug in reply, she blew out an exasperated breath and yelled, 'Where's Mark? Anyone seen Mark?'

'I think he went for a fag,' Steve, the best man, told her.

'Find him.' Sonia shoved the boy towards the door. 'And hurry up!'

Steve rushed outside. It might be Mark's wedding day but that hadn't stopped the sex-mad bastard from casting his net, and Steve had seen him and Ginger Jenny Abbot sneak out ten minutes earlier. They were nowhere to be seen, so he hurried round to the dark alley that ran down the side of the hall.

Mark had Jenny pressed up against the wall at the far end, her dress pulled up over her hips, his suit trousers on the floor around his ankles. He was going at her like a man who hadn't had sex in a year – which was what it felt like to him, considering that Amy hadn't let him near her in weeks. Not that he'd have wanted her even if she'd been willing, because he'd gone right off her since she'd bloated up like a beached whale. In contrast, Ginger Jenny was as thin as a rake – but that was the only good thing she had going for her, in Mark's opinion. That, and the fact that she was up for it, unlike Amy's mates who had all thought he was joking when he'd tried to chat them up.

Eyes shut now, Mark was mentally visualising all the girls he'd *rather* be shagging when he heard Steve calling his name. 'Piss off,' he grunted. 'I'm busy.'

'You'd best hurry up,' Steve whispered urgently. 'Amy's gone into labour.'

'Oh, fuck!' Mark croaked, scrabbling to pull his trousers up.

'You're not just going to leave me here like this, are you?' Jenny gasped, tugging her dress back down. 'I need a tissue.'

Mark was already walking backwards to where Steve was waiting. He pulled out of his pocket the serviette that he'd used earlier to spit a mouthful of rancid sausage roll into and tossed it to her.

'Sorry about the crumbs – it's all I've got. See you later.'

'When?' Jenny called after him. But Steve had already pulled him around the corner.

'You're a right one, you,' Steve whispered as they re-entered the hall. 'You've only been married two minutes, and you're at it already.'

'Last fling,' Mark retorted cockily.

'Thought you had that last night?'

'That was me last one as a single man,' Mark informed him, grinning as he pulled open the door to the inner hall.

The main lights had been turned on by now, and Amy had been moved onto a chair by the wall. Already furious that the ambulance wasn't here yet, despite it only being a couple of minutes since the call went out, Sonia lost her temper when somebody in the gawping crowd kneed her in the back as she knelt in front of her daughter.

'It's not a flaming sideshow!' she roared, shoving people roughly back. 'The party's over, in case you hadn't noticed, so why don't you all just piss off home!'

'Leave them,' Amy groaned, seeing no reason to deprive her mates of their fun just because it was over for her. 'There's loads of food left over from the buffet, and the DJ's booked till twelve.'

Mark pushed his way through the crowd and dropped to his knees in front of his wife. 'Are you all right?'

'Where have you been?' she demanded. 'I was shouting you.'

'Nipped out for a smoke,' he lied. 'Nearly choked on it when Steve told me what was going on.'

Amy spotted a smudge on his cheek and jabbed it with her finger. 'That'd better not be lipstick, 'cos if you've been messing around, I swear to God—'

'Don't be daft.' Mark rubbed his cheeks to remove the evidence. 'It'll be off that aunt of yours. She's been following me around all day.'

Another contraction robbed Amy of the energy to continue the argument. 'Oh, Mum, it hurts,' she cried.

'Whatever you do, don't start pushing,' Sonia ordered. 'Just breathe slow and hang on for the ambulance.'

'Anything I can do?' John asked, wringing his hands behind them. He'd managed to swerve away from Amy's birth and had no clue how to deal with this.

'Yeah, keep your big gob shut and your eyes to yourself,' Sonia snapped, still fuming about him flirting with Amy's friends.

The door opened and Ginger Jenny walked in. Blushing guiltily when all eyes turned her way, she self-consciously smoothed her frizzy hair. 'The, er, the ambulance is here.'

'Don't leave me,' Amy wailed when Mark stood up to make way for the paramedics.

'Don't worry, I'm not going nowhere,' he assured her.

'Promise?' She clung to his hand.

'Babe, I'm about to be a dad,' he reminded her proudly. '*Nothing*'s gonna stop me being there.'

Three hours later, baby Cassie had been delivered, cleaned, and fed – with a bottle, Amy having already decided that she would rather die than let anyone get even an accidental flash of her breasts. Cassie was fast asleep in a perspex cot beside the bed now, and Amy was gazing down at her in wonder.

'Isn't she gorgeous?' she purred, unable to believe that she had produced such a perfect little creature.

'The bomb,' Mark agreed, reaching for Amy's hand. 'I know I ain't always been the best, but you and that little girl are my world now and I'm gonna look after you like a proper husband and dad. Soon as I get home I'm gonna go through the paper and look for a job.'

Amy's eyes welled up and a tear trickled slowly down her cheek. 'I love you,' she whispered.

'Love you, too,' said Mark, glancing at his watch. 'Right, I'm off, before me mum thinks I'm stopping out and puts the bolts on.'

'Can't you stay?' Amy pleaded, nervous of being on her own with the baby. She'd babysat for other people's kids a few times but they had always been in bed by the time she got there so she'd never had to do anything. If Cassie woke in the middle of the night and started crying, she wouldn't have a clue what to do with her.

'What, and sleep on a chair when I've got a perfectly good bed at home?' Mark gave her a come-on-now look.

'I'm scared,' she admitted, her chin wobbling.

'You'll be fine,' Mark assured her, leaning down to kiss her before backing towards the door. 'You're gonna be a great mum – everyone says so.'

'Do you think so?' Amy sniffed.

'Deffo.' Mark opened the door. 'You've got the nurses to help you out if you need a hand, and I'll be back first thing.'

'Promise?'

Mark winked and slipped out quietly.

Amy wiped her eyes, then snuggled down and gazed at the slim gold band on her finger. Everyone had said they wouldn't last, but she and Mark had proved them all wrong. And now they had their beautiful daughter, the council would have to hurry up and give them a house of their own. It was kind of Mark's mum to let them move in with her but Amy didn't want to stay for one minute longer than she absolutely had to. She wanted it to be just her, Mark and Cassie in their own little palace. And when that dream came true, nothing and nobody would ever wipe the smile off her face.

'Who does she look like?' Ginger Jenny asked, sitting up when Mark had finished and swiping her hair out of her eyes.

'Spit of me,' Mark said proudly as he rolled over and reached into his jacket pocket for his cigarettes and lighter. 'Proper little stunner, she is. Loads of jet-black hair, and this dead cute little nose.'

Jenny turned her head and made a gagging face. She wasn't the remotest bit interested in the kid and had only asked so he wouldn't think she was being funny. It had been sickening enough watching him act all loved-up with that stupid bitch Amy at the reception. But she really felt like puking, listening to him spout off about the brat like it was some kind of fairy princess.

Mark lit up and lay back against the pillow. 'What's up with you?' He squinted at Jenny through the swirling smoke.

'Nothing.' She turned back with a smile. 'I was just thinking I'd best open the window. My mum'll be back in a bit, and she'll kick off if she thinks I'm smoking.'

Mark decided it was time to leave. He'd only called round to finish what he'd started earlier on, and now that he'd shot his load he was bored.

'You don't have to go,' Jenny said when he reached for his trousers. 'Just blow it out of the window so my mum can't smell it.'

'Nah, I need some kip.'

'When am I going to see you again?'

'Dunno.' Mark shrugged and stuffed his shirt tails in. 'I'm gonna be pretty tied up with the baby from now on. Oh, and not a word about me coming round here tonight. If Amy finds out, I'll know who to blame, won't I?'

'Didn't bother you a minute ago,' Jenny said sulkily.

'Yeah, well, I'm a dad now,' Mark reminded her. 'I've got responsibilities.'

When he turned and walked out, Jenny noticed that he'd left his cigarettes and was about to shout after him. But she changed her mind. Why should she do him any favours after the way he'd just spoken to her?

She heard the front door close down below and lit one of the cigarettes. Then she knelt on the bed to watch through the gap at the bottom of the net curtain as Mark hopped over the gate and sauntered down the road.

'*I'm a dad now,*' she mimicked under her breath. '*I've got responsibilities*. Yeah, well, let's see if Amy lets you anywhere near the kid after I tell her what we've just done.'

A taxi turned onto the road. Guessing that it was her mum, Jenny took a last tug on her smoke and flicked the butt into next door's garden before hopping back into bed. As much as she'd have loved to set Amy straight, she'd never have the guts to actually do it. Not only because Amy would kick the living crap out of her, but because Mark would probably never speak to her again. And, as angry as she'd been a minute ago, there was no way she was risking that.

She had worshipped Mark Taylor for years and had tried everything to get him to notice her, to no avail. Until tonight, when he'd not only noticed her but had dragged her away from her job helping her mum on the community-centre bar and made love to her on the other side of the wall from where his new wife had just gone into labour. And then he'd turned up here at the house straight after the birth of his baby and made love to her again, which must mean that he was interested.

Reassured, Jenny stroked the indentation that Mark's head had left in the pillow and held his Clipper lighter against her breast. So what if he'd put a ring on that stupid cow's finger and had a baby with her? That didn't mean anything. He was only sixteen and everyone knew that teenage boys couldn't stand kids. She'd give him two weeks, max, before he got bored and came back to her for seconds.

PART ONE
FIVE YEARS LATER

I

Mark slammed his fork down and glared at Amy across the table. 'Don't you ever stop fucking nagging?'

'I wouldn't have to if you came home when you were supposed to.' Amy jabbed her own fork into a lump of leaden mash. 'This was lovely when I made it, but look at the state of it now.'

'I was working. What am I supposed to do when the gaffer asks me to stay back? Tell him to fuck off, 'cos I'm gonna be late for me dinner?'

'You could have rung to let me know.'

'And get into trouble for using my phone at work?' Mark shook his head in disgust and shoved his plate away. 'You do my head in, you. All day I'm out there grafting, and all I get when I come home is nag, nag, fuckin' nag. I don't know why I bother.'

Amy looked down at her plate and pushed her shrivelled peas into a heap beside the mash. Maybe she was turning into a nag, but it wasn't easy being stuck in the house on her own all day with two kids to look after. It was all right for Mark, he could escape to work and have a laugh with his mates. But she was trapped in here day in, day out, with nothing but the washing, cooking, cleaning, shitty nappies and tantrums to keep her company. And Mark saw little enough of the kids as it was, so the least he could do was come home in time to see them for two minutes before they went to bed.

'I'm going out,' Mark said suddenly.

Amy jerked her head up at the sound of his chair scraping back. 'You've only been back five minutes. Just sit down and eat your tea.'

'Lost me appetite.' Mark strode out into the hall and snatched his jacket off the hook.

'Don't you dare go out and leave me on my own again,' Amy yelled after him. 'Mark . . . I'm warning you. I'm not joking.'

His answer was a harder than usual slam of the front door.

'*Bastard!*' She hurled her plate at the wall.

A few seconds later, the back door creaked open and Marnie from next door poked her head in. 'Is it safe?'

Amy nodded, and swiped at her tears.

'What was it this time?' Marnie stepped over the broken plate and eyed the mixture of mince, mash, peas and gravy that was sliding down the wall.

'The usual.' Amy stood up and snatched the dishcloth off the sink drainer. 'I've had a horrible day, but he doesn't give a toss. He just strolls in late and expects me to wait on him hand and foot.'

'That's men for you.' Marnie plonked herself down on the chair that Mark had just vacated and watched as Amy wiped the mess off the wall. 'They're all over you till they've got you, then they think they can treat you like shit. Wankers, the lot of 'em.'

'He's not that bad,' said Amy, automatically jumping to his defence like she always did when someone dared to criticise him. 'I'm just stressed out 'cos the kids have been playing me up. I shouldn't have taken it out on him.'

Marnie gave her a knowing look. 'You don't have to cover for him on my behalf, hon. I've heard the way he talks to you, and I think he's got a damn cheek calling you a nag.'

Amy turned her back and angrily rinsed out the dishcloth before reaching for the dustpan and brush and sweeping up the broken crockery. Nosy bitch must have had a glass up against the wall if she'd heard him say *that*.

'Oh, leave it,' Marnie urged when Amy reached for Mark's plate after depositing the rubbish in the bin. 'No point wearing yourself out, you won't get any thanks for it. Come round to mine and chill for a bit. I've got some wine.'

'The kids are in bed,' Amy told her, scraping the remains of Mark's dinner off the plate.

'They must be asleep by now. They'll be all right for half an hour.'

'No, I can't leave them. Mark will go mad if he comes back and I'm not here.'

'You'll be lucky. He'll be halfway to the pub by now. You won't see him again tonight.'

Amy's heart sank. Marnie was right. Once Mark hooked up with his mates and got the first few pints down his throat, he'd forget all about her and the kids. The mood he was in when he left, he'd probably crash at Steve's, then crawl home after work tomorrow full of apologies. That was how it usually panned out when he stormed off after a row.

Marnie's phone beeped. She took it out of her pocket, read the message and jumped to her feet. 'Oh, shit! Sorry, hon, got to go. I forgot Neil was coming round tonight. He's waiting outside, and I can't risk Fat Gemma seeing him or she'll be straight on the phone to his missus. See you tomorrow.'

Amy locked the door behind her, then finished clearing up and went into the living room. The kids had been watching

CBeebies before they went to bed, and stuffed toys were still prancing noisily around on the TV screen. She reached for the remote to turn it over, but hesitated when she caught sight of herself in the mirror above the fire. Her wedding photo, in pride of place on the mantelpiece below, showed a heavily pregnant girl with gleaming blonde hair, sparkling blue eyes, and a mile-wide smile. But the woman staring back at her from the mirror was a scrawny, dull-eyed, straw-haired replica of her mother. Worse, her *nan*. No wonder Mark couldn't be bothered to hurry home from work if this was all he had to look forward to.

Blinking back the tears of self-pity that were stinging her eyes when a peal of raucous laughter floated through the wall, Amy released a weary sigh. Mark had his faults, there was no denying that, but at least he wasn't a cheat like that pig Neil Foster. *His* poor wife had no clue what he was getting up to behind her back, and Amy hated bumping into her at the shops because she always felt as guilty as hell even though it had nothing to do with her.

Disgusted by the grunting sounds that were starting to filter through now, Amy decided to get an early night. Most of her and Mark's problems stemmed from the fact that he was always knackered from working so hard and she was always stressed out from dealing with the kids, so a good sleep would do her the world of good. Then, hopefully, she wouldn't be so quick to bite Mark's head off when he came home tomorrow – and he wouldn't be so quick to storm out again.

As Amy headed up to bed back home, Mark walked into The Junction and looked around for his mates, in desperate need of some light-hearted man-banter to shake him out of the mood that Amy had put him in. She was turning into a right old woman lately, always whining and bitching and making him feel like a cunt for coming home five minutes late. He loved his kids as much as she did, but he could do without having them forced down his throat every time he stepped through the door. And as for all that bedtime kissy-cuddly shit that Amy wanted him to do, that was *her* job, not his.

None of his mates were in, so Mark bought a pint and wandered over to the fruit machine in the corner. Made up when three cherries rolled around on his first go and ten pound coins rattled down into the tray, he shoved another fifty pence in, only for a further five quid to spew out. Mood lifting, he took a swig of his pint and dragged up a stool. It was his lucky night, and no fucker was getting near this machine tonight until he'd hit the jackpot.

It didn't happen, and by the time the bell rang for last orders he had precisely forty pence left to his name – not even enough to feed the machine one last time, never mind catch the bus to work in the morning. And definitely not enough to buy another drink to cushion him against the shit that Amy was going to throw at him.

Relieved to find the house in darkness when he got home, Mark let himself in quietly and slipped his feet out of his trainers. Then, keeping an eye on the stairs, he crept into the kitchen and pulled Amy's handbag out from the tray beneath Bobby's pram. Smiling when he looked in her purse and saw two ten-pound notes in the slot behind the change compartment, he slipped one into his pocket before putting everything back where he'd found it and heading up to bed. Amy would go mad when she realised the money was gone but he didn't care. He'd earned it, so he could do what the fuck he liked with it.

2

When the alarm woke Amy the next morning she reached out and switched it off, then stretched her arms above her head and yawned. She'd thought she was never going to get to sleep when Marnie and that stupid man of hers moved the action upstairs, but the cotton wool had shielded her from the worst of it – thank God.

She pulled the sticky little plugs out of her ears now and sat up. Surprised to see a lump on Mark's side of the bed, because she hadn't expected him to come home, she remembered the vow she'd made to be nicer to him and lay back down.

'Morning,' she purred, snuggling up to him and kissing the back of his neck.

'What time is it?' Mark rubbed at his eyes.

'Just gone seven.' She slid her fingers slowly down through the hairs on his stomach. 'You've got twenty minutes yet.'

When she reached his crotch, Mark's brain switched places with his dick and he rolled towards her and tugged at her nightie.

'Sorry about last night,' she murmured when he climbed on top of her.

'Sshhh,' he grunted, shoving her legs apart.

'*You* shush,' she gasped, giggling when he set the headboard banging against the wall. 'You'll wake the kids up.'

'Tell 'em we're playing doctors and nurses,' said Mark, clamping his mouth over hers to keep her from saying anything else.

They hadn't had sex for a while, mainly because they had been arguing so much lately. And when they argued, Mark always stormed off to the pub and came back late, if he came back at all, by which time Amy wouldn't have let him touch her even if she'd still been awake. So it was short and sweet now, and all over within a couple of minutes.

When they had finished, Mark jumped out of bed and had a quick wash before leaving for work. After he'd gone, Amy woke the kids and went downstairs to make breakfast, singing softly along to the radio as she toasted the bread and made herself a cup of tea.

She'd only been fourteen when she'd started going out with Mark, fifteen when she'd got pregnant, and sixteen when they'd got married. A pair of kids propelled into adulthood, they'd had more than their share of fights over the last five years, and she'd lost count of how many times one or other of them had demanded a divorce. But Mark had been her first love, and she felt as strongly about him today as she always had, so it was good to be back on track.

Now all she had to do was make sue she didn't let the kids get to her today and sour things by being moody when Mark got home this evening.

Thinking about the kids, she walked out into the hall and shouted, 'Cassie, hurry up. Your toast's going cold.'

'It's Bobby,' her daughter's complaining voice floated back. 'He won't let me put his jumper on. He keeps pulling his arms out and kicking me. And now he's locked 'isself in the bathroom.'

'Bobby, get out of there right now!' Amy yelled. 'And do as your sister says, or I'll be coming up to sort you out.'

Amused when she heard the bathroom bolt slide out of its hasp, followed by the sound of Bobby's pudgy little feet slapping on the floorboards above as he ran back to the bedroom he shared with his sister, Amy went back into the kitchen and finished her tea. She was rinsing her cup at the sink when she heard a tap on the window.

'Bit early for you, isn't it?' she teased when she opened the door. 'I thought you'd be hibernating for a week after the racket you and Neil made last night.'

'Don't mention that man's name to me,' Marnie grunted, pulling a face as she walked in. 'I told him from the off that I didn't want to get into anything serious, and he said he felt the same. But then he goes and gets all heavy on me last night, prattling on about leaving his wife and moving in with me.'

'You're joking!' Amy raised an eyebrow. 'What did you say?'

'Oh, believe me, I soon set him straight. I said, listen here, mate, I don't mind the occasional shag, but you can fuck *right* off if you think I'm giving up my freedom to wash your stinking boxers!'

'Bet he loved that. So, have you told him it's over, or are you just going to freeze him out?'

'The ice queen cometh.' Marnie grinned. 'And if that don't work, I'll get our Lee to kick his head in. Anyhow, I don't wanna talk about him.' She flapped her hand to indicate that the subject matter was as finished as the relationship. 'Fancy coming to town after you've dropped Cass off?'

'Yeah, why not?' Amy kicked off her slippers and sat down to pull her trainers on. 'Oi!' she protested when Marnie picked up a piece of toast. 'That's Cassie's.'

Marnie took a bite and grinned through the crumbs. 'Sorry, but I'm starving, and it was just sitting there asking to be scoffed. Fussy knickers probably won't want it anyhow, knowing her.'

'Bobby's the fussy one, not Cassie,' Amy corrected her. Then, noticing the time, she pushed past her and went back out into the hall, yelling, 'Will you two get a move on, I won't tell you again!'

Cassie came stomping down the stairs, tugging her little brother along behind her. 'Stop dragging your feet,' she warned, almost yanking him right off the last couple of steps. 'I've had just about enough of you for one morning.'

'Bless!' Marnie laughed. 'She sounds just like you, Ames.'

Amy turned her head so the kids wouldn't see the smile on her lips. Cassie had just turned three when Bobby came along, and she'd mothered him from the off. And, just like a real mother, her adoration was mixed with impatience, so she thought nothing of telling him off if he didn't do as she said, or giving him a little slap if she thought he deserved it. Amy's mum had told her off for letting Cassie get away with that, but Amy didn't see the harm in it as long as Cassie didn't hurt him. Anyway, she thought it was kind of cute to see a five-year-old acting like a full-grown woman.

As Amy manhandled Bobby into his anorak and strapped him into his buggy now, Cassie slotted a piece of toast between her teeth and pulled on her own coat. When she reached into her pocket for her mittens, a folded piece of paper fell out. She picked it up and handed it to her mum.

'What is it?' Amy asked, ushering her out into the hall.

'My teacher said to give it to you. It's about the trip.'

'What trip?'

'Chester Zoo, next week.' Cassie gazed up at her with a world-weary look in her eyes. 'You forgot, didn't you?'

'Oh, shit!'

'Language,' Marnie teased, grasping the buggy's handles and pushing it over the step.

Amy opened the letter and groaned when she saw that it was a reminder for payment: £9.50 – due today, or Cassie would be excluded from the trip.

'Sorry, love, I can't afford it.' She gave her daughter a regretful smile and tossed the letter onto the hall table. 'Maybe next time, eh?'

Tears immediately welled in Cassie's big blue eyes. 'I've got to go, Mummy. Everyone else is going, an' I don't wanna stay in the office with Mr Tunney. He smells.'

Amy sighed. Cassie was right: Mr Tunney, the deputy head, did smell. Correction, he *stank* – of BO and halitosis.

'I'm sorry,' she said again. 'I'd let you go if I could, but I've got to put credit on the electric and get a bit of shopping.'

'Don't be so tight.' Marnie gave her friend a disapproving look. 'It's horrible being the odd one out when you're a kid.'

'Can I?' Cassie's face was a picture of hope. '*Please*, Mummy? Ruby will sit with Shandi if I don't go, and they'll make bestest friends and won't play with me no more.'

'Right, fine,' Amy conceded, flashing Marnie a hooded look of annoyance as she yanked her handbag out from under the buggy. 'But don't bother asking for sweets for the rest of the week 'cos you won't be getting any.'

As Cassie nodded her eager agreement, Amy opened her purse – and frowned when she saw the lone ten-pound note.

'What's up?' Marnie asked when she started rifling through her bag.

'I've lost a tenner.'

'You probably spent it and forgot. I'm always doing that.'

'No, it was definitely there last night. I bought the kids an ice cream on the way home from school yesterday, and there were two of them. And I didn't go anywhere else after that.'

'Maybe Mark took it?'

'No, not without telling me.'

'You'll have put it somewhere safe, knowing you,' Marnie suggested. 'But can you look for it later, or we'll miss the bus. Don't worry, I'll pay.'

Amy knew that she hadn't taken the money out of her purse, but she could do without Cassie's teacher giving her another lecture about the importance of punctuality so she pushed it to the back of her mind, telling herself that if worse came to worst and she didn't find it, Mark would just have to stump up for the electric. He always pleaded poverty whenever she asked for money, but if he could afford to go drinking three or four nights a week he could certainly afford to keep the lights on at home.

By lunchtime, the tenner was burning a great big hole in Mark's pocket and he couldn't wait to get to the bookie's. It was another week and a half before he was due to be paid, and he needed cash asap. But he had no intention of telling Steve where he was going, because he could do without one of his mate's legendary lectures about the folly of throwing money away on gambling when he could be spending it on booze instead.

Hoping to avoid Steve now, he darted into the staffroom and changed out of his paint-splattered overalls. But Steve popped his head around the door just as he was pulling on his jacket and asked if he was ready.

'Er, no, I'm giving the pub a miss today,' Mark told him cagily.

'Yeah, right.' Steve smirked. 'And the pope's coming round mine for dinner tonight. Come on, the lads are waiting.'

'No, I'm serious,' Mark said, following him out. 'I've got an errand to run for Amy.'

'I don't mind subbing you a couple of pints if you're broke,' Steve offered.

'Cheers.' Mark gave him a grateful smile. 'But I promised Amy I'd check up on this thing she's waiting for from the catalogue.'

'Whatever,' Steve said dismissively, accurately guessing where Mark was really going. 'Just don't be late back.'

'I won't,' said Mark, grinning as he set off in the opposite direction.

Mark had no clue about form, or any of that other shit, so when he had the money to take a punt he generally picked out horses whose names gave him 'a feeling'. It was a shit system, and nine times out of ten he came out of the bookie's with less in his pocket than when he'd gone in. But not today. Today, luck was on his side, and he had two hundred and fifty quid in his hand by the time he realised he was late back to work.

Another race was about to start, and it was a real temptation. But he managed to drag himself away and ran all the way back to the depot.

The gaffer, Stan, was waiting when he sneaked in through the back door.

'What time do you call this?'

'Sorry, boss, an old lady fell over when I was on my way to the butty shop,' Mark lied. 'I had to call an ambulance, then wait with her till it came.'

'And that took two hours?'

'I know, it's shocking, isn't it?' Mark shook his head, the picture of innocence and indignation. 'I gave them a right mouthful when they turned up. I said, what are youse playing at, leaving an old woman lying on the pavement for that long? She could have froze to death.'

'Such compassion,' Stan drawled, not believing a word of it.

'What was I supposed to do?' Mark asked. 'Leave her lying there?'

'*Yes*, if it meant getting back to work on time,' barked Stan. Then, pointing a finger in Mark's face, he said, 'Do it again and you're out. Consider yourself warned.'

Mark gave a chastened nod and looked down at his feet until Stan had gone about his business. Then, smirking, he slipped his jacket off and his overalls on, and sauntered through to the workshop.

'Where've you been?' Steve hissed when Mark joined him at the paint-mixing machine. 'Stan's been going off his nut, threatening to sack you, and everything.'

'He's all talk,' Mark replied unconcernedly. 'I'm going nowhere.'

'I wouldn't be so sure,' Steve said grimly. 'You're pushing your luck, mate.'

'If you say so.' Mark smirked.

Amy had just sat the kids down in front of the telly and was about to make a start on dinner when Mark got home that evening. Surprised, because he was earlier than usual, she reached up to kiss him.

'I'm just putting dinner on. Go and sit down – I'll bring it in when it's ready.'

'No need.' Mark grinned. 'I stopped off on the way home and got these.'

A frown skittered across Amy's brow when he produced two pizza boxes from behind his back. Closing the door into the living room so the kids wouldn't hear, she whispered, 'What did you do that for? You know we can't afford it.'

'Yes, we can,' Mark assured her, putting the boxes down on the ledge. 'I got a bonus from work, so I thought I'd treat you.'

'A bonus? What for?'

'Employee of the month. Look.' Mark took a wad of twenty-pound notes out of his back pocket and fanned them out. 'Hundred squids.'

'Wow, that's fantastic,' Amy trilled, throwing her arms around his neck. 'I'm so proud of you.'

'You can thank me later,' said Mark, waggling his eyebrows to let her know that he meant in the bedroom. 'Now, hurry up and get that pizza out, 'cos I'm starving.'

'What are you going to do with the money?' Amy asked, reaching into the cupboard for plates. 'Only I could do with a bit for the electric, if you can spare it.'

'It's yours,' Mark told her, coming up behind her and putting his arms around her waist. 'I had to nick a tenner off you this morning, so I was going to buy you some flowers. But I figured I might as well just give you the dosh and let you get yourself something nice.'

'I can't take it all,' Amy protested. 'You earned it, you should have some as well.'

'I want you to have it,' Mark insisted, magnanimous in the knowledge that he had the same again and a little bit more still stashed in his pocket.

Amy looked at the money thoughtfully. Marnie had lent her thirty quid to buy Bobby a new coat and Cassie some shoes off the market this morning, but Mark would hit the roof if he knew she'd been borrowing, so she'd hidden them in the cupboard under the stairs, intending to produce them after his next wages went in. But now he'd given her this money, she could bring them out tomorrow and pretend she'd just bought them.

'Thank you.' She turned and kissed him. Then, to cover her guilt, she said, 'Why don't you give Steve a ring and see if he fancies going for a pint?'

'Are you sure?' Mark gazed innocently back at her, even though it was exactly what he'd expected her to say. 'I don't mind staying in with you and the kids.'

'No, you deserve a break,' Amy insisted. 'But get changed first,' she added, sniffing at his jumper and wrinkling her nose. 'You stink of sweat.'

'Must be all that hard work I've been doing,' said Mark, slapping her on the backside as she picked up the kids' plates and carried them into the living room.

Cassie and Bobby were sitting together on the couch watching TV. 'What is it?' Cassie asked, her eyes never leaving the screen as Amy held out her plate.

'Pizza,' Amy told her. 'Daddy's treat.'

Both children twisted their heads at the mention of their father. When they saw him in the doorway, they jumped up and ran to him.

'Steady on!' Mark yelped, squatting down to catch them as they launched themselves into his arms. 'I'm an old man, you'll break my back.'

'We haven't seen you for ages and ages,' said Cassie, hugging him tightly.

'We misses you,' added Bobby, wriggling to get closer.

'Yeah, well, now you've seen me you'd best give me some air before you kill me and I have to get buried with grandad Taylor,' Mark said, laughing as he pushed them gently off. 'And then I'll have worms in my eyes, and beetles in my mouth.'

'*Mark!*' Amy scolded, fetching in his plate in time to hear this. 'Don't say things like that. You'll give them nightmares.'

Mark exchanged a mock-contrite look with the kids and sat down to eat his dinner.

Half an hour later, he was washed, dressed, and ready for the off. 'I'll try not to be late,' he told Amy, kissing her goodbye.

'Don't worry about me.' She pushed him towards the door. 'I'm going to have a bath and go to bed with my library book. You just have a good time. And say hello to Steve.'

Watching through the window as he strolled down the road, Amy sighed. When they were like this, life was blissful, and she felt like the luckiest woman in the world.

3

Ginger Jenny had never been one for going out. In the past she'd avoided it because she'd been scared of bumping into the bitches who had made her life a misery at school. But in the last two years it had been because she'd been too busy nursing her mum to go any further than the local shops or the doctor's surgery. Today was the first time in as long as she could remember that she had been anywhere without the clunky old wheelchair preceding her every step, and it felt as if she'd had a limb amputated.

Everyone had been very kind, especially the vicar who had said some lovely things about her mum despite never having met her. But Jenny had kept her mouth firmly shut when he'd asked if anybody wanted to speak. There was nothing she had wanted to say – nothing that she cared to say in front of strangers, anyway. And that was what the other mourners were to her, truth be told. The small gaggle of elderly neighbours who had come along to pay their respects, for example.

Jenny had lived in the same house her entire life, and those neighbours had seen her grow from baby to teenager to the woman she was now. Yet none of them had bothered to call round to see how she was coping while her mum had been sick. And she would never forget the time she'd pushed her mum out in the wheelchair and seen old Mrs Peters scuttle back into her house to avoid them. But they had all turned up in black today, looking suitably mournful, as if they actually cared.

And the same went for the women from the cake factory who had worked alongside her mum for fifteen years before the cancer forced her to quit, only one of whom had ever bothered to call round to see how she was doing.

Still, at least the neighbours had bought flowers – albeit one poxy bunch between the three of them. And the factory girls had presented Jenny with the fifty-seven quid they had collected in a whip-round, so they weren't completely heartless.

Which was more than could be said for the bastards at the community centre where her mum had worked as a part-time barmaid for eight years. They hadn't even bothered to send a card, never mind show their faces.

As for family, the only ones who had turned up from her mum's side were two elderly aunts, Hetty and Lizzie, whom Jenny only vaguely remembered having visited as a child. None of her dad's side had shown up, but that was no surprise considering Jenny hadn't seen most of them since her dad had walked out when she was nine.

All in all, it was a pretty poor turnout, and Jenny was glad that her mum hadn't been there to witness how little she had meant to the world.

It was the first funeral Jenny had ever attended, much less had to arrange. She had completely forgotten that she was supposed to cater for the guests, so she'd been relieved when one of the neighbours had suggested going for a drink in The Junction instead. She was sitting between her aunts now, on a bench seat in the corner, and she was cringing as the elderly sisters bullied the other mourners – and anybody who was standing nearby and was foolish enough to look their way

– into joining in with their sing-song. When Lizzie launched into *On Mother Kelly's Doorstep* for the fourth time, Jenny stifled a yawn. It had been a long day and she was dying to go home, but none of the others seemed in any rush to leave and she didn't want to appear rude by being the first to go.

Icy air swirled around her ankles every time the door opened. Shivering when someone else walked in now, she glanced towards the door and nearly choked on her drink when she saw Mark Taylor. It was five years since she'd last seen him, but he hadn't changed a bit. His glossy black hair was a little shorter, but his face was every bit as handsome as she remembered. And as he and his friend Steve sauntered towards the bar he still exuded that air of self-confidence that she'd always found so attractive.

'Earth to Jenny.' Aunt Lizzie brought her out of her daze with a dig in the ribs. 'What's up, chuck? You look like you've seen a ghost.'

'It's nothing,' Jenny lied. 'I'm just a bit tired.'

'Best get yourself off to the bar before you drop off, then.' Lizzie scooped the pot money off the table and dumped it in her hand. 'Rum for Mrs P and Kenny. Scotch for Mrs J and them other two. Gin for me and Hetty. A lager for Bob. And whatever you're having.'

'Can't someone else go?' Jenny asked quietly.

'It's for *your* mam,' Lizzie reminded her, nudging her off the seat with her hip.

Aunt Hetty had already stood up to let her out from behind the table, so Jenny had no choice but to do as she'd been told. Dismayed to see that the only space at the bar was a tiny gap at the side of Steve, she slipped into it and pulled her hair down over the side of her face, conscious of her drab clothes and washed-out complexion.

When the lads had been served, Steve picked up his pint and turned to look for a seat. 'Sorry, love,' he apologised when he banged Jenny with his elbow. 'Didn't see you there.'

'It's all right,' she muttered, keeping her face averted as her cheeks flared.

'Coo-ee!' one of the factory women called just then. 'Stevie! Over here!'

Steve looked around and waved when he saw his mother sitting with Jenny's party. 'All right, Mam. What you doing here?'

'*Funeral*,' she mouthed. '*Her mam.*'

She pointed at the girl who was standing beside him, and Steve peered down at her. He was about to offer his condolences but hesitated when he recognised her. 'It's Jenny, isn't it?'

'Yeah.' She nodded.

'Sorry about your mum.'

'Thanks.'

'That's mine, in case you hadn't guessed.' Steve nodded back towards the table. 'Didn't know they knew each other. Small world, eh?'

Jenny gave him a tight smile and willed him to stop talking to her before Mark stopped chatting up the barmaid and spotted her. She'd dreamed about running into Mark so many times, but in those dreams she always looked amazing and he was always completely bowled over. But that was hardly going to happen if he saw her like this.

It was too late. Mark turned round.

'You remember Jenny, don't you?' Steve said.

Mark took a sip of his pint and gave her a bored look. Then, shrugging as if he'd never seen her before in his life, he said, 'Hurry up, the machine's free.'

'Sorry about that,' Steve apologised as his friend strode away. 'I'd, er, best go.' Unsure what else to say, he gave her an awkward smile and rushed after Mark.

Jenny stepped into the space they'd left at the bar and ordered the drinks she'd been sent for.

'Do you mind if we go after this?' she whispered to her aunt when she carried them back to the table. 'I'm getting a headache.'

'You get off whenever you like, chuck.' Lizzie patted her hand. 'You've had a hard day.'

'Aren't you coming?' Jenny asked, dismayed at the thought of going home on her own. 'I thought you and Hetty might stay over?'

'Oh, no, we've got to get home to the cats,' Lizzie informed her. 'But don't you worry about us. The fifty-seven stops round the corner from ours, so we'll just hop on that.' With that, she turned back to the others and clapped her hands together. 'Right, you lot, I bet you all know this one, so don't be shy about joining in . . . *She's only a bird, in a gilded cage . . .*'

As the oldies sang loudly along, Jenny downed her drink and slipped out quietly. It was freezing by now, so she pulled up the collar of her thin coat and walked quickly home.

The house was dark, and there wasn't a sound but for the soft tick-tock of her mum's brass carriage clock on the mantel-piece. Jenny made her weary way upstairs and pushed her mum's bedroom door slowly open. It was a week since she'd found her dead in her bed, and she hadn't set foot in there since the undertakers had removed the body. She'd been so busy with the funeral arrangements since then that she hadn't had time to stop and think what life was going to be like without her. But now, with everything done and dusted bar collecting the ashes, this was it.

No more Mother demanding she do this, that or the other. No more stinking sheets to change, or backside to sponge. No more wheedling pleas for morphine – or being called a selfish bitch for refusing to double the dose.

No more of any of it.

Jenny was free. At long last, she was free – and it felt really, really good.

4

Three weeks later Amy was sitting on the couch, folding the still-warm clothes she'd brought back from the launderette into piles. Bobby had fallen asleep on the way back so she'd carried him up to his bed. Thinking that he'd got up when she heard a noise in the hall, she looked round. But it wasn't Bobby who walked in, it was Mark. And he looked really glum.

'What's wrong?' she asked, shoving the washing aside. 'You're not ill, are you?'

'I've been sacked,' he muttered, dropping his jacket onto the couch and making his way into the kitchen.

Sure that she'd misheard, Amy jumped up and followed him. 'What did you say?'

'You heard.' Mark took a can of beer out of the fridge and flopped onto a chair.

'Are you serious?' Amy asked, hoping against hope that he would laugh and tell her it was a joke. When he didn't, a sliver of fear trickled down her spine. 'Oh God, Mark, what have you done?'

'Nothing.' He ripped the tab off the can and swallowed a mouthful of beer.

Irritated that he was being so cagey, Amy said, 'You can't get sacked for nothing. Stan must have given you a reason.'

Mark gripped his can and gritted his teeth. 'If you must know, I've been late a few times. Now drop it – I'm not in the mood.'

A frown of confusion creased Amy's brow. 'That can't be right. I always wake you up in the morning, and I make sure you're out of the house in plenty of time to catch your bus, so how could you be late? He must have got it wrong. Ring him. Tell him to check.'

'He's not talking about mornings,' Mark said quietly. 'He's talking about lunchtimes.'

'You've been back late from lunch?' Amy's frown deepened. 'Why? What have you been doing? And what about Steve? You always have lunch with him, so has he been sacked as well?'

'No.'

'Why not? That's not fair.'

Mark groaned and ran a hand over his eyes. He wished he hadn't told her now. Wished he'd just stayed out until it was his normal time to come home, then she'd be none the wiser and he wouldn't be getting earache.

But Amy wasn't about to drop it. She wanted answers, and she wanted them now.

'If you don't tell me what's going on, I'll ring Stan myself,' she threatened. 'Or, better still, I'll ring the head office. This is blatant favouritism, and I'm not having it. Where's that address book with the number in it?'

'Just leave it,' Mark groaned when she started rifling through the kitchen drawers.

'And let Stan get away with sacking you but not Steve? No chance!'

'It's got nothing to do with Steve. Stan's been looking for an excuse to get rid of me for ages, and now he's found one – end of.'

'That doesn't make sense.' Amy rounded on him, the address book in her hand. 'It's only a few weeks since he gave you that bonus for being employee of the month. Why would he pick you for that if he was planning to get rid of you?'

'Because he's a cunt!' Mark hissed, annoyed at himself for not thinking this through properly. 'Now put a sock in it, for fuck's sake. I've got a headache.'

'A headache?' Amy drew her head back and stared down at him in disbelief. 'You come home and drop a bomb like this on me, then tell me to drop it 'cos you've got a *headache*? Are you serious?'

'Back off,' Mark warned. 'I really don't need this.'

'*You* don't need it?' Amy squawked. 'What about me? And the kids – or have you forgotten about them?'

'Will you just shut the fuck up?' Mark yelled. 'I've had a shit day, and I just want to have a beer in peace.'

'Oh, I'm sorry! Pardon me for disturbing your beer, just 'cos I'm worried about how I'm going to feed my *kids*!'

Mark couldn't take any more. He lurched to his feet, kicked his chair across the kitchen and marched out, punching the door on the way.

'Oh, that's right, smash the place up,' Amy cried, running after him. 'And don't think you're going out,' she yelled, hurling the address book onto the living room table when he snatched his jacket off the couch and headed for the front door. 'We're going to talk about this whether you like it or not. Are you listening to me, Mark? . . . *Mark!*'

Furious when he walked out, slamming the door behind him, she yanked it open again and screamed, 'If you don't come back right now, we're finished! I mean it, Mark!'

He ignored her and carried on walking. Conscious of net curtains twitching at windows all along the road, Amy balled her hands into fists and cursed his retreating back. The bastard was lucky that Bobby was asleep and she couldn't leave the house or she'd have gone after him and given him what for.

The door of the house directly opposite opened and Amy's neighbour Gemma came out and waddled up the path. She dropped a plastic bag into the wheelie bin and then paused to wipe her hands on her jeans, before doing a comical double take.

'Oh, hello, Amy love. Didn't see you there. Everything all right?'

'Fine,' Amy snarled, seeing right through her little act. The bag had been practically empty, and it was obvious that the fat cow had only brought it out as an excuse to watch the show. Well, tough, it was over!

The phone started to ring. Amy slammed the door, marched into the living room and snatched up the receiver. '*What?*'

'Er, hi, Amy,' Steve said cautiously. 'Is Mark there?'

'No, he bloody well isn't,' Amy snapped. 'And if you see him before I do, you can tell him he'd best come straight back or he needn't bother coming back at all!'

She smashed the receiver back onto its cradle and slumped down on the couch with her face in her hands.

'Don't cry, Mummy.' Bobby's little voice came from the doorway.

Shocked, because she hadn't heard him coming down the stairs, Amy quickly pulled herself together and wiped her eyes on her sleeve.

'I'm not crying,' she lied, smiling as he clambered up onto the couch beside her. 'I've just got something in my eye, that's all.'

'I kiss it better,' said Bobby, holding her face in his hands.

Amy closed her eyes and let him kiss her on both eyelids. Then, giving him a cuddle, she glanced at her watch. 'Oh God, look at the time. It's lucky you woke up or we'd have been late for Cassie.'

'Cassie!' Bobby yelled, bouncing in excitement at the mention of his adored big sister.

Determined not to let this latest disaster affect him or Cassie, Amy strapped him into his buggy and set off for school with a smile on her lips. But it was hard to maintain the front when she felt as if she was clinging to the edge of a cliff by her fingertips. She couldn't wait for the day to be over.

Steve had been on his afternoon break when he rang Amy and she'd sounded so upset that it had made him feel like shit, even though it wasn't his fault. This was totally down to Mark, and Steve was pissed off with him for screwing up again. It was the fourth job he'd been sacked from in the last year alone, and Steve had warned him time and time again to stop pushing his luck. But the idiot had ignored him.

Still annoyed when he arrived home that evening and found Mark waiting for him on the communal stairs outside his flat, he gave him a disapproving look. But Mark was too busy feeling sorry for himself to notice.

'About time,' he grumbled, making a show of getting up stiffly. 'I've been sat here for hours. Can't even feel my arse, it's that cold.'

'Should have stayed at home in the warm, then, shouldn't you?' Steve said coolly.

'Don't *you* start,' Mark groaned. 'I've had enough shit off Amy already. Just make me a coffee and give us a fag. And hurry up with the door – I need to thaw out.'

Steve felt like telling him to go home. But there was no point, because Mark never did anything until he was good and ready. So he kept his mouth shut and let him in, then left him to wallow on the couch while he got changed and made a brew.

'Stan's a right cunt,' Mark complained when Steve handed his cup to him. 'I should have smashed his fucking head in. Should have seen him, sitting there giving it the big I am. *You've had your warnings*,' he mimicked. 'I'll give him fucking warnings.'

'You *were* warned,' Steve said bluntly, sitting on his chair by the window. 'You had more chances than you deserve, if you ask me, and you've proper taken the piss these last few weeks. I'm surprised he didn't do it ages ago.'

'Oh, cheers.' Mark flashed him a hard-done-by look. 'Nice to know I've got your support.'

'It's not just about you, though, is it?' Steve reminded him. 'You've got Amy and the kids to think about, an' all. Don't you think it's time you knocked the gambling on the head if it's causing this much grief?'

'Fuck off!' Mark sneered. 'Making out like I'm some kind of junkie, when all I've done is had a few bets on the horses. Everyone does that – even you.'

'Yeah, once a year on the Grand National. Hardly the same thing, mate. Anyhow, it's not just the horses with you. I'm always trying to get you off the fruit machine when we're at the pub. And what about all the scratch cards you left in your locker? There must have been about fifty when I looked, and they're all duds. How much did that cost?'

'Jeezus! What are you, my fucking therapist?' Mark sniped. 'If I wanted a lecture, I'd have stayed at home.'

'Maybe you should have,' Steve shot back. 'Amy sounded really upset when I spoke to her.'

Mark pulled a dismissive face. 'She's always upset about something. She does my head in, moaning all the time. And she wonders why I can't stand being around her.'

'Don't make out like this is her fault,' Steve berated him. 'She's put up with a lot of shit off you over the years, and she's stuck by you when plenty would have walked.'

'Careful, you're starting to sound like a woman,' Mark sneered.

'Say what you want about me.' Steve shrugged. 'It don't change the fact that you've messed up again. And that's not Amy's fault, it's yours.'

'Since when did you care about her?' Mark asked. 'If I remember right, *you* were the one who kept telling me to break it off with her before we got wed.'

'Only 'cos I knew you were messing around, and I didn't see why you couldn't just be honest if you didn't want to be with her.'

'Oh, yeah, 'cos you've never cheated on a bird, have you?'

'I'm not saying I haven't, but at least I've always finished with them before they found out. I haven't married them and made their lives a fucking misery.'

'Well, aren't you the shiny little saint?'

'This isn't about me. It's about *you*, and that problem of yours. And you can deny it all you want, but it *must* be a problem if you've gone and lost your job over it.'

'I've had enough of this.' Mark slammed his cup down on the table and jumped to his feet. 'You're supposed to be my mate, not my bleedin' mother. See you when you remember where you left your dick.'

'You'll have to face up to it sooner or later,' Steve called after him as he marched out. 'Think about the kids. They're the ones who are going to suffer.'

Mark slammed the door, stomped down the stairs and hit the pavement, anger propelling him towards the pub.

It was one thing Amy having a go – she was his wife, and that was what they did best. But mates were supposed to have your back in times of trouble, not make you feel worse. And as for Steve suggesting that he had a problem, that was just stupid. He didn't wake up sweating and shaking of a morning, desperate for a gambling fix; he just liked the occasional flutter. And Amy hadn't complained when he'd bunged her that extra cash the other week – even if he *had* lied about where it had really come from. The greedy bitch had almost snatched his fucking hand off.

Still brooding when he reached the pub, Mark bought himself a pint and headed defiantly for the fruit machine. Fuck Steve, and fuck Amy. It was his money, and if he wanted to blow it, it was none of their business.

Ginger Jenny was getting ready to meet up with her friends Fiona and Katie. Although she was no longer ginger, having finally shaken off the last shackles of her mother's control and visited a hairdresser.

She had pleaded with her mother for years to let her change her hair colour, convinced that it would make the bullies stop picking on her, make the boys fancy her, and make everybody in general realise how great she was and want to be her friend. Her mum had point-blank refused to spend money on something that she considered frivolous, so Jenny had been forced to suffer. And, even after her mother had died, she hadn't dared to do it, unable to shake the feeling that her mother was still there in spirit.

That feeling had eased after the council had taken the house back and moved her into a flat, and she had finally taken control of her life. A brunette now, with a style that was both trendy and easy to manage, Jenny felt pretty for the first time ever. And, having invested in a whole new wardrobe to complete her new image, she was ready to show herself off to the world, so when Katie and Fiona had asked her to go for a drink, she'd said yes – even though she'd never liked either of them.

Spurned and ridiculed by the cooler kids, the three of them had stuck together at school like a little band of lepers. Jenny had dropped the other two like a hot brick after leaving, and hadn't contacted them since. But Fiona had got back in touch after hearing about her mum passing away, and the pair of them had been bombarding her with phone calls ever since, seemingly convinced that she needed support and comfort.

When the carriage clock on the mantelpiece chimed softly, Jenny slipped her feet into her new stiletto heels and stepped back to check her reflection in the mirror, turning this way and that to make sure there were no unsightly bulges, or labels hanging out. As she preened, she glimpsed the urn on the windowsill out of the corner of her eye, and flashed it a sly smile.

'Something wrong?' she asked, as if responding to an unspoken muttering of disapproval from the ashes within. 'Skirt too short? Too much make-up?' She paused and cocked her head, as if waiting for an answer. Then, shrugging, said, 'Oh, well, it's not up to you any more, is it?'

Jenny felt great as she made her way to the pub, but her good mood dipped when she saw that Fiona and Katie weren't waiting outside as they had promised. She pulled her phone out of her bag and brought up Fiona's number.

'Where the hell are you?'

'Sorry,' Fiona apologised. 'But I'm sure we said half past, and it's not quite ten past yet.'

'What am I supposed to do now?' Jenny demanded. 'I only agreed to come because you begged me, but I wouldn't have bothered if I'd known you were going to let me down.'

'We didn't know you were going to be early or we'd have made sure we were there before you,' said Fiona, still apologetic even though it wasn't her fault. 'Look, we're leaving right now. We'll be there in ten minutes – I promise.'

'You'd better be,' snapped Jenny, disconnecting the call and shoving the phone back into her bag.

Annoyed, she reached out to open the pub door – at the exact moment that Mark pulled it open from his side. Their gazes met, and Jenny broke out in a cold sweat.

Mark was flat broke – and nowhere near drunk enough to forget his woes. But a pretty face always cheered him up, so he smiled, stepped back, and waved the girl in.

'After you, darlin'.'

'Thanks.' Legs like jelly, Jenny stumbled over the step.

'Steady.' Mark reached out and caught her. Then, cocking his head to one side, he peered at her closely. 'Do I know you?'

'It's Jenny,' she told him in a tiny voice. 'Jenny Abbot.'

Mark stared some more, then shrugged. 'Sorry. Doesn't ring any bells.'

Before she could stop herself, Jenny heard the words that had plagued her entire childhood coming from her mouth: '*Ginger* Jenny?'

Mark drew his head back and gave her a disbelieving look. 'You're joking!'

Pleased that he remembered her at last, albeit at the expense of her pride, Jenny nodded.

Mark looked her up and down. 'Wow, you look well different. I would never have recognised you.'

Jenny reached up and self-consciously touched her hair. 'It's been a long time,' she murmured. 'How's Amy?'

'All right,' Mark grunted, his good humour slipping at the mention of his wife.

'And the baby?' Jenny went on. 'Lassie, wasn't it?'

'Cassie,' Mark corrected her. 'Yeah, she's good. I've got a son now, an' all,' he added proudly. 'Bobby.'

'Wow, *two* kids. That's great. How old are they?'

'Five and two. What about you?'

'Me?' Jenny laughed softly. 'God, no! Still young, free and single. Not that I'm anti children, or anything,' she added quickly, fearing that she might have offended him. 'It's just not for me, if you know what I mean.'

Mark knew, all right. He'd lost count of how many times he'd wished he could go back to when he'd first met Amy, because if he'd known back then what life as a husband and father was going to be like he wouldn't have touched her with a rubber-coated barge pole.

Neither of them spoke for several long moments. Jenny shifted her handbag onto her other shoulder. Mark hadn't made any move to leave yet, and she wondered if it was possible that he wanted to talk some more. She might as well have been invisible for all the notice he'd paid her at school, and he'd completely blanked her on the night of her mum's funeral. But a lot had changed since then. *She* certainly had. She might never be as pretty as Amy, or any of the other girls who Mark had knocked about with back then, but she looked bloody good tonight.

'Look, I'm supposed to be meeting my friends,' she said, taking the bull by the horns. 'But I've got time for a quick drink if you fancy it?'

'Er, nah, best not.' Mark shuffled his feet. 'I left my wallet at home.'

'I'll pay,' Jenny offered, blushing as soon as the words left her mouth. 'Unless you've got to get back to Amy?'

Mark pulled a face and made a soft snorting sound. 'She'll see me when she sees me.'

'Oh, right,' Jenny murmured, her heart jumping for joy at the thought that maybe his marriage wasn't so perfect after all.

Mark was staring at her again. He'd been ashamed after having sex with her at his wedding, and had never dreamed that he would ever want to go there again. But he had to admit that she didn't look half bad now she'd sorted out her hair and put on some make-up. And, unlike Amy who had totally let herself go since having the kids, she was slim, and her tits faced him instead of the floor.

'You still live down by the Addy?' he asked, toying with the idea of persuading her to take him back there for a drink – and whatever else might be on the menu.

'No, I had to move,' Jenny told him. 'The council said the house was too big for me after my mum died.'

'Oh, yeah, I heard about that,' said Mark, vaguely remembering Steve having had a go at him for being so abrupt with her when they had walked in here on the night of the funeral. 'How've you been doing?'

'Okay.' Jenny shrugged.

'Bit shit taking your house off you at a time like that, though,' Mark said sympathetically.

'Actually, it's been easier since I moved,' said Jenny. 'Too many memories back there.'

'Suppose so,' Mark agreed. 'So where are you now?'

'Whalley Road. I've got the upstairs flat in a converted house. It was done up before I moved in, so I haven't had to do anything. And my downstairs neighbour is old, so he doesn't make a lot of noise, or anything.'

'Sounds good.'

'Suits me.'

They fell silent again. Jenny licked her lips, trying to summon up the courage to tell him that he was welcome to call round if he was ever passing. But the door opened before she had a chance, and her heart sank when Katie and Fiona walked in. She flashed Mark a look of desperation, willing him to say something – *any*thing – to indicate that he was interested in carrying on their conversation, in which case she would happily tell the girls to get lost. But he just smiled again and said, 'Well, it was nice talking to you. See you around sometime.'

'Hope so,' Jenny murmured when he reached out to open the door. 'It's number forty-seven,' she blurted out. But, as the door swung shut behind him, she wasn't sure he'd heard.

As soon as he was gone, Katie grabbed her arm. 'Was that who I think it was?' she gasped, her owlish glasses sliding down her nose in her excitement.

'Yes, it was!' confirmed Fiona. 'O . . . M . . . *Gee!* Mark Taylor – your first love!'

'Shut up,' Jenny hissed, glancing around in case anybody was listening. They were such a pair of losers, it was embarrassing to be seen with them.

'Sorry,' Fiona twittered. 'But it's so exciting. Did he mention *that night*?'

Her last words were mouthed, not spoken, and Jenny couldn't help but smile. As much as the girls irritated her, they were the only people she had ever told about her and Mark sleeping together.

'Yeah, we talked about it,' she lied. 'He said he's thought about me a lot over the last five years, and then he asked if

I'd like to go out with him sometime. But you turned up before I had a chance to answer.'

'Really?' Katie's eyes were on stalks. 'What about *you know who*?'

'Oh, he doesn't care about her.' Jenny flapped her hand in a dismissive gesture. 'He's only with her because of the kids.'

'Be careful,' Fiona cautioned, following as Jenny set off towards the bar. 'I remember what Amy was like at school, and she won't be happy if she finds out.'

'She doesn't scare me,' Jenny scoffed, waving to attract the barmaid's attention.

Fiona and Katie exchanged hooded glances behind her back. They had always known that she had a thing for Mark, but none of them had ever had a serious boyfriend – or *any* kind of boyfriend – so they had never really believed her story about sleeping with him. They'd thought it unlikely that *any* man would do something like that on his wedding day, especially with someone who hadn't even been invited but was only there to help out on the bar. But now, after seeing the way Mark had been looking at Jenny when they walked in, they weren't so sure. And that unsettled them. Not only because he was a married man but because Jenny was vulnerable right now, and they didn't want her to get hurt.

'We know you're still grieving for your mum,' Fiona said when they had got their drinks and found a table. 'And you probably think you need someone to fill the void. But you know you've got us, don't you?'

'We'll always be here for you,' Katie chipped in. 'Best friends for life.'

Both girls stuck out their little fingers and waited for Jenny to add hers to do the pinkie friendship pledge. But Jenny just smiled secretively and reached for her glass.

'You don't have to worry about me. I'm a big girl now.'

And you two are even more stupid than you look if you think I'm going to carry on hanging around with you after tonight.

Mark Taylor was the only one who could fill the so-called void in her life. And now that she had reconnected with him, the girls were as good as dead to her.

The house was dark when Mark let himself in, and he hoped that Amy had given up on him and gone to bed. But she was huddled on the couch when he walked into the living room, and he felt guilty when he heard her sniffing softly. He reached out to switch the light on and felt like the world's biggest bastard when she said, 'Don't bother. The electric's gone.'

'Sorry.' He shuffled his feet and gave her a hangdog look from the shadows.

'Your dinner's in the oven,' she murmured. 'It might still be a bit warm, if you're lucky.'

'Don't worry about it – I'm not hungry.' He sat beside her and held out his arms. 'Hug?'

Amy hesitated for a moment. Then, sighing, she leaned towards him.

'Sorry for kicking off,' Mark said softly, kissing her hair. 'I was wound up, but I shouldn't have took it out on you.'

'I didn't mean to make you feel worse.' Amy laid her head on his chest. 'I'm just worried how we're going to manage without your wages.'

'We'll be all right,' he assured her. 'I've been thinking about it, and I reckon Stan might give me my job back if I go and talk to him.'

Amy shook her head. 'He won't. He rang after you went out, said your P45's in the post.'

Mark's immediate response was anger at Stan for being so unreasonable. But it quickly changed to acceptance, and he gave a resigned shrug. 'Oh, well, I never liked it there anyhow. I'll just find another job, with better hours and pay.'

'What if you can't?' Amy gazed up at him. 'The electric's already gone, and I've got no money to put on the card. The rent's due on Monday, and I was expecting to do a big shop next week so I let the freezer run down. And I've got the phone bill to pay, and Sky, and the gas bill will be in any day.'

'I'll look for another job first thing,' Mark promised. 'And if I can't get one I'll sign on.' He raised her chin with his finger now and gazed down into her tearful eyes. 'I said I'd look after you, and I will.'

Amy squeezed her eyes shut and held onto him. She knew that he meant what he was saying, but she doubted it was going to be as easy as that. It had been hard enough for him to get this job after having been sacked so many times before, and she didn't hold out much hope of anyone giving him another chance now that it had happened again. It wouldn't even be easy to sign on, because there would be a whole load of forms to fill out and hoops to jump through before they saw any money. And what was she supposed to do in the meantime? The child benefit might just about cover their food, but there was no way it would cover the rent, or the other bills that were stacking up. And that was without the kids' school dinners, and all the other day-to-day expenses they incurred.

As he held her, Mark stared worriedly off into the darkness. He'd really blown it this time, and he didn't know how he was going to make it right. But Amy and the kids were depending on him, so he would have to try.

5

Steve cursed when he nicked his face with the razor, and splashed cold water onto the cut to wash away the blood. He was meeting his new girlfriend's parents for the first time tonight and he was already nervous, so the last thing he needed was to greet them with little bits of toilet paper stuck to his face.

Almost taking another chunk out of himself when somebody knocked on the door and made him jump, he tossed the razor into the sink, grabbed his shirt and ran out into the hall.

Fully expecting to see Layla when he opened the door, he was shocked to find Mark on the step. It had been over a month since their argument, and Steve had missed him. It would have been hard not to, considering they had been best mates since primary school and had done everything together for as long as he could remember. Like any good mates, they'd had loads of arguments over the years and it was always Steve who'd had to back down. But this time he had decided to give Mark a taste of his own medicine and wait it out – and it had taken the stubborn bastard a lot longer to come round than he'd anticipated.

'All right, mate?' Mark gave him a sheepish smile. 'Can I come in?'

'If you want.' Determined to play it cool, Steve stepped back.

In the hall, Mark shuffled his feet as Steve pulled the shirt on and buttoned it up. 'Going out?'

'Yep.'

'Sorry, I should have rung. I'll get off and leave you to it.'

Steve picked up on his friend's miserable tone and sighed. 'Come here, you dickhead.' He pulled him into a hug.

'Get off, you wuss,' Mark protested.

Laughing, Steve let him go and led him into the living room. 'How's it going? Amy and the kids all right?'

'Yeah, it's all good,' Mark lied, sitting on the couch and looking around. 'That new?' He nodded towards a stack hi-fi system that he'd never seen before on the shelf in the corner.

'Second-hand off eBay,' said Steve, reaching for his cigarettes and tossing one to Mark. 'But I wish I'd kept the old one, to be honest. One of the tweeters is fucked and it'll cost more to replace than I paid for the whole thing.' He lit up now and sat back. 'So, what's been happening with you? Found a new job yet?'

Mark was too busy sucking on the cigarette to answer immediately. It was his first smoke in three hours, and he'd been desperate for the nicotine. Exhaling slowly, he shook his head. 'Nah. I've tried, but there's nothing going.'

'Don't give up,' Steve said sympathetically. 'You're bound to find something eventually.'

'Yeah, I guess.' Mark shrugged as if he wasn't concerned, but Steve could see from his expression that he was already losing hope. 'Anyhow, never mind me,' he said more brightly. 'Where you off to tonight? Seeing a bird?'

'Yeah.'

'Anyone I know?'

'No, I only met her a couple of weeks back. Went to Zenith for Lippy's stag do, and Layla and her mates were sitting at the next table. We got chatting and just sort of clicked.'

'Cool,' Mark muttered, struggling to squash the envy that was clawing at his gut at the thought of Steve living it up at the nightclubs while he was so broke that he couldn't even afford a half at the pub.

'It's her twenty-first today and her folks are taking her out for a meal, so she asked if I could come,' Steve went on. 'Not really looking forward to meeting them, but me and Layla are coming back here straight after so I'll get through it.' He paused and took another pull on his smoke before saying, 'Want me to ask if you can come?'

Mark wrinkled his nose. 'Nah, you're all right. Not really into them family dinners, always feel like I've got to be on my best behaviour. Anyhow, you don't want me tagging along if you're bringing her back here.'

Steve tried to look suitably disappointed but he was secretly relieved that Mark had turned him down. He'd asked out of politeness – pity, even – but it wasn't really his place to invite anyone, and Layla's mum and dad would probably have thought he was taking the piss.

'So what's she like?' Mark wanted to know.

'Gorgeous.' Steve grinned. 'Long black hair, big brown eyes, and a really great figure. Bit like Amy Winehouse.'

'Amy Winehouse ain't gorgeous. What you on, man?'

'Come off it. She was well fit when she wasn't out of her head.'

'Fit, me arse,' Mark snorted, enjoying the banter, because he had missed Steve every bit as much as Steve had missed him. 'Now, Sharon Stone – *that's* fit.'

'Maybe twenty years ago,' Steve shot back. 'But it'd be like shagging your nan nowadays. Anyhow, I like them dark. *You*'re the one who likes blondes. And gingers,' he added slyly.

'Fuck off!' Mark snorted, taking the dig in good humour. Then, 'Subject of ginger, I bumped into that Jenny the other week.'

'Yeah, I know, I was there,' Steve reminded him. 'At The Junny, after her mam's funeral. You said you didn't remember her, but I reckon you were just ashamed.'

'No, it was after that,' Mark told him. 'This was the day me and you fell out. She's gone dark now. Looked pretty fit.'

'You having a laugh?' Steve gave him a disbelieving look.

'Nah, serious.' Mark shook his head and sucked on his cigarette.

A car horn tooted down below. Steve pulled the curtain back and waved before standing up. 'Sorry, mate, got to go.'

Mark was already on his feet. 'Have a good 'un. And don't do anything I wouldn't.'

'So, basically, anything goes, then?' Steve quipped, grinning as they headed out into the hall.

He slipped his jacket on and checked his hair in the mirror before picking up the slim gift-wrapped package from the table. But, just as he was about to open the door, Mark said, 'Don't suppose you've got a few quid to lend us, have you?'

'Sorry, I haven't,' Steve told him regretfully. 'Layla's present cost an arm and a leg. Only got enough left for a cab back from town.'

'No worries.' Mark stepped out onto the landing. 'Forget I said anything.'

Steve felt terrible. Mark would never have asked if he wasn't desperate and, even though he'd brought it on himself, Steve wished he could help.

'Look, why don't you come round tomorrow?' he suggested as they walked down the stairs. 'My wages should have gone into my account by then. I'll get some beers, and we can watch the footie and have a proper catch-up.'

'Yeah, that'll be good.' Mark smiled. 'I'll ring first, though, eh? Give you and your bird time to get dressed.'

'Cheers, bud.' Steve reached out and touched fists with him. Then, pulling his cigarettes out of his pocket, he shoved them into Mark's hand. 'Here, take these.'

'You sure?'

'Yeah, I've got another pack in the drawer,' said Steve, adjusting his cuffs as they emerged from the stairwell.

A bronze Lexus was idling at the kerb, and as they walked out onto the path a pretty girl in a long black dress stepped out of its back door.

'*Wow.*' Mark whistled through his teeth.

'Told you,' Steve said proudly.

'You look nice,' the girl said, her eyes gleaming as she reached up to kiss Steve on the cheek.

'So do you,' he murmured, conscious of her dad staring out at him from the driver's seat. 'This is Mark, my best mate,' he said as he introduced them. 'Mark, this is Layla, my . . .'

'Girlfriend,' said Layla when he trailed off.

'Pleased to meet you.' Mark grinned. 'And happy birthday.'

Layla thanked him and waved her hand at the occupants of the car.

'This is my mum and dad,' she said when they stepped out. 'Mum, Dad . . . this is Steve.'

Layla's father was a good foot shorter than Steve, but he had the brooding intensity and stocky physique of a pro boxer, and Steve was conscious of his knees knocking as he held out his hand.

'Pleased to meet you, Mr . . .' He realised he didn't know their surname and gave Layla a helpless look.

'It's Gerry.' The man grasped his hand and pumped it. 'And it's nice to meet you, too, son. Good to finally put a face to the lad who's had my girl mooning around like a lost puppy all week.'

'*Dad!*' Layla hissed. 'You're embarrassing me.'

'That's my job,' Gerry chuckled. 'You should be used to it by now.'

'Behave,' his wife scolded, stepping forward and giving Steve the once-over. 'I'm Janice – mother of the bride.'

'Oh, my *God*!' squealed Layla, a look of mortification on her face.

'Hi.' Smiling, Steve offered his hand to Janice. But she was having none of that.

'It's so lovely to meet you at last,' she gushed, pulling him into a hug. 'Layla's told me all about you.'

'All good, I hope?'

'Do you think I'd be hugging you if it wasn't? I'd be setting Gerry on you.'

Mark smirked as he watched his friend being sucked into the family like a long-lost relative. Poor sod didn't know what he was letting himself in for. The dad looked like he'd stepped straight off the set of *The Sopranos* and the mum was like a middle-aged Barbie, all fake tan, peroxide hair and killer boobs. Layla was very pretty, though, he'd give Steve that.

'Right, we'd best get moving before they give our table away,' said Gerry. 'Nice to meet you.' He gave Mark a nod before climbing back into the car.

Janice smiled and walked back round to her side, while Steve held the back door open for Layla – giving Mark a look of terror before climbing in beside her.

Mark maintained his smile as he watched the car drive away, but his heart felt like a lump of lead in his chest. It had taken a lot for him to swallow his pride and come begging to Steve. But he'd promised Amy that he would get some money and none of his other mates had any, so he'd had no choice.

He lit one of the cigarettes that Steve had given him and started walking slowly home. It was the last place he wanted to go, because he and Amy had been tearing lumps out of each other all day and he'd had a gutful of it. He'd already admitted that he'd fucked up by getting the sack, and he was trying his best to rectify it. Hell, he'd been down to the job centre so many times in the last month that he was surprised they hadn't set up a bed for him. But that wasn't good enough for Amy. According to her, he was useless . . . useless husband, useless dad, useless excuse for a man.

As he mentally replayed the argument they'd been having just before he walked out, Mark's anger began to resurface. Amy had never had a job in her life, and yet she had the cheek to call him a loser just because he was temporarily out of work. Well, she'd better watch out, because his luck was bound to change before too long. And when it did and she came running to him for money, he was going to tell her right where to shove it.

Almost home by now, he stopped at the corner and stared down the road towards his house. If he went in without the money Amy would go off her nut and they would end up having another barney – and *he* would end up walking out again. It was as inevitable as night following day, and the only way to avoid it was by not going home in the first place.

Decided, he did an abrupt about-turn and strode off in the opposite direction.

*   *   *

Jenny hadn't felt well when she woke that morning, so she'd stayed in bed and had spent the day watching TV, reading magazines, and generally feeling sorry for herself.

Restless after her soaps had finished in the evening, she got up and had a bath, then wandered into the kitchen to make herself a sandwich. She was just making her way back to bed when the doorbell rang. Cautious, because she didn't usually get visitors at night, she crept down the stairs and peeked through the spyhole. A man was standing on the step, but he had his back turned so she couldn't see his face.

'Who is it?' she called through the wood.

'Er, hi . . . it's me – Mark.' He turned and looked at the spyhole. When she didn't respond after a few seconds, he frowned. 'Sorry, is this a bad time?'

'No, it's fine!' Jenny blurted out, snapping out of the trance she'd gone into at the unexpected sight of his face. 'Just a sec. I'll get the key.'

She fled back up the stairs, tugging the towel off her hair on the way. In the bedroom she dropped her dressing gown and quickly pulled on a pair of jeans and a jumper. Then, running the brush through her damp hair and slicking a quick coat of mascara over her ginger eyelashes, she grabbed her keys and ran back down.

'Sorry about that. I wasn't expecting anyone, so I'd already locked up for the night.'

'Don't worry about it.' Mark stuffed his hands into his pockets. 'I was just passing and remembered you said you'd moved here, so I thought I'd call in and make sure you're okay.'

'Thank you, that's so nice,' Jenny murmured, touched that he cared. 'Do you want to come in?'

'If I'm not disturbing you?'

'No, course not.'

Jenny went up the stairs ahead of him and switched on the lamp and the TV before drawing the curtains to conceal the urn containing her mother's ashes.

'I'll put the kettle on,' she twittered nervously. 'Tea or coffee?'

'Whatever you're having.' Mark perched on the edge of one of the two black leather couches.

'Sugar?'

'Two, please.'

Left alone when she rushed off to the kitchen, Mark sat back and looked around. The room was surprisingly well furnished, with a fancy fireplace, a massive mirror, and a decent-sized plasma TV. There were only two pictures on the wall, one of a woman who Mark assumed to be Jenny's mum, the other of Jenny herself – but as she looked now, he noticed; no trace of the ginger freak he'd known and taken the piss out of at school.

Amused by her attempt to rewrite history, Mark reached for the TV remote and flicked idly through the channels. When Jenny came back a few minutes later with two steaming cups in her hands, he smiled up at her. 'This couch is well comfy. I'd have been asleep if you'd been much longer.'

'I know, it's lovely, isn't it?' Jenny agreed, passing his cup to him and taking a seat on the other couch. 'The bereavement counsellor advised me to get rid of some of the old stuff so I wouldn't be constantly reminded of my mum.'

'Did it help?'

'Oh, yeah, loads.'

Mark took a sip of his tea and gazed around again. Never mind getting rid of *some* of the old stuff, she'd obviously chucked the whole lot out and started from scratch. And that would have cost a fair bit, because these couches weren't cheap, so either she had a well-paid job or she'd inherited a bundle. Either way, she was beginning to look more attractive by the second.

Annoyed when Steve's phone went to voicemail, Amy slammed the phone down and paced the living-room floor. Mark still hadn't come back, and while she wouldn't usually be bothered, because he always went awol after a row, this time she was fuming. He knew that the kids hadn't eaten, and he'd promised to borrow some money so she could get them something from the chippy. She wouldn't even have cared if he'd posted it through the letter box and pissed off again, just so long as they got fed. But, as per usual, he was putting his own selfish needs before theirs. And now he'd switched his phone off and none of his friends claimed to have seen him, so there was nothing else she could do.

She turned around and abruptly stopped pacing when she saw her daughter standing in the doorway. 'What's the matter, love?'

'I can't get to sleep,' said Cassie, a wobble in her voice, dark shadows circling her sad blue eyes. 'Bobby's crying. He says his tummy's poorly.'

Amy felt like crying, too. But that wasn't going to put food in their stomachs. So, making a decision, she said, 'Go and get your coat on. And put Bobby's on him for me.'

'Are we going out?' Cassie asked.

'I hope so,' Amy murmured, shooing her back out into the hall before reaching for the phone.

Sonia Clark was lying on the couch in her nightdress, watching reruns of *Only Fools And Horses* and snacking on cheese and crackers. John was at the pub, and she was thoroughly enjoying not having to sit through another football or snooker match – just about all the boring bugger ever wanted to watch these days. When the phone rang, she brushed the crumbs off her chest and reached over her shoulder to pick it up.

'Hello?'

'It's me,' said Amy. 'Just checking you're in.'

'Why?' Sonia frowned. 'I hope you're not thinking of coming round, 'cos I'm already in bed,' she lied.

'Oh. Sorry. Didn't mean to disturb you.'

Sonia caught the unhappiness in her daughter's voice and sighed. 'What you after?'

'Nothing,' Amy muttered. 'It doesn't matter.'

'Well, it obviously does, or you wouldn't be ringing.' Sonia reached for the remote and paused her programme. 'Come on, spit it out. And it'd best not be money, 'cos you haven't paid me back from the last time yet and your dad's already giving me flak over it.'

'I don't want money,' said Amy plaintively. 'I just need something for the kids to eat. There's nothing in, and our Bobby's crying. Can I bring them round?'

'You're having a laugh,' Sonia said coolly. 'Have you seen the time? And you're gonna drag them kiddies all the way over here in the cold?'

'I wouldn't if I wasn't desperate,' Amy replied, a sob betraying the fact that she was crying now. 'Oh, just forget it,' she said before her mum could respond. 'I'll wait for Marnie to come home and ask her.'

'And what time will that be?' Sonia demanded. 'It could be four in the morning, knowing her, and you'd have had them kids sat there starving all that time.'

'Don't you think I know that?' Amy wailed. 'That's why I rang *you*, 'cos you're their nan and I thought you cared. But you're in bed, so don't worry about it.'

'Stop being such a drama queen,' Sonia berated her. 'Fetch them round. But don't you dare make them walk. Get a taxi. I'll pay when you get here.'

'Thanks, Mum. I'm really sorry. It's just been a difficult week.'

'It always is with you. And that's half the trouble – you never learn.'

Sonia dropped the receiver back onto its cradle and slammed her plate down. Peace shattered, she shoved her feet into her slippers and shuffled into the kitchen to take some fish fingers and chips out of the freezer. Putting them on to cook, she looked for her purse, then went out onto the step to wait.

This was the first time Amy had brought the kids round so late, but it certainly wasn't the first time she'd relied on Sonia to fill their little bellies. Everyone knew it was hard to feed a family in this day and age, and Sonia knew it wasn't Amy's fault that the DSS was messing her about and her benefits hadn't come through yet. But Amy couldn't keep expecting Sonia and John to cough up willy-nilly. It was the fault of that useless husband of hers, all this, and it was about time Amy stopped making excuses for him and gave him a kick up the arse.

When the taxi pulled up outside her parents' house ten minutes later, Amy guiltily dipped her gaze when her mother stepped forward to pay the driver.

'Sorry,' she mumbled, herding the kids inside and taking Bobby's coat off while Cassie shed her own. 'If there'd been any other way, I'd have—'

'I don't want to hear it,' Sonia cut her off, shoving her purse into her dressing-gown pocket and marching into the kitchen. Coming back with two plates of food, she handed them to the kids, telling Amy, 'I didn't make you any, but you can get yourself a butty if you're hungry.'

'I'd rather go home, if you don't mind,' Amy said quietly. 'Mark's gone walkabout, and I want to be there when he gets back.'

Sonia gave her a scathing look. 'I never thought I'd raised an idiot but I'm seriously starting to wonder about you.'

Amy flashed a cautious glance at the kids. 'Please don't start, Mum. I'm not stupid, but he's my husband. What am I supposed to do . . . kick him out 'cos he can't find another job? He's been trying, but it's not that easy these days.'

'There you go again, making excuses for him.' Sonia sneered. 'I wouldn't even mind if you knew where he was, but you haven't got a clue, have you? He could be up to all sorts, for all you know. What if he's cheating on you – have you even thought about that?'

'I'm going,' said Amy desperate to get out of there. She leaned down and kissed the kids. 'Be good for Nana, and I'll see you in the morning.' Then, thanking her mum again, she rushed out and set off on the long, cold walk home.

6

Mark woke to the delicious scent of fried bacon.

'What time is it?' he asked, sitting up when Jenny put the tray she was carrying on the bedside table.

'Half-ten,' she told him, taking a cup of tea off the tray and walking around to the other side of the bed.

'At night?' Mark's eyes swivelled towards the curtains.

'No, morning. I would have woken you earlier, but you looked so comfortable I didn't want to disturb you.'

Mark groaned, shoved the quilt off and looked around for his clothes. He couldn't remember coming into her bedroom last night, never mind getting undressed. After the tea Jenny had cracked open a bottle of Scotch, and the last thing he remembered was her giving him a blow job. And he could only imagine that it had been a belter for everything that had come after it to be erased. But, good or not, nothing was worth the grief he was going to get off Amy when she got her hands on him.

'You might as well eat your butty before you go,' said Jenny, hoping to keep him a little while longer. She'd slept with a couple of lads in the years since their first encounter, but none had ever matched up to Mark. And she had never spent a full night with any of them, so it had been absolutely magical to wake up beside him this morning.

Mark shook his head. He didn't even want to speak to her just now, never mind eat the flaming butty.

'You're not angry with me, are you?' she asked. 'I did try to wake you, but you were completely out of it. Hope I haven't got you into trouble.'

With his back turned towards Jenny, Mark heard the threat of tears in her voice and rolled his eyes. Why did women always turn on the waterworks when you were trying to get away from them?

'Look, don't worry about it,' he muttered, pulling his socks on. 'I'll sort it.'

'How?' Jenny wanted to know. 'Where will you say you've been?'

'Steve's. That's where I usually go, so she'll believe me. Just hope she hasn't spoken to him already.'

'Maybe you'd best ring him and check?'

'I'll call in on the way home,' Mark said, zipping his fly. 'I was supposed to be going round there today, anyway.'

Jenny hugged her knees and watched as he hurriedly pulled on the rest of his clothes. She didn't want him to leave but she was in no position to ask him to stay. Not yet, anyway.

When he was ready, Mark gave her an awkward smile. 'Right, well, I'll, er, see you, then.'

'Okay.' Jenny smiled back. 'See you.'

Already at the door, Mark hesitated. He'd borrowed one hundred quid off her before the Scotch had come out last night, and he had fully expected her to use the loan to try and force him into some kind of relationship. By rights, she ought to be grateful that he'd shagged her in the first place, considering that he was cool and she was a ginger freak

– albeit brunette now, and not really all that freaky any more. But she didn't seem to care that he was leaving, and he couldn't help but wonder why. Embarrassed when it suddenly occurred to him that he might have performed badly, he gave her a quick nod goodbye and fled.

Jenny stayed where she was until she heard the front door click shut behind him, then ran to the window and watched as he walked away. She felt physically sick at the thought of him going home to Amy. The bitch would probably make him grovel, and then they would probably end up in bed having great make-up sex.

Unable to bear the thought, she shook it out of her head and climbed back into bed. She had loved Mark since the first time she'd ever laid eyes on him, but she'd never dreamed she stood a chance with him, because boys like him didn't go for girls like her, they went for girls like *Amy* . . . pretty, popular Amy, with her perfect blonde hair and her sickening self-confidence. That was why she'd been so shocked when Mark had taken her down the alley on his wedding night – and even more so when he'd called round later that same night to pick up where they had left off. When he'd told her that he wouldn't be coming back, she'd refused to believe that it was over and had started hanging around at the corner of his mum's road in the hopes of catching him on his own. But Amy and that stupid baby of theirs had always been with him whenever he came out, so she hadn't been able to approach him. And then they had moved into their own place, and Jenny hadn't known any of his friends well enough to ask for the address without raising suspicion, so she'd been forced to give up and accept that she had lost him.

But now, beyond her wildest dreams, he was back in her

life. And this time Jenny was determined to make sure that he stayed.

Mark got no answer when he knocked on Steve's door a short time later. Assuming that he and his new bird were still in bed, Mark switched his mobile back on and rang him.

'Shit, man, I'm sorry,' Steve apologised. 'I totally forgot you were coming round. I'm in town with Layla.'

'Oh, cheers,' Mark muttered, miffed that his friend had so easily forgotten him when they had only just made up after their argument. Showed how much *he* cared.

'Look, the match starts at five, so why don't you come round then?' Steve suggested. 'I'll get those beers and treat you to a takeaway. Oh, and sorry I didn't answer your call last night, by the way.'

'My call?'

'Yeah, your name came up, but we were in the middle of dinner and I thought it'd be rude, so I switched my phone off.'

Mark guessed that it must have been Amy calling from the house phone, and said a silent thank-you to God that she hadn't got through.

'Couldn't do us a massive favour, could you?' he asked. 'Only me and Amy had a bust-up last night and I didn't go home. If she asks, can you tell her I stopped at yours?'

'Oh, mate,' Steve groaned. 'I'm a shit liar. She'll know as soon as I open my mouth.'

'*Please*,' Mark pleaded. 'She probably won't ask, but I just need to know you're gonna back me up if she does.'

Steve went quiet for a moment. Then, sighing, he said, 'Right, fine. But don't ask me to do it again, 'cos I like Amy and I don't want to get involved in whatever's going on.'

'Nothing's going on.'

'So why don't you just tell her where you really were instead of dropping me in it?'

'It's complicated,' Mark said evasively. 'Look, I'd best go. See you later. And cheers for that.'

Relieved to have an alibi, Mark sauntered out of the flats and set off for home with the money that Jenny had lent him weighing heavy in his pocket. Amy was doing her best, but he felt guilty every time she cried because she couldn't afford to give the kids a treat, or go to the launderette, or put the lights or heating on. One hundred quid was all well and good, but how much happier would she be if he handed her *two* hundred . . . or three, or four?

As an excitement that he hadn't felt in weeks began to stir in his gut, Mark turned on his heel and headed back to the bus stop. Lady Luck was an elusive lover, and only a fool would turn his back on her when she came a-calling. And whatever else he might be, Mark Taylor was no fool.

Amy woke up with a start and stared in dismay at the clock on the bedside table. It had been gone five a.m. before she'd finally fallen asleep, and it was almost noon now. Dreading the tongue-lashing she was bound to get off her mum, she jumped out of bed and ran downstairs to ring her.

'I'm so sorry,' she blurted out. 'I know I promised to pick the kids up early, but I didn't—'

'No use saying sorry to me,' Sonia cut her off. '*I'm* not the one who sat here all morning in tears waiting for you.'

'Oh, God,' Amy moaned guiltily. 'Tell them I'm coming now. I just need to get dressed.'

'Too late,' said Sonia. 'Poor little buggers deserved a treat, so your dad and Uncle Ricky took them to Chester Zoo for the day. I'll ring you when they get back, but I'll warn you now, your dad's fuming. Cassie's told us all about you and that waste of space arguing in front of them.'

'That's not true,' Amy protested. 'We never argue in front of the kids, we always wait till they've gone to bed.'

'It doesn't matter if they're in the same room or up the bloody stairs, they can still *hear* you, and they're frightened to flaming death.'

'It's not that bad.'

'So you're calling Cassie a liar?'

'No, but . . .'

'Oh, shut up!' snapped Sonia. 'You're pissing me off now, Amy, you really are. I told you from the start you were too young to get wed and have kids, but you always knew better than everyone else, didn't you? *I'll be fine*, you said. *I'll be a great mum.* Well, I haven't seen any evidence of it so far. Your house is a pigsty, and those kids look like they haven't had a bath in weeks, never mind a decent meal. But all *you*'re bothered about is that pillock who can't even keep a job for more than two minutes!'

Amy's chin was wobbling, but she blinked back the stinging tears. 'It's not Mark's fault.'

'Well, whose *is* it, then?' Sonia demanded. 'It sure as hell isn't mine or your dad's, but we're the ones who have to keep picking up the pieces whenever he screws up. It's a good job the kids have got us to watch out for them, 'cos *you* obviously don't give a toss. You should be ashamed of yourself!'

When her mum slammed the phone down, Amy sank down onto the couch and sobbed. But with the tears came anger. How *dare* her mum accuse her of not caring about her kids! They were her life, and she was doing her best to bring them up decently. It wasn't easy, carrying on as normal when her world was falling apart and no one was lifting a finger to help, but that didn't mean she wasn't *trying*.

When the tears finally stopped, Amy looked around the room. Her mum was right about one thing – she *had* let it get into a state. A thick roll of dust lay along the join between the laminate flooring and the skirting board, and there were overflowing ashtrays on the coffee table and window ledge. The kids' breakfast bowls were still on the couch from yesterday morning, along with a pile of old sweet wrappers and comics. And her own stuff was also contributing to the mess, from the hairbrush on the mantelpiece to the magazines stuffed down the side of her chair. And there were cups everywhere she looked, some empty, the rest half full of filmy wasted tea.

Disgusted with herself for letting it get so bad, and determined to prove her mother wrong, Amy shoved up her sleeves and set to work, moving from room to room, clearing, polishing and vacuuming until the house was spotless from top to bottom.

She was just putting the vacuum cleaner back into the cupboard under the stairs when Marnie knocked on the back door.

'Don't shoot, I come in peace!' Marnie teased, holding up her hands when she saw the thunderous look on Amy's face.

'I'm having a bad day.' Amy snatched the kettle off its base and carried it to the sink.

'Mark pissed you off?' Marnie ventured.

'How did you guess?' Amy snapped sarcastically.

'Sit down, I'll do that,' Marnie ordered, prising the kettle out of her friend's hand and pushing her towards a chair. 'You've been at it for hours. And don't say you haven't, 'cos you've been banging around so much I thought you were being raided.'

'I'm better off keeping busy,' Amy insisted, sidestepping her and taking two cups out of the cupboard.

'There's busy, and there's manic,' Marnie said when Amy slammed the cups down on the ledge. 'And this is manic to the max, hon. Cass and Bobs won't know where they are when they get up, it's that clean.'

'I like it clean,' said Amy, spooning sugar into the cups. 'And they're not here.'

'No *way*!' Marnie clasped her hands to her breast and stared at Amy as if she couldn't believe what she'd just heard. 'You mean Mark's actually took them out to give you a break? Hallelujah, kingdom come!'

'Has he hell. They're at my mum's.'

'Typical.' Marnie tutted. 'And there was me thinking he'd remembered he was a dad at long last. I take it he's still in bed while you're wearing yourself out?'

'He didn't come home last night,' Amy told her. 'He was supposed to be borrowing some money, but I've phoned all his mates and no one's seen him.'

'So they say.' Marnie gave her a cynical look. 'Bet he was sitting right there while you were on the phone. Born liars, the lot of them. Or, as I like to call them, pricks with dicks.'

When Amy cracked a sad smile, Marnie said, 'That's better. Who needs men when you've got mates like me to cheer you up, eh? Now sit down and let me pamper you for a bit.'

Too weary to argue, Amy flopped onto a chair. But when the kettle switched itself off a few seconds later, and Marnie said, 'Oh, oh, I think the electric's gone,' she fell to pieces all over again.

'Oh, God! I can't take any more of this!'

'Hey, it's not the end of the world.' Marnie rushed over and gave her a cuddle. 'We'll just go round to mine for a brew instead.'

'I don't want a stupid brew,' Amy sobbed, fresh tears streaming down her cheeks. 'I just want my l-life back.'

'I know it's hard,' Marnie said soothingly, pulling up a chair and sitting beside her. 'But this is just a little blip, hon. Everything will start picking up soon, you'll see.'

'*How?*' Amy cried. 'Mark's not even trying. He just leaves everything to me, then walks out when I ask him to do anything. And the social are saying we're not entitled to full benefits 'cos it's Mark's fault for getting sacked. I've got no food, no electric, and the phone's about to get cut off. I don't know how much more I can take, Marn, I really don't.'

'Right, that's enough,' Marnie said firmly. 'You're one of the strongest women I've ever met, Amy Taylor, and if anyone can get through this, you can.'

'I couldn't even give the kids their tea last night,' Amy admitted tearfully. 'That's why they're at my mum's. Mark promised to get some money so I could go to the chippy, but he didn't come back. And then Bobby started crying, and my mum had a right go at me, and I just . . . I just . . .'

Unable to go on, Amy covered her face with her hands and sobbed. Marnie held her in silence. There was no point saying anything, because money was the only thing that would make her feel better and Marnie had none to give. She could cheerfully kill Mark for walking out and leaving Amy to deal with all this on her own, but she didn't want to add to her friend's distress, so she kept her thoughts to herself.

When she was cried out, Amy got up and splashed cold

water onto her swollen eyelids. 'Sorry. Didn't mean to break down on you like that.'

'That's what friends are for,' Marnie reminded her, taking her cigarettes out of her pocket and lighting one. 'You've done it enough times for me in the past. Christ, there've been times when I probably would have slit my wrists if you hadn't been there.'

Drained, Amy sat down and held out her hand. 'Give us a drag.'

Marnie drew her head back. 'You don't smoke.'

'I need *some*thing.'

'Not that. You've seen the state I get in when I run out, and you expect me to get you started?'

'Just bloody give me some,' Amy groaned.

'Right, fine.' Marnie passed the cigarette over. 'But don't blame me if it makes you sick.'

Amy took a deep drag, and was instantly whisked back to her teens by the taste and the sensation of giddiness in her head. Before she got caught with Cassie, she'd been a twenty-a-day girl. She had given up as soon as she found out she was pregnant and had never touched one since. But this was a whole new level of low and, the way she was feeling right now, if somebody had offered her crack she would probably have taken it.

Soothed by the nicotine, but also a little nauseous, Amy passed the cigarette back to Marnie after a couple of drags. Getting herself hooked on fags wasn't going to solve her problems. And nor was making excuses for Mark. Her mum had been spot on about that, because Amy had been covering for him ever since they'd first got together. She'd lied for him, provided him with alibis, defended him, and even physically fought over him. And all he'd ever given in return was his last name, and two kids who, precious as they were, had effectively ended Amy's life outside these four walls. From waking up in the morning till she went back to bed of a night, her whole life revolved around them. Mark, on the other hand, was spending even less time with them these days than when he'd been working. Apart from when he was forced to get up to sign on, he stayed in bed all day, and only got up after the kids had gone to bed so he could play on his Xbox without being disturbed. And if Amy dared to complain, he flew off the handle and walked out.

Well, enough was enough. She was done with being a doormat, and when Mark showed his face she was going to give it to him straight: *Sort it out, or pack your bags and piss off back to your mum's.*

Or, better still . . .

'I'm going to stay at my mum's,' she declared, pushing her chair back.

'Really?' Marnie raised an eyebrow. 'How long for?'

'Who cares?' Amy shrugged. 'Don't see why I should sit here suffering while he's out doing God knows what. If he asks, you haven't seen me. Let him figure it out and come running after me for a change.'

As Amy packed a bag of clothes for herself and the kids and called a cab to take her to her mum's, Mark walked out of the bookie's with a face as grey as the storm clouds that were brewing overhead.

It had taken him less than half an hour to lose every penny of the hundred quid that Jenny had lent him, and he was absolutely gutted, because he'd been banking on the money to cheer Amy up and make her overlook the fact that he'd stayed out all night.

It was far too early to go to Steve's, and too cold to hang around on the street, so he set off for home with a list of excuses going round in his head.

The house was deathly quiet, and full of shadows. Mark tried to switch the hall light on, but nothing happened. Even in the gloom, he could see and smell that the living room and kitchen were spotlessly clean. Hoping that Amy wasn't too mad after all, because she rarely cleaned when she was in a mood, he went back out into the hall and called her name. When he got no answer, he went quietly up the stairs to see if she and the kids were sleeping. But both rooms were empty, and when he saw the open drawers and missing clothes a sickly feeling stirred in the pit of his stomach.

He ran round to Marnie's and banged on the door. 'Marnie . . . open up. I know she's in there. I just need to talk to her.'

After several more knocks, and a fruitless peer through the window, he was about to climb over Marnie's locked side gate to go round the back when Gemma came out of her house.

'Coo-ee!' she shouted. 'If you're looking for your Amy, she went off in a taxi about an hour ago. With a suitcase.'

Muttering 'Thanks,' Mark went home and picked up the phone.

'Yes, she's here,' said Sonia when she answered his call. She turned to Amy who was sitting on the couch with her feet up and a cup of tea in her hand, and mouthed, '*Mark.*'

Amy shook her head.

'I'm sorry, she doesn't want to talk to you,' Sonia told him. 'And don't come round, 'cos John will be back soon and he's already gunning for you.'

Sonia rolled her eyes at Amy when Mark pleaded with her to let him speak to his wife, and said, 'No, I'm sorry. She's made her decision, and you're just going to have to give her a bit of space to think things through.'

Amy drew her knees up to her chest and listened to her mum's side of the conversation.

'Yes, I know they're your kids, but they're safer here with us for the time being . . . No, of course I'm not trying to punish you, I'm just supporting my daughter . . . It's got absolutely nothing to do with me, this is her decision, not mine . . . Well, if that's the way you've been talking to her, I don't blame her for leaving you . . . Goodbye!'

'What did he say?' Amy asked when her mum slammed the phone down, even though she'd already guessed most of it.

'That it's not all his fault,' said Sonia. 'That you're not as perfect as me and your dad seem to think, and if you weren't so lazy he wouldn't get so mad and keep going out. Oh, and the kids are as much his as yours and you've got no right to keep them away from him, and if you try he'll take you to court.' A pious look on her face, she sat down and pressed the button on the side of her chair to elevate her legs. 'Like to see how he's going to get a solicitor when he can't even afford to put the lights back on.'

Amy would have been amused if she hadn't felt so sick. Her mum had been so mad on the phone this morning that she'd half expected her to slam the door in her face when she'd turned up. But as soon as Sonia saw the suitcase and realised that Amy was serious about sorting her life out, she had welcomed her daughter with open arms. And she was in full mother-tiger-protecting-her-young mode now, determined not to let Mark anywhere near until Amy was good and ready.

And, right now, Amy was nowhere near ready. She just

wanted to relax and let the stresses of the last few months drift off her shoulders.

Cold, miserable, and totally pissed off with Sonia for refusing to let him talk to his wife, Mark sat down and willed Steve to hurry up and ring so he could go round to his place. He'd feel better once he had food and beer in his belly, and the footie would chill him out enough to stop the conversation he'd just had with his bitch of a mother-in-law from going round in his mind.

He didn't know who the fuck she thought she was, but if she thought she was going to get away with treating him like a prick she had another think coming. And John fat-bastard Clark wasn't going to stop him, either. He might think he was a hard man just because he was six foot something to Mark's five-eleven, and fifteen stone to Mark's ten. But size wasn't everything, and Mark would mash him up if he tried to get in his way.

Still brooding when his mobile rang at half-four, he saw Steve's name on the screen and pushed himself up in his seat. 'At last! I was starting to give up on you. I'll be there in ten.'

'Sorry, mate, change of plan,' said Steve. 'I was about to get on the bus, but Layla's mum rang and told her to bring me home for dinner.'

'You had dinner with them last night.'

'Yeah, I know, but I couldn't very well say no, could I?'

'What about the footie?' Mark whined. 'And you promised me a takeaway.'

'I can see you any time,' said Steve, pissed off with his friend for trying to make him feel guilty. 'And you've let me down loads of times, so what you acting up for?'

Aware that he sounded like a sulky brat – or, worse, a scorned girlfriend – Mark said, 'Yeah, I know. Sorry. Just forget I said anything.'

'Look, she's special,' Steve told him, almost whispering now. 'But you're me best mate, and I don't want us falling out over her.'

'We won't,' Mark assured him. 'Everything's cool. Go and have your dinner, and give us a ring when you're free for that catch-up.'

He disconnected without waiting for an answer and slumped back miserably in his chair. Now what was he supposed to do? No electric, no food, no booze, and no cigs. He was going to be crawling up the walls before the night was through, and all he had to look forward to tomorrow was more of the same.

He snatched his phone up and dialled another number.

'All right, Mum?'

'What do you want, Mark? I'm a bit busy just now.'

'That's nice. Can't I call my mother to say hello without her thinking I'm after something?'

'Well, you never have before, so that'd be a no,' Jane Taylor answered bluntly. 'Seriously, Mark, I'm up to my eyes in it here. The am-dram are doing *Grease*, and I've only got a week to finish the costumes.'

'Tell 'em to do their own.'

'It doesn't work like that. I'm wardrobe mistress.'

'Well, I hope they're paying you for all the time you're putting in.'

'Oh, so that's why you've called?' Jane said knowingly. 'Should have guessed. You're after a borrow, aren't you? Well, sorry, son, you're out of luck, 'cos the bank of mum is closed for the foreseeable.'

'I wasn't even gonna ask for dosh,' Mark lied, injecting as much hurt into his voice as he could manage. 'I just wanted to say hello, but if you can't be arsed talking to me, I won't bother in future. Oh, and by the way, Amy's left me and took the kids. See ya!'

With that, he cut the call and threw the phone down angrily. When it immediately began to ring and his mum's name appeared on the screen, he switched it off. Fuck her, and fuck Amy's stuck-up bastard parents. He'd get Amy back if it killed him. And when he did, they could all go to hell if they thought he was letting them see his kids again.

7

Jenny was settling down to watch *Big Brother* when the door-bell rang. She wasn't expecting anyone so she ignored it. But when the letter box flapped open and Mark called her name, she leapt off the couch and ran into the bedroom as if her heels were on fire. Quickly changing her cosy fleece dressing gown for a more sexy satin one, she brushed her hair and spritzed herself with perfume, then ran downstairs.

'Sorry,' she told Mark breathlessly. 'I couldn't find my keys.'

'Not disturbing you, am I?' He eyed her nightclothes.

'No, I'm just watching telly,' she said. Then, seeing his miserable expression, she asked, 'Is everything all right?'

'Amy's left me,' he told her glumly. 'She's took the kids and gone to her mum's.'

Jenny's heart lurched so hard she had to put her hand against the wall to steady herself. 'Has – has she found out about us?'

'No.' Mark shook his head. 'Least, I don't think so.'

'Why has she left you, then?'

'I don't know. Everything.' Mark shrugged. 'Me not having a job, never having any money, kids doing her head in . . . It's all just got on top of her.'

'Has she said it's over?' Jenny probed, waving for him to come in and leading him upstairs. 'Has she asked for a divorce?'

Mark frowned deeply as he sat down on one of the couches. It hadn't even crossed his mind that Amy might ask for a divorce, and he didn't know what he would do if she did. As much as she pissed him off, he didn't want to lose her. And it would totally crack him up if they split and Amy got together with another bloke and the kids started calling him Daddy.

Jenny switched the lamp on and poured two glasses of Scotch. Mark looked crushed, and she wished she could sit next to him and hold his hand. But she wasn't brave enough, so she handed his glass to him and carried her own to the other couch.

Mark swallowed a mouthful and closed his eyes, relishing the burn as the liquid slid smoothly down his throat.

'You know she can't stop you seeing the kids, don't you?' Jenny said supportively. 'Dads have got rights now as well as mums.'

'Nah, she's not like that.' Mark shook his head and opened his eyes. 'It's not as bad as I'm making out. She'll come back if I get things sorted.'

Disappointed, but determined not to show it, Jenny gave him an understanding smile. 'How are you going to do that?'

'Money,' Mark said bluntly. He took another swig of his drink, then looked her in the eye. 'I know I already owe you but I could really do with some more. It'll only be for a few weeks, till my dole comes through. They owe me a fair bit, so I'll be able to pay it all back in one go.'

Jenny's heart sank, and she took a slug of her own drink. So *that* was why he was here. Not because he wanted to see her, just because he wanted more money.

'I'm sorry, I haven't got any,' she murmured.

'I can wait till tomorrow if you need to go to the bank,' said Mark, thinking that she meant she didn't have any more cash here.

'There's nothing in there either,' Jenny told him.

Mark gave her a questioning look. 'You can't have spent it all already?'

'Spent all what?'

'Your inheritance.'

'What inheritance?'

'The money your mum left you. I know you've bought all this new stuff, but there must be *some* left?'

'You're joking, aren't you?' Jenny snorted. 'My mum didn't leave me anything. And she's lucky she's already dead,' she added bitterly, "cos I'd have killed her all over again if I'd known about the unpaid bills she'd been stashing under her mattress. She didn't even bother telling me she'd stopped paying her funeral plan, so I got lumbered with that as well.'

Mark was confused. 'How did you afford all this new stuff if you're in that much debt? These couches must have cost a bomb.'

'Credit card,' Jenny admitted. 'But I'm totally maxed out – so I can't use it again, before you ask.'

'I wasn't going to,' Mark lied. A look of sheer misery on his face, he finished his drink and put the glass down on the table. 'Sorry, I shouldn't have come. I'm just scared I'm going to lose my kids.'

'I thought you said Amy wouldn't stop you from seeing them?' Jenny reminded him.

'I'm trying to put a positive slant on it,' Mark said with bitterness in his voice. 'Truth is, there's no telling with her, 'cos she's not right in the head. That's why I need to get the kids home, so I know they're safe.'

'She wouldn't hurt them, would she?'

Conscience refusing to allow him to accuse Amy of something as serious as that, Mark shook his head. 'No, course not. It's just . . .' He tailed off and shrugged. 'Well, she's not really been keeping on top of things lately. She just lies on the couch all day, watching telly. The kids would have starved by now if it wasn't for me.'

Jenny's eyes flashed with disgust. She had never particularly wanted children, but if she ever *did* have them she would do her damnedest to take good care of them. Especially if a good man like Mark had fathered them. Amy was a selfish, lazy bitch, and she didn't deserve Mark *or* their kids.

'That's why I need this money,' Mark went on. 'But it's not your problem, so just forget I said anything.' He stood up and gave her a sad smile. 'Thanks for the drink, and listening, and that. I'll see myself out.'

Jenny felt sick as he walked towards the door. For one beautiful moment she'd thought that he was here because he wanted to see her, and it hurt to think that he was only after money to lure Amy back. But having some of him was better than having none at all – and that was what she would get if she let him walk out.

'Wait,' she said. 'There is someone who could help you.'

Mark turned back with hope in his eyes.

'I know a man who does loans,' Jenny went on, reaching for the bottle to refill their glasses. 'But if I tell you his name you've got to swear you won't mention me, because he's a family friend – and he won't be happy if he thinks I've been talking about him.'

'Course I won't,' Mark promised, sitting back down, beside her this time.

'I want you to promise me something else as well,' Jenny added quietly.

'Anything.'

She passed his glass to him and looked him in the eye.

'Promise you won't dump me when Amy comes back to you.'

'Do you even need to ask?' Mark reached for her hand. 'Why do you think I'm here?'

'For the money,' Jenny replied bluntly.

Mark smiled and shook his head. 'If it was only that, I'd have gone to Steve. But I came *here* because I wanted to see *you*.'

Jenny inhaled deeply. 'Really?'

'Look, I don't know about you, but I think we've got something special going on here,' Mark purred. 'And I don't see why we shouldn't go for it – as long as Amy doesn't find out. I don't give a toss about her, but I can't lose my kids. You can understand that, can't you?'

Jenny's head was spinning. He looked and sounded sincere, but was it really possible that he felt the same about her as she did about him?

Mark had never jumped through hoops for any girl, and he resented having to do it now. But he could see that Jenny was weakening, so he leaned towards her and kissed her. Surprised when his dick twitched, because sex hadn't even entered his mind until then, he took her glass out of her hand and put it on the table, then pushed her gently down on the couch.

Clinging to him when he peeled her knickers down and slid into her, Jenny gasped, 'I love you!'

Mark's hard-on immediately began to soften. Groaning '*Ssshhh!*' he closed his eyes and visualised the last porno he'd watched in order to bring it back to life.

Ten minutes later it was all over, and Mark stood up and pulled his pants up.

'Are you going now?' Jenny asked, self-consciously covering herself.

Mark smiled and reached for his glass. There was nothing for him back at the house. Amy definitely wasn't going to come back tonight, and there was no way he was sitting there in the cold and dark when he could be snug as a bug right here.

'Fill us up,' he said, handing the glass to her. 'Might as well make a night of it now I'm here, eh?'

In the morning, Jenny let him out and stood shivering on the step. 'Will you ring me?' she asked. 'Or should I ring you?'

'Don't ring me,' Mark said quickly. 'I'll try to call but I can't promise when, 'cos Amy always checks my phone. Best just wait till I get a chance to come round.'

'When will that be?'

'No idea.'

Jenny's expression clearly showed her disappointment. She wanted to know exactly when he would be coming so she could make sure that she was ready for him. But she didn't want to make it any more difficult for him, so she forced a smile.

'Okay, I suppose I can wait. But please don't leave it too long. I need to see you – soon.'

'I'll try.' Mark smiled and started backing away. 'Cheers again for helping me out.'

'Don't forget, you can't mention me,' Jenny called after him in an urgent whisper. 'He doesn't like people knowing his business, and he'll go mad if he thinks I've been sending people to him.'

'I won't say a word,' Mark assured her. 'I'll tell him an old mate told me about him.'

He waved goodbye and set off down the road. He could feel Jenny's stare burning into his back as he walked and wished that she would piss off back inside. She'd served her purpose, and that was an end to it as far as he was concerned.

8

The Beehive pub in the heart of Moss Side had only recently reopened after a spate of murders and several drug busts some months earlier. Mark hadn't been in there in years, and had tended to avoid the area in general since the Somalians had taken over. Large groups of them hung around on every corner, and it was intimidating even for someone like Mark who had grown up in Hulme and had loads of black mates. These new guys were a different breed from the regular black guys. They didn't want to integrate, they just wanted to stick with their own, and they eyeballed anyone who dared to enter their territory.

Edgy as he walked past them now, Mark breathed a sigh of relief when he made it into the pub unscathed. Smacked in the face by the familiar fug of ganja smoke, he nodded hello to a couple of Rastas who were propping up the bar and looked around.

Len Yates was sitting with another man at a table in the corner. Mark wasn't sure it was him when he first spotted him, because he was a lot smaller and skinnier than Mark had expected. If it hadn't been for the white patches that Jenny had mentioned on his already pale face, Mark wouldn't have picked him out as a moneylender in a million years. The other one, maybe, because at least he had the build; but not the skinny fella.

Less apprehensive now that he knew he wasn't dealing with a bruiser, Mark strolled over. The men had been laughing, but they stopped abruptly when he reached them, and four suspicious eyes turned on him. Strangely, given what he'd just been thinking, it was Yates's stare that unnerved him the most. His tiny eyes were the palest shade of blue that Mark had ever seen, and there was an icy coldness in them that sent a shiver down his spine.

'What do you want?' the bigger man demanded.

Mark swallowed nervously. 'I'm a friend of Coxy's. He said you were the man to talk to about . . .' He paused and glanced around before whispering, '*A loan*.'

'That right?' Yates's voice was as thin as his face, and as whispery as his fair hair.

Mark nodded and shuffled his feet.

'Fuck off,' the big man snarled, rising up from his seat.

He was huge, and Mark took a step back and held out his hands. 'All right, mate, I'm going. No problem.'

'Just a minute,' said Yates, still staring at him. 'Do I know you?'

'I don't think so,' Mark replied, nervously eyeing the other man.

'You look familiar. Where do you live?'

'Hulme.'

'Do you drink in The Junction?'

'Yeah, sometimes.'

'I think I've seen you in there. Take a seat.' Yates nodded at the chair beside his.

The big man cast a hooded glance at his friend, but when Yates gave a surreptitious shake of his head he picked up his pint and walked over to the bar.

Legs shaking, Mark shuffled around the table and sat down.

Yates turned towards him and stared him in the eye. 'So when did Coxy tell you about me, then?'

'A few weeks back,' Mark lied. 'Not sure. Could be a bit longer.'

Yates draped his arm around the back of Mark's chair and smiled a sinister smile. 'Psychic, are you?'

'Sorry?'

'Well, you'd have to be if you spoke to Coxy a few weeks back, seeing as he's been *dead* for four months.'

Mark felt the colour drain from his face, and his heart lurched when Yates grabbed him by the hair and dragged his head down until they were nose to nose.

'Who really told you to come to me? And none of your bollocks this time.'

Mark felt something hard press against his ribs and almost fainted when he glanced down and saw the glint of a blade in Yates's hand. All pretence at loyalty flying out of the window, he was about to blurt out Jenny's name. But before he had a chance, someone called out his.

'All right, Tayls! How's it hanging, star?'

It was Clive, a Jamaican guy who had worked with Mark at the paint-mixing shop. They hadn't really known each other all that well, but Mark had never been more pleased to see anybody in his entire life.

'All right, Lenny.' Clive walked up to the table and touched fists with the man.

'Killa.' Yates nodded. Then, jerking his head in Mark's direction, 'Pal of yours?'

'Yeah, he's cool,' said Clive, touching fists with Mark now. 'Used to work at our place – till he got sacked.' He chuckled now, and turned to Mark. 'I hear the missus wasn't too pleased about that? Stevo reckons she gave you a right bollocking.'

'Yeah, she did,' Mark replied quietly, still conscious of the knife despite Yates having slid it back into his pocket.

'Tough break,' Clive said sympathetically. 'Stan's a bastard for kicking you out when you've got kids to feed. Have you found anything else yet?'

Mark shook his head.

'Soon come,' Clive said supportively. 'Anyhow, I'll leave youse to it.' He rubbed his hands together and grinned widely. 'Got me a fine lickle lady to wine and dine.'

'In here?' Yates scoffed. 'Fuck me, you know how to push the boat out, you lot, don't you?'

Mark winced and glanced up at Clive to see if he'd taken offence. But Clive just grinned, and drawled in an exaggerated patois, 'Man, me c'd tek her t' Nandos an' she still be purrin' like a lickle kitty cat. Darker da bee, sweeter da honey – seen?'

'Me see, mon, me see,' said Yates, mimicking him, badly.

Clive laughed out loud and touched fists with them both again before making his way over to the bar.

Yates turned back to Mark. 'So you've got kids?'

'Yeah, two.'

'And you've just been sacked, so I'm guessing you need money to tide you over?'

'Yeah.' Mark nodded. 'But I totally understand if you don't want to give me any after what I said about Coxy.'

'Coxy was a snake,' Yates said sharply. 'And you're lucky you didn't get your bollocks sliced off like him,' he added with a sly grin. 'But now I know you're mates with Killa, that's different. How much you after?'

'A-a couple of hundred,' croaked Mark, licking his lips, which were as dry as sandpaper.

'Address?' Yates demanded. Sitting back when Mark had

told him, he said, 'I'll call round in an hour. Make sure you're there, 'cos I don't like being fucked about.'

Mark nodded and stood up quickly. Unsure what to do now, he held out his hand, but immediately withdrew it when Yates ignored it and reached for his pint.

'Thanks,' he said instead. 'I really appreciate it.'

Yates took a swig of his beer and looked right through him as if he was no longer there. Taking that as his cue to leave, Mark walked out, waving goodbye to Clive on the way. Then, head down, he hurried past the Somalians and rushed home to wait for his money.

An hour later, a shabby silver Vauxhall Vectra pulled up at the kerb outside the house. Mark jumped up off his chair when he saw Yates climb out and ran to open the door.

Yates walked straight past him into the living room and looked around. Narrowing his eyes when he spotted the framed wedding photo on the mantelpiece, he picked it up.

'The missus?'

'Yeah. Amy.'

'Pretty.' Yates put the photo down and nodded at a picture of the kids on the wall. 'They the little 'uns?'

'Cassie and Bobby, yeah.'

'How old?'

'Two and five.'

'Family man, eh?' Yates smiled and pulled a thick wad of notes out of his pocket. 'There's five hundred there.' He handed it to Mark. 'Count it if you want.'

Mark's eyes widened as he gazed down at the money. 'Are you sure you want to give me this much?'

'That's my minimum,' Yates told him. 'You'll pay me back at fifty a week. Bring it to The Bee, five o'clock every Monday.

Don't be late, and don't even think about not turning up, because I *will* come round, and you *will* pay. We clear on that?'

'Absolutely,' Mark agreed without hesitation. 'Every Monday, five o'clock. I'll be there, no worries.'

Yates nodded and walked back out into the hall. He paused before he opened the door, and said, 'Just so you know, first time I have to come round for it I'll be breaking something before I leave. Second time . . .' He tailed off and smiled. 'Let's just say there won't *be* a second time.'

Mark gulped nervously. Moments earlier, the money had felt as light and as lovely as gold dust, but now it felt like a lead weight. He contemplated handing it back, but he had a feeling that wouldn't be an option now that he'd accepted it.

Amy had just put the kids to bed when Mark turned up at her mum's house at eight that night. Her parents had gone to the MRI to visit her aunt who'd just had an operation, so she was alone – and bored.

She had enjoyed being back home to start with, eating her mum's cooking, listening to her dad's lame jokes, and sleeping in her old bed. But the gloss had worn off within a couple of hours of getting up this morning, and she remembered exactly why she'd been so desperate to escape in the first place. Mark called *her* a nag, but she had nothing on her mum.

Don't leave that there . . . Stop slurping your tea . . . Close your mouth when you're eating . . . Don't let the kids touch that . . .

She made Amy feel like a five-year-old, and it wasn't nice. And it *definitely* hadn't been pleasant to be reminded of her dad's farts. Every two minutes he let one go, and Bobby thought it was so funny he'd been copying him all day. Only he hadn't quite mastered the fart without the follow-through yet, so Amy had had to change him four times before dinner.

Desperate to be back in her own house with her own things around her, and missing Mark far more than she dared to admit to her mum who seemed to think that she was home for good, Amy's heart leapt with joy when she gazed into his eyes as he stood on the doorstep. But, determined not to let him think she was a pushover, she folded her arms and played it cool.

'You shouldn't be here. My mum told you not to come.'

'I don't care about your mum,' said Mark, holding out the bunch of flowers he'd bought from the garage on the way. 'All I care about is you and the kids. Please come home, babe. I can't stand it when you're not there. I need you.'

'It's too soon,' Amy replied, already mentally packing her bags and pulling the kids out of bed. 'I need more time.'

'It's killing me,' Mark moaned. 'I just want my family back. You're my life. I don't want to live without you.' He sank down to his knees now, and thrust the flowers at her again. 'I've been stupid, and selfish, and you deserve someone better. But you're my wife, and I love you with all my heart. Please come home, darlin'. I'll change. I'll do anything you want. I'm *begging* you.'

Despite her resolve to stay strong, Amy melted. Mark was a clown, and she'd long ago learned that he would say anything to get his own way. But no other man had ever made her feel the way that he did when he looked at her the way he was looking at her right now. His soppy eyes and little-boy pout were so cute. And when he called her *darlin'* like that she just wanted to dive into his arms and stay there for ever.

'Not tonight,' she said, struggling to maintain her composure. 'The kids are in bed, and I'm not getting them up to take them back to the house while the electric's off. Sort that out, and I might think about it.'

'Already sorted,' Mark told her, grinning as he stood up and brushed the dirt off his knees. 'And I've been shopping, so there's food in, an' all.'

'*You*'ve been shopping?' Amy drew her head back and gave him an incredulous look. 'I didn't think you knew where the shops were. Well, not the ones that sell food, anyhow. You only ever go for booze and cigs.'

'That was the old me,' Mark said softly, moving closer. 'I just told you, I'm gonna change. Whatever it takes to get you back, I'll do it. 'Cos I love you. And you love me – don't you?'

He was so close by now that Amy could smell the scent of his skin, and she couldn't keep up the act any longer.

'You know I do,' she murmured, falling into his arms and burying her face in his shoulder. 'But this is your last chance,' she whispered. 'I can't keep doing this on my own.'

'I know,' Mark crooned, stroking her hair and kissing her neck. 'But we're gonna be all right, you'll see. We've got money now, so you don't have to worry about anything.'

'Did the benefits come through?' Amy gazed up at him. 'How much?'

'Three hundred,' Mark lied. 'And there's more to come. But let's not talk about that now. I just want to get you home.'

'No kidding,' Amy teased, pressing her hips against his when she felt his erection.

'Get the kids,' Mark growled. 'I'll call a taxi.'

Sonia was confused when she and John returned from their hospital visit to find the house in darkness. It was only nine, and that was far too early for Amy to have gone to bed. Concerned when she checked Amy's room and saw that the bed was empty, she rushed to the spare room to check on the kids. If Amy had gone out and left them on their own, she would bloody kill her.

The kids weren't there but, unlike Amy's bed which was still neat from Sonia having made it that morning, their beds had obviously only recently been vacated – and they were a right mess: chocolate smeared on the sheets and pillowcases, and a big wet patch in the middle of Bobby's.

'They've gone!' she yelled down to her husband as she came back out onto the landing.

'I know,' John called back from the bottom of the stairs. 'She left a note on the kitchen table.'

Sonia marched down and snatched the note out of his hand.

Gone home, call you tomorrow X

'Ungrateful little mare,' she hissed, pushing John out of the way and going into the living room.

'Leave her be, she knows her own mind,' John said placidly as he followed her. Shaking his head when she snatched up the phone, he switched the TV on, then sat down and kicked off his shoes.

'Don't get too comfortable,' snapped Sonia, tapping in Amy's number. 'If he's forced her to go back, we'll be going right round there to pick them up again. And that no-good swine will know about it if he tries to get in my way.'

'Don't interfere,' John warned, shifting to one side to let out a fart. Straightening up, he reached for the TV remote with one hand and picked his nose with the other.

'Get a tissue,' Sonia ordered, pulling a face as she waited for Amy to answer.

John ignored her and wiped his snot on the underside of the chair arm.

Amy took a long time to answer the call, but when she did Sonia launched into her.

'What the bloody hell do you think you're playing at, dragging those kids out of bed in the middle of the night? And you'd better not tell me *he* made you do it, or I'll have his bloody head on a plate!'

Amy pulled the quilt up over her breasts and rolled her eyes at Mark.

'The kids are absolutely fine,' she replied evenly. 'And Mark didn't make me do anything. I'd already decided I wanted to come home.'

Amy winced when her mother started shouting and held the phone away from her ear. Giggling when Mark licked her neck, she tried to wriggle away. But he held her down and started tickling her.

'Amy, are you listening to me?' Sonia's shrill voice blared out of the receiver. 'AMY . . . ? *AMY!*'

'Mum, I've got to go,' Amy gasped when Mark dived under the quilt and forced his head between her legs. 'Call you in the morn-*ahhh*!'

'Don't you dare hang up on me!' Sonia barked. The line went dead. She stared at the receiver in disbelief, then tapped it and listened again, as if she expected it to have been reconnected.

'Told you to leave her be,' John droned.

'If I wanted your opinion I'd ask for it,' Sonia snapped, giving him a dirty look as she pressed redial. Furious when the phone just rang and rang, she slammed it down. 'Just wait till she calls me back. I'll roast her bloody earholes!'

'If I was you, I'd keep me nose out,' John cautioned her

for the fourth time. 'You know what she's like. She won't thank you for interfering.'

'Oh, so I'm good enough for a shoulder to cry on, and she doesn't mind using me as an unpaid bloody babysitter. But I'm not allowed to be concerned about my grandchildren being dragged out of their beds in the middle of the night?'

'It's only nine,' John reminded her. 'And they're her kids, not yours, so I suggest you keep your gob shut if you don't want her to stop you seeing them.'

Sonia clamped her mouth shut and flounced into the kitchen. There was no point talking to John about stuff like this; he was a man, they didn't understand emotions. It wasn't just the situation with the kids that was pissing her off, it was the whole bloody lot of it. There wasn't a day went by that Amy wasn't on the phone complaining about Mark, but it never occurred to her to ask if Sonia had better things to be getting on with than listening to the same old gripes over and over. And who was the first one she came running to when she needed money, or food, or a bed for the night? Muggins, that was who! But let Muggins dare to speak up when madam didn't want to hear the truth, and madam thought nothing of falling out with her.

Well, bugger her. Sonia had had a gutful, and when she spoke to Amy again she would bloody well tell her so.

9

Amy rang her mum first thing the next morning and tried to explain that she was happy, that Mark had promised to change and she was convinced that he really meant it this time. But her mum hadn't wanted to hear that so they'd had a massive argument, culminating in her mum telling her that she was washing her hands of her and Amy saying that was fine by her, but that she needn't think she was seeing the kids again.

That little blip aside, Amy was blissfully happy during the next few weeks. She and Mark were getting on better than they had in ages and, still under the impression that the dole had already paid them three hundred pounds, she was delighted when they received a cheque for a further seven hundred. And, to cap it all, their sex life was better than ever, so she was walking around with a permanent smile on her lips.

Mark was also happy – far too happy to be bothered to go and see Jenny like he'd promised. In fact, he'd totally pushed her out of his mind, along with the money he owed her.

The loan he'd taken out with Len Yates wasn't so easy to forget, however, and he had been fastidious about making his repayments on time. Which was all well and good when he was flush, but not so good when the money began to run out.

As usual when he had a bit of cash in his pocket, Mark had been completely unable to resist the lure of the bookie's. And that, along with his first love, the fruit machine, soon put a dent in his stash.

It didn't help that Amy had been splashing out on the kids, buying them a load of new clothes, and treating them to days out at the pictures, bowling and swimming. But when Mark came home from the bookie's one day to hear that she'd ordered them each a new bed, he almost had a heart attack.

'Why have you done that?' he demanded. 'There's nothing wrong with the ones they've got now.'

'Bobby's pissed in his so many times the mattress is starting to rot,' Amy told him. 'And I couldn't get him one without getting Cass one as well, or she'd think I was playing favourites. Anyway, that's what the money's for. We wouldn't even be getting it if we didn't have the kids.'

Mark couldn't argue with that, so he just begged her not to buy anything else unless it was absolutely necessary, reminding her that they would soon be relying on just the weekly benefits and telling her that he didn't want them to go back to scrimping and scraping.

Amy calmed her spending down after that. But they were soon back to square one and Mark realised he was in trouble when he tried to withdraw Yates's money out of the hole in the wall one Monday afternoon, only to see on the screen that there was the grand total of seven pounds fifty left in the account. With just half an hour to go before he was due to pay up, he rang Steve.

'Mate, I need a massive favour. I need to borrow fifty quid asap. I'll pay you back first thing next week.'

Steve whistled softly through his teeth. 'Sorry, man, no can do.'

'*Please*,' Mark begged. 'It's urgent.'

'I *can't*,' Steve told him. 'Honest, I'm really skint. Layla's folks are away, and I've been stopping round at hers, so I've had to—'

'Fuck Layla,' Mark squawked. 'This is an emergency. I'm your best mate!'

'And Layla's my woman,' Steve reminded him sharply. 'So don't ever disrespect her like that again, or we're gonna fall out big time.'

'Sorry,' Mark bleated. 'But I really, really need this money.'

'Well, I haven't got it,' Steve repeated coolly. 'Sorry, can't help you.'

Mark cursed when Steve disconnected the call, but he had no time to waste so he tried his mum instead. She was out, so he went through the rest of the friends whose numbers were in his phone. And, finally, when there was absolutely nobody else left, he rang Jenny.

'Oh, so you've remembered my number, have you?' she said frostily when she heard his voice. 'Aren't I the lucky one?'

'Don't be like that, babe.' Mark forced himself to sound contrite. 'You don't know what it's been like since Amy came home. It's been a nightmare. She's been on my case day and night.'

'Should have thought about that before you begged her to come back.'

'I didn't beg her. And it wasn't even about her, I did it for—'

'The kids,' Jenny finished for him, a sarcastic edge to her voice. 'Yes, I know how devoted you are to your kids, thank you.'

Already pissed off about having to creep to her again,

Mark felt like telling her to fuck off. But she was his last hope, so he said, 'I know you're upset with me, but I genuinely haven't had a chance to get away.'

'Or pick up a phone?'

'Don't think I haven't wanted to. You've been in my head day and night. You don't know how hard it's been, waking up and seeing *her* lying next to me of a morning when all I want is you.'

Jenny went quiet, and Mark wondered if she had cut him off.

'Jenny?' he said. 'Are you still there? *Jenny?*'

'I'm here.' She sighed. 'But I don't want to talk over the phone. I want to see you.'

'And I want to see you too,' Mark purred. 'But I can't right now. I'm in a spot of bother and I need to get it sorted. You know that bloke you put me onto?'

'What about him?' Jenny asked warily.

'I'm supposed to be paying him this week's instalment in, like . . .' Mark glanced at his watch and groaned. 'Shit, I've only got twenty minutes left.'

'You'd better get off the phone, then,' said Jenny. 'Call me when you've finished.'

'I can't pay him,' Mark blurted out before she had a chance to hang up. 'My money's not gone into my account yet.'

'Oh, I see.' Jenny's voice hardened. 'So *that*'s why you rang, so you could tap me up again.'

Mark's heart sank. He supposed he couldn't blame her for cold-shouldering him after the way he'd messed her about, but if she wasn't going to help there was no point continuing the conversation.

He put his thumb on the disconnect button, but just as he was about to press it, Jenny said, 'All right, come round. I'll have to go to the machine, but it's not too far so I should be back by the time you get here.'

'Can't you bring it to me?' Mark asked, reluctant to schlep all the way over to her place when he was already on borrowed time.

'No,' Jenny said firmly, determined not to let him think she was a complete pushover. 'If you want it, you'll have to come for it.'

'Okay,' Mark agreed. 'I'll be there in five. But I won't be able to stay.'

Jenny murmured something that sounded suspiciously like 'We'll see' before she hung up. Mark kissed his teeth in irritation and set off at a rapid stride.

Jenny knew that Mark was using her, and she wished that she was strong enough to tell him to get lost. But she desperately wanted to see him. It had been hell waiting for him to come round after his last visit, jumping up and running to the window every time she heard a noise and sleeping with her phone in her hand in case she missed a call. She had even gone to his house last week and walked up and down on the opposite side of the road in the hope of catching a glimpse of him. Her heart had almost stopped when Amy had pushed the buggy out onto the path, but it had positively shattered when Mark had come out and kissed the bitch.

That had almost destroyed her and she had gone home in bits, vowing never to talk to Mark again. But now, as she stood on the step watching him walk up the path towards her, her resolve crumbled.

'Come in,' she said quietly.

'I can't,' said Mark, eyeing the money she was holding in her hand. 'I've only got ten minutes.'

'Considering how long it's been, I think you can spare me one minute,' Jenny insisted.

Mark gritted his teeth when she turned and walked up the stairs.

'I've missed you,' she said when he joined her in the living room.

'Yeah, me too,' Mark lied. 'And I wish I could stay, but I really need to get going. So, if I can just . . .'

'Why did you lie to me?'

'What?'

'You said it's been a nightmare since Amy came back.'

'It has.'

'So how come you're still kissing her like you love her?'

'Am I fuck!' Mark scoffed. 'Who told you that?'

'I *saw* you,' said Jenny.

'You what?'

'On your doorstep, last Wednesday. She came out with the buggy, and you kissed her.'

Mark drew his head back and narrowed his eyes. 'Have you been spying on me?'

'*No.*' Jenny blushed and folded her arms. 'I went to see a friend round the corner and had to walk past yours on my way home.'

'Jeezus!' Mark spluttered, running his hands through his hair. 'Are you stupid? Have you got any idea what Amy would have done if she'd seen you and put two and two together?'

'Left you?' Jenny was defiant.

'Is that what you're trying to do?' Mark demanded. 'After everything I said about my kids?'

'It wasn't the kids you were kissing, it was *her*.'

'A peck on the cheek is *nothing*. And if it keeps her happy and stops her from taking off with the kids again, what's wrong with that?'

'Are you still sleeping with her?'

'*What?*'

'You heard me.'

'Are you having a fucking laugh?'

'No, I want to know,' Jenny said firmly. 'You said I was special, so I've got a right to ask. Or maybe I should just go and ask Amy? I'm sure *she*'d tell me the truth.'

'You stay away from Amy,' Mark warned her angrily. 'And I'd better not catch you anywhere near my house again, neither.'

'If you came round when you said you were going to, I wouldn't have to come looking for you,' Jenny retorted sulkily.

Mark had heard enough. She was acting like a jealous wife and it was freaking him out. 'I'm out of here,' he muttered, turning and heading for the door.

'What time are you coming back?' Jenny asked. 'I'm thinking of getting a takeaway for dinner. Which do you prefer – Indian or Chinese?'

Mark spun round and gaped back at her in disbelief. 'Are you for real?'

'There's no need to be nasty.' Jenny gave him a hurt look. '*I*'m the one who should be angry after the way you've messed me around. All I want to know is what time you're coming back so I'll know when to order the food. What's so bad about that?'

'You seriously think I'm coming back after this?' Mark was incredulous. 'You're not right in the head, you.'

Aware that she'd gone too far, Jenny ran after him when he started trotting down the stairs.

'Mark, wait! I'm sorry! I shouldn't have said anything about you and Amy, but I just get so jealous when I think about you and her together.'

'She's my wife,' spat Mark, tugging his arm free when she grabbed it. 'The mother of my kids.'

'I know, and I'm sorry,' Jenny said again, tears of desperation streaming from her eyes. 'I just love you so much, and I don't want to lose you. Here, take the money.' She thrust out the notes that she was holding.

'I don't want it.' Mark shoved her hand away. 'It ain't worth the hassle.'

'Please,' Jenny implored. 'I swear I'll never mention Amy again. And you *need* it. Len will kill you if you don't pay him. *Please* . . . just take it.'

Mark wanted out of there so bad, but she was right, he did need the money. So he took a deep breath and, as if he was doing her a favour, said, 'Okay, I'll take it. But don't you ever do anything like that again or we're finished – for good.'

'I won't,' Jenny promised.

'I've got to go.' Mark opened the door.

Jenny bit her lip and nodded. 'Will – will you call me?'

'If I can.' He stepped out and pulled the door shut.

Jenny went back upstairs and watched through the net curtains as he ran down the road. When he'd disappeared from view, she turned to get a tissue out of the box on the coffee table. Pausing when she caught sight of the urn, she snarled, 'What are you laughing at? At least mine still wants me. Yours couldn't wait for you to *die*.'

Mark ran all the way to The Beehive, but as he turned the corner he saw the Vectra pulling out of the car park with Yates at the wheel and Keith, the moneylender's big sidekick, in the passenger seat. He waved and shouted, but they didn't see him. Guessing they were on their way to his house, he put his head down and legged it home.

Yates had been okay with him over the last few weeks, and Mark had felt like they were on their way to becoming mates when they bantered about the footie, even though Mark was a diehard red and Yates a committed blue. He hadn't forgotten the warning that Yates had given him at the start about what would happen if he was late making payments, but he was hoping that the man would be lenient seeing as this was the first time. And at least he had the money, so it wasn't like he was trying to get out of paying.

Relieved when he turned onto his road and saw that Yates's car wasn't there yet, Mark quickly let himself into the house and ran into the living room.

Amy was lying on the couch, reading a magazine. 'What's wrong with you?' she asked when she heard how out of breath he was.

'Nothing.' Mark pressed his nose up against the window.

'Well, who are you looking for?' Amy wanted to know. 'Is someone after you? What have you done?'

'*Nothing*,' Mark repeated irritably. 'Where are the kids?'

'Bobby's asleep, and Cass is playing with her dolls. Why?'

'Take them out.' Mark reached for her hand and pulled her to her feet.

'I can't wake Bobby up, he'll have a fit,' Amy protested. 'Anyway, I don't want to go out. I'll be starting dinner in a minute.'

'Get some chips and go to the park.' Mark pushed her towards the door.

'Stop it,' she complained, standing her ground and putting her hands on her hips. 'What's going on, Mark? And don't say nothing, 'cos I can always tell when you're lying.' Suspicion in her eyes now, she said, 'Is it a girl? You haven't been messing around, have you?'

'What? *No!*' Mark reached out and stroked her hair. 'Course not. Don't be stupid. I love *you*.'

'Well, what is it then?' Amy jerked her head away. 'You might as well tell me, 'cos I'm not going anywhere till I know.'

'All right, I might be in a bit of trouble,' Mark admitted, glancing out of the window again. 'I owe a bloke some money, and I was supposed to pay him at five, but I didn't make it so I think he's on his way over.'

'You've been borrowing money?' Amy was shocked.

'It was before the dole got sorted,' Mark told her. 'When you left me and took the kids to your mum's. I didn't tell you 'cos I didn't want you to worry. I'll explain later, but you've got to take the kids out before he gets here.'

'Why?' Amy was struggling to take it all in. 'What's going to happen?'

'Hopefully nothing,' said Mark. 'But he said he'd come and break something if I didn't pay on time, and I was late today.'

'You're telling me some bloke thinks he's coming into *my* house, and I'm just supposed to stand here and let him smash it up?' Amy's confusion changed to indignation. 'I don't *think* so!'

'What are you doing?' Mark asked when she pushed past him and reached for the phone.

'Calling the police.'

'*No!*' He lurched towards her and snatched the receiver out of her hand. 'You'll make everything ten times worse.'

Yates's car pulled up outside. Mark spotted it and groaned.

'Is that him?' Amy demanded, glaring out at Yates when he stepped out of the car. 'Right, I'll soon set him straight.'

'Stay here!' Mark ordered, his legs starting to shake when Keith got out as well. 'I'll deal with this.'

'No way,' Amy said huffily. 'I'm gonna tell him to get lost.'

Mark physically blocked her path and shoved her back into the room. 'I said *I'll* deal with it. Now stay there.'

Yates rapped on the front door. Mark took a deep breath and pulled the money out of his pocket. Then, smiling, he opened up.

'All right, mate? Bet you've been cursing me, haven't you? I've got your money, but you were leaving when I got to the pub and you didn't hear me shouting after you so I had to run all the way back.'

'Tough.' Yates barged past him. 'I told you what'd happen if you made me come round for it.'

Flattened against the wall when Keith squeezed past, Mark followed as they strolled into the living room.

'Just let me explain, Len. It's not my fault I was late. One of the kids was sick, and Amy was at her mum's, so I had to wait for her to get back before I could come out.'

Yates turned and grabbed his face, digging his fingernails hard into his cheeks. 'You were warned, and you took the piss, so now you're gonna be punished.'

'Get your hands off him!' Amy yelled. 'And get out of my house or I'm going to call the police.'

Before she could move to carry out her threat, Keith spotted the phone on the table beside the window and yanked the lead out of the socket.

'What the hell do you think you're doing?' Amy demanded. 'How dare you!'

'Feisty, your missus, ain't she?' Yates grinned at Mark.

'Amy, shut up,' Mark spluttered, his lips puckering from the pressure of Yates's grip. 'I told you I'd deal with this. Go upstairs.'

Scared now, Amy began to edge towards the door. But Keith grabbed her and pulled her back.

'Not so fast, sweetheart. We want you where we can see you.'

'Please don't do this,' Mark croaked. 'I've got your money, and I swear I'll never be late again. But this has got nothing to do with Amy, so please don't hurt her.'

'Who said I was going to hurt *her*?' Yates snatched the money and slotted it into his back pocket. Then, smirking, he drew his head back and butted Mark.

'*Stop it!*' Amy screamed when a horrible cracking sound rang out and blood spurted from Mark's nose. 'Leave him alone!'

Mark's knees buckled and he sank to the floor with his face in his hands. Amy struggled like a wildcat to get to him, but Keith was too strong and she could only watch as Yates set about Mark. Tears already streaming down her face, she cried out when she heard footsteps coming down the stairs.

'Cassie, don't come in! Go back to your room!'

It was too late – Cassie had already opened the door. And when she saw her father on the floor with blood all over his face she started screaming.

Yates immediately stopped what he was doing and, thin chest heaving, smiled down at the little girl. 'It's all right, sweetheart, no need to be frightened. Daddy's been a naughty boy so I'm just telling him off, that's all.'

'Don't you dare talk to her,' Amy hissed, wriggling free and rushing to Cassie. She shoved her back out into the hall, and glared at Yates. 'She's only five, you sick bastard!'

Yates chuckled softly, and squatted down beside Mark. He

grabbed him by the hair and turned his head around. 'I'm going. But I'll be back tomorrow, so make sure you've got my money.'

'He's just given you your money,' Amy reminded him angrily. 'Now get out, and don't come back.'

Yates straightened up and patted his pocket. 'This is interest for making me come for it, darlin'. And if you don't want me coming back every day, I suggest you make sure he's got the rest when I get here tomorrow.'

When he and the other man walked out, Amy pulled Cassie into her arms and hugged her. 'Please stop crying, baby. The nasty men have gone, and they won't be coming back. Just go back to your room and make sure Bobby's all right while I see to Daddy. Okay?'

Calmed by her mum's soothing tone, Cassie gulped back her tears and ran up the stairs. Shaking all over, Amy bolted the front door and rushed to Mark.

'Are you all right? Let me see your face.'

'Don't touch it,' Mark cried, still cradling his nose. 'I think it's broke.'

'I'll call an ambulance.' Amy reached for the phone but, when she heard no dial tone, remembered that the wire had been ripped out and looked for her mobile instead.

'Leave it,' Mark croaked, using the couch to pull himself up. 'They'll only fetch the police.'

'Good!' Amy tossed cushions aside as she searched for her phone. 'He's an animal, and he can't be allowed to get away with what he's just done.'

'I said *leave* it,' Mark yelled, his face contorting with pain. 'He'll only come back and do worse if we grass him up.'

'He's coming back *anyway*,' said Amy. 'And what's to stop him having another go at you?'

'He won't,' Mark insisted. 'I'll give him his money, and he'll be cool.'

'We haven't *got* any money till the child benefit goes in on Wednesday,' Amy reminded him. 'And while we're on the subject, I thought we were skint, so where did you get the money you just gave him?'

'Not now,' Mark moaned, clutching at his ribs as he hobbled into the kitchen. 'I feel bad enough without you quizzing me like I'm some kind of fucking criminal.'

'I've got a right to know what's going on in my own house,' Amy argued as she followed. 'You've already lied about borrowing the money in the first place, so now I want to know what else you've been hiding.'

'Nothing.'

Mark turned on the tap, and Amy watched as he gingerly washed the blood off his face. Lumps and bruises were springing up all over, and she could tell from the hunched way he was standing that he was hurting. But she was too angry to care. He'd brought danger into their home, threatening the safety of their children.

'I know you're hiding something, and I want the truth. Where did you get the money you just gave to that thug?'

'Off Steve.'

'So you borrowed money off that animal, and now you've borrowed off Steve to pay it back? How stupid are you?'

'Stop fucking blaming me.' Mark turned on her angrily. 'This is all *your* fault, so if you want to call anyone stupid you'd best take a look in the mirror!'

'I beg your pardon?' Amy's mouth dropped open in shock. 'How dare you try and blame me for this! I didn't even *know* about the money.'

'Didn't mind spending it, though, did you?' Mark said

accusingly. 'And I wouldn't have even needed it if you hadn't fucked off and left me with no food or electric.'

'And *why* didn't we have food and electric?' Amy shot back furiously. 'Because *you*'re a loser who can't keep a job for more than five minutes – *that*'s why!'

Mark snatched a cup off the draining board.

'Go on, I dare you!' Amy challenged, guessing from the look on his face that he wanted to throw it at her. 'But if you do, it'll be the last thing you *ever* do.'

'Oh, 'cos you're so hard, you're gonna do *what*?' spat Mark.

'Get out,' Amy hissed, a cold calmness settling over her. 'I mean it, Mark, just get the fuck out! I've given you chance after chance, and you always say you're gonna change. But you won't, 'cos you're a born liar.'

'And you're perfect,' Mark retorted nastily. 'Little Miss fucking Perfect, always looking down her fucking nose at everyone. Well, you want to take a good look at yourself, 'cos you're no better than that skank of a mate of yours.' He jerked his thumb towards the wall that separated their house from Marnie's. 'Only difference is, you've got a mug of a husband to sponge off, while she just shags every random bloke she meets and bleeds the fuckers dry.'

'Get *out*,' Amy said again, her teeth gritted, her eyes flashing with fury.

'You know what, I think I will,' Mark agreed, adrenalin making him temporarily forget the pain. 'At least then I won't have to look at your ugly fucking face.'

He hurled the cup at the wall and walked out, slamming the door behind him.

'Mummy?' Cassie's scared little voice floated down the stairs. '*Mummy?*'

Amy inhaled deeply through her nose to calm the storm

that was raging inside, and said, 'It's all right, baby, I'm here. I'm just going to clean up this broken cup and then I'll put dinner on. You can come down and watch telly, if you want.'

'Bobby's wet his bed,' Cassie told her.

'Bring him down,' said Amy, sighing as she reached for the dustpan and brush.

This was all Mark's fault, and it was typical of him to walk out and leave her to deal with his traumatised children. Well, fine, she'd do what she had to do. But if he thought he was going to stroll back in when he felt like it and everything was going to be all right, he was in for a shock, because he wasn't setting one foot in here until he'd sorted things out with that horrible man.

Mark was halfway to Steve's before he remembered that his friend had said he was staying at his girlfriend's house. Doing an abrupt about-turn, he went to his mum's instead. After he'd knocked several times and shouted through the letter box, she finally answered. She was wearing a dressing gown and looked a little flustered, but Mark was too interested in his own woes to notice.

'What are you doing here?' she asked. 'You should have rung first.'

'I didn't have time,' he said, edging past her when she seemed in no hurry to move out of his way. 'I need somewhere to kip for a few nights.'

'Oh, my God!' Jane exclaimed when he stepped under the hall light and she saw the state of his face. 'What the hell happened? Have you had an accident? Are Amy and the children okay?'

'They're fine,' Mark grunted, shrugging her off when she pulled him round to get a better look. 'I just need to sit down and have a cup of tea. And a fag, if you've got any going spare.'

'You can't go in there,' Jane yelped when he headed for the living room. 'I've got company.'

Mark had already opened the door.

A fat, bald, very naked man was lying on the rug in front of the fire.

'What the *fuck* . . . ?' Mark turned and gaped at his mum.

'It's not what it looks like,' Jane spluttered, blushing guiltily. 'Alan – Mr Dobbs – is from the am-dram, and we're rehearsing for a play we're thinking of putting on.'

'What, *Emmanuelle*?' Mark snorted. 'Do me a favour, Mam, I wasn't born yesterday.'

Jane recovered her composure and raised her chin. 'Yes, well, neither was I,' she replied defiantly. 'I'm old enough and ugly enough to do what I want, and if you don't like it, go home.'

'And leave you and Free Willy to do God only knows what?' Mark sneered, tossing the man a contemptuous look. 'Oi, fatso, shift it.'

'Don't you move!' Jane ordered when Alan Dobbs started to get up.

He stayed put, his hands covering his genitals, a look of mortification on his face.

Jane turned back to Mark. 'How dare you come in here and push my friends around. And why *are* you here, anyway? I don't see hide nor hair of you for months on end, and you only ever call me when you want something. So what is it this time? Hmmm?'

'I just told you, I need somewhere to stay,' Mark reminded her, angry that she was talking to him like this in front of a stranger. 'Me and Amy have had a row.'

'Oh, don't tell me,' Jane said knowingly. 'She's caught you messing around with another girl, hasn't she? Well, like I told you last time, you make your bed, you bloody well lie in it.'

Mark flicked the man on the floor a hooded glance and, lowering his voice, said, 'It's got nothing to do with birds. I owe a bloke some money, and he's just been round to the house.'

'And did that to you?' Jane eyed his battered face. 'In your house, in front of Amy? And then she kicked you out?'

Mark nodded and looked sorrowfully down at his feet, waiting for his mother to say that his wife was a bitch, and of course he could stay. But Jane just shook her head, and pursed her lips disapprovingly.

'You never learn, do you? Ever since you were a kid you've been bringing shit to my door and blaming everyone but yourself for it. God knows I've never been Amy's biggest fan, and I always said you were asking for trouble getting wed so young. But I don't blame her for kicking you out. How do you think she must have felt, having some nasty piece of work beat you up in front of her? She must have been bloody terrified. And where were the kids while all this was happening?'

'In their room.'

'Well, at least that's one good thing,' said Jane, folding her arms. 'But you're not stopping here.'

'Why not?' Mark frowned. ''Cos of *him*?' He gave a scornful jerk of his head in Dobbs's direction.

'It's got nothing to do with Alan,' Jane said sharply. 'I'm just not having you hiding out here, eating me out of house and home and scrounging all me fags when you should be back home looking after your wife and kids.'

Mark locked stares with her for several long moments, then

sneered. 'Fine, I know where I'm not wanted. I'll leave you and Viagra Man to it.'

'Don't be so bloody rude,' Jane scolded, following him as he stomped out into the hall. 'It's about time you grew up and realised that the world doesn't revolve around you, Mark Taylor. I might feel different if you hadn't brought it on yourself, but you have, so now you'll have to deal with it.'

'Yeah, whatever.' Mark cast one last bitter look back at her, then walked out.

Everything was aching by now, and his head was banging. All he wanted was a bed for the night, and a bit of tea and sympathy, but no one gave a fuck. His wife had kicked him out straight after watching him get his head kicked in, and his mother had chosen her pet Shrek over him. And Steve was more interested in getting his end away than in helping out his best mate.

Feeling increasingly sorry for himself, Mark walked to Jenny's flat. The rest of them might not care if he lived or died, but she would never turn him away.

Jenny was overjoyed when she answered the door and saw Mark on the step. But the joy quickly turned to horror, and her hands flew to her mouth. 'Oh, my God! Did Lenny do this?'

Mark nodded and gave her a pitiful look. 'Sorry about earlier, I shouldn't have spoken to you like that.'

'It doesn't matter.' Jenny reached for his hand and pulled him inside. 'Come and sit down. You look terrible.'

The fire was on in the living room. Mark flopped down on the couch in front of it and sighed as the heat immediately started to seep into his body. He was exhausted, and wished that he could just curl up and sleep for a week.

'Let's get you comfortable, then I'll make you a cup of tea,' said Jenny, arranging the cushions behind him.

Mark gave her a weak smile. 'I'd rather have Scotch, if there's any left?'

'Yeah, course.' Jenny rushed into the kitchen, grabbed two glasses and poured two shots: a small one for her, a very large one for him.

Mark took a sip and flopped his head back.

'Did he do this because you were late with his money?' Jenny asked, perching on the other couch. 'Is it my fault for keeping you talking earlier?'

'Nah.' Mark shook his head. 'I was already going to be late – it's my own fault.'

'Are you sure?' Her voice was loaded with guilt.

'Positive.'

It was a lie – Mark *did* partially blame her. But he wasn't about to admit that and risk having her kick him out as well.

'You haven't got any painkillers, have you?' he asked. 'My head's splitting.'

'I think I've still got some of my mum's strong ones. Won't be a sec.' Jenny jumped up and rushed back out to the kitchen. 'Do you want a bath?' she asked when she came back and handed a couple of small capsules to him.

'That'd be nice,' Mark said gratefully. 'You're an angel.'

Jenny smiled a shy little smile and went to run the bath. Alone, Mark swallowed the capsules and looked around. With the warmth of the fire, the TV in the corner, and the lamp casting a mellow glow, the room was really cosy. Add to that a willing woman running round after him like he was some kind of wounded hero, and no wife nagging or kids making a mess and demanding attention, and it was just about heaven.

He took another swig of his drink and closed his eyes.

He was fast asleep when Jenny came back, and her heart melted as she gazed down at him. He'd said some horrible things to her this afternoon, but she blamed herself for letting jealousy take control of her mouth. She'd been mentally kicking herself ever since, convinced that she had ruined everything before it had really even started. But Mark obviously felt something for her if this was the first place he had thought to come to in his time of trouble.

And if this was where he wanted to be, he was welcome to stay for as long as he liked.

10

Amy tossed and turned all night, unable to sleep for worrying about Mark. After the anger had died down the guilt had crept in, and she felt terrible knowing that he'd only borrowed that money to persuade her to come home. But instead of thanking him, she had blasted him, and then she'd kicked him out knowing that he was in pain. She was a horrible person, but she would make it up to him when he came home if it was the last thing she ever did.

It had already started to get light outside before she'd finally dropped off, so she was exhausted when the alarm clock woke her just a couple of hours later. Dismayed to see that Mark's side of the bed hadn't been slept in, she got up and got the kids ready for school.

She'd left her mobile phone on the living-room table, and she could hear it ringing when she opened the front door after dropping the kids off. Praying that it would be Mark, she ran in and snatched it up.

'Mark? Is that you? Where are you? Are you okay?'

'It's not Mark, it's me.'

'Oh.' Amy was disappointed to hear her mother-in-law's voice.

'Are you out?' Jane asked. 'Only I've been trying the house phone for ages. I don't really like calling mobiles, it's so expensive.'

'Sorry, the plug came out,' Amy told her. 'Do you want me to ring you back?'

'Never mind, I'll keep it short,' said Jane. 'I was only checking on Mark. I thought he'd go home after he left mine, but I guess he didn't.'

'Did he stay at yours?' Amy asked, hoping that he'd not long left and was on his way back.

'No, he came round, but we had words and he went off in a huff,' Jane told her. She paused now, and sighed before adding, 'Look, I know we haven't always seen eye to eye, Amy, and your mum made it clear when we were organising the wedding that you're her daughter and I'm not to interfere. But that doesn't mean I don't care about you and the kids.'

'Yeah, I know,' Amy said softly. 'Thanks, Jane, I really appreciate that. But we're fine. It's Mark I'm worried about. He was in a right state when he left last night.'

'I know,' Jane murmured. 'But like I told him, whatever's happened, he's brought it on himself so he'll have to deal with it. You just look out for yourself and those little 'uns.'

'I will,' said Amy, touched that Jane was being so caring. They had never been particularly close, because Jane had made it clear from the start that she didn't approve of them having a baby and getting married so young. She'd never outright said it, but Amy suspected that Jane thought she'd got pregnant on purpose to trap Mark. And her mum felt the same about Mark, hence the frostiness between the two mothers.

Feeling less guilty now that she knew she wasn't the only one who thought Mark was out of order, Amy promised to ring Jane as soon as he got home to let her know that he was all right. Then, determinedly pushing her worries to the back of her mind, she reminded herself that she and Mark had had much worse arguments than this in the past and he'd always come back. Anyway, he would never leave her and the kids at the mercy of that horrible man, so she had every faith that he would be back by five with the money to pay him off.

At five on the dot, the Vectra pulled up at the kerb – and Mark was still nowhere to be seen. Furious with him for leaving her to deal with his shit, Amy sent the kids upstairs and told them not to come down until she called them. Then, raising her chin to let the men who were already knocking on her door know that she wasn't going to tolerate a repeat of yesterday's nonsense, she opened up.

'Mark's not here.'

'No probs, we'll wait.' Yates stepped forward.

'Not in here, you won't.' Amy stayed put despite her shaky legs. 'And before you think about trying to force your way in, you should know that some of the neighbours are watching. And, believe me, they're nosy enough round here to call the police if they think something funny's going on.'

Yates stepped back and peered at her with a glint of amusement in his piggy eyes. 'Now, that's not very nice, is it, darlin'? And there was me thinking you and me were friends.'

'Never!' spat Amy. 'Thanks to you my children haven't seen their dad all day, and they're missing him, so I hope you're proud of yourself.'

Yates smiled and started to walk away. But he stopped after a couple of steps and looked back at her. 'By the way, I'll be adding an extra hundred to the tab every day he don't show up. And if he ain't back in a week, the debt passes to you.'

'Get lost!' Amy slammed the door shut and leaned against it with the thud of her racing heart roaring in her ears. For an awful moment she'd thought he was going to call her bluff and push his way in. Thankfully, they had gone for now, but that wasn't an end to it, and she dreaded to think what would happen if Mark wasn't back by the time they called again.

Dragged back to the here and now by an enormous thud from up above, followed by the piercing sound of Bobby crying, Amy's taut nerves jangled. 'What the hell's going on up there?' she yelled.

'Bobby fell off his bed,' Cassie called back, adding guiltily, 'I didn't push him.'

'Bobby, come down and let me look at you,' Amy ordered. 'And you'd better get that room tidy before I come up, madam!'

'But I'm hungry,' said Cassie. 'Can't I do it after dinner?'

'Do as you're bloody well told!' Amy bellowed.

When Cassie started bawling, Amy squeezed her eyes shut and clenched her fists. This wasn't their fault, and she shouldn't be taking it out on them. Blinking back her tears, she ran up the stairs.

Cassie gave a squeak of fear when Amy walked into the room, and ran to the other side of her bed. 'I'm sorry, Mummy, I'll clean up.'

'Come here.' Amy sank down on the bed and held out her hand. 'I'm not going to hurt you.'

Still sniffling, Cassie came tentatively towards her. Amy picked her up and sat her on her knee, then reached out and pulled Bobby into the embrace.

'I'm sorry.' She kissed each of them on their wet little cheeks. 'I shouldn't be shouting at you, and I won't do it again. You know I love you more than anything else in the whole world, don't you?'

Cassie nodded, then, perceptively, asked, 'Is you angry with Daddy?'

'A bit,' Amy admitted. 'But it's nothing for you to worry about.'

'Did the nasty mens frighten him away?' Cassie probed, her eyes filled with such concern it almost broke Amy's heart. 'Is that why he doesn't want to live with us no more?'

'Don't be silly,' said Amy. 'Of course Daddy wants to live with us. He's just had to go and visit Nanny Jane for a bit, that's all. He'll be back any time now, you watch.'

Bobby had his head on her chest, and his eyes were starting to droop. 'Want din-dins,' he murmured.

'Come on, let's go down before you fall asleep,' said Amy, holding onto him as she stood up.

'Can me and Bobby sleep with you tonight?' Cassie asked, clasping Amy's hand tightly as they made their way out onto the landing. 'I won't let him wee 'isself.'

'Course you can,' Amy agreed, smiling even though her blood was boiling.

Bobby didn't really know what was going on, but Cassie had to be seriously scared if she felt the need to sleep in Amy's bed. Mark had a lot to answer for, and he was going to get it with both barrels when he decided to show his face.

'We should have gone in,' Keith said as Yates drove away from the house. 'He was probably hiding.'

'Nah, she was telling the truth,' Yates said with conviction.

Keith wasn't so sure, and if it had been his shout he'd have gone in and searched the gaff from top to bottom. But it was Len's money, and if Len wanted to believe the tart that was his business.

'Where we going?' he asked when Yates turned onto the main road and stopped at a red light.

'I'm dropping you off, then I'm going for a bath,' Yates told him, gazing out thoughtfully through the windscreen.

'What time are you picking me up for Degsy's party?'

'You'll have to make your own way. I've got something to take care of.'

'On your own?'

'Yep.' Yates grinned slyly. 'This is definitely a one-man job.'

Over at Jenny's house just then, Mark was lying in bed, half dozing, half watching a DVD. Jenny's mum's leftover painkillers were so strong that he'd gone out like a light last night, and he'd taken more when he woke this morning aching like a bastard, his body black and blue. Fully anaesthetised, he'd been drifting in and out of consciousness all day while Jenny ran round after him, fetching him food and drinks, plumping up his pillows, and generally treating him like a king. She had even bought him a carton of cigarettes and a bottle of Jack Daniel's, so he was feeling pretty damn good right now.

In his more lucid moments, he couldn't help but compare Jenny to Amy. The way Amy had gone off on him, anyone would have thought it was her who'd been battered. She hadn't shown the slightest concern for him, it had all been about her – her and her house, her and her kids. But Jenny had been the complete opposite. From the second she'd seen his face she hadn't been able to do enough for him, and it was making him look at her in a whole new light. First time round, he would rather have died than admit that he'd shagged Ginger Jenny. Second time – a brunette by then and quite fit – Jenny had been little more than a purse with a pussy. But she was starting to grow on him, and he thought he would probably carry on seeing her after he went home.

The thought of going home made him sigh. He knew he'd have to do it sooner or later, but he felt so tired and weak right now that he wasn't sure he could get out of bed, never mind walk all that way.

Maybe he'd ask Jenny to lend him the money for a cab.

Later.

In a day or two.

Jenny walked into the bedroom, carrying a tray. She smiled when she saw that he was awake, and laid the tray gently down on his legs. Mark's mouth watered when he looked down at the thick juicy slab of steak, the chunky chips, and the chopped tomato and coleslaw.

'Wow, this looks great.'

Thrilled that he appreciated her efforts, Jenny said, 'There's apple pie and ice cream for afters. Would you like a drink?'

'Coke, please.' Mark picked up his fork and stabbed it into a chip. But as Jenny turned to go, he reached out and grabbed her hand. 'Thanks.' He gazed up at her. 'I know I don't deserve it after the way I've treated you, but you've been brilliant.'

'It's my pleasure,' Jenny said shyly. Then, blushing, she blurted out, 'I love you,' before hurrying from the room.

11

Yates turned onto Amy's road at just gone midnight and parked up in the inlet halfway down the block. It was pitch dark by then, and cold enough for the residents of the surrounding houses to have closed their curtains and locked themselves in for the night. He peered around to make sure that no one was about, then pulled up his hood and slipped on a pair of gloves before climbing out.

A clutch of scruffy bushes sat at the rear of the inlet, behind which a broken fence separated the road from the overgrown field which sprawled out behind the houses. Yates pushed his way through the foliage and slipped through the fence. Then, treading carefully to avoid the tangled heaps of bicycles, rubbish bags and discarded household goods that were strewn along the fence-line, he counted his way along, coming to a stop at the fifteenth house down.

A sliver of light was showing through a narrow gap in the curtains when he peeked over the fence. He'd done his homework and knew there were no kids living on either side, so when he saw the dark shape of a child's trike in the middle of the garden and the swing in the corner, he was confident he'd got the right house.

Amy was sitting at the kitchen table, chain-smoking her way through the pack of cigarettes she had scrounged off a reluctant Marnie earlier that evening.

'God, you must be stressed if you're smoking again,' Marnie had said disapprovingly. 'That Mark wants a good slap. You just wait till he comes back – I'm gonna give him a right earful.'

Amy had so wanted to confide in her friend about what was really stressing her out, but she decided it would be safer to keep it to herself. Marnie was too gobby, and if she saw the men she was likely to run out and have a go at them. Amy didn't want her to get dragged into this mess, so she'd kept her mouth shut and let Marnie believe that it was just Mark's disappearance that was upsetting her.

In truth, she wasn't just upset about that, she was furious. But Mark's mates were claiming not to have seen him, so there was nothing she could do but wait for him to stop being a coward and face the music. The man had said that he would give Mark a week, and Amy hoped that meant that he and the other thug would stay away until then. But she'd locked all the windows and bolted both doors all the same.

She'd just stubbed out a cigarette and was about to light another when she heard a scraping noise at the back door. Praying that Mark had tried his key at the front and, unable to get in, was now trying the back, she leapt to her feet.

'Mark? Is that you?'

Flooded with relief when he whispered, 'Yeah . . . hurry up and let me in,' she quickly pulled the bolts back.

'Where have you been?' she demanded as she yanked the door open. 'I've been worried si—'

The word froze in her mouth when she found herself looking into Yates's eyes. She tried to slam the door in his face, but when he stuck his foot in the gap and gave it a hard shove, she lost her footing and toppled over.

Yates strolled calmly in, locked the door behind him and pocketed the key. 'I take it he's not back yet?'

'No.' Amy pushed herself away from him with her heels and stood up. 'And I don't know where he is, so you might as well go.'

'I'll go when I'm good and ready,' Yates drawled, walking over to the table and helping himself to a cigarette.

Amy edged towards the door as he lit up, but just as she was about to dart out into the hall Yates pulled out a chair and banged its feet down hard on the floor.

'*Sit.*'

Amy shook her head. He was ugly, and the blotches on his face made him look like he had some kind of disease. But it was his eyes that really spooked her; as pale as ice – and twice as cold.

'I've already told you Mark's not here. And I've got no money, so you're wasting your time.'

'We'll see,' said Yates, sitting on the chair himself and putting his feet up on the table. 'If you don't wanna sit with me, you might as well put the kettle on.'

Amy saw dog shit on the sole of one of his trainers and said, 'Can you take your feet off my table, please? My kids have got to eat their breakfast there in the morning.'

Yates chuckled softly. 'Tell you what, darlin', I'll do you a deal. You make us that cuppa, I'll put me feet down.'

Amy didn't want him in her house, but she sensed it was more of an order than a request. She just hoped he would go once he'd had his drink.

With her back turned as she filled the kettle at the sink, she heard a thud behind her and twisted her head to see what he was doing. Her heart lurched when she saw a small black cosh lying on the table where his feet had just been.

And then she noticed his gloves.

'Wh-what are you going to do?' she stammered.

'Haven't decided yet.' Yates shrugged. 'Depends how welcome you make me feel. See, I'm big on all that you-scratch-mine-and-I'll-scratch-yours stuff – if you get me drift?'

Amy was near to tears, and her heart was hammering in her chest. 'Please just go,' she croaked. 'I swear I don't know where Mark is, and this has got nothing to do with me. M-my kids are upstairs.'

'Mmmm.' Yates smiled. 'Pretty little girl, that. Takes after her mummy.'

When Amy's chin started wobbling and the tears spilled over, Yates frowned. 'What you fuckin' crying for? I ain't even done nothing yet. Pisses me right off, that does.'

'You're scaring me,' Amy admitted. 'You've already beaten Mark up, so why can't you just leave it at that?'

Yates pulled a face. 'Nah, it don't work like that. See, when I lend someone my hard-earned money, they agree to pay me back on time. And when they don't, I have to punish 'em. It's all part of the contract.'

'But Mark's the one who owes you, not me,' Amy reminded him tearfully.

Yates sat back and raked his gaze down her body as he took another deep pull on his cigarette.

'You're not a bad-looking bird, you. Bit fat, but that's to be expected when you have kids at your age. How old are you, anyhow? Seventeen . . . eighteen?'

'Twenty-one.'

'Don't look it.' Still staring, Yates took another deep drag on his fag and blew a smoke ring. 'Tell you what, darlin' . . . forget the tea, you can give us a suck instead.'

'*What?*' Amy's mouth fell open with shock.

'You heard,' said Yates, already unzipping his jeans as he stood up.

'*No!*' Horrified, Amy backed towards the door. 'That's disgusting. *You*'re disgusting.'

The smile disappeared from Yates's face and he stabbed the cigarette down on the tabletop. 'I'm offering you a way out here, and if you want me to keep on being nice I suggest you do as you're fuckin' told.'

Amy carried on backing away. When she banged into the wall, she dived to the side, dodged him and ran to the back door.

'Forgetting something?' Yates took the key out of his pocket and dangled it in the air.

'I'll scream,' Amy spluttered when he pulled out his cock and started stroking it.

'And I'll cave your head in,' Yates warned, his stare boring crazily into her. 'Don't think the little 'uns will be too happy when they come down for brekky and find Mummy chopped up on the kitchen floor, will they?'

Unable to move when he pressed himself up against her and started pawing at her breasts, Amy squealed and tried to slap his hands away. But, as thin as he was, Yates easily overpowered her, and she gagged when he clamped his mouth over hers and slithered his foul-tasting tongue between her teeth. She tried to force her knee up between his legs, but he just jerked his hips back and laughed.

'Wanna play rough, do we? Okay, my turn!'

When he headbutted her, Amy saw stars, her legs buckled, and she dropped to the floor like a sack of flour.

'Now quit playing hard to get and we might still be friends when we're finished,' Yates said throatily as he climbed on top of her.

'No,' Amy groaned, groggily moving her head from side to side as she felt her jeans being tugged roughly down over her thighs. 'Please don't . . . *Please* . . .'

'Oh, yeah, baby, you just keep on begging,' said Yates, pushing her legs apart.

Amy clamped her eyes shut and screamed a silent scream when he entered her roughly. Her head smashed against the bottom of the door with every thrust, and she felt like her insides were being ripped to shreds. Finally, after ten agonising minutes, Yates stiffened and a strangled squealing sound came out of his mouth before he collapsed on her and panted his rancid breath all over her face.

When his heart had slowed, Yates lifted himself up on his fists. 'Look at me.'

Tears streaming from her closed eyes, chest heaving with silent sobs, Amy shook her head.

'I said, look at me,' he repeated, grasping her face in his hand.

It hurt so much that Amy was forced to obey.

'Don't be scared,' Yates said softly when he saw the fear in her eyes. 'You're mine now, and I look after mine.'

Amy's face crumpled all over again, but this time she couldn't keep the noise inside and a howl slipped out.

Yates put his hand over her mouth. 'You wanna wake the kids up? Want them to come down and see you like this? Want them to think I'm some kind of bad man?'

Amy bit down hard on her lip and shook her head.

'Say it,' Yates ordered, squeezing her mouth into a pucker. 'Say, no, Lenny . . . you're not a bad man . . . Come on. I wanna hear you.'

'No, Lenny,' Amy mumbled. 'You're n-not a b-bad man.'

'And we're gonna have a nice time.'

'And . . . and we-we're gonna have a good time.'

'*Nice* time! Get it right.'

'Nice time.'

Yates grinned and pushed himself off her. Then, reaching for her hand, he hauled her to her feet and pressed her up against the door.

'I like you, so I'm gonna trust you to behave yourself,' he said, gently brushing her hair back off her face. 'But if I find out you've betrayed me, it won't just be you I'll be fucking, it'll be her upstairs an' all. You get me?'

Amy's insides gave way and hot piss streamed down her legs. Yates looked down when he heard it and smiled slyly.

'Yeah, you got it,' he drawled, letting her go. 'Now hurry up with that brew, 'cos I've got a party to get to.'

I2

Two weeks later, Amy dropped the kids off at school and then scuttled home without stopping to chat to any of the other mothers like she usually would have. She couldn't face them: she felt too dirty, and she was convinced that they would be able to see her sins in her eyes.

She still hadn't heard from Mark, and every day that passed she became more convinced that something terrible had happened to him. None of his friends had seen him, and he hadn't been back to his mum's. It was as if he had just vanished off the face of the Earth. He might never have been as hands-on a dad as she'd have liked, but he *did* love the kids, so she couldn't believe he would abandon them like this. But he hadn't even called to ask if they were okay, and that wasn't like him at all.

She suspected that Yates had caught up with him and done something awful, and she had picked up the phone on numerous occasions. But she was never brave enough to press the 9 for the third time, too scared of Yates finding out and carrying out the threat he'd made against Cassie. Even if the police picked him up, with only her word to go on they wouldn't be able to hold him for long, and then she really would be in trouble.

Yates had been coming every night, letting himself in with the key he'd stolen and then raping her. Amy had found a way of switching off while he was actually doing it, but it wasn't so easy when he'd gone and she was left alone with her thoughts. She put on a brave face for the kids' sake, but she was sinking deeper and deeper by the day.

When she reached her road now, she put her head down and rushed past Marnie's house. Dismayed when Marnie waved at her through the window, she pretended she hadn't seen her and rushed up her own path. But Marnie came out before she'd had a chance to put her key into the lock.

'Oi! Not so fast!' Marnie pulled her door shut and climbed over the small fence. 'I've been trying to catch you all week, but you never answer the door. Have you fallen out with me, or what?'

'No, I've just been busy,' Amy lied.

'Well, you're not busy now, so you can make me a brew, can't you?'

'I've got no milk.'

'I'll have it black.'

Marnie pushed her inside and herded her up the hall into the kitchen. Mouth dropping open when she saw the mountain of dishes in the sink, the rubbish all over the ledges, and the black bags heaped up beside the bin, she said, 'Fuck a duck, girl, it looks like a bomb's exploded in here. And what's that horrible smell?'

'Bobby's been pooing his pants, so I've had to put him in nappies,' Amy admitted, blushing as she filled the kettle.

'And you're keeping the dirty ones in here – where you *eat*?' Marnie wrinkled her nose. 'Not being funny, hon, but don't you think you'd best put them in the wheelie bin before you get mice, or cockroaches, or something?'

'I've lost the back-door key. Anyway, no one asked you to come round so, if you don't like it, go home.'

'I'm your best mate. I'm worried about you.'

'Well, there's no need.' Amy wiped her nose on her sleeve. 'I'm fine.'

'You don't bloody look it,' Marnie said bluntly. 'And what's with the curtains being shut all the time? Are you hiding from someone?'

'Everyone's too nosy round here,' Amy replied frostily. 'I'm sick of being watched.'

'No one's watching you.' Marnie sat down and gazed worriedly up at her. 'I could bloody kill Mark for what he's doing to you, babe. You deserve so much better.'

Amy bit down on the inside of her cheek as a tear spilled over and trickled down her cheek. Swiping it away with the back of her hand, she turned when the kettle switched off. She poured boiling water into Marnie's cup, then mashed at the tea bag with a spoon that had bits of cereal stuck to it.

'Amy, talk to me,' Marnie implored. 'Scream, shout, do whatever you want, so long as you let it out, 'cos it's not good to bottle things up like this – for you, *or* the kids.'

'The kids are fine.'

'No, they're *not*. I've seen their faces when they walk past, and they look as miserable as sin.'

'They're missing Mark. What do you expect?'

'I'm sure they are, but you're not exactly helping them to come to terms with it, are you? It must feel like a bloody prison in here. They need fresh air.'

'They get it at school.'

'They need to play out in their own back garden, with their own toys,' Marnie insisted. 'When was the last time you let them out, 'cos I haven't seen them?'

'I've lost the key,' Amy repeated irritably. 'And there's nothing for them to come to terms with, so stop trying to make out like Mark's abandoned them. He'll be back. He might be on his way right now, for all you know.'

Marnie felt really sorry for her friend, but there was no point beating around the bush. Amy needed to be told straight, or she was never going to get over him.

'He's not coming back,' Marnie said quietly. 'And I really wish I didn't have to tell you this, but you need to know.' She paused and licked her lips. 'He's got another woman.'

'*What?*' Amy's head shot up as her heart fell through the floor. She turned round, her hands clutched to her breast.

'It's true,' Marnie said regretfully. 'I'm so sorry, hon. I didn't want to tell you, but I can't just sit back and watch you make yourself ill over him. He's shacked up with some tart called Jenny. And I only found out yesterday, so please don't think I've been hiding it from you.'

'*Jenny?*' Amy repeated blankly.

Marnie shrugged. 'That's all Gemma told me. She's mates with the mum of some girl called Fiona who used to go to your school, and *she* told her. They're supposed to have been at it for years.' She took a deep breath before adding, 'The girl reckons it started on the night of your wedding reception.'

Amy shook her head. It wasn't possible. She'd have known if Mark had another woman, she'd have seen the signs.

As she was frantically trying to convince herself that it wasn't true, an unwelcome memory leapt into her mind.

Amy in her wedding dress, crying with pain and shouting for Mark . . . Mark rushing in with lipstick on his cheek . . . Ginger Jenny coming in a few seconds later, flustered and bright red in the face.

'*No . . .*' she moaned. 'He wouldn't. Not *her.*'

'Do you know her?' Marnie asked, feeling guilty for having been the bearer of such horrible news.

'Not really,' Amy said sickly. 'She was just some girl who went to our school. No one liked her, 'cos she was a massive suck-up. And she was dead ugly. And *ginger*. There's no way Mark would go near her.'

So why was he outside at the same time as her at the wedding reception?

Amy gritted her teeth and tried to force the thought out of her mind. But it wouldn't go, and she felt the tears building afresh in her eyes and the scream bubbling up in her throat.

'Can you go now, please?' she said, struggling to contain her emotions. 'I've got things to do.'

'Babe, don't push me out,' Marnie said quietly. 'I'm only telling you what Gemma told me.'

'You should know better than to listen to her gossip,' Amy snapped. 'Mark wouldn't do that to me – not with a skank like *her*.'

'So, where is he?' Marnie raised an eyebrow. 'And who *is* he with if he's not at his mum's or with any of his mates? He can't have just disappeared into thin air.'

Amy couldn't answer that, but right now she'd have preferred it if Mark *had* just disappeared. In all the agonising she'd been doing, it hadn't even crossed her mind that he might be with another woman. Dead, yes, but *cheating* . . . ?

'You haven't half gone pale,' said Marnie. 'I hope you're not thinking of doing anything stupid.'

'Just go.'

'Not till you talk to me. I'm your friend – I want to help.'

'Well, you can't.'

'Not if you won't let me, no. But you can't keep on like this. You're a mess, and the kids are suffering. It's not fair.'

Amy's nostrils flared and she glared at the floor.

Marnie sat forward and looped her hands together on the

tabletop. 'Look, I know you're probably going to tell me to mind my own business, because you would have told me if you wanted me to know. But why don't you just forget about Mark and concentrate on your new boyfriend?'

'*What?*' Amy gaped at her.

'I've seen him letting himself in of a night,' Marnie admitted. 'And before you say anything, I wasn't being nosy, and I haven't told no one. Mark's gone, so you can do what you want. And if the new fella makes you happy, I'm pleased for you.'

'You haven't got a clue what you're talking about,' said Amy. 'But you're right, it's none of your business. Now get out.'

'Okay, have it your way.' Marnie flapped her hands in a gesture of helplessness and stood up. 'You know where I am if you need me.'

When she'd gone, Amy sank to the floor and sobbed her heart out. But as the raw aching pain began to subside, an icy anger crept in to take its place. She couldn't believe that Mark would cheat on her with an ugly bitch like Ginger Jenny. But there was only one way to find out: she would have to go round there and see for herself.

She refused to give Gemma more gossip to spread by asking her for the bitch's address, so she rang Steve instead. His phone had gone straight to answerphone every time she'd tried to call him recently, and when it did it again now she figured that he must be screening his calls in order to avoid talking to her. Which could only mean one thing: that he knew where Mark was.

Plan formulating in her mind, Amy called her mother.

'Well, blow me down,' Sonia said sarcastically when she heard her voice. 'To what do I owe this pleasure?'

'Sorry, I know it's been a while,' Amy apologised. 'I've been meaning to call for ages, but things have been a bit difficult.'

'When are they ever not with you?'

Amy closed her eyes and inhaled deeply. 'I didn't call for an argument, Mum. I need to ask a favour.'

'Straight to the point, as ever. Come on, then, out with it. How much?'

'I don't want money,' Amy said quietly. 'I just need you to have the kids for the night.'

She bit her lip and waited for the inevitable earbashing. But her mum just went quiet for several long moments, then sighed, and said, 'Bring them round in time for their tea. I'll get some fish fingers. Your dad'll be chuffed,' she added, as if she herself couldn't care less either way. But Amy could tell that she must have been dying to see them.

'Thanks,' Amy murmured gratefully. 'They've really missed you. And . . . I'm sorry.'

Fresh tears stinging her eyes, she hung up. There was time enough for emotional reunions later, but right now she needed to get her head straight or she wouldn't stand a chance of putting her life back in order.

Steve hadn't long got home from work that evening when someone knocked on his door. Assuming that it was Layla, he answered it with a grin on his lips, all set to tell her that it was her own fault if he smelled bad, because she was early and he hadn't had a chance to shower yet.

Surprised to see Amy standing there, and then concerned, because she looked terrible, he said, 'Has something happened? Mark's not had an accident, has he?'

Amy's heart sank. She'd hoped that it would turn out that Gemma's source was lying and Mark had been staying here all along. But obviously not.

'Can I come in for a minute?' she asked.

'Yeah, course.' Steve stepped aside. 'Sorry, it's a bit messy.'

He rushed into the living room and scooped a heap of newspapers, plates and cups into the corner. 'My girlfriend's always telling me off for being scruffy, but you know how it is.' He shrugged and gave Amy a sheepish smile. 'Can I get you a drink?'

'No, I'm not staying.' Amy stood by the door and shoved her hands into her pockets. 'Do you know where Mark is?'

Steve frowned and folded his arms. 'I haven't seen him for a few weeks. Why? Has he gone awol again?'

Amy bit her lip and nodded. Then, swallowing deeply, absolutely dreading his answer to her next question, she said, 'Did you know about him and Ginger Jenny?'

Just as she'd known would happen, Steve's face gave him away. His cheeks flared a bright shade of crimson, and his eyes were everywhere but on her.

'Oh, my God,' she croaked. 'It's true.'

'I never said that,' Steve blurted out guiltily.

'You didn't have to,' she cried. 'Is that where he's staying? If you know, just tell me. *Please*.'

'Amy, I swear I haven't seen him, and that's God's honest truth.'

'But you did know he'd been seeing *her*?'

'No, I honestly didn't. I just . . .' Steve ran his hands through his hair and exhaled wearily. 'Look, I didn't think it was serious. I told him to steer well clear.'

Amy couldn't bear it. If it had been anybody else telling her this she wouldn't have believed them. But, unlike Mark and all the other dickheads they'd hung around with at school, Steve had always been a gentleman, and she *knew* that he was telling the truth. Once, a long time ago, he had asked her out but, fool that she was, she'd chosen Mark. And, right now, she'd never regretted anything more in her life, because

Steve would never have put her through the hell that Mark was putting her through. And he would never have left her to fight off Len Yates on her own.

'I'm so sorry.' Steve walked over and pulled her into his arms. 'I could kill him for hurting you, I really could.'

Amy closed her eyes and laid her face against his chest. Her heart was absolutely breaking and she wanted so desperately to pour everything out. But then Steve might get hurt, and she had no right to do that to him.

She pulled herself free after a moment and raised her chin. 'Do you know where she lives?'

'No idea,' Steve replied truthfully, his eyes gleaming with guilt and pity.

'Can you find out?' Amy asked. 'I've been told that's where he's been staying, and I have to see him. He's left me in a mess, Steve. A really bad mess.'

Steve nodded. 'I'll try. No promises, but if I hear anything I'll ring you.'

Amy thanked him and wandered home in a daze, unable to come to terms with the fact that Mark had been seeing Ginger Jenny behind her back. If it had been any other girl, she might have understood. But *her*? What could he possibly see in *her*? And what could she possibly be giving him that he would choose her over Amy?

Amy knew that she hadn't been looking her best since having Bobby, but even on her worst day she was a million times better than Ginger Jenny. But Mark obviously felt something for the bitch, or he wouldn't have run to her after Yates had beaten him up. It hurt to think that he'd been eating her food, watching her TV, sleeping in her bed, while Amy and the kids had been suffering because of him. But it was the push that she needed to put an end to this situation once and for all.

13

Yates was surprised to find Amy sitting at the kitchen table when he let himself into the house that night – and even more surprised that she had the light on, because she was usually huddled on the couch in the darkened living room.

He narrowed his eyes and looked around the room for signs that her husband had finally found his balls and come home. Not that it made any odds, because Amy was part of the deal now whether the cunt liked it or not.

'Where is he, then?'

'No idea.' Amy forced herself to meet Yates's piggy gaze. 'But he won't be coming back, so if you want your money you'll have to find him. It's not my problem any more.'

'Is that right?' Yates walked slowly around the table. 'Think you're calling the shots now, do you?'

Amy winced when he stopped behind her chair, but she was determined to stand her ground.

'I mean it,' she said quietly. 'It's his debt, not mine, and if you touch me again I'm going to call the police and tell them everything.'

'Brave words,' Yates said nastily. 'But we both know it ain't gonna happen, 'cos the debt passed on to you when hubby decided to do a runner. I handed the money over in this house, so this is where I'm getting it back from.'

'It's . . . *not* . . . *my* . . . *debt*,' Amy repeated slowly. 'I didn't ask for any money, and I don't see why I should have to pay for it. You've had all you're getting from me. This ends *now*.'

Yates leaned down and put his lips to her ear. 'Let's go and see what little Cassie thinks about that, shall we?'

Amy shuddered at the feel of his breath on her skin, and said, 'She's not here.'

Yates ignored her and ran upstairs to check the bedrooms for himself. Thundering back down a few seconds later, he grabbed Amy by the throat and slammed her up against the fridge.

'Think you're fuckin' clever, do you? You'd better tell me where she is before I rip your fuckin' heart out.'

'She's somewhere where *you* can't get your hands on her,' hissed Amy, adrenalin making her fight back for a change. 'And I don't care what you do to me, 'cos I'd rather die than let you hurt my daughter, you dirty bastard!'

Yates tightened his grip and brought his face close to hers. Eyes glinting with malice, he said, 'I thought you had more sense. I thought you and me were starting to get somewhere.'

'*Never!* I hate you. You *disgust* me.'

Yates's breathing sounded harsh in his chest as he stared into Amy's eyes for several long moments. Then, seizing her by the hair, he dragged her across the room, demanding, 'Where's your phone? Give me your fuckin' phone!'

'You're hurting me,' she squealed, slapping at his hand as he hauled her into the living room.

'So fuckin' *what*?' barked Yates, renewing his grip when she fell over and pulling her along the floor. 'You had your chance to play nice and you blew it, so now we play it my way!'

All the time he was talking, he was looking around for her

phone. But when he spotted the address book on the window ledge he hurled her onto the couch and snatched it up.

'Bingo!' he said when he'd flipped through the pages and found what he was looking for. 'Mum and Dad . . .'

Amy jumped up and tried to wrestle the book away from him, but Yates put his hand flat over her face and shoved her, sending her sprawling across the floor.

'Thirteen Coniston Avenue, Stretford,' he read out. 'Not far, that. Think I'll go round and see if Granny and Grandad are taking good care of my little girl. That *is* where you've sent her, isn't it?'

'Don't you dare!' Amy screeched, scrambling to her feet and flying at him again. 'Don't you dare!'

Easily dodging her punches, Yates grabbed her, threw her down on the couch and sat astride her.

'My dad will rip you to pieces,' Amy warned him breathlessly. 'He was in the TA – he's trained to kill!'

'You reckon?' Yates laughed and reached into his pocket. 'Got one of these, has he?'

Amy's eyes widened when she saw the gun, and her mouth went bone dry when he stroked the tip of the barrel over her lips.

'I've been good to you,' he said quietly. 'I could have killed you, but I let you live. And this is how you repay me? Talking down to me like I'm a piece of shit.'

'I'm sorry,' Amy whimpered. 'I didn't mean it.'

'Oh, I think you did,' said Yates. 'See, that's the trouble with nice-looking birds, they think they can get away with anything. But you've picked the wrong one to fuck around with this time, darlin'.'

'I'm not trying to,' Amy sobbed, tears spilling down her cheeks and wetting the cushion beneath her head. 'I–I'm just trying to protect my ch-children. I'll do anything you want, but please don't hurt them. I'm begging you.'

'Too right you'll do what I want,' said Yates, grinning as he unzipped his fly.

Amy gagged when he rammed his cock into her mouth, but he wrapped her hair around his hand so that she couldn't move her head.

'Oh, yeah, you like that, don't you?' he said as he thrust in and out. 'Look at me . . . I said fuckin' *look* at me!'

Tears still streaming down her face, Amy opened her eyes. Yates stared into them, his ugly face contorting with pleasure.

'You're gonna earn me some good money with that tongue,' he gasped as he picked up speed. 'Punters'll be queuing round the block for a bit of this.'

Amy's eyes bulged with shock.

Punters?

The word screamed in her head. Surely he didn't intend to make her have sex with men for money?

Yates groaned and held her face tight up against his crotch. Amy choked as his semen spurted down her throat and she tried to push him off, but he didn't move until he was good and finished. Then, climbing off her, he zipped himself back up as if nothing had happened.

'What you looking at me like that for?' He smirked as Amy covered herself up. 'Hope you ain't expecting a kiss and a cuddle, 'cos them days are over. You could have been my woman if you'd played your cards right, but now you're gonna pay your debt in full.'

'But it's not *mine*,' Amy sobbed, sitting up and giving him a pleading look. 'It's Mark's, and he's left me. Please, Lenny, I've already told you I'll do anything you want. Can't we just carry on as we are?'

'Nah. You get one chance with me,' Yates replied coldly as he scooped the address book up off the floor. 'And you've blown yours.'

'I thought you liked me?' Amy clutched at his hand.

Yates yanked it free and gripped her by the face. 'Maybe I did, but I don't no more. You're just a whore to me now – a whore who owes me five grand.'

'*What?*' Amy felt her world go into a spin. 'I'll never be able to pay that.'

'Sooner you get working the better, then, eh? I'll pick you up at twelve tomorrow night. Wear a short skirt, and don't keep me waiting.'

'I *can't*. The kids will be back by then.'

'They'll be asleep,' Yates reminded her unconcernedly. 'And you'll be home before they wake up – if you're good.'

He started to walk out but stopped when her mobile started to ring. Turning back, he snatched it up and frowned when he saw the name on the screen.

'Who's Steve?'

'M-Mark's best friend,' Amy stammered.

'Why's he ringing you at this time of night?' Yates gave her an accusing look. 'You been shagging him behind my back?'

'*No!*' Amy gasped. 'I saw him earlier, and he said he'd let me know if he hears from Mark.'

'Answer it.' Yates handed the phone to her. 'Put it on loud-speaker so I can hear what he says. And don't say nothing about me, or Mummy and Daddy will be getting that visit straight after I leave here. And after I've finished with them, I'll work my way through the rest, from A to Z.'

When he patted his pocket to remind her that he had the addresses of everybody she cared about, Amy's hands shook so badly that she almost dropped the phone.

'Sorry it's so late,' Steve blurted out when she answered. 'I meant to ring earlier, but Layla dragged me out to the pictures and I totally forgot. I didn't wake you up, did I?'

'No, it's okay,' Amy said quietly.

'Good. Anyhow, I only wanted to tell you that I've asked around, but no one knows where Mark is. I'll keep asking and let you know as soon as I hear anything. Are you and the kids all right? Do you need anything?'

Yes, we need you to come and rescue us! Amy cast a nervous glance at Yates.

'No, we're fine,' she lied. 'I just need to find Mark.'

'You and me both,' Steve said darkly. 'If you need anything before he turns up, just ring me, yeah?'

'Thanks,' Amy murmured. Then, when Yates made a cutting gesture across his throat, she said, 'I've got to go – I can hear one of the kids getting up. Bye.'

'I don't want you seeing him again,' Yates said when she'd disconnected. 'And I don't want you calling him neither. And I'll be watching you,' he added ominously. 'So be warned.'

Amy stayed on the couch after he'd gone and cried the rest of the night away. She wished that she could pick the kids up and run away to somewhere where nobody knew them, but she didn't have a penny to her name so it was an impossible dream. Anyway, Yates would hurt her parents and friends if she ran away. She was totally and utterly trapped, and there was only one way to survive: do whatever Yates wanted and hope that, one day, somehow, something would happen to bring the torture to an end.

Physically, mentally and emotionally drained by the time morning came around, Amy decided to ring her mum and ask if she would keep the kids for a while. She would make the excuse that she needed time to sort her head out, and would promise to pick them up in the mornings and take them to school, then deliver them back in the afternoon after they'd had their tea.

That was the plan, but before she had a chance to reach for the phone, her dad's car pulled up outside.

'I want a word with you,' Sonia said when Amy opened the door. 'In the kitchen.'

'In a minute,' said Amy, hugging the kids. 'I want to spend a bit of time with them before they go to school.'

'Now!' Sonia insisted, shoving her up the hall. 'Turn the telly on for them, John,' she called back over her shoulder.

When they were both in the kitchen, Sonia closed the door and gazed around with a look of horror on her face.

'Bloody hell, Amy! I knew it was going to be bad, but not *this* bad.'

'It's not as bad as it looks,' Amy said defensively, stepping in front of the sink to hide the unwashed dishes.

'Are you blind?' Sonia spluttered. 'It's absolutely filthy. And it stinks.'

'I haven't been able to put the bins out 'cos I've lost the key.' Amy folded her arms. 'I'll sort it out after the kids have gone to school.' She paused now, and bit her lip before adding, 'It'd help if you could have them for a couple of weeks.'

Sonia gave her a knowing look. 'Oh, yes, you'd like that, wouldn't you? Lump them on me and your dad so you're free to go gallivanting with your fancy man.' She pursed her lips when Amy gave her a blank look, and said, 'Don't bother denying it, because Cassie's already told us all about him. And before you accuse her of lying, Bobby said it as well – and he wasn't even in the room when she mentioned it, so he wasn't just copying her.'

Amy was confused. The kids were always fast asleep by the time Yates called round, and they couldn't possibly have seen him because their room was at the front and he always used the back door. She supposed it was possible that one of them had woken up and heard him talking, but there was no way she could admit to it now without making everything a million times worse.

'They must have been dreaming,' she said, fronting it out. 'Until Dad came in just now, there's been no man in here since Mark left.'

Sonia shook her head. 'I can always tell when you're lying; your nose goes even redder than your face. I told your dad on the way over . . . I said, there's no point asking her 'cos she'll only lie. And here you go, proving me right again. How could you do it, Amy? Mark's only been gone five minutes. Don't you think the children are hurting enough?'

Amy gritted her teeth and reached for the door handle. 'I haven't got time for this. I need to get the kids ready for school.'

'No, lady, what you need to do is stop thinking about yourself and start thinking about the effect all this is having on *them*.' Sonia pointed at the wall behind which the children were waiting. 'I've never cared for Mark, as you well know, and I'll be the first to dance at the divorce party. But if you're going to replace him, at least have the decency to wait till the kids have got over the split.'

'For the last time, there is no other man,' said Amy, irritated that her mum was talking to her as if she didn't care about her children. They were precisely the reason she was in this position, because they were her life and she would rather sacrifice herself than see any harm come to them.

'I don't believe you,' Sonia said coolly. 'But I know you don't care what I think, so I'll say no more about it. I just want you to promise that you won't move this man in – whoever he is. And sort this place out, because it's a health hazard,' she added, casting another look of disgust at the bin bags. 'I know you're upset, but that's no excuse to neglect your children.'

'I am *not* neglecting them,' Amy protested. 'They're clean and fed.'

'Clean?' Sonia raised an eyebrow. 'Bobby soiled himself twice yesterday, and once again this morning. It's a good job you left some of his pants the last time you stayed over, or he'd have a bare bottom right now.'

Amy guiltily dipped her gaze. 'I meant to bring his nappies, but I forgot.'

'Don't you think you're missing the point?' Sonia asked. 'He knows how to use the toilet, but the fact that he's started doing it in his pants again says a lot about what's going on in here, and here . . .' She pointed from her temple to her heart. 'He's obviously disturbed, but how can you help him if you can't even look after yourself?'

'Why are you blaming me?' Amy snapped. 'This is Mark's fault, not mine. He's the one who's pissed off with someone else. I'm doing my best, but it's not easy trying to do everything by myself.'

'I'm not saying it's your fault. But you're the one who's got to look after the children, because you're their mum.'

'And you're mine, so you're supposed to be looking after me, not having a go because I haven't washed the stupid dishes.'

'You're a grown woman,' Sonia said calmly. 'And you've made it quite clear that you don't appreciate me sticking my nose in, so I'm staying out of it. But I refuse to keep my mouth shut when it comes to my grandchildren. They're the priority here, not you, so pull yourself together and sort it out.'

'Thanks,' Amy said bitterly. 'Nice to know I've got your support.'

'The Lord helps those who help themselves,' Sonia retorted piously.

'Don't preach at me,' Amy yelled, too upset and angry by now to care who heard. 'You haven't got a clue what I'm going through! I need help, not criticism, but you're too busy looking down your nose at me to see that, aren't you? And how can you accuse me of neglecting my kids when you *know* how much I love them?'

'If you loved them as much as you claim to, we wouldn't be having this conversation,' Sonia argued. 'Luckily for them *I* do, so at least they're going to school clean and fed today. But I'll be buggered if I'm taking them off your hands so you can flit around like a free woman.'

'Oh, just get out.' Amy yanked the door open.

'We'll drop the children off, seeing as we're already here,' Sonia told her. 'It'll give you a chance to make a start on the house. And then I'd have a bath, if I was you, because you don't smell very nice.'

She walked out now and strode up the hall with her nose in the air, calling, 'John . . . kids . . . I'm ready.'

Amy managed to muster up a smile when the children trooped miserably out of the living room. 'See you later,' she said, giving them a quick hug before her mum herded them out.

Her dad looked weary as he shuffled his feet in the doorway. 'Sorry about your mum. I wanted to ring you and warn you she was on the warpath, but she didn't give me a chance. Are you all right?'

'I'll manage,' Amy assured him, folding her arms. 'You'd best hurry or you'll get it in the neck an' all.'

'You know where we are if you need us.' Her dad gave her a peck on the cheek and then stepped out with his head down.

Amy slammed the door behind him and slid to the floor in despair. She was alone, totally and utterly alone. And now that her mum had refused to take the kids she had a real problem.

14

When Amy came home after picking up the kids from school that afternoon, she saw Marnie chatting to Gemma across the road. And she could tell from the guilty look on her friend's face that they were talking about her.

'All right, love?' Gemma called, her enormous breasts spilling over her arms as she leaned on the gate.

Amy gave her a dirty look and hustled the kids inside without answering. Seconds later, Marnie was at the door.

'Babe, we weren't gossiping,' she said when Amy gave her an accusing glare. 'I was just asking if she knew that bird's address so you can go and find Mark.'

Amy's heart lurched. 'And?'

'Sorry.' Marnie shook her head. 'Her mate's daughter reckons they lost touch after she moved.'

'Right,' Amy said flatly, flicking a glance at Gemma who was smoking now and trying to pretend that she wasn't watching. 'I've got to go. The kids need their tea.'

'I hope you're not still mad at me for what I said about your new man?' Marnie asked. 'I'm pleased for you, I really am. I just don't know why you didn't want to tell me about him.'

She looked hurt, and Amy sighed, because she knew that she'd feel the same if Marnie was keeping things from her like this. They were best mates – they told each other everything.

Or, at least, they *had* until Yates had come along and put the fear of God into her.

'There's nothing going on,' she said quietly. 'He's just an old friend who's looking out for me, that's all.'

'So why's he been going round the back like you've got something to hide?'

'Because I didn't want anyone to see him and start spreading it about that I'm cheating on Mark.'

'Oh, right, I get you. But we're all right, yeah? You've not fallen out with me?'

'Course not,' said Amy. Then, tentatively, she asked, 'I, er, don't suppose you'd babysit for me tonight, would you? Only my friend wants to take me out for a couple of drinks.'

Marnie gave her a knowing smile. 'Does he, now?'

'Oh, just forget it,' Amy snapped. 'I don't even know why I bothered asking.'

'Don't be daft,' Marnie said placatingly. 'You know I'd do it if I could. But it's our Pearl's birthday, and we're going clubbing. Why don't you send them to your mum's?'

'She had them last night.'

'I'm sure she'd have them again if she knew your *friend* was taking you out.'

The emphasis she'd placed on the word didn't escape Amy, and it sickened her to know that Marnie didn't believe her.

'Actually, I've changed my mind,' she said. 'Don't really feel up to going out at the moment. Tell your sister happy birthday from me.'

'What did she say?' Gemma asked when Marnie walked back across the road.

'Well, she's admitted there's a new man,' Marnie told her conspiratorially. 'But she reckons he's just an old friend, and she didn't want anyone to know about him in case they thought she was cheating on Mark.'

'Which, of course, she isn't.' Gemma smirked.

Marnie raised her eyebrows in a *you-know-as-much-as-I-do* gesture, and said, 'She asked me to babysit so she can go out for a drink with him, but I'm going out. Pity, 'cos I know men, so I'd know as soon as I got a proper look at him if something was going on.'

Gemma resisted the urge to say *You should know men, you've had enough of 'em*. Instead, she smiled, and said, 'I'll keep an eye out. Wonder if Mark knows?'

'Doubt it,' said Marnie, glancing at her watch. 'Shit, best get going. I need to get a fanny tickler for our Pearl.'

'You what?'

'Don't ask.' Marnie grinned. 'Let me know if you see anything.' She jerked her head back towards Amy's house before waving goodbye.

Amy struggled through the rest of the afternoon and evening. Nerves totally shot at the thought of what Yates had lined up for her, she was bad-tempered with the kids, shouting at them every time they made a noise and even smacking Bobby for knocking over a glass of milk, before sending them both to bed in tears.

She already felt terrible about taking her stress out on them, but the guilt intensified when she peeped into their room at five to twelve and saw them snuggled together in Cassie's bed. As she gazed at them – Cassie with her long black hair and serious little face, Bobby so fair and angelic – her tears began to flow all over again. The poor little things knew that something was wrong, and it was heartbreaking to think that they had turned to each other for comfort instead of to her. She was their mummy, the one who should be cuddling them and reassuring them, not hurting them and making them cry.

A car drove slowly past the house just then and, as the glow of its headlights illuminated the thin curtains, Amy squeezed her eyes shut and whispered, 'I'm so sorry, my babies. Please don't wake up.'

Yates was parked up in the inlet and he glared at Amy when she climbed nervously in beside him, wearing a hoodie and jeans. 'I thought I told you to wear a short skirt.'

'Sorry,' she mumbled. 'But I haven't worn skirts since before I had the kids, and none of them fit me.'

'Get a new one for next time,' Yates ordered, throwing the car into gear and taking off at speed.

Amy huddled against the door and sniffled softly.

'Pack that in!' Yates lashed her across the face with the back of his hand.

'I c-can't,' Amy sobbed, holding a hand over her stinging cheek. 'I'm worried about the kids.'

'Like I told you last night, do a good job and you'll be home before they wake up,' Yates said uncaringly. 'Mess me about, and you'll be there all fuckin' night. *If* I decide to let you go home,' he added menacingly.

'Wh-what do you mean?' Amy stammered, terror for her children forcing her to speak even though experience had already taught her that it would be safer to keep her mouth shut.

'I mean,' said Yates, his eyes more piggy than ever as he stared at the road, 'if you mess me about, I might just kill you and dump you on the moors. And then I'll go back to yours and have a bit of fun with them brats of yours.'

Unable to bear the noise when Amy started to wail, Yates slammed his foot on the brake and seized her by the throat. 'Shut the fuck up! This is your last warning!'

Amy bit down hard on her own hand to keep her sobs inside, but her chest was still heaving.

'Right, I've had enough of this,' Yates snarled, pulling a small tablet out of his pocket. 'Take this.'

Amy stared at it and shook her head.

'I'm not fucking asking!' Yates growled. 'Open your mouth!'

He was almost on top of her by now, and he was squeezing her cheeks so hard it was impossible for Amy to keep her teeth clamped together. She had no idea what the tablet was but, apart from the odd spliff, she'd never taken drugs in her life and she was absolutely petrified. She gagged when he shoved it onto her tongue, and tried to spit it out, but Yates covered her mouth with his hand and dragged her head so far back by the hair that she had no choice but to swallow.

Yates made her open her mouth so he could check that she wasn't hiding the pill under her tongue. Then, satisfied that it was gone, he restarted the car and drove on, saying, 'You'll feel better in a minute.'

Amy hugged herself tightly. Her life was in tatters and she didn't see how she was ever going to feel better again. She just hoped the pill would make her sick and Yates would be forced to take her to the hospital. Then she would tell the nurses about the kids and get them to send someone round to rescue them. They might get taken into care, but at least they would be safe – even if Yates then went berserk and killed everybody else in her address book.

Fifteen minutes later, Yates turned along an alley behind a row of run-down houses in Longsight. He switched the ignition off and looked at Amy slumped in her seat, her head lolling, her eyes glazed and unfocused.

'Told you you'd feel better,' he said, easing her jacket aside and sliding his hand inside her top. Getting no resistance when he squeezed her nipple between his finger and thumb, he grinned and climbed out of the car.

He pulled her out and walked her into a pitch-dark back-yard, propping her against the wall before rapping on the door.

'It's me,' he hissed when he heard the shuffle of feet on the other side.

Two bolts were drawn back and a man opened the door. Yates shoved Amy into a dingy passageway and said, 'Got my money?'

'Upstairs,' the man said, licking his lips as he eyed Amy.

Barely conscious, Amy stared at the brown carpet that seemed to be undulating like a stream of filthy water beneath her feet as Yates pushed her up a flight of stairs.

Two more men were upstairs, lounging on a shabby sofa and watching a porn movie on a huge flat-screen TV. The only other furniture in the room was an unmade bed, and a coffee table littered with overflowing ashtrays, spirit bottles, traces of coke, and several pieces of blackened tinfoil.

When the first man handed over a wad of notes, Yates snatched it and shoved Amy down onto the bed. 'I'll be back in two hours. And I don't wanna see no marks on her, so don't get too rough.'

'No worries,' the man agreed, rubbing his hands together as he gazed at Amy staring unseeingly up at the nicotine-stained ceiling. 'How old did you say she was again?'

'Fourteen.'

'She looks older.'

'They all look fuckin' older these days. Do you want it, or not?'

'Yeah, yeah, leave her. What's she had?'

'Rope,' said Yates, heading for the door. 'Laters.'

He trotted back down the stairs and let himself out. The low-life kiddie-fiddlers preferred them even younger than fourteen, but Mancunian kids were too streetwise nowadays so it wasn't as easy to get hold of little ones as it had been when he'd started out a decade earlier. Still, she was there now, so they would fuck her regardless.

15

'Mummy . . . Mummy, wake up. Bobby's wee'd, and I need to get ready for school. *Mummy!*'

'Gerroff!' Amy flapped her hand at Cassie who was shaking her shoulder.

'I need to get ready for school,' Cassie repeated with a wobble in her voice. 'But I can't find any clean knickers.'

Amy groaned, pulled herself into a sitting position and looked around. She was confused to see that she was on the couch. Her body was aching all over, her head banging, and she had a very vague memory of having gone out the night before – but none whatsoever of *being* out, or coming back.

'We haven't had breakfast,' Cassie was saying now. 'And Bobby's been naughty in the kitchen.'

'What you talking about?' Amy grimaced at the foul taste in her mouth.

'He tried to make an egg butty,' Cassie told her. 'But it spilled on the floor and maked a mess.'

'Didn't,' Bobby protested, sidling guiltily into the room. 'Wasn't me.'

'Yes, it was!' Cassie turned on him accusingly. 'Don't lie. It's naughty to lie.'

'Just go and clean it up,' Amy said irritably as a wave of nausea washed over her. 'And put some cereal out while you're there.'

Cassie sighed as if she had the weight of the world on her little shoulders and went miserably into the kitchen to do as she'd been told.

'Want hug?' Bobby asked Amy, clambering onto the couch beside her.

'Oh, God, just give me some space,' she snapped, shoving him away.

Her temper flared when he started whining and Amy slapped him on his bare leg. It was so unexpected that Bobby was momentarily stunned into silence. But then he breathed in sharply and burst into tears. Unable to bear it as the sound ricocheted around inside her head, Amy raced up to the bathroom, making it just in time.

When she came back downstairs a few minutes later, Cassie was cuddling Bobby on the couch and spoon-feeding him the last powdery bits of Coco Pops that had been in the box. Overcome by guilt, she sat down next to them.

'I'm sorry for shouting. I just don't feel very well today.'

'It's okay,' Cassie said quietly.

'No, it's not.' Amy stroked the child's hair. 'And I'm sorry for smacking you, baby,' she told Bobby, gently wiping the tears off his cheeks. 'I won't do it again, I promise.'

Despite her best efforts, both children were late for school, and Amy felt sick all over again when Cassie's teacher cornered her and lectured her about the importance of bringing Cassie in on time for assembly. Making a contrite promise not to be late again, she went home with her head in bits. She didn't know what day it was, never mind what time, and hazy images kept flashing through her mind like pieces of a nightmarish disjointed jigsaw.

When she turned the corner and saw Marnie and Gemma talking, at Marnie's gate this time, she huddled deeper into her jacket. Just like the previous day, she could tell from the looks on their faces that they had been talking about her, and her heart started to race as she got near.

As she passed, Gemma folded her arms and gave her a dirty look. 'You're a disgrace, you. Call yourself a mother? Going out and leaving them kids alone in the house like that. You want locking up.'

'You talking to me?' Amy turned and glared at her.

'Yeah, I am,' Gemma retorted aggressively. 'And don't bother denying it, 'cos I saw you going off with your fancy man.'

'We're not having a go,' Marnie chipped in, trying to soften the blow of Gemma's words. 'But you asked me to babysit last night, so we know the kids must have been at home.'

'I took them to my mum's,' Amy lied, tossing a betrayed look back at her friend as she marched up her path and slotted her key into the lock.

'No, you didn't, you lying bitch,' yelled Gemma, as if she wanted the whole street to hear. 'I was watching, and no one left that house last night except you.'

'Think what you like,' Amy muttered, stumbling through her door and slamming it shut.

Inside, she leaned against the wall and gasped for breath. Oh, God, it was true, she *had* gone out and left the kids. But why couldn't she remember it? And what had happened while she was out? And how had she got back? Her mind was a complete blank.

She jumped when the postman pushed a couple of envelopes through the letter box. Both were brown and, guessing that they were bills that she had no chance of being able to pay, she left them where they were and went into the kitchen to look for something to ease the throbbing pain in her head. All she could find was an old bottle of Calpol, but she swallowed what little was left of it, then hauled herself up the stairs and climbed into bed. Shivering wildly, Amy wrapped the quilt around herself and tried to sleep it off.

Mark was messing around on the Internet when his mobile rang at half-three that afternoon. Cautious, because he didn't recognise the number, he said, 'Hello?'

'Mr Taylor?' asked the woman on the other end. 'This is Mrs Burns from Princess Nursery. Your wife hasn't been to collect Bobby yet, and we can't reach her on the phone, so we're going to need you to come and get him.'

'What, now?' Mark frowned.

'Well, yes,' the woman said, sounding surprised that he wasn't already running for the door. 'I appreciate that it may be inconvenient, but he *is* your son. Unless I've dialled the wrong number, in which case I apologise.'

'No, it's the right number.' Mark ran a hand through his hair. 'I'm, er, just a bit busy, right now. Can't you ask one of the other parents to drop him off?'

'As all the other parents collected their children on time and have now gone, *no*, I can't,' said Mrs Burns tartly. 'If you're refusing to come, I'll try your wife again. But please be aware that if I can't reach her in the next ten minutes, I'll have no option but to pass it over to social services.'

'All right, I'm coming,' Mark said reluctantly. 'But you'll have to give us twenty minutes, 'cos I'm out.'

'Ten minutes,' said Mrs Burns before hanging up.

'What's going on?' Jenny asked, walking into the room just as Mark put the phone down. 'Who was that?'

'Nursery.' Mark scraped his chair back and reached for his trainers. 'Amy's not been to pick Bobby up, and they can't get hold of her so I've got to go.'

Scared that if he bumped into Amy she might persuade him to go home, Jenny said, 'You can't! What if Len sees you and beats you up again?'

'At school?' Mark gave her an irritated look and bent down to tie his laces.

'All right, I'll come with you,' Jenny said, her hands already shaking at the prospect of coming face to face with Amy. She desperately didn't want to see her, but right now she was more afraid of letting Mark go on his own and risking losing him.

'No, you stay here,' Mark insisted. 'If she hasn't got Bobby, she won't have got Cassie either, and I don't want them seeing you.'

'Why not?' Jenny was offended.

'I just don't,' Mark snapped. 'See you in a bit.'

'Call me and let me know what's happening,' Jenny called after him as he pulled the hood of his jacket up over his head and rushed out.

Bobby was sitting in the corridor outside the office when Mark reached the nursery, and he looked as forlorn as could be.

'All right, mate?' Mark squatted down in front of him. When Bobby gazed blankly back at him, he said, 'It's me . . . Daddy.'

At last there was a reaction, and Bobby's face lit up as if the sun had just come out. He squealed with joy and launched himself into Mark's arms, hugging him with all his might.

'Thank you for coming so quickly,' said Mrs Burns, walking out of the office. 'May I have a word?'

'Yeah, sure.' Mark stood up with a clinging Bobby in his arms. 'What's up?'

'I have a couple of concerns, actually,' said Mrs Burns. 'This is the first time your wife has been late to pick Bobby up, but his teacher has informed me that he has been coming in quite late recently.'

'The alarm clock's not working properly,' Mark lied. 'I'll have a look at it when I get home and make sure it doesn't happen again.'

'I haven't finished,' Mrs Burns called after him when he started to walk away. 'Another concern is the issue of Bobby soiling himself.'

Embarrassed, because he had already guessed from the smell that Bobby had crapped his pants, Mark shifted his son onto his other arm. 'I'll talk to his mum about it.'

'I already did, but I'm not sure she understood the seriousness of the situation. We don't mind dealing with the occasional accident, but my staff cannot be expected to deal with it on a routine basis – as is becoming the case with Bobby. We expect our children to be toilet-trained in advance of being given a placement here, and if this continues I'm afraid we'll be forced to reassess Bobby's suitability.'

'I said I'll talk to his mum, and I will,' Mark said sharply, irritated at being lectured as if he was to blame. Bobby had been toilet-trained when he had been living with him, so whatever had happened since he left was Amy's fault, not his.

Pissed off, he marched out and went next door to the primary school.

'I'm Cassie Taylor's dad,' he informed the woman on reception. 'Her mum's busy, so I'm picking her up today. Where's her class?'

'Down the corridor, second left,' the woman told him. 'Just wait outside; they'll be finished in ten minutes.'

Mark thanked her, walked down to Cassie's classroom and peered through the glass panel in the door. Inside, the teacher was reading to the kids who were sitting in a semicircle on the floor. Cassie was at the back. All the others were listening, with their legs and arms crossed, but she was fidgeting as though she was bored off her skull. Then, as if she'd felt him looking at her, she suddenly twisted her head round. Beaming when she saw his face, she waved like a lunatic. Mark waved back and blew her a kiss.

'Daddy!' she screamed, hurtling out of the classroom and into his arms when the bell went at last. 'Where have you been? We've missed you!'

'Missed you too, buttercup.' Mark gave her a hug. Then, conscious of the other parents giving him curious looks as they arrived to collect their offspring, he said, 'Go get your stuff.'

When she came back out with her coat and bag, Mark held her hand and walked quickly out.

'Excuse me?' a woman called, rushing after him. 'Are you Cassie's dad?'

'Yeah.' Mark hesitated. 'Why?'

'I'm not being funny,' the woman said quietly, 'but can you do something about her nits? I've had to do my Ruby's hair twice in the last few weeks, and it's getting beyond a joke 'cos she just picks them straight back up off your Cass. I don't want to tell my Rubes not to play with her, but if it don't stop . . .'

She left the rest unsaid, but Mark got her point loud and clear. 'I'll sort it,' he promised, pulling his hood back up and herding Cassie down the path.

With Bobby stinking to high heaven in his arms, and Cassie scratching at her head every couple of steps, Mark walked them down the road and in through the park gates.

'Go and play for a bit,' he told them. 'Daddy needs to make a call.'

When the kids ran towards the climbing frame, Mark sat on a bench and pulled his phone out of his pocket. There was no way he was going near the house and risk bumping into Yates, so Amy would just have to come here and get them. Annoyed when Amy didn't pick up after several attempts to reach her on both her mobile and the landline, he reluctantly tried Marnie instead.

'I haven't seen her since this morning,' Marnie told him coolly. 'And I don't really want to talk to you after what you did, so don't ring me again.'

'I've got the kids,' Mark blurted out before she had a chance to hang up. 'She didn't pick them up from school, and no one can get hold of her.'

'So what do you want me to do about it?'

'Knock on at hers and see if she's there. Please, Marnie, I can't keep them with me.'

'Bring them home, then. You've got a key.'

'It's not as easy as that. I can't come near the house. It's too dangerous – for them, not me.'

Marnie sighed. 'Look, I don't approve of what you did, Mark, but youse are both out of order if you ask me. You haven't seen the kids in God knows how long, and Amy might as well not be there for all the notice she's been paying them lately. The house is a mess, and the kids are filthy. And I don't even know what Amy's on, but I'm surprised her new fella's still giving her the time of day 'cos she looks disgusting.'

'She's seeing someone?' Mark frowned.

'Yeah – but don't bother kicking off about it, 'cos you left her so she can do what she wants,' said Marnie. 'Anyhow, I'm at the door, so just a minute.'

Still frowning, Mark listened as Marnie knocked on Amy's front door and shouted her name. He'd been living with Jenny for a while now and had made no move to contact Amy in the whole time he'd been gone, so he supposed he shouldn't have been surprised that she'd met someone else. But he was. No, more than surprised, he was shocked – and more than a little jealous. Jenny wasn't as pretty as Amy, or anywhere near as good in bed, but she was a better cook, and she never nagged, so he'd lulled himself into thinking that he was content. But the thought of Amy moving on enraged him.

'She's not answering.' Marnie came back on the line. 'What do you want me to do?'

'Keep trying,' said Mark, determined now to speak with his wife and find out what the hell she thought she was playing at.

'To be honest, I don't see why I should,' Marnie replied. 'She can hardly be bothered to talk to me when I see her these days, and I'm not impressed with her for going out and leaving the kids alo—' Old loyalties kicked in when she realised what she'd been about to say, and she pulled herself up short. But it was too late.

'What do you mean?' Mark demanded.

'Nothing,' she murmured. 'I'll knock one more time, then I've got to go.'

'No, wait!' Mark yelled. 'I want to know what you meant. Has she been going out and leaving the kids on their own in the house? I've got a right to know.'

Marnie was quiet for a moment, then said, 'Right, I'm only telling you this 'cos I'm worried about the kids. But, yeah, we think she left them last night. I didn't see her go out,' she added, not wanting to get the blame if it all blew up as a result of what she was telling him. 'But Gemma did, and she reckons she didn't come back till the early hours. Amy denied it when we confronted her this morning, and told us the kids had stayed at her mum's. But Gemma never saw her mum bringing them back this morning, and Amy took them to school, so they must have been there the whole time.'

Mark was watching the kids as Marnie talked. They were playing, but not as enthusiastically as they usually would have been. And now that he was looking, they did seem pretty grubby.

'Is there anything else I need to know?' he asked.

'Well, we have been wondering if she might be on something,' Marnie admitted. 'But that didn't come from me, and I'll deny it if you say it did. All I know is you need to come home and sort it out before something happens.'

'Like what?'

'Like someone reports her and the kids get taken off her,' said Marnie. 'Anyhow, I'll give her another knock, and then I'm going.'

Mark mulled everything over while he waited to see if she got an answer. When she didn't, he made a decision.

'I'm taking the kids home with me. When you see Amy, tell her I've got them – and if she wants them back she'll have to take me to court.'

'Oh, God, Mark, come on,' Marnie spluttered, panic in her voice now, because Amy was definitely going to blame her for this. 'She'll freak out.'

'That's her problem,' Mark said coldly. 'She's obviously not looking after them, and I'm not losing them just 'cos she's more interested in some bloke. I'll fight her all the way, and I guarantee I'll win.'

He cut the call now and stood up. Jenny might not be too happy when he turned up with his children in tow, but she'd soon get used to them. And if not, he'd just go to the council and get himself put into a hostel.

'Come on, kids,' he shouted. 'Let's go home.'

Distraught to think that she'd caused the already bad situation to spiral even further out of control, Marnie tried to call Mark back to plead with him to reconsider. When it went straight to answerphone, she hammered on Amy's door again until, at last, she got a response.

'What do you want?' Amy stared down at her from the bedroom window.

Marnie stepped back and peered guiltily up at her. 'Come down, Ames. I need to talk to you. It's urgent.'

Amy was still annoyed with Marnie for not sticking up for her when Gemma had been having a go at her. But her friend seemed genuinely upset about something, so she said, 'Wait there.'

'Oh, God, I'm so sorry,' Marnie blurted out, rushing in when Amy opened the door. 'Mark rang, and—'

'What?' Amy interrupted with a gasp. 'When? Where is he? He didn't come round, did he? Oh, God, I was asleep.'

'Babe, *listen*.' Marnie grasped hold of Amy's hands. 'He's got the kids. The school rang him when you didn't go to pick them up, and he couldn't get hold of you so he rang me and asked me to knock on your door.'

'Is he bringing them home?' Amy asked, her heart racing at the thought of being reunited with him.

Marnie inhaled deeply and shook her head. 'He says he's keeping them, and if you want them back you'll have to take him to court.'

Amy gaped at her as if she didn't understand what she'd just said. Mark had hardly been dad of the year when he'd been living here, so what did he think he was playing at, taking the kids off her just because she was late picking them up from school? More importantly, where had he taken them? It had better not be to that bitch's house, or Amy would be going down for murder when she got her hands on him, never mind taking him to court.

'He can't do this,' she said, her already pale face drained to a sickly shade of deathly white. 'Tell me exactly what he said.'

Marnie shuffled her feet and folded her arms. 'I think he's heard about your new fella,' she mumbled, her cheeks flaring. 'And he asked me if you'd been leaving the kids on their own.'

'Oh, my God!' Amy felt the world go into a spin. 'Did *you* tell him that?'

'No, of course I didn't,' Marnie lied. 'One of the kids must have said something.'

Amy didn't believe her, but she had more pressing things to deal with right now.

'Where's he taken them, did he say?'

'No, he just said he was taking them home. I tried to call him back, but he's switched his phone off.'

'Move.' Amy shoved her out of the way and ran upstairs to get her shoes.

'Where are you going?' Marnie asked when she ran back down a few seconds later with her mobile phone pressed to her ear.

'To get my kids.' Amy yanked the front door open. Furious when Mark's answerphone came on, she marched across the road and banged on Gemma's door. 'I need that slag's address,' she snapped when her neighbour answered.

Gemma folded her arms and smirked at her. 'Even if I knew it, I wouldn't tell *you*.'

'This isn't a joke,' Amy squawked, anger making her forget her fear of the lairy cow. 'He's got my kids.'

'Good for him,' spat Gemma. ''Bout time someone realised you weren't fit to have 'em. Look at the state of you.' She looked Amy up and down with a sneer of disgust. 'You look like you've been sleeping in a fucking skip.'

Amy wanted to lunge at her and tear her eyes out, but she managed to hold it together and said, as calmly as possible, 'Please, Gemma, I'm begging you. If you know where she lives, just tell me.'

'No,' said Gemma coldly. 'It's your own fault, and if you ask me you're lucky it's Mark who's took 'em, 'cos I was about to call the social services on you. Now piss off!'

When she slammed the door shut, Amy pounded on it with her fists, screaming, 'You can't do this! I want my kids! I want my *kids*!'

'Amy, stop it!' Marnie rushed up the path and pulled her away. 'He'll bring them back when he gets fed up – you know what he's like. Trust me, they'll be home by this time tomorrow.'

'What if they're not?' Amy peered at her through the tears. 'What if he keeps them?'

'He won't,' Marnie insisted, putting an arm around her shoulder and leading her across the road. 'It's all been getting on top of you lately, so it's not like you couldn't do with a break, is it? Let Mark have them for the night, while you have a nice long soak in the bath and a good sleep. You'll feel a lot better, and your head will be clearer so you'll know what to say if you need to call the police.' She pushed Amy's door open now and led her inside. 'Come and sit down. I'll make you a nice cup of tea.'

'Electric's gone,' Amy muttered, wiping her eyes on her sleeve.

'Again?' Marnie gave her a pained look. Sighing when Amy gave a miserable little shrug, she said, 'You've got to get a grip, Amy, 'cos this doesn't look good if the social services get involved.' She waved a hand to indicate that she was talking about the mess. 'You've proper let yourself go since Mark left, but it's time you stopped thinking about him and started thinking about the kids, or you're never gonna get them back.'

Amy squeezed her eyes shut and held her pounding head in her hands. Marnie was right, but she didn't even know the half of it. This wasn't just about Amy, Mark and the kids. Yates wasn't going to walk away just because Amy had a crisis on her hands. He still wanted his money, and until he got it they were all in danger. She just wished she could remember what had happened last night, but her mind was still woolly. All she did know was that she'd been seen going out and leaving the kids on their own, and then she'd over-slept and missed picking them up, so now Mark had kidnapped them. It was one big mess – and it was getting bigger and messier by the minute.

16

Yates was pissed off. The nonces had demanded a refund, complaining about Amy's baby-stretched fanny and saggy tits. He would ordinarily have kicked the shit out of the lot of them for daring to ask for their money back, but he'd agreed to a partial refund in the end, figuring that they were good regular customers – when the goods were satisfactory.

Forced to rethink his plans, he decided to put Amy to work on the streets instead. But he'd been waiting in the car for ten minutes now and the stupid bitch still hadn't shown her face. Infuriated to think that she was daring to disobey him after everything he'd said, he slammed his fist down on the steering wheel. Right, that was it! No more Mister Nice Guy!

Amy was curled up in the corner of the kids' bedroom, her face streaked with dried tears, her eyes so badly swollen that she could barely see. She held her breath when she heard Yates letting himself in through the back door, and covered her head with her arms.

Yates stormed up the stairs and into her bedroom. When he saw that her bed was empty, he checked the bathroom. Then, finally, he burst into the kids' room. Eyes quickly adjusting to the dark, he spotted Amy in the corner and marched over to her.

'There you are, you little bitch!' He seized her by the hair and hauled her to her feet, smacking her around the head and face. 'Thought you could hide from me, did you? Thought I wouldn't find you?'

'He's got my kids!' Amy screamed, scratching at his hands and trying to get at his face as well. 'He's got my kids, and it's all your fault!'

'And how do you work that one out?' Yates laughed, wrapping his arms around her and staring down into her eyes. 'Wasn't me who borrowed money and tried to weasel out of paying up, was it? Wasn't me who broke my contract and ran away to avoid my punishment like a little wuss. No, it was that fucking husband of yours. He owes me, so now I *own* you. And I don't give a flying fuck about your kids!'

He dragged her out of the kids' room now and threw her down onto her own bed. Winded, Amy stared up at him and tried to catch her breath.

'What are you doing?' she gasped, shoving herself up the bed with her heels when he pulled something out of his pocket.

'Something I should have done at the start,' said Yates, straddling her and shoving his glove into her mouth before grasping her wrists tightly.

He looked around and, seeing a belt among the mess on the floor, snatched it up and tied her hands together. When she bucked beneath him and tried to kick out, he punched her in the face. Her head lolled to the side, and he climbed off her and went downstairs to get a spoon. Coming back, he took a syringe and a wrap of heroin out of his pocket and prepared a hit, using the faint light of the moon coming in through the window to see by.

When it was ready, he rifled through the drawers until he found a scarf. He was tying it around Amy's arm when she came to. Eyes bulging with terror when she saw the needle, she wet herself as he plunged it into her vein.

When, seconds later, she sank down into the mattress like a deflated balloon, Yates smiled. 'There you go,' he said softly as he pulled the glove out of her mouth and untied her hands. 'All better now.'

Amy didn't respond. She couldn't. Her blood had stopped raging and was now flowing through her veins like a river of molten gold.

17

Jenny and Mark had just had sex and now she was snuggled up to him, playing her fingertips through the fine hairs on his chest. It had been a long day and they were both exhausted. But Jenny was especially so, having spent the last few hours trying to deal with Mark's kids – neither of whom, despite her best efforts, seemed to like her. The boy had cried non-stop and kept soiling his pants. And the girl was a sullen little madam who hadn't said two words all day, and had flat-out refused to eat the lovely dinner that Jenny had cooked so Mark had run out and got her a McDonald's Happy Meal instead. Which had pissed Jenny off no end, because she saw it as the girl getting one over on her.

Still, it was early days, and Jenny was nothing if not patient.

'We'll have to get another bed,' she said now, already planning ahead. 'And a waterproof sheet for Bobby's.'

'Maybe,' Mark murmured. 'But let's not rush into anything. Amy won't want them to stay too often after she gets them back, so I don't think we should waste money on new beds, and that.'

'But they're not going back.' Jenny gazed up at him. 'You said we're keeping them.'

'Might not be that easy,' said Mark. 'She won't give them up without a fight.'

'She's got no chance,' Jenny asserted. 'We're a couple, and we can give them a clean, loving home. She's been neglecting them, so no judge in his right mind is going to hand them back to her. That's why you need to see a solicitor as soon as possible and start divorce proceedings.'

Mark pulled a face. Jenny was getting well ahead of herself, and he wasn't too happy about it. Divorce was the last thing on his mind. He was pissed off with Amy for finding a new man, and really pissed off that she'd supposedly left the kids on their own in order to go out with the bloke. But that didn't mean he wanted to divorce her. Or keep the kids for ever. Sure, he'd said that when he'd first brought them home, but that had just been anger talking.

'You do want a relationship with the kids, don't you?' Jenny asked slyly.

'Yeah, course.' Mark was starting to get irritated. 'What's that got to do with anything?'

'Just think you need to be careful,' said Jenny. 'She's not going to be too happy with you for taking them today, and if she gets them back she'll probably put a block on you seeing them again. You see these things on the news all the time: parents split, mum gets spiteful, and dad hasn't got a leg to stand on. You need to think ahead, that's all I'm saying. They were a mess when they came and, if they go back, they'll be worse next time you see them – *if* there's a next time. And what's to say one of them won't get seriously hurt in the meantime because she left them in the house on their own? Someone could break in and kill them, or abduct them, or anything.'

'I need to go to sleep,' Mark muttered. He felt like she was railroading him, and it was making him feel sick. Grateful as he was to her for welcoming his kids, he needed to think things through on his own, and come to his own conclusion about what was best for him and them.

'Yeah, it's late,' Jenny agreed, sensing that she'd nudged him as far as she could for one night. 'We'll talk again tomorrow. But I still think we should get that bed, because Cassie's a big girl and she needs her own space.'

'Yeah, whatever,' Mark conceded, rolling over. 'Night.'

'Night.' Smiling to herself, Jenny put her arm around him and kissed his back before closing her eyes. One little step at a time was enough for now.

In the next room, Cassie had been woken by Bobby crying. The room was icy cold, and the thin quilt was doing nothing to keep them warm but her brother felt hot and clammy in her arms.

'Want Mummy,' he sobbed, his little chest heaving. 'Want M-Mummy.'

'So do I,' said Cassie, licking at her own salty tears as she rocked him.

'Wan' go home,' Bobby croaked, his eyes drooping as she comforted him.

'Sshhh,' said Cassie, stroking his sweaty hair. 'Go back to sleep, baby.'

Through the wall she'd heard her father and his new girl-friend talking. She hadn't been able to make out what they were saying but she hoped it was about taking her and Bobby home, because she didn't like it here. And she especially didn't like Jenny.

Jenny had pretended that she didn't mind when their daddy had brought them home from school, but Cassie knew different. Jenny had smiled and said nice things to them, but she'd called their mummy a nasty name to their daddy, and said that she was ugly and didn't deserve to have children if she couldn't look after them properly.

Cassie hadn't really understood that last bit, but she'd known it wasn't nice because of the nasty way Jenny had said it. She did, however, understand what 'ugly' meant, and therefore knew that Jenny was a big fat liar, because their mummy was the prettiest lady in the whole wide world – much prettier than Jenny, with her skinny hands, her mean eyes, and the orange stripe in the parting of her hair.

Poor Bobby didn't understand any of what was going on, so Cassie was having to look after him. She didn't mind, because she loved him, but she really hoped that he didn't wet the bed tonight because she had a feeling that Jenny was the kind of lady who would rub his nose in it.

The talking had stopped now, and Bobby's breathing had slowed. Cassie closed her eyes and tried to pretend she was in her own bed. When her daddy had first left home she had missed him like mad. But now they were with him, she was missing her mummy far more.

'Night-night, Mummy,' she whispered as another tear trickled out of her eye and rolled slowly down onto the pillow. 'Love you the whole wide world.'

18

As the week rolled on with no word from Mark, Amy felt as if she was living in a nightmare from which she couldn't wake up. Mark's phone was still switched off, so she'd called the police to report him for kidnapping the kids – only to be told that he had equal rights, and therefore wasn't committing a crime.

She hadn't eaten and had barely slept all week. It felt as if her heart had been ripped right out of her chest and a gaping hole left behind. She missed seeing her babies' beautiful faces and hearing their voices; missed making their dinners and watching them eat, giving them their baths and watching over them to make sure they brushed their teeth properly. She even missed the tantrums and the mess. But most of all she missed the smell of them, and the feel of them in her arms.

She had almost given up on ever hearing from Mark again, so when her phone rang now his was the last name she expected to see on the screen.

'Where are you?' she demanded, sitting bolt upright. 'Why haven't you been answering my calls?'

'I didn't want to talk to you,' Mark replied coldly. 'And I don't want to now, so I'll keep this short. I'm going for custody.'

'What are you talking about?' Amy gasped. 'You can't! I'm their mum – they need me.'

'Don't make me laugh,' said Mark. 'They were a mess when I got them, and I've got the pictures to prove it. I'll be handing them over to the solicitor to prove you're not fit. Oh, and while I'm at it, I'm starting divorce proceedings.'

'*What?*' Amy felt as if she'd been physically kicked in the stomach.

'You heard me. You don't seriously think I'm staying married to you after you cheated on me, do you?'

'I didn't!' Amy protested. 'You're the one who left *me*.'

'And who could blame me?' spat Mark. 'Marnie told me all about your fancy man sneaking in the minute my back was turned. I bet you were at it the whole time we were married, weren't you? Slipping them in the back way every time I went to work, and shagging 'em in my fucking bed.'

'Don't be stupid!' Amy snapped, offended that he could think such a thing when she had never even looked at another man in the whole time they had been together. 'There's never been anyone but you.'

'Save it for the judge,' Mark said coldly. 'Doubt he'll believe you, though, 'cos you've been lying through your teeth so long you wouldn't know the truth if it walked up and bit your fucking nose off.'

Angry now, because he seemed determined to twist everything around to make it look like she was the bad one, Amy said, '*You*'re the liar and the cheat. I can't believe I kept forgiving you, and now you're treating me like *this*.'

'This is different. You're a mother – you should know better.'

'So it's all right for you to shag that ginger bitch behind my back, but I'm not allowed to find another man?'

'Never mind Jenny. Just tell lover boy I'll be naming him in the divorce.'

'Tell him yourself,' snarled Amy. 'If you've got the balls – which I kind of doubt, seeing as you were so shit scared of him you ran away and left me to deal with him.'

'You what?' Mark sounded far less cocky all of a sudden. 'You'd best not be saying what I think you're saying.'

'What? That I'm shagging Lenny Yates?' said Amy, digging the knife in and twisting it. 'So what if I am? What are you gonna do about it?'

Mark's head started to spin, and he was momentarily struck dumb. He'd been jealous when Marnie had told him about Amy seeing someone else, but he'd managed to convince himself that it wasn't true; that Amy had put her up to it to get a reaction out of him. That was why he had left it a week before contacting her, thinking that she would be so desperate when he finally *did* call she would beg him for forgiveness. He'd only mentioned going for custody and applying for a divorce to punish her for winding him up, but the last thing he'd expected was for her to admit that there was another man. And not just any man. Len Yates. The man who had kicked and beaten him to within an inch of his life.

'You dirty fucking slag,' he hissed when he recovered the power of speech. 'You deserve everything that's coming to you.'

Before Amy could respond to that, she heard Jenny's voice in the background: 'Mark, *sshhh* . . . ! The kids are in the bath, and they can hear you shouting.'

White-hot with rage, Amy yelled, 'What the fuck's *she* doing bathing my kids? If she lays one finger on them, I'll kill her!'

'It's none of your business,' Mark said icily. 'She's their mam now, not you. And I was gonna let you see them but you can fuck that, 'cos there's no way *he*'s going anywhere near them.'

'You can't do this!' Amy screeched, tears cascading down her face. 'They're my kids!'

When the line went dead in her hand she tried to call him back, but he'd switched his phone off again. Screaming at the top of her lungs, she jumped up and started smashing her way around the room.

Next door, Marnie heard the commotion and jumped up off the couch. She and Amy still weren't speaking, but it sounded like holy hell was breaking out in there and she couldn't just ignore her.

Afraid that Amy might be being attacked, Marnie ran round and banged on her door. But she got no answer, and the screaming and banging continued.

'Amy, it's me!' she yelled through the letter box. 'Let me in, or I'm calling the police!'

Almost immediately, an ashtray flew through the window, sending a shower of glass every which way. Marnie jumped back in time to avoid being hit and was about to go home to carry out her threat when a car drove slowly past. She recognised it, and ran out onto the pavement, waving frantically at the driver to stop.

'Oh, thank God!' she cried, running around to the driver's-side door. 'I'm Amy's friend, I live next door.'

'Yeah, I know.' Yates frowned up at her through the open window. 'What's up?'

'I don't know!' Marnie glanced worriedly back at the house. 'Someone's smashing the place up, but Amy won't let me in so I don't know if it's her or someone attacking her.'

Yates switched the car's engine off and jumped out, just as Gemma waddled over. 'What's going on?' She stared at the glass littering Amy's front lawn and path. 'Shall I call the cops?'

'No, I'll sort it,' Yates told her.

Gemma squinted up at him. 'You're her new fella, aren't you? I've seen you picking her up of a night. Decided to go public at last, have youse?'

'*Gemma!*' Marnie hissed. 'She didn't want anyone to know.'

'Ah, well, no point hiding it if everyone's already sussed us,' Yates said philosophically. 'I'll go and see what's up. Thanks for telling me, love.' He nodded at Marnie, then took a run up to the locked side gate and hauled himself over.

'Let me know if you need any help,' Marnie shouted as he dropped down the other side.

'Well, that's a turn-up,' said Gemma, turning to Marnie with a smirk on her lips. 'No wonder she didn't want anyone to fucking see him. Did you see the mush on it? Talk about ugly.'

Marnie couldn't disagree, but the man had seemed friendly enough, so she shrugged, and said, 'Amy obviously likes him, so he can't be that bad. Anyway, Mark was handsome, and look where that got her.'

'Suppose so,' Gemma conceded. 'Never trust a good-looking bloke, my mam always used to say. If they're not giving some other slag the glad eye, they're too busy checking themselves out in the mirror to notice you.'

'True,' Marnie agreed, folding her arms and looking at Amy's broken window. 'Hope she's all right.'

'It's gone quiet now, so I guess he's got it under control,' said Gemma.

'He must really care about her,' Marnie murmured. 'Can't think of many blokes who'd put up with her the way she's been acting lately.'

'Yeah, well, I did try and tell you what she was like.' Gemma drew her chin in, instantly tripling it in size. 'You lot might have fell for the Little Miss Sunshine act, but I had her number from the off. Snotty bitch, she is; looking down her nose at the rest of us just 'cos her hubby had a job. Well, she ain't so fucking high and mighty now, is she?'

Marnie shook her head slowly, then sighed, and said, 'I'd best go in. Got a pot of soup on the stove – don't wanna burn the house down.'

'I'm going out in a minute,' said Gemma, glancing at her watch. 'But I'll have me mobile on me, so make sure you give us a ring if anything else kicks off.'

Inside Amy's house just then, Yates had his hand clamped over her mouth and was dragging her into the kitchen. Her hands were covered in blood, and the front room was destroyed: mirror shattered, broken ornaments littering the floor, couch overturned, and tea dripping down the wall from where she'd hurled the cup at it. It was her wedding picture that had caused the cuts to her hands. Not satisfied with just smashing it, Amy had torn the photograph out through the jagged spikes of glass, shredding her flesh in the process. But she hadn't cared about the pain, she'd just wanted to tear Mark to pieces the way he'd done with her heart.

Yates shoved her down onto a chair and warned her to keep her mouth shut before taking his hand away. Then, tipping the dirty dishes out of the washing-up bowl, he filled it with warm water and carried it to the table.

'Are you fucking stupid?' he demanded as he grabbed one of her hands and plunged it into the water. 'Your mate was about to call the pigs when I got here. And if you thought you had it bad now, it's nothing to what they'd have done if they'd clocked the state of this place.'

'I don't care,' Amy snarled. 'He's got my kids, and he's never giving them back because he thinks I'm having an affair with *you*!'

Yates chuckled softly and hauled her hand out of the bloodied water to check the damage.

'Get off me!' Amy yelled, tugging her arm out of his grasp. 'You've destroyed my life, you bastard! My husband's shacked up with some tart, my friends think I'm scum, and my mum and dad aren't talking to me 'cos they think all of this is my fault. I *hate* you!'

'My, we *are* feeling sorry for ourselves, aren't we?' drawled Yates, reaching for her other hand. 'Seems to me you brought all this on yourself by marrying the dickhead in the first place. What kind of a man runs out on the woman he's supposed to love and leaves her to pay his debts? If you ask me, I did you a favour.'

'*GET OUT!*' Amy screeched, leaping up and punching and clawing at his face. 'Just get out of my fucking *house*!'

Pissed off when she got blood on his jacket, Yates head-butted her. When she collapsed, smashing her head on the hard tile floor, he took a syringe out of his pocket and rooted through the sink for a spoon. She was getting too emotional, and that was dangerous, because she could drop him right in it if she mouthed off to the wrong person. But this would soon sort her out.

After preparing the syringe, he pulled his belt out of its loops and knelt beside Amy.

'Don't,' she croaked, coming to as he shoved her sleeve up. 'Please . . .'

'Don't beg.' Yates grinned. 'You know I can't resist you when you beg.'

Amy cried out and arched her back when he plunged the

spike into her flesh. But, seconds later, her mouth fell open and her eyes rolled back.

'There we go,' Yates said softly. 'Few more of them and you'll soon forget about them kids of yours.'

Marnie had been watching through the window the whole time Yates had been inside Amy's house. When she saw him walk towards his car a short time later, she ran outside.

'Is she okay?'

'She's asleep.' Yates quickly adjusted the smirk on his lips into an expression of weariness and concern. 'She's just upset about that ex of hers.'

'It's terrible what he's done to her,' Marnie said angrily. 'I could kill him, I really could.'

'She'll be all right,' Yates sighed. 'She's got me now. I'll look after her. Just off to get some wood for the window.' He opened the car door. 'Couldn't do us a favour and listen out for her, could you?'

'I'll sit in with her, if you want,' Marnie offered.

'Thanks, love, but best not.' Yates gave her an embarrassed smile. 'It's a bit of a state in there, to be honest. And she's, er, taken something,' he added quietly, glancing around as if he didn't want anyone else to hear. 'I'm not too happy about it, 'cos I'm not into drugs, but she reckons she needs it.'

'I knew it,' Marnie said flatly. 'I asked her if she was on something and she denied it, but I just knew it. Let me guess . . . smack?'

'Keep it to yourself, eh?' Yates urged. 'I'm going to get her off it, but it ain't gonna be easy. It's already messed her head up. She tells me all this stuff, and I know half of it ain't true, but what can I do?' He sighed again as if he had the weight of the world on his shoulders. Then, shrugging, he said, 'Best go so I can get back before she wakes up. Cheers again for your help, love.'

'No problem. I'm Marnie, by the way.'

'Lenny.' He held out his hand.

'Nice to meet you.' She shook it. 'And I'm, er, just next door if you ever need anything. Even if you just want a chat, or a brew, or whatever.'

Yates nodded and gave her a grateful smile before climbing into the car.

Marnie stepped back onto the pavement and watched as he drove away. He was ugly, there was no denying that, but he seemed to genuinely care for Amy, and Marnie couldn't help but wish that a man would feel like that about *her*, instead of just wanting to shag her and run. Amy had been mooching around like a tramp for weeks, snapping at people when they tried to talk to her and locking herself away behind closed curtains. It amazed Marnie that any man would look twice at her right now, never mind tolerate her crazy outbursts. But she'd hooked herself a good one there.

Envy stirring in her gut, Marnie went back into her house and turned down the TV volume to listen out for Amy – not for Amy's sake, for Lenny's. She was disgusted with her friend for sinking so low as to get hooked on smack. They'd all had their hearts broken at some time or other, but they hadn't all used it as an excuse to turn into a dirty junkie.

It was no wonder that Mark had taken the kids, because he obviously knew how bad Amy really was. And Gemma had been right about her, as well. In fact, it seemed like everyone except Marnie had seen her for what she really was.

But Marnie wouldn't be falling for any more of her lies. She'd given the bitch the benefit of the doubt too many times and had it chucked right back in her face. But it would be that poor man who would be getting her support from now on, not Amy. And he was going to need it, because he obviously didn't know what he was letting himself in for.

On his way to the job centre just then, Mark was still chewing over the conversation he'd had with Amy. The custody and divorce thing had been Jenny's idea, and he'd only said it to Amy to hurt her. But now she'd admitted that Yates was the mystery man that Marnie had told him about he didn't see how he could ever go back.

He had his head down as he walked, and his hood pulled right over his head. As he passed the timber merchant's on Chorlton Road, he didn't notice the car about to head into the parking lot. But the driver saw him, and pulled right in front of him.

'All right, stranger – long time no see.'

Mark's heart dropped down through his feet at the sound of Yates's voice. Apart from when he'd picked the kids up last week, he'd hardly stepped foot out of the flat for fear of bumping into Yates. And he wouldn't be out now if the bastards at the DSS hadn't refused to let him switch to signing on at a different office.

'I don't want any trouble,' he stammered, holding his hands out in front of him. 'Please, Len . . . I'll pay you back, I swear I will. I've just—'

'Don't worry about it,' Yates interrupted, enjoying watching him squirm as he climbed out of the car. 'Your missus is taking care of me, so we're square.' He paused, lit a cigarette, and grinned. 'Right little goer when she gets started, ain't she? Proper knows her way around a cock.'

The blood drained from Mark's face as Yates's words scored a direct hit, but he kept his mouth shut.

'How's that pretty little girl of yours?' Yates asked now, squinting at Mark through the smoke. 'Hope you're looking after her?'

'Yeah, course,' Mark muttered sickly.

'Good.' Yates nodded his approval. 'Between you and me, I reckon they're better off with you, 'cos their mam ain't exactly equipped to look after them – if you get me drift? Bit too fond of the old . . .' He held up his hands and mimed chasing the dragon.

Satisfied that he'd fucked the man's day up when he saw the pain in Mark's eyes, Yates took another drag on his smoke and smirked. 'Oh, well, best let you go. Make sure you give your little 'un a kiss from Uncle Lenny when you get home, won't you?'

As Yates climbed back into his car and drove away, Mark struggled to control the seething anger and jealousy. Much as it was a relief to know that he was off the hook for the money, because it had been horrible being stuck in the flat with Jenny twenty-four-seven, he just couldn't get to grips with the thought of Amy and Yates seeing each other.

As his head began to clear, an icy coldness settled over him. It was over. And as soon as he'd signed on, he was going to see a solicitor and start the ball rolling for real.

19

Three weeks later, Yates drove into a darkened parking lot at the rear of a cash-and-carry in Levenshulme, switched off the engine, and nudged Amy with his elbow.

She stirred and peered blearily out through the window. Confused to see that they weren't at the back of Piccadilly Station where he had been dropping her off every night, she said, 'Where are we?'

'You're shit on the streets, so you ain't doing that no more,' Yates told her as he unbuckled his seat belt and hopped out. 'You're gonna be working here from now on, where someone can keep an eye on you.'

Amy wasn't really listening, but even if she had been she wouldn't have cared. In the weeks since Mark had dropped his divorce bombshell, she'd thought she would never climb out of the black hole he'd pushed her into. But now she had the smack to take her mind off it, none of it seemed to matter quite so much any more.

Yates walked her through an open gate and up to a metal door at the rear of the building, above which a single security light highlighted a small faded sign that read *Hawaii*. A spyhole was drawn back when he knocked and a dark eye peered out.

'We're not open. Come back in half an hour.'

'Do I look like a fuckin' punter?' Yates snapped. 'It's me, you plank. Mani's expecting me.'

The door opened, and a black security guard waved them in. 'Sorry, couldn't see you properly. He's in the office.'

Yates shoved Amy ahead of him up the stairs. At the top, another door opened onto a dimly lit corridor. 'Stay there,' he ordered.

When he disappeared into a room at the far end of the corridor, Amy swung her head around at the sound of laughter to her right. Through a partially open door she could see several women lounging on shabby couches, each of them wearing short dressing gowns and sucking on cigarettes. One who looked much older than the rest seemed to be holding court from a chair in the corner. Fat, with enormous breasts, she had a scabby feather boa draped around her shoulders, unnaturally black hair, and a face so thick with make-up that Amy thought she looked like Alice Cooper's mother.

'So I told him straight,' the woman was saying, waving her long cigarette holder around as she spoke and leaving a trail of purple smoke in the air. 'I said, Andy, if I wanted a horse, I'd go to the bloody stables. Put it away before you do some serious damage, you naughty boy.'

'Who's Andy?' a younger girl asked.

'Warhol, of course,' said the old woman. 'Had 'em all in my time, I have.'

'Yeah, in your dreams,' scoffed another girl, heading towards the door. She yanked it open and stopped in her tracks when she saw Amy. 'Who the fuck are you?'

Too spaced out to be bothered to answer, Amy stared back at her without speaking. Recognising a fellow junkie, the girl smiled slowly. 'Got any gear on you?'

Before Amy could respond, Yates called her name and waved for her to come to the office. She pushed herself away from the wall and walked towards him, the old woman's voice floating along behind her: 'Did I ever tell you girls about the time I visited the Earl of Whatjamacallit in his castle? Bedroom as big as this whole place – and a todger to match . . .'

In the office, a fat Asian man was sitting behind the desk. He looked Amy up and down when she came in, then smiled and waved for her to sit on the sofa against the wall.

'Well?' Yates raised an eyebrow.

'Very nice.' The man stood up and came around the desk to shake his hand.

Yates turned to Amy. 'Right, I'm off. I'll pick you up at five. Do as Mani tells you – and no messing about or there'll be trouble.'

Mani locked the door behind him and turned back to Amy with a leering smile on his flabby wet lips.

'Right, then, blondie.' He unzipped his fly. 'Let's see if you're as good as he says you are.'

PART TWO

SIX MONTHS LATER

20

Two letters had arrived that morning, and Amy had read and reread them several times throughout the day. But she still couldn't get her head around them.

Decree Absolute . . .

She stared at the words and wondered why solicitors could never speak in plain English. Why not just get straight to the point and say: *Ha! Loser! He don't love you no more!* Because that was effectively what it meant.

She screwed the letter into a ball and hurled it at the wall. It bounced off and landed inches away from the other one: the one informing her that Mark had been granted temporary custody of the children and that, due to her unreasonable behaviour and continued abuse of illegal substances, access – if allowed – would be restricted to a secure location, under strict supervision.

Bastards! Dirty, lying, fucking bastards!

Clean yourself up and come to court, they'd said. *The judge will see that you're making an effort and be more inclined to view your situation kindly.*

And Amy had tried, she really had. She'd dressed nicely, and had tried to stay calm and speak politely even when they were saying horrible things about her. But if her own mother hadn't been able to bear to look at her, she'd stood no chance with the officials.

'*You should be ashamed of yourself,*' her mother had said when they left court. '*I didn't bring you up to be a tramp, but that's exactly what you've become. And I'm glad Mark and Jenny have got the children,*' she had added as a cruel parting shot. '*At least they know how to look after them properly.*'

Her hands shaking violently as the memory replayed itself in her mind, Amy snatched up the blackened strip of tinfoil and tipped the last of her heroin onto it. Then, stuffing the rolled-up note she'd taken from Cassie's old Monopoly game into her mouth, she held her lighter flame beneath the foil and greedily sucked up the smoke.

It took effect quickly and she slumped back in her seat, sighing as the anger and pain began to drift away. It had been ages since she'd seen the kids, and she hated Mark for making it so difficult. But she'd deal with him later.

When she was better.

And she *would* get better.

Eventually.

When people stopped making her life hell.

She was still gouched out when Yates walked in a short time later, and he booted her in the leg.

'Oi! Get the fuck up. You're gonna be late.'

'Ugh?' Amy peeled her eyes open and gazed blearily up at him.

'Look at the state of you,' he spat. 'How many times have I told you to lay off the gear till you've finished work? Think the punters want to look at *that* when they're trying to get their ends away?'

Amy was wasted, but not so wasted that she didn't know better than to argue.

'Get up the stairs!' he growled, dragging her off the couch and hurling her towards the door. 'And make sure you get a proper wash, 'cos you fuckin' stink,' he added, booting her in the arse as she stumbled into the hall. 'Rate you're going, you'll still be turning tricks from your fuckin' grave before you've paid me back, you piss-taking slag!'

Properly awake now, Amy scuttled up to the bathroom and dashed water over her face before running into the bedroom and changing into a short skirt and low top – both of which were stained, but they'd be coming off soon enough, so she didn't care. Lastly, she spritzed her underarms and mouth with perfume before running back down to where Yates was waiting in the hall.

He pushed her out of the door and walked her swiftly to the car. Out of the corner of his eye, he saw Marnie come out onto her step and quickly dropped the scowl as he shoved Amy onto the passenger seat.

'At it again?' Marnie asked.

Yates gave a *what-can-you-do?* kind of shrug.

'You're a bloody saint,' said Marnie, shaking her head in disgust.

She herself had long since given up on Amy. Every word that came out of her mouth was a lie, and the one time Marnie had made the mistake of feeling sorry for her and letting her in for a brew Amy had nicked a tenner off the mantelpiece on her way out.

'I can only try,' Yates said humbly as he headed around to his side of the car. 'See you later.'

'Are you coming round?'

'If I can.' Yates winked, waved, and hopped into the car.

Amy glowered out at Marnie as they set off. The bitch thought that Amy didn't know she was shagging Yates, but little did she know that Yates had told Amy all about it. It was all part of the game to him, and he got a kick out of knowing that the neighbours had fallen for his *innocent-boyfriend-trying-to-keep-his-wayward-woman-on-the-straight-and-narrow* act. If Marnie did but know it, Amy was actually grateful that she'd taken some of Yates's attention away from her. He hadn't stopped sleeping with Amy altogether, but any day that he wasn't forcing himself on her was a good day.

Amy couldn't, however, so easily forgive Marnie for the rest of it. Once, way back in the agonising weeks after Mark had first snatched the kids and Amy was at rock-bottom, she'd broken down and spilled her guts to Marnie. But instead of supporting her, the back-stabbing bitch had relayed every word to Yates, earning Amy the beating of her life. And now Marnie looked at her as if she was a piece of shit – as did everyone else who was supposed to care about her. And they wondered why she needed the smack to keep her going.

When Yates dropped her off outside *Hawaii* a short time later, Amy rushed inside. As much as she still hated the actual work, she did enjoy coming here. Not only because it was the only time she ever got out of the house now that Yates had more or less moved in, but also because it felt good to talk to the other girls without being sneered at and looked down on.

'Evening.' Kelvin, the doorman, smiled as he let her in. 'And how are you tonight?'

'Fine, thanks.' Amy smiled back. 'You?'

'Can't complain.' He shrugged. 'See you later.'

'Yeah, see you.' Amy waved and tripped up the stairs.

Kelvin was a nice man, and *very* good-looking. The other girls were always flirting with him and going on about what they'd like to do to him given the chance, but Amy didn't dare get too friendly in case Yates found out. She'd made the mistake of saying hello to a male neighbour a while back, and Yates had battered her before threatening to petrol bomb the man's house. It had taken ages to convince him that she wasn't flirting with the man, and she'd never made the same mistake again.

As usual, Betty Bullshit was holding court in the staffroom, ever-present cigarette holder clamped between her yellow teeth. She had been on the game for ever and swore she was only fifty, but they all knew she was closer to seventy. Rumour had it that she'd been the mistress of Mani's father and that was why Mani kept her on despite it being several years since any of the punters had so much as sniffed in her direction. Whether or not that was true, her ludicrous stories brightened what would otherwise be a dismal job.

'Ah, here she is.' Betty broke off from her current story when she spotted Amy. 'Shove the kettle on, there's a good girl. And drop a nip of this in mine.' She pulled a small bottle of whisky out from between her gargantuan breasts and tossed it to Amy. 'So, where were we?' She picked up her thread. 'Oh, yes . . . Well, I was whipping Frank with my suspender belt, when Elvis wakes up . . .'

'Know who she's talking about, don't you?' Ella whispered, joining Amy at the sink as she filled the kettle. 'Only reckons Frank Sinatra flew her to LA for a threesome with Elvis.'

'Really?' Amy raised an eyebrow.

'As if!' Ella snorted. 'Must be fuckin' nice being her, though, eh? Living in a land of total make-believe.'

'She's harmless,' Amy murmured, glancing quickly back over her shoulder to make sure no one was eavesdropping. 'Did you get it?'

Ella nodded and slipped a tiny wrap into her hand. 'Don't forget to pay us before you go, though, 'cos I need to pay my guy first thing.'

'I won't,' Amy promised, slipping the wrap into her bra. If she'd been brave enough she'd have smoked some in the loo, but there was no way she was risking it while Mani was prowling around. The man had a nose like a sniffer dog on heat and, while anything else might go in here, drugs were an absolute no-no and anyone caught using on the premises would be out on their arse in a flash – and Yates would kill Amy if that happened.

'Well, we laughed so much,' Betty was saying when Amy handed her tea over a few minutes later. 'I said, Elvis, you'd better bloody stop or I'm not gonna be able to walk by the time you've finished.'

'Who's Elvis?' Trudy, the youngest girl, asked, still soaking it all up like a sponge despite having been told a thousand times that it was all rubbish.

'Presley,' Betty told her. 'The undisputed king of rock and roll.'

'You've shagged a *king?*'

'Oh, for God's sake.' Ella shook her head and rolled her eyes at Amy.

Amy smiled and settled down to drink her tea.

Mani walked in a few minutes later and demanded to know why they were all still sitting here gassing.

'Punters are queuing up round the block out there,' he said, clapping his hands together. 'Come on . . . get moving.'

Amy finished her brew and wandered down the corridor to her room. A few minutes later, a tap came at the door. Sighing, she said, 'Come in, Jimmy.'

'How d'you know it was me?' the man asked as he sidled in.

'You're the only one who ever knocks,' Amy told him. 'What's it to be?'

'Usual, please.' Jimmy closed the door and fumbled with his belt.

Amy turned her back to take her top off. When she turned

round, Jimmy was already naked and lying on the bed, worm in hand, racing heartbeat causing his paper-thin chest to vibrate visibly. He was by far the gentlest and most polite of the punters, but his puny body and rotten teeth disgusted her.

'Can you do a special?' he asked huskily when she strad-dled him.

Amy swallowed the bile that had risen into her throat and shuffled up the bed on her knees until she was squatting over his face.

'Do it,' he gasped.

'I'm trying,' she muttered.

'*Please*,' he urged. 'I'll give you an extra twenty.'

Amy squeezed her eyes shut. This was so humiliating, but the extra money meant that she'd be able to pay Ella for the gear instead of sneaking out at the end of her shift as she'd intended.

'Oh, thank you,' Jimmy moaned as the hot liquid began to trickle over his ecstatic face. 'Thank you so much.'

Kelvin was outside having a cigarette when Yates pulled up at five a.m. He waved, dropped the fag, and went back inside to tell Amy her ride was here.

'You look done in,' he said, watching from the staffroom door as she slipped her shoes on and reached for her jacket.

'I'm wiped,' she agreed, covering a yawn with her hand.

'Your man don't look too happy,' Kelvin warned her quietly. 'Gave me a right stare just now. You gonna be all right?'

Amy shrugged and stood up. There was no way of knowing until Yates showed his hand. Sometimes he was fine, but more often than not a wrong look or word could send him into a violent rage. The beatings she could handle, but it was torture when he punished her for whatever he thought she'd done by withholding her fix. Still, she had the wrap Ella had given her, so she'd be all right tonight.

'Take it easy,' Kelvin said now as he walked ahead of her down the stairs.

Amy nodded and rushed out with her head down. As soon as she climbed into the car she knew that Kelvin had been right about Yates being in a mood. He was drumming his fingers on the steering wheel, and his eyes had the too-bright gleam that told her he'd been doing coke. Aware that it pissed him off when she moved too much, she sat rigid in her seat.

Yates drove home in silence, then followed Amy inside and slammed the door shut.

'How many did you do tonight?'

'Eleven or twelve.' Already trembling, Amy rubbed at her arms and gazed up at him nervously.

'You taking the piss?'

'No. That's all the men who came. Honest.'

'You lazy fucking *bitch*!' Yates snarled, spittle flying out through his clenched teeth and splattering her face. He seized her by the throat and slammed her up against the wall. 'Think this is a game? Think I ain't got better things to do than chase after my fuckin' money week in, week out?'

'It's not my fault,' Amy squealed, struggling to breathe as he squeezed ever harder. 'Please, Lenny, I did my best. But Mani rotates them so all the girls get the same.'

'Well, it ain't good enough!' Yates was staring at her with such intensity that she felt physically sick. 'You owe me, and I'm getting sick of waiting for it.'

Amy could have reminded him that, apart from the odd backhander, she never saw a penny of what she earned, because Mani always handed it straight to Yates. But she kept her mouth shut and braced herself for the beating that she felt sure was coming.

'And what's with that cunt back there eyeballing me?' Yates asked now. 'You been talking to him?'

'No, course not.'

'*Liar!*' Yates punched her in the stomach.

'I'm not!' Amy cried, clutching at her midriff. 'I don't talk to anyone.'

'Think I don't know what goes on in there?' Yates slapped her around the head and knocked her down to the floor. 'Think I ain't got people reporting back to me?' He kicked her in the stomach. 'Want me to shoot the cunt, do you? Want me to shoot *you*, then go after your brats? 'Cos that's what I'm gonna do if you carry on taking the piss.'

Amy curled into a ball and covered her head with her hands as the kicks kept coming. Finally, what felt like an hour later, Yates stopped and stared down at her.

'You're mine,' he hissed. 'And if I catch you so much as looking at that black cunt, or any other man, you're dead.'

Amy stayed where she was for several minutes after he walked out. Then, dragging herself up painfully, she reached into her bra for the wrap that Ella had given her. She was sweating with fear and the paper felt damp. Scared that the powder might be too, she hobbled into the front room and quickly tipped some out onto her foil.

The sound of muffled voices came to her through the wall as she was putting the Monopoly note into her mouth. Sneering, she sucked up the soothing dragon-smoke and lay down, pulling the dirty clothes that were heaped at the end of the couch over herself. Marnie and Yates would be on their way to bed any time now, and Amy had no intention of going upstairs and listening to them at it.

Woken by the sound of her mobile phone ringing the next morning, Amy rooted down the side of the couch cushions and dragged it out. Shocked to see Mark's name on the screen, because they hadn't spoken in weeks, she sat bolt upright.

'Hello . . . Mark? What's up? Are the kids all right?'

'Like you care,' spat Mark. 'It's your daughter's birthday, but you've obviously forgotten.'

'Course I haven't,' Amy lied, guilt washing over her like a red-hot wave. 'But I couldn't send a card 'cos you won't tell me your address.'

'Too right I won't. Think I want you turning up and kicking off every time you feel like it? Anyhow, don't worry about it, 'cos me and Jenny are doing a party for her.'

'Can – can I see her?' Amy's chin had started to wobble, and tears were scorching her eyes.

'I just told you, we don't want you round here,' said Mark. 'And the kids don't, neither.'

'So why did you ring me?' Amy cried, guessing that he'd done it to hurt her.

Mark didn't answer. As it happened, he *had* only rung to rub it in that he wouldn't be letting her see Cassie on her birthday. Long as they had been apart now, he was no less angry with her for betraying him. But if hearing about Cassie's party had hurt her, his next news was guaranteed to cut her to pieces.

'I wasn't just ringing about Cassie, actually,' he said, an edge of spite in his voice. 'Me and Jenny are getting married, and the social worker reckoned I should tell you before you got wind of it and took it into your head to try and stop us. I wouldn't, though, if I was you, 'cos Cass is proper excited about being a bridesmaid, and I'd hate for her to have her big day ruined.'

'You bastard,' Amy hissed.

'Yep, that's me.' Mark laughed nastily. 'Anyhow, got to go. Jenny's baking a special cake, and I've got to go and get some candles and balloons, and that.'

When the line went dead, Amy buried her face in her hands and sobbed. She had completely forgotten that it was Cassie's birthday, and it killed her to think that she wouldn't be able to see her. She was the one who had always organised the kids' parties in the past, and if Mark had even made it back from work in time to see them blow out their candles, he'd usually sneaked out again before the smoke had cleared. But all of a sudden he was the world's best daddy, and he was letting that bitch play mummy and do all the things that Amy had always done. It wasn't fair, it just wasn't fair.

Unable to bear it, Amy went to the kitchen and rooted through the bin for one of the spikes that Yates had used on her. She was still terrified of needles, and never injected herself if she could get away with it. But she didn't have enough gear left to wipe out the pain by smoking it, and desperate times called for desperate measures.

'What did she say?' Jenny asked when Mark put down the phone. 'Did she say anything about me?'

'She was fuming when I told her you were baking a cake,' Mark muttered sickly. Jenny had been nagging him to ring Amy and tell her about the wedding for ages, and he'd got quite a kick out of it while he was actually doing it. But the satisfaction had been short-lived. He and Amy had been together for a long time and, however many times he'd cheated on her, she'd always been the one. Still, it was done now, so there was no point thinking about it.

'She's only got herself to blame,' Jenny said self-righteously. 'If she'd been a proper mum, the kids would still be with her. Not my fault I'm better at it than her.'

Mark didn't think Jenny's mothering skills were a patch on Amy's, and if things had been different he'd have been happy to let the kids go home, because full-time parenting was much harder than he'd thought it was going to be. But that wasn't an option since the social services had declared Amy unfit, so Jenny would have to do.

'Best go and get those candles,' he said, getting up and pulling his jacket on.

'You won't be long, will you?' Jenny asked, kissing him on the cheek.

Mark shook his head and glanced at Cassie. It was Saturday, so there was no school, but far from looking happy at the prospect of spending her birthday at home Mark had never seen her so miserable.

'What's up, darlin'?' He walked over to the couch and squatted down in front of her.

'Nothing,' she whispered, sad eyes downcast.

'You don't look very happy.' Mark stroked her hair. 'If you're not feeling well, why don't you go and have a little lie-down with Bobby while Daddy gets the stuff for your party?'

'I wanted to talk to my mummy,' Cassie mumbled, casting a wary side-glance at Jenny.

'I know,' Mark said quietly, the guilt intensifying and making him feel like a cunt. 'But she's not very well at the moment, so she couldn't talk. Maybe later, eh?'

'Don't worry, I'll cheer her up,' said Jenny, touching him on the shoulder to tell him to leave Cassie be. 'You go and get the candles. And don't forget the pop. Can't have a birthday party without pop, can we?' She smiled down at Cassie.

'Thanks.' Mark stood up and gave her a grateful smile. 'Won't be long.'

Jenny waited until she heard the front door close, then turned to Cassie and scowled.

'What do you think you're playing at, you little bitch? Your daddy's going to a lot of trouble to give you a nice birthday party, and I won't be happy if you ruin it for him. You'd better get that look off your face and start acting like you're having fun – or else.'

Tears welling in her eyes, chin quivering uncontrollably, Cassie whimpered, 'I want my m-mummy.'

'*Boo-hoo! I want my mummy!*' Jenny mimicked nastily. Then, sneering, she said, 'You're a stupid little girl. Stupid and ugly, just like your precious mummy. Well, guess what . . . she doesn't want you. That's why she wouldn't talk to you, and that's why she gave you away, 'cos she can't stand the sight of you.'

Cassie drew her knees up to her chin and buried her face in them. But Jenny was having none of that. She grabbed the child's hair and dragged her head up, hissing, 'You'd better stop this before your dad gets back, or you know what'll happen, don't you? Bobby will get hurt. And you don't want that, do you?'

Tears streaming down her cheeks, Cassie shook her head.

'Make sure you remember that,' spat Jenny, letting go of her and heading for the door. 'I'm going for a bath. Make sure that brat doesn't touch anything of mine when he wakes up or I'll chop his hands off.'

Her little chest still heaving, Cassie listened out for the sound of the bolt going across on the bathroom door. Then, easing herself off the couch, she tiptoed across the room. Mark had left his phone on the arm of the other couch. Cassie had never used a mobile in her life, but she'd watched her mum and dad doing it loads of times, so she thought she knew what to do. Hands shaking wildly, she stared at the door, picked up the phone and pressed the redial button.

Amy had just finished preparing her fix and was trying to summon up the courage to inject herself when her mobile rang again. Red mist descending when she saw Mark's name on the screen, she snatched it up and yelled, 'Fuck off and die, you bastard! I hate you, and I never want to see you or hear your horrible voice again!'

Shocked and heartbroken, Cassie dropped the phone and ran into the bedroom, dived under the quilt, curled into a little ball and buried her face in the pillow to cover the sound of her sobs.

All she'd wanted was to hear her mummy sing *Happy Birthday To You* like she'd always used to do on their birthdays. And she'd wanted to tell her that she loved her, and missed her, and didn't want to be a bridesmaid because she hated Jenny and didn't want her daddy to get married to her. But more than anything she'd wanted to tell her mummy to come and get her and Bobby and take them home.

But that was never going to happen, because Jenny had been telling the truth. Her mummy *did* hate her.

22

As usual, Kelvin Brown was smiling when he opened the door for Amy that night. But his smile soon slipped when he caught sight of the bruise on her cheek and the livid markings on her throat.

'Oh, my days,' he murmured concernedly. 'What's he done now?'

Amy blushed and self-consciously covered her face with her hand, murmuring 'I fell over' as she rushed towards the stairs.

Was that before or after you walked into the door? Kelvin wanted to ask, but she had already gone.

He shook his head and went back into his booth. It wasn't the first time he'd seen bruises on Amy, and it definitely wouldn't be the last. But, if she wasn't careful, she was going to end up like the last girl that Yates had brought here.

Like Amy, that girl had always had a haunted look in her eye and an air of resignation about her. And, like Amy, she had regularly come to work with bruises on her face. But it hadn't been long before the scars had started to appear; scars that became progressively deeper and nastier, until her pretty face was no longer pretty. And then, one night, she hadn't turned up – and nobody had seen her since.

Kelvin had three sisters, and his mother had been widowed when he was only nine, so he'd grown up in pretty much an all-girl household. But, annoying as girls could undoubtedly be, he could never imagine a time when he would want to cause them pain. Not only because it would shame his father's memory, but because it would send his mother into an early grave.

She was so proud of him for holding down a full-time job – a rarity in their neck of the woods. And every time one of the neighbourhood boys succumbed to the evils of drugs or guns, she thanked the Lord for having given her the tools to guide her fatherless boy onto the right path. But Kelvin knew that she wouldn't be so proud if she ever found out *where* he worked, so that was one thing he'd never told her.

He personally saw nothing wrong with a girl choosing to sell her body – as long as she was doing it of her own free will. The problem arose when they were forced into it, and he despised the men who abused them in that way. Men like Yates, who dropped them off and picked them up in order to maintain control; and who took all the money they earned, and then beat them for not earning more.

Kelvin had been working at *Hawaii* for three years now, and he'd seen it all. Girls came and went, and they all had their reasons for doing what they did. Most were addicts who chose this line of work because it was the quickest way to get the money for a fix without putting themselves in danger on the streets. Some did it because they were struggling to feed their kids, having been abandoned by the fathers or getting no help from them. For the odd few, like old Betty, it was simply the only way of life they had ever known. But then there were the ones like Amy, who Kelvin could see from a mile off didn't really want to be there. And they were the ones that made him question what *he* was doing here.

The first punter of the night arrived, and Kelvin pushed Amy to the back of his mind. Saturdays were the busiest night of the week, and also the night when trouble was most likely to flare, so he had to stay on his toes at all times.

The night went by quickly and with little incident, but Kelvin's instincts prickled when a group of lads who didn't look old enough to shave, never mind have sex, turned up at two in the morning.

'How much for me mate?' one of them asked as the others sniggered behind him. 'It's his birthday, and he's a virgin, so we wanna get him laid.'

'Sorry, lads,' Kelvin told them through the spyhole. 'You're not old enough.'

'We've got fifty quid,' the lad persisted, holding up the money to show him. 'Come on, mate. We just wanna give him a good time. The rest of us are just gonna watch.'

'Sorry,' Kelvin said again. 'Come back in a couple of years.'

'Yo, cunt!' the lad shouted, hammering his fist on the door when the spyhole slid shut. 'Who d'ya think you're talking to? I ain't one of your homies, you ain't dissin' *me* like that and getting away with it. Come out here if you think you're a big man – I'll fuckin' show you!'

The rest joined in, and Kelvin listened as they started booting the door in unison. Soon the walls were echoing with the sound of missiles being hurled at the door. He wasn't concerned about that, because he knew they would never get through it. But when he heard the sound of glass smashing up above, he ran up the stairs.

A brick lay in the middle of the staffroom floor, and shards of glass were scattered everywhere. The girls were huddled around Betty, who was sitting shocked in her chair in the corner, blood trickling from a cut on her forehead.

Down below, someone screamed, and Kelvin ran to the

broken window and peered out into the darkness. He winced when he saw the gang attacking a man, dragging him down to the floor and kicking him from all sides. Sickened when he saw the one who'd been mouthing off at him leap up into the air and slam his foot down on the poor man's head, he turned back to the girls.

'Get dressed. I'm going to have to call the police.'

As the girls ran to their rooms to retrieve their clothes, Kelvin squatted down in front of Betty. 'You okay, sweetheart?'

'It's just a nick,' she told him, sounding as old as her actual years for once. 'I'll just go and have a lie-down. I'll be right as rain in a minute.'

Kelvin frowned. The cut was a good inch long, and the skin around it had already swelled so much that it was splitting apart even more as he looked. But it was the ashen paleness of her face that he was particularly worried about, and her breathing sounded unhealthily shallow.

'I think we need to get you looked at,' he said decisively. 'Just stay there – I'll call an ambulance.'

As he stood up, he spotted Amy huddled in the corner, and asked, 'Are *you* all right?'

She nodded and hugged herself. She wasn't all right at all. In fact, she was far from it. Already withdrawing when she'd arrived tonight, her body now felt battered, and her head was hurting so much that it felt like it was going to explode. And her skin was raw and crawling with invisible insects.

'Can you keep an eye on Betty?' Kelvin asked. 'I won't be a minute.'

Amy nodded again, dragged herself up off her seat and hobbled over to Betty.

'Sit down,' Betty said quietly, patting the seat beside hers. 'You look worse than me.'

After calling the police and ambulance, Kelvin let the girls out through the secret door that separated *Hawaii* from Mani's cash and carry down below. Watching through the broken window as the police arrived and tackled the gang, he waved for Amy to help Betty up when the ambulance finally arrived.

'You'll have to go to the hospital with her,' he said as they helped the old lady down the stairs. 'I'll have to stay here till Mani shows up.'

Amy flicked him a worried look and shook her head. 'I can't.'

'Don't worry, I'll tell him what's happened,' said Kelvin, guessing that she was concerned about Yates. 'He can't blame you for this, can he?'

Amy wasn't so sure about that. But Betty was clinging to her hand so tightly that she didn't have the heart to make her go to the hospital by herself.

Yates wasn't amused when he turned up to collect Amy at five only to be told that she had gone to the hospital a few hours earlier. It was getting light by then, so he could clearly see the dents in the door, the broken window up above, and the bricks and other debris strewn all around the yard. He even had to sidestep the pool of blood that had congealed at the gate from where the innocent passer-by had been attacked. But none of that made any difference. Amy should have been here waiting, and the fact that he would now have to drive to the other side of town to get her infuriated him.

Amy's nerves were jangling like live wires as she sat in the hospital waiting room. The cut on Betty's forehead had been glued together when they first got here, but just as they had been about to release her, she'd had a heart attack. Scared out of her wits when the crash team had leapt into action, Amy had sat back down to wait for news.

Still sitting there when the door opened and Yates appeared, she almost jumped out of her skin.

'Out,' he hissed, jerking his thumb at her.

The receptionist had told Amy that she would let her know as soon as she had any news about Betty, and Amy flicked her a guilty glance as she slid quietly off her chair and went to Yates.

'I'm sorry,' she mumbled when she reached him. 'B-Betty had a h-heart attack.'

'I don't give a fuck about Betty,' Yates snarled, dragging her out and marching her towards his car. 'You know how much you've just cost me in petrol, making me drive all the way over here? And who said you could go fuckin' walkabout anyhow?'

'I had no choice,' Amy protested, banging her head on the door as he shoved her roughly into the passenger seat.

Yates jumped into the driver's side and slammed his door shut. 'You ever fuck me about like this again, you're dead!' he bellowed, slamming his fist into her face.

Amy screamed in pain when her lip exploded. But Yates was more concerned about the blood that had sprayed out onto the dashboard.

'Now look what you've fuckin' done!' he roared, grabbing her by the back of her head and smashing her face against the instrument panel. 'Wreck my fuckin' car, will you? Wreck my fuckin' *car*?'

'Stop it!' Amy squawked, her body convulsing when he grabbed her wrist and bent it right over. 'You're hurting me!'

'I'll do more than fuckin' hurt you,' Yates hissed, applying even more pressure.

A sharp snapping sound rang out, and Amy's eyes bulged

with shock and pain. Aware that he'd broken her wrist, Yates threw the car into gear and reversed out of the parking space.

'Shut up and keep still,' he ordered as he drove out onto Oxford Road and spotted the patrol car parked up on the opposite side. 'I'm warning you. If you draw attention to us and he pulls me, I'm gonna shoot the pair of you.'

When he slid the gun out of his pocket and rested it on his thigh, Amy forced herself to stop squirming and screaming.

'I'll give you a fix as soon as we get back,' Yates told her, driving on.

'What's happened?' Marnie asked when Yates went round to hers after dropping Amy off and sorting her out. 'Where's all that blood come from?'

'Amy's been in a fight,' he told her, flopping down on her couch. 'I had to split it up and calm her down.'

'Who was she fighting with?' Marnie asked, rushing to get him a drink. 'Another *prostitute*?' She spat out the last word, her face already contorting into a sneer of disdain.

'Yeah.' Yates sighed. 'Ripping chunks out of each other when I got there, they were. Think she might have bust her wrist.'

'Serves her right,' said Marnie, sitting beside him.

'I don't know what I'm gonna do with her,' Yates went on wearily. 'I've tried, I really have, but there's just no reasoning with her.'

'I know how hard you've tried,' said Marnie supportively. 'God knows why, though, when she keeps throwing it back in your face.'

Yates shrugged, and took a sip of his drink. 'She needs me. What am I supposed to do? Turn my back on her, like the rest of them have?'

'Hon, I know your heart's in the right place, but you've done more than your fair share,' Marnie said softly. 'She's brought it all on herself, and you can't keep trying to rescue her.'

'I hear what you're saying, but I can't just abandon her,' Yates replied. 'Suppose I'll just have to try a bit of tough love.'

'How?' Marnie asked. 'You can't tie her up and keep her prisoner.'

'No, but I can try and stop her going out, at least till her wrist's healed,' said Yates. 'She wouldn't go to hospital, she just wanted a fix.'

'And you gave in and let her have one?' Marnie shook her head. 'You're too soft for your own good, Lenny Yates. She'll be the death of you if you don't watch yourself.'

Yates grinned and reached for her hand. 'Good job I've got you to keep me sane, then, eh?' he said, placing it on the bulge in his pants.

Marnie smiled as she unzipped his fly. 'What *would* you do without me?'

Yates put his arms behind his head when she sucked his cock into her mouth, and he watched as her head bobbed up and down. Women were all the same. Wouldn't give you the time of day when you were single, but let them think they were scoring points at the expense of their mates and they couldn't get enough of you. Throw a bit of cash into the equation and the sky was the limit to what they would do for you. Marnie was a pretty enough bird, and her body was half decent, but he'd got her number from the second they met. She was a slapper who liked to think she was in control. But he was the only one in control around here – and if she ever stepped out of line, she would learn that the hard way.

23

Kelvin had guessed from the expression on Yates's face when he'd arrived to pick Amy up that he was pissed off with her for leaving work without his permission, and he'd spent the rest of the night worrying about her.

Betty was still in a bad way when he called in at the hospital on his way home, so he hadn't stayed long. Before he left, he asked if Amy had got home okay, only for Betty to tell him what one of the nurses had told her: that a man had dragged her out of the waiting room and into a car.

Already concerned about that, Kelvin was even more worried when Amy didn't turn up for work the next night. So he pulled Ella aside and asked if she knew Amy's address.

'I've never been there, but I think it's off City Road,' she told him. 'Round the back of The Mancunian, I think she said. Might be Ford Road. Why?'

'No reason,' Kelvin lied. 'Just thought I saw her round by mine this morning, but it must have been someone else.'

After leaving work that morning, he took the bus into Hulme. Yates's car was parked outside a house halfway along Ford Road. Aware that he couldn't go round there while Yates was in because it would make things ten times worse for Amy, Kelvin clocked the house number and went home.

The car was nowhere in sight when he went back a few hours later, so he walked up to the door and knocked.

Yates had left the house at noon. He'd given Amy a fix before he went, and had left a wrap for her to smoke throughout the day to ease the pain. She was spaced out now, but nowhere near as much as she would have been if her wrist hadn't been throbbing so painfully. It had ballooned to twice its normal size, and was purple all the way around and halfway up her arm.

Afraid of jolting it, she hadn't dared to move off the couch all day, and had no intention of getting up to answer the door when someone knocked on it now. But she quickly changed her mind when the letter box flapped open, and a familiar voice called, 'Amy . . . are you there? I was worried about you, so I just wanted to check you're okay.'

Terrified that someone would see him, she leapt up and, grimacing as the agonising pain shot up her arm, hobbled to the door.

'Oh, my God,' Kelvin groaned, taking in the bruised eyes, the split lip, and the clearly broken wrist she was cradling. 'What the hell has he done to you, girl?'

'It's none of your business,' Amy retorted shakily. 'Now, just go away before someone sees you. *Please*.'

'I can't leave you like this,' he protested. 'You need to go to hospital. I'll take you. And if you're worried about Yates, he needn't even know I've been here.'

'Are you crazy?' Amy gasped. 'Of course he'll know. He knows *every*thing.'

Kelvin gazed at her, his dark eyes gleaming with concern and pity. 'Jeezus, he's really done a job on you, hasn't he?'

'Kelvin, just go,' Amy pleaded. 'You're just going to make everything worse. Please, I'm begging you.'

Reluctant to leave her like this, Kelvin reached into his back pocket and pulled out a ten-pound note.

'There's a café on Deansgate called Orange,' he told her, shoving the money into her undamaged hand. 'I'll be waiting there for you. Get a cab.'

'I can't,' she hissed.

'Half an hour,' Kelvin said firmly. 'If you don't come, I'm coming back. And this time I'll be bringing the police.'

'Don't be stupid,' Amy squawked, but he was already walking away.

She closed the door and paced up and down the hall in a state of panic. Kelvin meant well, but all it would take was for one person to have seen him and say something to Yates and they were both as good as dead.

Amy didn't want to meet up with him, but he'd been deadly serious about the police – she'd seen it in his eyes. And if they got involved, everything was going to explode and nobody would be safe. There was only one thing for it. She would have to go and talk to Kelvin, try to persuade him to back off.

Kelvin had already drunk two cups of tea and had begun to think that Amy wasn't going to show when she walked in. Her face was ashen, and she'd wrapped a dirty old bandage around her arm, but he could tell by the way she was holding it that she was in serious pain.

He stood up as she approached his table and pulled out a chair for her. 'Sit down. I'll get you a drink. Tea or coffee?'

'I don't want anything,' she said. 'I'm not staying. I only came to tell you to leave me alone.'

'How can I do that?' Kelvin asked quietly, sitting back down and peering at her across the table. 'Look at you.'

'You've got the wrong end of the stick,' Amy lied. 'Lenny didn't do this. I fell over.'

'That's what you said the other night about the bruise on your cheek, but this is way worse. Can't you see what he's doing?'

'No, all I can see is *you* sticking your nose in where it isn't wanted and causing trouble. Now just back off and stay out of my business.'

'Leave him,' Kelvin blurted out when she started to walk away. 'I've got a spare room – come and stay with me. I'll look after you, get you back on your feet.'

Amy turned and gave him an incredulous look. 'Christ, Kelvin, you must have some whacked-out kind of marriage if you think your wife won't mind you bringing a junkie prostitute home.'

'I'm not married.'

'Yes, you are.' Amy pointed at the ring on his third finger. 'Forget to take it off, did you?'

Kelvin smiled and twisted the gold band. 'It's my dad's. He passed away when I was a kid, and my mum gave it to me when I left school. This is the only finger it fits.'

'Oh,' Amy murmured. 'Sorry.'

'Don't worry about it.' Kelvin waved his hand dismissively. 'Look, seriously, just think about it, yeah? My mum's a retired nurse – she'll know how to help you. And you're welcome to stay as long as you like. No strings.'

Amy saw the sincerity in his eyes and wished with all her heart that she could take him up on his offer. But it was impossible. Yates would never let her go.

'I can't,' she said quietly. 'And please don't come round to the house again. It's not as bad as you think. Lenny's usually all right, he just gets a bit jealous if he thinks I'm being too friendly with other men.'

'But he doesn't mind you sleeping with them?' Kelvin said bluntly. 'As long as he gets the money?'

'I owe him,' said Amy. 'And it's none of your business.'

Kelvin exhaled loudly and flopped back in his seat. He was fighting a losing battle, and he knew it.

'Fine.' He shrugged resignedly. 'Go back, take your chances. Just do me one favour. Take my number, and call me if you ever change your mind.'

'Okay, if it gets you off my back,' Amy agreed. 'Here.' She jutted her hip out. 'My phone's in my pocket. You'll have to get it, 'cos I can't use my hand. But put it in a girl's name.'

'How about Ella?'

'Yeah, whatever. Just hurry up.'

In serious pain by the time she got home, Amy rushed into the living room and grabbed her foil. Her heart was racing, and the rush of adrenalin brought on by the shock of Kelvin turning up had made her feel sick. Crying in frustration when she opened the wrap and some tipped out onto the carpet, she fell to her knees and carefully scooped it onto the foil. Her hands were shaking wildly, but she managed to smoke it. Then, sighing as the terrible jumbled thoughts began to drift out of her mind, she lay down on the couch and closed her eyes.

She was fast asleep when Yates strolled in at eleven that night, but she woke with a start when he prodded her sharply in the shoulder.

'Got something to tell me?' he asked.

'No.' She shook her head.

'That right?' He gave her a nasty smile and cracked his knuckles. 'So, what's been happening while I've been out? Had any visitors? Been anywhere?'

The blood drained from Amy's face. *Oh, God, he knew.*

'A m-man called round about d-double glazing,' she stammered, blurting out the first thing that came into her mind. 'And I went t-to the shop for some painkillers. But that's all.'

'Where are they?' Yates looked around. 'The painkillers . . . where are they?'

'I didn't get any,' Amy whispered. 'I forgot I d-didn't have any money.'

Yates leaned down and gripped her face in his hand. 'You'd better not be lying.'

'I'm not,' she whimpered.

'Swear on your kids' lives.'

'Lenny, please. My arm's h-hurting, I can't think straight.'

'Swear . . . on . . . your . . . kids' . . . *lives,*' he repeated through gritted teeth, his stare boring into her eyes.

Amy's mouth had gone so dry that it felt like her tongue was sticking to the roof of her mouth. But this was life or death, so, saying a silent prayer to God to forgive her, she forced out the words.

'I s-swear on the kids' lives.'

'Wasn't so difficult, was it?' Yates sneered, letting go of her and wiping her tears off his hand. Then, smiling slyly, he reached into his pocket and pulled out a small wrap. He dangled it in front of her nose, but snatched it away as soon as she reached for it.

'Ah, ah, ah . . . not so fast. You've already missed a night's work, so that's more interest added to your debt. If you want this, you'll have to earn it.'

'What do you want me to do?' Amy asked, willing to do just about anything right now.

'I'm thinking about branching out,' said Yates. 'Them broke-arse punters at twenty quid a pop ain't making a dent, so it's time we got some proper dosh coming in. I'm thinking of making a film.'

'A film?' Amy repeated, the blood running cold in her veins.

'Yes, a *film*,' said Yates as if he was talking to a child. 'One of them things men like your spineless ex wank over. I can put it on the net, and invest in some DVDs to flog around the pubs.' He laughed as a thought occurred to him. 'Here, how funny would it be if your old dad got hold of a copy? Be a bit of a shocker, that. Settling down for a nice little tug, and up pops baby girl in all her glory.'

'No,' Amy wheezed, shaking her head. 'Please don't, Lenny, I'm begging you. I'll do anything, but not that.'

Yates stared down at her with a sneer of disgust on his lips. 'I'm way past the stage of giving a fuck what *you* want, sweetheart. That debt of yours is racking up by the minute, and every second you spend on your arse is adding to it. I'm a generous man, but I've got my limits – and you've reached yours. Now, here . . .' He tossed the wrap to her. 'Sort yourself out and start thinking about how you're gonna make yourself presentable for the camera.'

Amy hugged herself when Yates walked out, but was surprised to hear him climb into his car and drive away instead of going round to Marnie's. She checked that he'd really gone and then reached for her foil. She tipped some of the powder out of the wrap onto it, but instead of lighting up she sat and stared at it through her tears.

She didn't want this any more. The smack numbed the

pain, but it wasn't taking away the cause of that pain. That was always there, gnawing away at the edge of her consciousness, and it was only going to get worse. And if it wasn't bad enough that Yates had forced her to sleep with strangers, he was now going to expose her to hundreds, maybe even thousands of men. That was an unbearable thought, and she knew that she couldn't allow it to happen.

Hand shaking, vision completely blurred, she screwed the foil into a ball and reached for her phone.

Yates hadn't gone far, and he was already on his way back as Amy made her call. Marnie had rung him earlier and told him about Amy's afternoon caller and her subsequent trip out. But if that had pissed him off, her next bit of news had cheered him right back up again.

She was pregnant.

He was going to be a daddy.

It was a day he'd thought would never come, and he couldn't have been happier, because the thought of a little Lenny running around town, a little mini-me that he could mould in his own image, thrilled him. Mates were all well and good, but blood was the thing upon which truly great empires were built. And the blood bond between a father and his son was the strongest, most invincible bond of all.

Marnie was in town right now at a girls-only karaoke party in a backstreet bar. She'd said she would be back by two and, intending to surprise her with a special little celebratory party, Yates had just nipped over to the Moss to pick up his supplies: three grams of coke, a few bottles of fizzy stuff, and a bunch of flowers.

As he turned the corner now, he spotted the light going on in Amy's bedroom and narrowed his eyes. He'd just given her a gram of smack, so she ought to be completely gouched out, not moving about upstairs. And she was moving pretty damn fast, he noticed as he watched her silhouette shifting from one side of the room to the other as he neared the house.

Suspicious, he carried on driving and parked up in a dark spot on the neighbouring estate. Then, pulling his hood up, he climbed into the field at the back of Amy's house. It was months since he'd had to sneak in the back way, but the bitch looked like she was up to something and he wanted to catch her unawares.

Unable to reach Kelvin on the phone, Amy had run upstairs to pack some things. She hadn't really thought it through, she just wanted to get out of there before Yates came back. But as she stepped out onto the landing, he appeared at the foot of the stairs.

'Going somewhere?' he asked, walking slowly up.

'No!' She took a step back. 'I'm – I'm just putting some rubbish out.'

Yates snatched the bag when he reached her and tipped out the contents. Her toothbrush, a bra, and a couple of pairs of knickers fell out, along with a rolled-up pair of jeans, a crumpled sweatshirt, and her empty purse.

'Rubbish, eh?' Yates kicked the stuff aside and advanced towards her again.

'I can't do a film,' Amy squealed, holding her undamaged hand out in front of her as she backed into the bedroom. 'I'm sorry, Lenny, I just can't. It would kill my mum.'

'Your mum doesn't give a flying *fuck* about you,' Yates snarled, lashing her across her face and knocking her onto the bed. '*No* one does – haven't you got that yet?'

He jumped on top of her now and put his hands around

her throat. She bucked beneath him and tried to fight him off, but then she suddenly went limp and her eyes rolled back in their sockets. Yates let go of her throat and shook her. When she didn't respond, he leapt off the bed and stared down at her. Shit! He hadn't meant to *kill* her. What the fuck was he supposed to do now?

Fire!

As soon as the word entered his mind, he fled back down the stairs. Nobody had seen him come back into the house, so all he had to do was set it on fire and get out of there, and they would never be able to pin any of it on him.

24

Gemma was in her usual spot on the chair by the window, from where she could watch TV while keeping an eye on the goings-on outside. Knitting needles flying, her latest cardigan half-grown in her lap, she froze when she noticed a thin swirl of smoke rise into the air across the road. Curious, she pulled her net curtain aside and squinted to get a better look. Shocked to see a faint orange glow at Amy's bedroom window, and wispy smoke filtering out through the top of the frame, she jumped up and reached for the phone.

'Fire!' she spluttered. 'The house across the road is on fire . . . And I think the girl's in there. Hurry!'

Marnie had been having a good time at the karaoke, but when her head started to spin she realised she'd had one too many and, conscious of the new life nestled in her womb, told her girlfriends that she was going home.

She sobered up fast when the cab turned onto her road and she saw blue flashing lights. She rolled the back window down and leaned out to see what was going on. Shocked to see a fire engine, two ambulances and several police vehicles blocking the road ahead, she realised where they were and, fearing the worst, gasped, 'Oh, my God! That's my house!'

Gemma was standing with a group of neighbours. When she saw Marnie climb out of the cab and come running down the road, she waddled over to her as fast as her fat legs would allow.

'It's Amy,' she blurted out. 'The house was on fire and she was in there. I called the emergency as soon as I saw it. They've just brought her out.'

'Oh, God, she's not . . .' Unable to say the word, Marnie threw a hand over her mouth.

'Don't know,' Gemma admitted grimly. 'No one's telling us nothing. But they didn't look too happy when they carried her to the ambulance.'

'Where's Lenny?' Marnie worriedly searched the faces of the onlookers.

'He's not here,' Gemma assured her, patting her hand. 'Bleedin' lucky, though, 'cos he called round about half an hour ago. But I saw him go off again, so he's definitely safe. Why don't you give him a ring if you're worried?'

'Yeah, I will,' Marnie murmured, her voice thick with relief.

She pulled her mobile out of her pocket and moved away so that Gemma wouldn't hear her. Her friend obviously knew that something was going on, but Marnie hadn't actually admitted to it, and Gemma hadn't outright asked. It would be common knowledge soon enough now that the pregnancy test had confirmed her suspicions but, under the circumstances, it hardly seemed appropriate to announce it right now.

'Lenny, it's me,' she said quietly when he answered. 'Where are you?'

'At my mate's,' he told her. 'You still in town?'

'No, I'm home, but there's a problem,' said Marnie, her gaze following the ambulance as it drove past her.

'Was that a siren?' Yates asked. 'What's going on?'

'There's been a fire,' Marnie told him. 'It's Amy. I think you'd best get over here.'

Yates arrived ten minutes later. The road was still blocked, so he left his car at the corner and ran down to the police tape that was stretched from pavement to pavement.

'What's going on?' he yelled to a policewoman who was standing on the other side. 'That's my girlfriend's house . . . where is she? Amy . . . *AMY!*'

'Calm down, sir.' The policewoman came over. 'We got her out. She's on her way to hospital.'

Face contorted with worry, Yates reached across the tape and grabbed her arm. 'Is she . . . is she okay?'

'We haven't heard anything yet, but we'll let you know as soon as we do.'

'She was fine when I left her. Everything was fine. How could this happen?'

'We'll know soon enough,' the policewoman assured him. 'When did you last see Mrs Taylor?'

'I don't know.' Yates shrugged. 'About an hour ago. Why?'

'Could you just come through here for a moment while I take your details?' She lifted the tape and waved him towards one of the police cars.

'My name's Yates,' he told her when he was sitting in the back of the car. 'Leonard Yates. I live at thirty-seven Langley Court, but I stay here most of the time.' He gazed out of the window now and peered at the house as if he was in agony. 'I can't believe this. I should have been here. I should be with her now. Where've they took her?'

'Don't worry,' said the policewoman, jotting his details down. 'You'll be able to see her as soon as we've finished here. Can you just tell me where you've been since you left the house?'

'Why?' Yates screwed up his face. 'What's that got to do with anything?'

'Just routine.'

Before Yates could answer, a voice came over the radio and the policewoman excused herself and stepped out of the car. Keeping an eye on her, Yates slid his mobile out of his pocket and rang Keith.

'It's me. Don't ask questions 'cos I ain't got time to explain. If anyone asks I've been at yours for the last hour watching a DVD. I don't know. What've you got? Yeah, that's fine. Laters.'

He disconnected just as the policewoman came back to the car, accompanied by a male officer. 'Was that about Amy?' He gave her a questioning, dread-filled look when she opened the back door. 'She's not . . .'

'Could you step out of the car, please, sir? We'll need you to come down to the station to answer some questions.'

'Are you having a laugh?' Yates stepped out and jerked his arm away when the male officer tried to grip it. 'I'm not going nowhere except to the hospital to see my girlfriend.'

'It shouldn't take long, if you cooperate,' the policewoman assured him.

'I'm going nowhere,' Yates repeated, still resisting as the officer now tried to cuff him. 'I ain't done nothing wrong. I've been at my mate's watching *Terminator* for the last hour. Ring him if you don't believe me.'

'Here, what's going on?' Gemma yelled when she noticed the commotion. 'He was nowhere near when the fire started. I saw him going out with me own eyes, and he ain't been back 'cos I'd have seen him. I've been out here the whole time, and I'll swear to that on any Bible!'

Amy came round and winced when the bright lights scorched her eyes. 'Where am I?' she croaked. 'What's going on?'

'You're in hospital,' a nurse told her. 'And your wrist is broken, my love, so I'm going to need you to lie as still as you can until we can get it set. Do you think you can do that for me?'

Amy nodded and squeezed her eyes shut as a hacking cough rose up from her chest to her throat.

A young PC came into the room. After a quiet word with the nurse, he sat down on the chair beside the bed.

'Hello, Amy, I'm PC Gibson. I just need to ask you a few questions, if that's okay?'

'About what?' Amy eyed him nervously.

'About the fire, to start with.' He flipped his notepad open.

'*Fire?*' Amy frowned.

'I know it's probably a bit hazy, but it's important that we try to build a picture of what happened,' said Gibson. 'Do you remember how it started?'

'No idea,' Amy answered truthfully.

'Your boyfriend . . .' Gibson looked at his notes. 'Leonard Yates, is it?'

Amy tensed at the mention of Yates's name. Gibson noticed and sat forward on his seat. 'Did he do this to you?'

'I don't know what you mean,' Amy mumbled.

'It's obvious that you've been assaulted,' Gibson said quietly, guessing that, like most abused women, she was probably too scared to talk. 'We've taken Yates in for questioning, so he can't get to you if that's what you're worried about. If he *did* do this, it'll be easier for us to hold him if you tell us what happened.'

A sob escaped Amy's raw throat, and she threw her undamaged arm over her eyes and rocked her head from side to side on the pillow.

'I'm sorry, you'll have to leave it for now,' the nurse intervened. 'We need to treat her injuries and give her some pain relief. She's an addict,' she added quietly, gesturing with a motion of her eyes at the track marks scarring both Amy's arms. 'If she starts withdrawing it'll be difficult for us to work on her – and even more difficult for you to get any sense out of her. I'll call you back in when she's fit to talk.'

Half an hour later, her wrist set, Amy felt much more comfortable. She'd been given a shot of morphine for the pain but, thankfully, it hadn't been enough to knock her out, so when the nurse went off to find the policeman Amy was able to reach into the bedside cupboard and pull out her jeans. When she found her mobile phone still in the back pocket, she said a silent thank-you to God. Then, aware that she had very little time, she pressed redial – and sobbed with relief when, this time, Kelvin answered.

25

Yates scowled at the desk sergeant who opened the holding cell door the following morning. 'Letting me go, are you? Realised you've got nothing on me?'

'Come and get your stuff,' the sergeant said coolly.

Yates followed him out to the reception desk with a cocky swagger in his step, complaining all the way: 'My girl's been in hospital all night on her own thanks to you lot, so I hope youse are fuckin' pleased with yourselves. And I'm gonna sue youse for locking me up, an' all. I'm an innocent man, and this is an infringement of my civil liberties, this.'

Unfazed, the sergeant pushed the clear plastic bag containing Yates's belt, wallet, watch, loose change, cigarettes and lighter across the counter. 'Check it and make sure it's all there, then sign this.' He slapped down a form.

Yates tore the bag open and rifled through it. 'Where's me coke?'

'Very funny,' the sergeant drawled, disappointed that no drugs had been found on Yates, because he'd have taken great pleasure in charging the scrote had there been the slightest trace.

'You're a joke, mate,' sneered Yates. 'A total fuckin' joke, the lot of you.'

'If you say so.' The sergeant smiled and nodded towards the door. 'Off you go, there's a good boy. But make sure you behave yourself, because we'll be watching you.'

'For what?' Yates glowered at him. 'You ain't got nothing on me, or you wouldn't be letting me go.'

The sergeant leaned forward and clasped his hands together on the counter. 'We all know you did it, and it's only a matter of time before we prove it, so I'd watch my back if I was you.'

'You're the one who needs to watch your back,' Yates retorted with a smirk. ''Cos if I see any of your lot following me, I'll be doing you for harassment.'

The sergeant held his gaze for several long moments, then smiled again and turned his back.

Yates sucked his teeth and strolled out, shouldering past a PC who was on his way in.

Marnie was sitting on a bench outside. She was smoking a cigarette, but she dropped it when she saw him and ran up the path.

'Are you okay? Did they treat you all right? What did they say?'

'Not now, I'm tired,' Yates muttered, eyeballing the occupants of a panda car that was driving slowly past. 'What you doing here?'

'I wanted to see you,' said Marnie, linking her arm through his. 'I couldn't sleep, I was too worried.'

'You ain't been sat out here all night, have you?'

'No, your friend Keith came round to pick your car up, and he gave me a lift. He's waiting round the corner. Have you heard anything from the hospital?'

'No, but I'm gonna go up there now. I'll drop you at home and give you a call when I know what's going on.'

'I'll come with you, if you want?' Marnie offered.

Yates shook his head. 'I need to see her on my own. Find out what she's been saying about me.'

'What *could* she have said? You weren't even there.'

'They think I did it,' muttered Yates, nodding hello to Keith as they neared the car. 'She was smacked out of her head when I went round there last night, and I walked out on her. You know what she's like. She could have said anything to get back at me.'

'Yeah, well, she'll have me to deal with if she tells any lies about you,' Marnie said indignantly. 'Gemma saw you going out well before the fire started, so we all know you weren't there. And if she says different, I'll knock her out.'

'You'll go home and keep your mouth shut,' said Yates, grinning as he stroked her stomach. 'You've got Junior to think about now, so there'll be no scrapping or arguing. You just leave all that to me.'

Marnie smiled and climbed into the back of the car. It wouldn't be long now before everyone knew their news, and she couldn't wait. Lenny had tried his best, but even *he* would have to admit now that Amy was beyond help. If the drugs and the prostitution hadn't been enough to make him see sense, surely Amy setting the house on fire would. She hadn't been right in the head since Mark walked out on her, but instead of getting better she'd been getting progressively worse, and now she was an actual danger to herself. And God only knew what would have happened if the fire had spread to Marnie's house.

That didn't bear thinking about, and Marnie was determined to make sure that the bitch was never allowed to move back in after the council fixed the house up. She had her baby to think about now, and she would kill Amy before she would let her put it in danger.

After dropping Marnie off, Yates drove straight over to the MRI. Furious to hear that Amy had discharged herself just ten minutes before he got there, he jumped back into the car and set off for Stretford, sure that she must have gone to her parents' place.

'Go easy,' Keith cautioned when they stopped a few doors down from the house. 'If she's told them anything, they'll be straight on the blower to the pigs when they see you.'

'They've got nothing on me,' Yates reminded him. 'Anyway, it'd look a bit odd if I didn't call round to check on her, wouldn't it?'

'I suppose so,' Keith conceded. 'Just don't go kicking off if it doesn't go your way.'

'I'm cool,' said Yates, smiling as he got out of the car.

He had no intention of kicking off and giving the fuckers ammunition to throw at him. He just needed to see the bitch, find out what she'd been saying – and make sure she didn't say anything else.

Sonia Clark was weeding in the back garden when she heard the doorbell. She peeled her gloves off and walked down the path to the side gate. 'Can I help you?' She peered out at Yates through the bars.

'Oh, hello, love, sorry to disturb you.' Yates stepped around the wheelie bin and smiled at her. 'I'm a friend of your Amy's. The hospital said she'd been discharged, so I figured she'd probably come here, what with the house still being taped off, and that.'

'Sorry?' Sonia frowned. 'What are you talking about?'

Yates immediately knew that she hadn't heard from Amy, and held up his hands. 'My apologies. I presumed you knew.'

'About what?' Sonia demanded. 'Has something happened to Amy?'

'There was a fire,' Yates told her. 'But it's okay, she wasn't hurt. They just kept her in overnight to keep an eye on her.

I was in London and I couldn't get back till this morning, but she'd already left by the time I got there.'

A little less alarmed now that she knew Amy wasn't hurt, Sonia said, 'Who did you say you are?'

'Just a friend.'

'And you say there was a fire? At Amy's house?'

'Yeah. The police reckon it started in her bedroom. They think she might have fell asleep with a lit fag, or something.'

A spark of disapproval glinted in Sonia's eyes, and she muttered, 'More like she fell asleep smoking drugs.'

'Wouldn't know anything about that, love.' Yates gazed innocently back at her. 'Anyhow, sorry for worrying you, but I've got an idea where she might have gone, so I'll get off. Shall I give her your love when I see her?'

'Thank you for telling me,' said Sonia, sidestepping his question.

Yates smirked when she went back to her gardening. No wonder Amy was so fucked up with a mother as cold as that. But attention-starved girls were a godsend for a man like Yates, because he could do whatever he liked to them safe in the knowledge that nobody cared enough to stop him.

'What did she say?' Keith asked when Yates climbed back into the car. 'Is she there?'

'No, they haven't seen her.'

'So what now?'

'Got three gees of white in the boot, so we're going back to yours for a few lines,' said Yates, throwing the car into gear. 'Then, when me head's clear, I'm going to track her down.'

'Don't you think it's time to knock this on the head?' Keith suggested as they set off. 'You nearly killed her last night – ain't that enough?'

'Is it fuck.'

'So what you gonna do when you find her? Finish the job? 'Cos you know the pigs are gonna come after you if anything happens to her now, don't you? They already think you battered her and started the fire.'

'Thinking it and proving it are two different things.'

'And what about that other bird's baby?'

'What about it?'

'How you gonna be a dad to it if you're banged up?'

'I ain't gonna get banged up,' snapped Yates. 'Now shut the fuck up – you're starting to do my head in.'

Keith shook his head in despair and gazed out of the window. There was no point trying to reason with Yates, because he never took any notice. He'd treated girls badly in the past and got away with it, but even Keith didn't know the full extent of what he'd done to them – or where they went to when they suddenly disappeared.

Yates was his best mate, and Keith would always have his back, but he had a bad feeling about this one. When it had first started, Keith had thought it was just about the money, but he'd soon realised that Yates was more interested in the girl herself. Unfortunately, *she* hadn't been interested in *him*, so it hadn't been long before Yates had turned nasty and started pimping her out. And now he'd escalated to actually trying to kill her. But instead of thanking his lucky stars that he hadn't succeeded and leaving well enough alone, Yates was determined to find her and push his luck even further by doing God only knew what.

Keith just hoped that the girl had had the sense to go somewhere far, far away – for Yates's sake as well as her own.

26

Kelvin had been horrified when Amy told him what had happened, but he hadn't been overly surprised to hear that Yates had upped his violence to a murderous degree. He didn't know the man on a personal level, but he knew the type all too well, and they were never satisfied until they had crushed everyone around them into submission. And those they couldn't crush they tried to destroy instead.

Unable to leave work at the time he received the call, and aware that there was nothing he could actually do then anyway, Kelvin had struggled through the rest of his shift with a set smile on his lips, determined not to give anything away to Mani and to the other girls. One tiny seed of suspicion would be all that Yates needed to put two and two together, and if Kelvin was to stand any chance of helping Amy to escape he would have to carry on as normal and fool everybody into thinking that he knew nothing.

Already nervous when he picked Amy up from the hospital this morning, he kept an eye out for Yates as he helped her into the back of a black cab.

Amy was silent on the ten-minute ride, but when they pulled up outside a semi-detached house in a nice part of Fallowfield she gave Kelvin a curious look. 'I thought you said you lived in a flat?'

'I do.' Kelvin paid the driver and reached for her hand to

help her out. 'This is my mom's place. I thought it would be better if I brought you round here for something to eat before we decide what to do next.'

The front door opened, and an elderly woman appeared on the step. Kelvin smiled and ushered Amy up the path. 'Mom, this is my friend Amy. She's just come out of hospital. Got anything nice in the pot to help her get better?'

Claudine Brown's grey eyebrows puckered together as she gave the girl the once-over. Her son had dated a few nice girls in the past, and one or two that Claudine had seriously disapproved of. But this one looked the worst of the lot. Still, she could hardly shut the door in her own son's face, so she stepped back and waved them in.

'Tek off your shoes,' she ordered Amy when she'd shown her into the lounge. 'Do you want some soup? I'll get you some soup.'

'No, I'm fine,' said Amy, her stomach turning at the thought of eating. 'Please don't put yourself out.'

'She'll have some.' Kelvin overruled her. 'I'll come and help you.'

'*Shoes,*' Claudine barked over her shoulder as her son hustled her out of the room.

Amy slipped her shoes off, perched on the couch and gazed around, awed by the spotlessness of the room and the enormous array of gleaming ornaments. Everywhere she looked there was a china figurine, a vase filled with artificial flowers, or a framed photograph. It was a massive contrast to the squalor of her own home, and it made her feel even dirtier than she already knew she was.

In the kitchen, Kelvin had briefly explained the situation to his mother, and she wasn't impressed.

'It's not your problem,' she said, frowning as she ladled

soup out of the enormous pot on the cooker top into a bowl. 'Why you gettin' involved?'

'She's a nice girl,' Kelvin told her. 'I want to help her.'

Claudine gave him a piercing look. 'You an' she up to no good, boy?'

'No, course not. It's not like that.'

'So where you meet her?'

'At work.'

'She work?' Claudine's eyebrows shot up in disbelief.

'Well, she *did*, but I doubt she'll be going back after this,' said Kelvin. 'Look, don't worry about it, Mom. It's not going to affect me in the slightest, I promise. I just want to make sure she's safe while she gets better.'

'And how long that gon' take?' Claudine wiped her hands on her apron and placed the bowl on a tray.

'I don't know.' Kelvin shrugged. 'She's got a broken wrist, and . . .' He managed to catch himself before he let slip about the drugs. His mother was already concerned, but the mention of heroin would send her fleeing to the pastor for spiritual intervention. 'She needs to rest,' he said instead.

'If you ask me you is headin' for trouble,' Claudine intoned grimly, reading between the lines. 'You may t'ink she a good girl, but just remember the devil can smile like a h'angel when he huntin' soul.'

Amused, Kelvin leaned down and kissed her on the cheek. 'Don't worry, my soul is safe.'

'Me hope so, son,' Claudine said quietly, picking up the tray.

Amy sat bolt upright when the door opened and Kelvin's mother came in. 'Thank you,' she murmured when the tray was laid on her lap. 'It smells lovely.'

'Eat it while it hot,' ordered Claudine, going over to the chair beside the fire.

Amy dipped the spoon into the soup and prayed that she wouldn't throw up when it touched her tongue.

'How would you feel about staying here for a while?' Kelvin asked, perching on the end of the couch and watching as Amy toyed with the soup. 'I don't think you should be on your own just now, and my mom and my sister would be able to look after you while I'm at work.'

Amy's head shot up. So that was why he had brought her here instead of to his flat? He was trying to palm her off.

'No.' She shook her head. 'I'll go to my mum and dad's.'

'I thought they weren't talking to you?'

'They'll be okay when they see me. Anyway, I'm not your mum's problem. It's too much to expect her to look after me.'

'She doesn't mind,' Kelvin insisted. 'Do you, Mom?'

Claudine jerked her chin up in a gesture that could have meant anything. Sensing that it was negative, Amy shook her head again.

'No, really, it wouldn't feel right. And you've done enough for me already.'

'All I've done is pick you up from the hospital and bring you to my mom's for something to eat,' Kelvin said softly. 'That's nothing.'

'That's *more* than enough,' said Amy, meaning it sincerely. He barely knew her, and yet he'd already shown her more concern and compassion than anybody else had done in a long time.

The doorbell rang, and Claudine arched her neck to peer out through the window. 'Sister Hampson.' She hauled herself to her feet. 'Stay here while me see what she want.'

As soon as she had left the room, Amy whispered, 'Please don't think I'm being rude, Kelvin. Your mum's lovely, but she doesn't want me here, and I don't blame her. Look at this place and then look at me. She must think I'm a total tramp.'

'She's a good Christian woman,' Kelvin whispered back. 'She'd never turn anyone away if they needed help.'

'I don't *want* to stay,' Amy insisted, tears flooding her eyes. 'I'm not fit to be around good people. If you don't want me at your place, I'll just—'

'Hey, settle down,' Kelvin interrupted softly. 'I only suggested it because I thought it'd be better if someone was looking after you. Course you can stay with me. But it's probably best if we don't tell my mom, so I'll say I'm taking you to your parents – okay?'

'Thank you.' Amy sighed. 'And, don't worry, I won't stay too long. I'll ring the council first thing, see if they can put me in a hostel.'

'You can stay as long as you like,' Kelvin assured her, reaching for the spoon. It was obvious that she didn't want to eat the soup, and his mother would be more offended to come back and find the bowl full than by the thought of Amy's dirty feet and greasy hair touching her nice clean carpet and sofa.

The door opened while he was eating, and a girl strode in wearing a dressing gown, her hair wrapped in a towel. She stopped in her tracks when she saw him, and drew her head back.

'What are you doing here so early?'

'Just picked my friend up from the hospital.' Kelvin nodded towards Amy. 'Her house was set on fire last night. Amy, this is my sister Eve.'

'*Evangeline*,' the girl corrected him tartly, looking Amy up and down as she spoke. 'What you playing at, bringing ragamuffins into Mommy's house?'

'Hey, Amy's my friend!' Kelvin scolded. 'Have some respect.'

'Say 'gain?' His sister jutted her jaw out and gaped at him in disbelief.

Claudine came back just then from speaking with her church friend and, clocking the expression of annoyance on her son's face, and her daughter's cocky stance, she guessed what was going on and cuffed the girl on the shoulder as she passed her.

'Don't even t'ink about startin' none a your foolishness,' she warned. 'Your brother welcome to bring him friend home, and if you don't like it, go to your room.'

The girl kissed her teeth and tossed Amy a look of undisguised disgust before marching out.

'I'm calling a cab,' Kelvin told his mother when she'd gone. 'I'm going to take Amy to her mum and dad's.'

'It's for the best,' Claudine said approvingly. Then, smiling down at Amy, she nodded at the almost empty bowl. 'You c'yan eat no more?'

'No, that was really filling,' Amy lied. 'And absolutely delicious. Thank you.'

The taxi arrived five minutes later. Claudine gave her son a hug goodbye before turning to Amy. 'You tek care, y' hear? An' stay 'way from dem bad mens in future.'

'Oh, don't worry, I will,' Amy agreed, desperate to get out of there. Kelvin's mother had been very nice, but if looks could kill Amy would have been stone dead within a minute of stepping foot in the house. And the sister would happily have helped her on her way with a knife between the eyes.

Kelvin's flat was on the third floor of a tower block in a rundown part of Rusholme. It was the first place the council had offered him, and his family and friends had said he needed his head testing when he told them he was taking it, but it was exactly what he'd been praying for. If his mother had had her way, she'd have kept him tied to her apron strings for life. But a twenty-five-year-old man needed his own space, and Kelvin still got a kick out of being able to go home and close the door on the world. Nobody ever bothered him there, and it was only a ten-minute bus ride to work and a fifteen-minute one to his mother's house, so it was perfect.

He led Amy in and waved her into the tiny living room, saying, 'I'll show you to your room in a bit. Just let me find some sheets. It's only a fold-down bed, by the way. I hope that's okay?'

'I'd sleep right here if I had to,' Amy assured him, flopping down on his couch and relaxing for the first time all day.

Her wrist had started to throb again, so she reached into her pocket for the painkillers that the hospital pharmacist had given her before she discharged herself. The doctor had wanted her to stay another night to make sure there was no internal damage from the smoke she'd inhaled, but Kelvin had arrived by then and she'd been desperate to get out before Yates turned up. If he had got his hands on her, smoke damage would have been the least of her worries.

Kelvin brought her a glass of water to wash her tablets down, and said, 'I'll make you a cup of tea when the kettle's boiled. And I'll run you a bath, if you want to get cleaned up. You should be all right if you put a plastic bag over the plaster.'

'You don't have to wait on me,' Amy said guiltily, aware that he'd come straight to the hospital from work. 'Go to bed. I can look after myself.'

'Just want to make sure you've got everything you need first,' said Kelvin, putting his cigarettes and lighter down on the table beside her. 'Help yourself if you want a smoke. And I know you're not really hungry, but do you think you could manage a piece of toast? The nurse reckoned those tablets are really strong, so I think you should have something in your stomach.'

'Considering all the smack I've taken over the last few months, I doubt the pills are going to do me any harm,' Amy murmured.

Kelvin gave her a worried look. 'Do you think you'll be able to cope without it?'

'I don't know,' Amy admitted. 'But I've got to try, or Mark will never let me see the kids.'

As soon as the words left her mouth, Amy's face crumpled. Kelvin sat down and pulled her into his arms.

'Hey, don't cry. He's bound to let you see them once he knows you're making an effort.'

'What if he doesn't?' Amy sobbed. 'I miss them so much.'

'Trust me, he will,' Kelvin whispered. 'Now stop worrying. I'm here, and I'm going to look after you.'

Amy closed her eyes and laid her head against his broad chest. Mark had always told her that he would look after her, but while she had always known that he meant it she'd never fully believed that he was actually capable of doing it. But Kelvin wasn't like Mark. He wasn't weak, and he didn't speak just for the pleasure of hearing his own voice. He was strong, and genuine, and he treated his mother with respect – the mark of a real man, in Amy's eyes. It was going to be tough, but with Kelvin's support she truly believed she could beat the addiction.

What she would do after that, she had no idea. But, for now, she just had to take it one step at a time.

★   ★   ★

The withdrawal kicked in with a vengeance a short time after Kelvin went to bed, and Amy felt like she was going insane as she paced the room from window to wall and back again. The craving was all-consuming, and only one thing would take it away: a fix. Just one little fix. One tiny little fix to take the edge off, and then she'd be able to start kicking it.

She stared at the people walking by on the street down below and contemplated going out to ask if any of them knew where she could score. She was completely broke, but Kelvin's jacket was draped over the back of the couch and, as the agonising cravings grew, so too did the temptation. Unable to resist, she slid her hand into his pocket.

There was nothing in there, and she was flooded with shame when it occurred to her that Kelvin might have emptied it before he went to bed because he had known that she would search it. He had been so kind, and yet, first chance she'd got, she had been about to steal from him.

Disgusted with herself, she went to bed and prayed for sleep to release her. But it didn't come, and as the minutes ticked slowly by, the pain grew and grew.

Kelvin got up at five and tried to persuade Amy to eat something, but she couldn't stomach anything. He looked in on her again before going to work, and wished that he could magic the pain away when he saw her shaking from head to toe. But they had talked about this earlier, and Amy had insisted that no matter how bad it got or how much she pleaded, he wasn't to cave in and get her anything.

'I've got to go,' he told her, squatting beside the bed. 'Are you going to be all right?'

Amy gritted her teeth and nodded.

'I know you're not really supposed to drink with those

painkillers,' Kelvin went on softly, 'but if it gets too bad there's a bottle of JD on the sideboard. And if you need me, ring me and I'll come straight back. Okay?'

'Just go,' said Amy, wishing that he would stop fussing. He was lovely, but her nerves were already screaming, and the sound of his voice was making her feel physically sick.

Kelvin sighed and stood up. He gazed down at her for a moment, then looped his bag over his shoulder and left.

When Amy heard the front door click shut behind him she released the sob she'd been holding in. It was already unbearable and she didn't know how she was going to manage another minute, never mind hour, or day. But she had to try – if not for herself, then for the kids.

As she tossed and turned the next few hours away, Amy struggled to keep an image of the kids at the forefront of her mind. But all she could think about was smack. She wanted it, needed it, and every fibre of her being was craving it.

The bed was already sweat-soaked, but when she threw up on the duvet cover she dragged herself into the living room. Unable to sit still, and too weak to pace, she stepped out onto the tiny balcony. Tears streamed from her eyes when the wind whipped into her raw flesh like a million knife slashes, and she put her foot on the bar at the bottom of the iron railing and stared down at the road below, wondering how long it would take to land if she fell.

Terrified of merely breaking something and causing herself even more pain, she quickly stepped down and rushed back inside. The blister pack of tablets was still sitting on the table. She grabbed the bottle of JD and twisted the cap off, then popped all the tablets out of the pack and shoved them into her mouth.

The kids already didn't want to see her, and they would soon forget all about her if she was gone. And it would certainly be a weight off Mark's mind, because he'd be free to get on with his life without worrying about her popping up to ruin things. And her mum and dad would be relieved, too. They had already washed their hands of her, and she couldn't blame them because she had shamed them in the most unforgivable way. She just hoped that they would find it in their hearts to bury her so that she wouldn't have to spend eternity in an unmarked grave. But she would understand if they didn't want to waste any more time or money on her.

Tears rolling down her cheeks, she drank from the bottle until it was empty, then lay down on the couch and waited for death.

Kelvin eased the bedroom door open when he got home from work the next morning. Knocked back by the stench of vomit and sweat, he saw that Amy's bed was empty and went to the living room. Amy was lying on the couch with his coat pulled up over her shoulders. Her face was grey, and she didn't seem to be breathing.

'Oh, no,' he moaned, dropping his bag and running to her. 'Please, no . . .'

He touched her face, but snatched his hand back when he felt the icy coldness of her skin and pulled his mobile phone out of his pocket. About to call for an ambulance, he hesitated when Amy made a noise.

'Amy?' He dropped to his knees beside her and shook her gently. 'Amy . . . wake up.'

'What's wrong?' she whispered, peeling her eyes open.

'Oh, thank God!' he croaked. 'I thought you were dead. Don't ever do that to me again.'

'Sorry. I must have fallen asleep.'

'How are you feeling?'

'Not too good, everything's aching.'

Kelvin looked around for her tablets, and a cold chill ran through him when he saw the empty packet lying on the floor next to the empty bottle. 'Oh, Jeezus, Amy, please don't tell me you tried to kill yourself?'

'No.' Amy blushed and shook her head. 'I just wanted to forget about it all.'

'Swear?'

'I swear.'

Kelvin was shaken, but he wanted to believe her – *had* to, because the alternative would make it impossible to leave her on her own again.

'Right, I'm going to ring my doctor when the surgery opens,' he said decisively. 'This obviously isn't going to be as easy as we thought, so I'll get him to do a home visit – see if there's anything he can give you to help you through it.'

'No!' A look of terror leapt into Amy's eyes. 'I can't see anyone. What if Lenny—'

'Don't worry about him,' Kelvin interrupted. 'I've already seen him, and he doesn't suspect a thing.'

'How do you know?'

'He turned up at work just before we opened last night and asked if anyone had seen you. I played dumb, and the girls obviously couldn't tell him anything, so it's all good.'

'You sure he believed you?'

'I doubt I'd still be here if he hadn't,' said Kelvin, smiling as he stood up. 'Think you can manage a cup of tea?'

'I'll try,' said Amy, pushing the coat off her legs. 'Have you got a washing machine? I made a bit of a mess of your sheets, but I'll wash them in the bath if you haven't got one.'

'Don't worry about it,' Kelvin said, pushing her gently back down when she tried to get up. 'You just stay there and rest. I'll fetch you my quilt.'

'No, you need it,' Amy protested. 'I'm all right with your coat.'

'Quit arguing and let me look after you,' Kelvin ordered. 'I've got a blanket in the cupboard – that'll do me. Now just lie down.'

Amy thanked Kelvin when he fetched his quilt and laid it over her. Shivering by now, she pulled it up around her throat and closed her eyes when his scent rose up to her nose. It smelled clean and manly, and it made her feel even more dirty than she already knew she was. It was no wonder he hadn't wanted to tell his mum that he was bringing her here: he was probably ashamed of her – and rightly so.

She was asleep when Kelvin came back with her tea, so he left the cup on the table and tiptoed into her room. After stripping her bed and putting the soiled sheet and duvet cover into the washing machine, he jumped in the shower and then climbed into bed.

He was already knackered, and this was going to get a lot more tiring before it was over, he was sure. But he was all Amy had right now, so he would just have to find the strength to deal with it.

27

It was three weeks before Amy turned the corner, but she knew she was through the worst when she woke up one morning thinking about the kids instead of craving heroin. But as bad as the physical pain had been during that time, it was nothing compared with the guilt that now swamped her. Without the smack to dull her thoughts and stop her from feeling, the full horror of what she'd exposed the kids to hit her. She would never forgive Mark for bringing Yates into her life, but she had to admit that he'd done the right thing in taking their children away from her. Cassie and Bobby were her life, but she'd neglected them when they had needed her the most, and she was grateful to Mark for saving them. And, as much as it still killed her to think of Ginger Jenny taking her place, she was even grateful to *her*, because at least the children were being looked after by somebody who cared about them and wouldn't put them in danger like she had done.

But that didn't mean that she was going to let the bitch steal her children from her for good. It wasn't going to be easy to convince the social workers that she was fit to have them back, but she was determined to do it. The first thing she had to do was find a new place for them to live. Even if the old house was still standing after the fire, she couldn't go back. She had too many enemies round there; too many idiots who had been taken in by Yates and would probably get straight on the phone to him if they saw her. It saddened her, because that house had been her and Mark's first proper home together, and everything she owned was still in there. But that life was over, so she was just going to have to get over it.

Filled with a new determination to get her life back on track, she got up and took a bath, then set about cleaning the flat to repay Kelvin for putting up with her.

Kelvin was surprised when he came home from work to find not only the flat spotless, but Amy looking and smelling clean, with a light in her eyes and a fresh glow to her skin. It was the first time he had ever seen her like this since he'd met her, and he liked it.

'Does this mean you're feeling a bit better?' he ventured.

'A *lot* better,' said Amy, smiling for the first time in ages. 'Sit down – I'll make you a cup of tea. I'd make you some toast as well,' she added sheepishly, 'but I finished the bread. Hope you don't mind?'

'*Mind?*' Kelvin followed her to the kitchen and leaned against the door frame. 'I'm made up that you've finally got your appetite back, babe.'

As soon as the word left his mouth, Amy blushed, and Kelvin mentally kicked himself. So many men had already taken advantage of her, and now she probably thought he was trying to do the same. *Idiot!*

'I'll, er, go and get cleaned up,' he said. 'Won't be long.'

Amy put her hands on the counter top when he'd gone and exhaled a shaky breath. The word hadn't meant anything, and Kelvin had obviously been horrified by her reaction because he hadn't been able to get away fast enough. She was a stupid, stupid woman, and she wouldn't blame him if he never spoke to her again.

'I've decided to ring the council when the office opens,' she told him when he came back.

'Oh, right,' Kelvin murmured, trying not to let his disappointment show. 'Are you sure you're ready?'

Amy shrugged. 'Probably not, but I've got to do it sooner or later or I'll never get the kids back. Anyway, I've been here long enough, and you need your own space back.'

'I'm cool,' Kelvin assured her, annoyed with himself for scaring her off. God only knew where she was going to end up now thanks to his over-familiarity. A hostel, a park bench, maybe even back to Yates – any of which would be bad, and it would be his fault if anything happened to her. But he could hardly ask her to stay now that she'd made it clear that she wanted to go.

After drinking his tea, Kelvin went to bed. But, exhausted as he'd been when he'd left work, he couldn't get to sleep. It hadn't been a barrel of laughs watching Amy suffer, but her presence was all over the place and he would miss her when she was gone. He'd always thought she was pretty, but without the stress she was beautiful. And, as rare as they were, her smiles lit up the room – and his heart.

He was still lying there deep in thought when Amy eased the door open a short while later.

'Are you awake?'

'Yeah, what's up?'

'I've just spoken to a woman at the council.'

'Oh, yeah?' Kelvin sat up. 'What did she say?'

'It's all a bit of a mess,' Amy told him miserably, sitting down on the end of the bed. 'She said my rent hasn't been paid in ages. They must have cut my benefits off after I stopped signing on, but I was out of my head back then so I couldn't keep track of when I was supposed to do what. Anyway, they sent someone round to see me about it, but one of the neighbours told them I'd done a runner, so now they're in the process of getting a repossession order.'

'Shit,' Kelvin murmured. 'What you gonna do?'

'I don't know.' Amy shrugged. 'I told her I had no choice about leaving, 'cos someone set the house on fire while I was in there and I was too scared to go back. But she reckons I need to get a crime number off the police before they'll consider stopping the court proceedings.'

'Well, you can get that, can't you?'

'No.' Amy shook her head. 'I never told the police anything when they questioned me. I didn't even know about the fire, and there was no way I was going to grass Lenny up for hitting me, so none of it was logged.'

'It *is* a bit of a mess, isn't it?' Kelvin said thoughtfully. 'But there must be something they can do. Do you want me to talk to them?'

'No. I didn't tell them I was staying with you in case they thought something was going on. You know what they're like.'

'So what now?'

Amy shrugged again. 'She says she'll make me an appointment to talk about getting me into a refuge while my case is being assessed. But I've got to take ID, and everything's back at mine.'

Kelvin sighed and flopped back on his pillow. He didn't like the idea of her going into a refuge, but if it was the only way she could start the process of getting her kids back, he wasn't about to stand in her way.

'Tell me what you need and where it is, and I'll go and get it,' he said.

'No, you can't – it's too risky,' Amy argued. 'Someone might see you.'

'Not if I go straight from work in the morning,' said Kelvin. 'Just ring her back and make your appointment, and leave the rest to me.'

28

Marnie was up, dressed, and sitting at the dressing table drying her hair by seven. It usually took a firework up her backside to get her out of bed before noon, but she had an appointment for a 3-D antenatal scan at a private clinic this morning, and she'd hardly slept for excitement at the thought of seeing her baby for the first time.

Yates was still asleep and snoring loudly in the bed behind her. Marnie glanced at him in the mirror and smiled. When Amy had disappeared, so too had some of the initial thrill that Marnie had got from sleeping with her man. She couldn't help it; she'd always preferred attached men. It was the ego boost of knowing that the blokes would rather shag her than their own wives and girlfriends that did it – that, and being able to tell them to fuck off when she was done with them, knowing that they couldn't harass her for fear of wifey finding out.

It was a hard habit to break, so she had carried on sleeping with a few of her other men for a while after she and Lenny got together. But she'd stopped all that as soon as she'd found out she was pregnant. And now that Lenny had effectively moved in, she knew she wouldn't be getting rid of him so easily. But she didn't really mind. It was a bit weird having to take someone else into consideration after years of doing her own thing but, pros versus cons, she'd rather have him here when the baby was born, because the thought of having to look after it by herself filled her with dread. She just hoped it didn't come out looking like him. But if worse came to worst and it was an ugly little fucker, at least it would be the best-dressed ugly little fucker in Manchester.

Dragged from her thoughts by a noise on the other side of the wall, Marnie cocked her head. Nobody had set foot in Amy's house since the fire, and she wondered if the council had finally decided to clear it out. Curious when she heard footsteps clattering down the uncarpeted stairs, she rushed to the window and eased the edge of the curtain back in time to see a man come out with a sports bag over his shoulder and a plastic bag in his hand. He walked down the path with his head down but, when he paused at the gate and glanced up at her window, she gasped.

'What's up?' Yates woke with a start and reached under the bed for his cosh.

'A man just came out of Amy's,' Marnie told him. 'I thought it might be council, but I'm sure it's the bloke who called round there the day I found out I was pregnant. Remember I told you about him?'

'You what?' Yates jumped up, rushed to the window and shoved her out of the way.

'Ow!' she yelped, rubbing at her elbow when it banged against the wall. 'That really hurt.'

'There's no one out there,' said Yates, peering down the road. 'You sure you didn't imagine it?'

'No, I bloody didn't,' Marnie snapped. 'I heard him in there, then saw him walk out clear as day.'

'Can't be the same bloke,' Yates muttered, reaching for his jeans. 'Amy said he was selling double glazing.'

'Well, she obviously lied,' Marnie said huffily, pissed off that he was more concerned about Amy than about having hurt her. 'And where are you going?'

'To catch him.' Yates shoved his sockless feet into his trainers. 'See if he knows where Amy is.'

'*Why?*' Marnie stepped in front of the door to stop him from leaving. 'You're with me now, what you still thinking about *her* for?'

Angry when Yates pushed her aside and trotted down the stairs, she ran out onto the landing and yelled, 'You'd better not be long. We've got the scan, and I'm not going on my own.'

Yates ignored her and ran outside. Pissed off when he remembered that he'd left the car with Keith last night because he'd been too bladdered to drive himself home, he legged it down the road. A bus was just pulling away from the stop when he turned the corner, and he quickly ducked out of sight when he spotted a familiar face peering out of the window.

Marnie was standing on the step when he got back to the house, arms folded, scowl on her face. 'Find out what you wanted to know, did you?' she sniped.

Too angry to answer, Yates ran up the stairs and slammed the bedroom door shut. Eyes blazing, chest heaving, he snatched his mobile phone off the bedside table. He couldn't believe Mani's security guard had dared to show his face around here. Twice Yates had seen him since Amy had fucked off, and both times the cunt had looked him in the eye and smiled like butter wouldn't melt, when all the time he'd obviously known where she was.

'It's me,' he said when Keith answered his call. 'Fetch the car. And whatever you've got planned tonight, cancel it, 'cos we've got a job on.'

Amy had been on pins all morning, waiting for Kelvin to come home. Terrified that he might have been seen or, worse, caught, she was so relieved when he walked in unscathed she almost hugged him. But she folded her arms to prevent herself from overstepping the mark, and asked, 'What happened? Did anybody see you?'

'Don't think so.' Kelvin slipped his jacket off and looped it over the hook behind the door. 'His car wasn't there, and all the curtains were shut so I don't think your friend was up.'

'Probably not,' Amy agreed. 'She always stays in bed late.'

'Well, hopefully I got everything you need so you won't have to go near the house again.' Kelvin handed the bag to her.

'Thanks.' Amy opened it and smiled when she saw her purse and her mobile phone charger. There was no money in her purse, and no credit on her phone, but it was good to have them all the same.

'Brew?' Kelvin headed for the kitchen.

'I'll do it.' Amy followed and put her bag down on the ledge. Kelvin leaned back against the fridge and watched as she filled the kettle. 'I, er, thought we might go out for a walk later,' he said. 'You've got that appointment in the morning, and I know you're nervous, so I thought it might help if we do a trial run.'

Already shaking at the thought of going out, Amy murmured, 'Thanks.'

'No problem.' Kelvin gave her an understanding smile. 'And I've got a hoodie you can wear, in case you're worrying about someone recognising you.'

Amy nodded, forced out a smile, and blinked back the tears that had sprung into her eyes. A couple of minutes ago she'd felt great, but now she felt sad, as if she was about to lose something precious. But she pushed the emotion aside and got on with making the teas, reminding herself that the sooner she was out of here, the sooner she would get her kids back.

29

Yates was scowling as he drove through the deserted streets of Levenshulme at 5:30 the next morning. He'd been awake for almost twenty-four hours by now, and he was wired to the max. It was Marnie's fault. She'd pissed him off good style, calling Amy all the dirty junkie whores under the sun, and slating him for sticking it out when everyone else had seen Amy for what she was and given up on her. Even the scan hadn't shut her up, and she'd mouthed off in front of the nurse to the point of being an embarrassment. If it hadn't been for the worm-like child in her belly that he'd seen on the screen, Yates would have battered the fuck out of her as soon as they left the clinic. But, instead, he'd dropped her off at the house and gone to his flat to get his head together.

When he reached the road at the back of Mani's cash and carry he switched off the headlights and, using the silvery dawn light to guide him, reversed into the yard of the closed-down shop unit at the end of the block.

'How long do you think he'll be?' Keith asked, covering a yawn with his hand. He'd only had a couple of hours' sleep thanks to Yates turning up in the early hours with a shitload of coke and a pack of cards, and he was absolutely knackered.

'Half an hour, give or take.' Yates pulled a pack of cigarettes out of his pocket and tossed one to Keith before lighting his own. 'He'll do his rounds after the tarts have gone, then come past here on his way for the bus.'

'What about the boss?'

'He goes straight to his office.'

'Isn't that where he keeps the CCTV monitor?'

'Yeah, but it's behind his desk so he won't be looking at it.'

'What if he hears us?'

'For fuck's sake! Are you just gonna moan all fuckin' morning?'

'I'm only asking.'

'Well, don't. I know what I'm doing, so just keep it zipped and do as you're told.'

They sat in silence for the next half hour, the peace fractured only by the *thud, thud, thud!* of Yates's fingertips drumming on the steering wheel. It was seriously starting to do Keith's head in, so he was glad when a couple of girls walked past.

Slouched low in his seat, Yates counted those who followed. When the last had gone, he pulled on his gloves and tugged his balaclava down over his face before stepping out of the car.

'What d'ya bring that for?' Keith hissed, spotting the gun in his friend's waistband as he climbed out the other side. 'I thought we was just gonna do him over and find out where Amy is.'

'We are, but he's a big fucker so I'm not taking any chances,' Yates hissed back, his eyes scanning the road. 'Pull your bally down and come on.' He jerked his head and set off at a trot.

They slipped into the shadows of the cash and carry's yard and darted into the narrow alley at the side of the metal door. Then, squatting behind a wheelie bin, they waited.

It was another ten minutes before the heavy back door creaked open and Kelvin came out. He closed it with a loud bang, and Yates and Keith listened as the key turned in the lock. When Kelvin turned to make his way towards the gate, they pounced, grabbing him from behind and dragging him into the alley.

Kelvin's survival instincts kicked in and he easily twisted free of Yates's grip. But it was harder to shake off the larger man, and they fell to the floor in a struggling heap. Kelvin managed to draw his fist back, but they were wedged too tight between the walls for him to get a clear shot at the man's head so, when he saw a flash of flesh between his glove and jacket cuff, he sank his teeth in – hard. When the man screamed and released his hold, Kelvin scrambled to his feet and aimed a kick at his head. He winced at the sound of crunching bone, but this was no time for conscience because they wouldn't have jumped him if they didn't want to cause him serious harm.

He drew his foot back to kick again, but froze when a voice snarled: 'Yo, cunt, start praying.'

He hadn't had time to stop and think about who he was fighting, but there was no mistaking that voice. His heart lurched when he turned and saw the gun pointing at him, but the adrenalin was pumping too hard to let him stand and wait for the bullet, so he put his head down and ran.

Yates fell when Kelvin shouldered him out of the way, and a shot rang out as he involuntarily squeezed the trigger. Kelvin carried on running, but just as he reached the gate another shot was fired, aimed this time, and he went down.

'What's going on out there?' Mani's scared voice floated down from a window above. 'I can see you! I know who you are, and the police are coming to get you!'

Yates and Keith hauled themselves to their feet and, pausing just long enough to look at Kelvin's body, hobbled out of the yard and back to the car.

'What the fuck did you do that for?' Keith squawked, pulling the balaclava off and stuffing it into his pocket. 'We were only supposed to be putting the frighteners on him to get him to tell you where Amy is, you didn't have to fuckin' kill him!'

'Did you want me to let him kick you to death?' snapped Yates, shoving the key into the ignition and tearing out of the yard.

'I was all right,' Keith argued, gingerly wiping his bloodied nose on his sleeve. 'He was only trying to put me down. He'd have left it after a minute.'

'Wasn't how it looked to me,' said Yates, swerving into an alley when he heard the sound of sirens heading their way.

'Yeah, well, you still didn't have to kill him,' Keith repeated, exhaling loudly as his heart began to slow down. 'We'll have to go on the hop now. The boss recognised you. They're probably already looking for us.'

'He was bluffing – he didn't see klish,' Yates said confidently.

'How can you be so sure?'

'I heard it in his voice. Anyhow, I'm not going nowhere till I've found her.'

'Oh, man!' Keith groaned and covered his face with his hands. 'This is getting way out of hand. I can't keep doing this.'

'Fine.' Yates shrugged. 'I'll do it meself.'

'Do what?' Keith twisted around in his seat and stared at him. 'Kill her? *Why?* What's she done that's so bad?'

'She owes me ten grand.'

'Does she fuck!' Keith slammed his fist down on his thigh. 'Her hubby only borrowed five hundred. But this ain't even about the money any more, is it? You're just pissed off 'cos she escaped.'

'She's *mine*,' Yates said through gritted teeth. 'And no one treats me like shit and gets away with it. *No* one.'

'Jeezus, I get it now,' Keith snorted. 'You fuckin' fell for her, didn't you? You fell for her, like a dick, but she wouldn't play along, so you've been punishing her ever since.'

'Did I *fuck* fall for her!' Yates replied with vehemence. 'I just told you, she owes me. Now, shut up, 'cos you're boring me.'

Keith shook his head and gave a mirthless laugh. He was right, and they both knew it. But Yates was never going to admit it, and he would only get mad if Keith kept pushing him on it. And then he'd go off by himself and do God only knew what. And, considering what had just happened, that would be dangerous, because he was bound to get nicked, and then Keith would get dragged right down with him.

Whether he liked it or not, Keith was going to have to stick with him until he'd found the girl. And when he did find her, Keith would have to do whatever it took to make sure that she got out alive.

30

Claudine Brown was still in her nightclothes when two police-women knocked on her door later that morning. She'd just made herself a cup of tea and had been about to carry it back up to bed, but her legs gave way when they told her why they had come, and the cup fell from her hand and shattered on the floor.

'Lord, don't tek my boy away from me,' she wailed, her hands clutched to her breast, her tearful eyes raised to the ceiling. 'Tek me . . . tek *me!*'

Already running down the stairs, having been woken by the noise, Evangeline gave the officers an accusing look as she rushed to her mother's side and helped her up. 'What have you said to her? Why's she so upset?'

'Are you her daughter?'

'Yeah, why?'

'There was an incident outside your brother's workplace this morning,' the officer explained. 'We need to get your mother over to the MRI as soon as possible.'

'No!' Evangeline clutched her mother's arm. 'He's not . . .? Please tell me he's not . . .'

'He's in surgery,' the officer told her. 'But he's not good, so we really should leave now.'

Evangeline inhaled deeply and pulled herself together.

'Come, Mommy . . .' She took her mother's hand. 'Let's go and get dressed.'

'No time,' said Claudine, wrapping her dressing gown tighter around herself. 'My boy need me. Tek me to my boy.'

Evangeline ran up the stairs as the officers led her mother outside, and she quickly threw on some clothes. Then, grabbing a coat from her mother's wardrobe, she snatched up her keys and ran back down to join them in the car.

Kelvin was still in theatre when his mother, sister and the policewomen arrived at the hospital. A nurse showed them into a small room and brought them a cup of tea.

'Do you mind if we ask you some questions?' one of the officers asked when they were settled.

'We weren't there,' said Evangeline. 'We can't tell you nothing.'

'Don't be rude,' chided Claudine, sounding uncharacteristically old and defeated. 'Me never raised you t' be rude.'

'I'm not,' Evangeline argued. 'I'm just telling them that we don't know anything.'

Claudine patted her hand to shut her up, and looked at the officers. 'Ask me anyt'in, an' if me can help, me help. She, too.' She jerked her chin at Evangeline.

'We need to know if your son is involved in any sort of gang activity,' the officer asked.

'No, he's not!' spat Evangeline, instantly on the defensive. 'You think just because he's black that means he must be a gangster? Well, you're wrong. Our Kelvin's an honest, hardworking man, and you won't find anyone as lovely as him if you tried!'

'We appreciate that this is difficult,' the officer said gently when she saw the tears glittering in the girl's eyes. 'But your brother has been shot, and we need to find out who did it before somebody else gets seriously hurt. We're aware that his line of work has probably brought him into contact with some—'

'What you mean, him line a work?' Claudine interrupted.

'Your son works at a massage parlour,' the officer explained, 'and we're trying to ascertain if this was a personal attack, or work-related.'

'Don't talk shit,' Evangeline snapped. 'Sorry, Mommy,' she apologised when her mother gave her a disapproving look. 'But our Kelvin's not like that, and I'm not having them say he is. As *if* he'd work at a dirty place like that!'

'Me don't care where he work,' Claudine said wearily. 'Me just want him home safe. And if me knew anyone who want to hurt him, you'd already know the name. But he a good boy, an' everyone who know him love him.'

'Excuse me . . .' The nurse popped her head around the door. 'Kelvin's out of surgery, and the doctor will be along to speak to you shortly, if that's okay?'

'Fine,' one of the officers answered, guessing that she was asking if the interview was over. 'We'll leave you to it, Mrs Brown, Miss Brown. But if you think of anything else in the meantime, no matter how insignificant it may seem, please don't hesitate to let us know.'

The doctor who came to speak with them a few minutes after the officers had left was still wearing his theatre scrubs, and Claudine stared at the blood spots dotted over the top as if in a trance.

'We managed to remove the bullet,' he told them. 'And Kelvin is stable. But he lost a lot of blood, so we'll be keeping him under close observation for the next forty-eight hours.'

'He's going to be all right, though, yeah?' Evangeline clutched her mother's hand tightly.

'He's stable,' the doctor repeated gently. 'And that's better than we could have hoped for, considering the location of the bullet. He's a very lucky young man.'

'He strong,' Claudine said with conviction. 'And the good Lord will see him through.'

The doctor nodded respectfully and stood up. 'He's heavily sedated at the moment, and probably won't come round for several hours, so I'd recommend that you go home and rest while you can. Someone will ring you if anything changes.'

'No, me stay,' said Claudine, pulling the coat that Evangeline had brought closer around her shoulders. 'T'ank you for your concern, doctor, but my boy need me here when he wake up.'

'Mommy, you should go,' said Evangeline. 'You've had a shock. I'll stay with Kel.'

'Me said me *stay*,' Claudine repeated firmly. 'If you want to help, you can go to 'im flat and get some bits and pieces.'

'Like what?'

'Pyjamas, soap, toothbrush . . . You know how clean he is, he'll want to get fresh when he wake up. And find a vest. He'll need a vest to keep him warm.'

'Fine.' Evangeline sighed and turned to the doctor. 'Is my brother's stuff here? I'll need his keys.'

'I'll ask one of the nurses to check,' said the doctor, heading for the door. 'Please don't worry, Mrs Brown. We'll look after him.'

'Me not worried,' Claudine replied serenely. 'Like me already say, the good Lord gon' see him through.'

Amy was clock-watching and chewing on her fingernails. Kelvin was usually home from work by seven, but it was almost ten now and he still hadn't shown. He sometimes called in on his mother on the way home, but he never stayed for this long, and that worried her. And it worried her even more that he wasn't answering his phone, because he always got straight back to her as soon as he realised he'd missed a call.

She had started to imagine all sorts of terrible things when she heard the key in the lock. More relieved than she'd ever been in her life before, she ran out into the hall to greet him – only to find herself face to face with his sister.

'Who the hell are you?' Evangeline demanded.

'Kelvin's friend,' Amy told her. 'Amy. I met you at your mum's a few weeks ago.'

Evangeline squinted at her as if she'd never seen her before in her life. Then, scowling when recognition kicked in, she spat, 'What the hell are *you* doing here?'

'I've been staying,' Amy murmured, quickly adding, 'In the spare room,' in case the girl got the wrong end of the stick.

Evangeline was glaring at her as if she wanted to rip the face right off her, but Amy's stomach was churning for a different reason. Kelvin had told her that he deliberately hadn't given his family a key in order to avoid unannounced visits like this. But he hadn't come home, and now his sister had let herself in. Something was wrong.

'Where's Kelvin?' she asked, dreading the answer. 'Has something happened to him?'

'Nothing that concerns *you*,' said Evangeline, remembering why she was here. 'I need some things. And *you* can get your stuff and get out.'

'Please just tell me,' Amy begged.

Evangeline narrowed her eyes with suspicion. 'You know who did this, don't you?'

Her fears confirmed, Amy's eyes brimmed with tears. 'Oh, God, he's hurt him, hasn't he?'

'Who's *he*?' Evangeline demanded, grabbing her by the hair. 'If you know who shot my brother, you'd better tell me so I can tell the police, you skanky bitch!'

Amy's legs gave way and she fell back against the wall. She could hear the girl shouting at her, but it sounded like it was coming from a distance. Her head was spinning, and her body felt numb.

Yates knew! He'd found out that she was staying here and he'd shot Kelvin – and now he would be coming after her.

'I've got to go,' Amy gasped, tearing herself free and running into her bedroom, oblivious to the pain as she left a clump of hair behind in the other girl's hand.

'You're going nowhere!' Evangeline yelled, going after her. 'Not until you've told me who shot my brother?'

'I don't *know*!' Amy lied, fighting to get past her. 'There's no time for this. We've got to get out of here or he'll kill us both.'

'Who's *he*?' Evangeline demanded again.

'I can't tell you.' Amy grabbed her bag and backed towards the door. 'Just *go* before he gets here, *please*!'

She turned now and ran out into the hall. Pausing to snatch Kelvin's hoodie off the hook, she yanked the front door open and fled.

Spooked by the girl's obvious terror, Evangeline gathered together the things she needed and quickly followed.

Already hiding behind a wheelie bin in a takeaway yard across the road, Amy watched as Evangeline ran out onto the pavement and hailed a passing cab. She wished that she could escape so easily, but she had no money and nowhere to go.

She couldn't even risk going to her appointment with the housing people because Yates could turn up at any minute now that he knew she'd been staying here, and if he spotted her on the street she was dead. She would have to wait here until night fell, and then try to find a cash machine. Her card was in her purse, and even though her benefits had been stopped there might still be a few pounds in her account.

She hoped so, anyway. If not, she didn't know what she was going to do.

Back at the hospital, the police officer who was stationed on a chair outside Kelvin's room stood up when Evangeline approached. He held out his hand to prevent her from going in. In no mood for messing about after an already fraught morning, she sucked her teeth and tried to push past him. But he held her back.

'Sorry, miss, no one's allowed in there without authorisation.'

'I'm his sister,' she snapped. 'I've just been to pick some things up for him.'

'Have you any proof of ID?'

'Yeah, *this*.' Evangeline waved her hand in front of her angry face.

Before the officer could answer, the door opened and the nurse who had shown them to the waiting room earlier came out and confirmed that Evangeline was family. He nodded and stepped back. Evangeline gave him a dirty look and flounced into the room.

Kelvin was lying unconscious in the bed, surrounded by a mess of tubes and beeping monitors. Their mother was sitting in an armchair, fanning her face with a magazine.

'Who put that fool on guard?' Evangeline asked, leaning

down to kiss her mother on the cheek before handing over the bag she was carrying. 'Axin' me for proof of ID, like it ain't obvious I'm Kel's sister.'

'You is too sparky,' said Claudine wearily. 'Him only doing 'im job. Or would you rather them didn't bother protecting Kelvin?'

'Yeah, all right, point taken.' Evangeline sighed. 'Have they told you anything yet?'

'Only what the doctor already tell us.'

Evangeline pulled another chair up beside the bed and sat down. She reached for Kelvin's hand and gazed at his handsome face, willing him to wake up. There was a seven-year age difference between them, so they had never hung out together as mates. But Kelvin had always been her hero, and she was his little princess, so this was all wrong. He wasn't supposed to be lying here fighting for his life; he was supposed to be looking after her like he always had done. The main man in her life since their father had passed away when she was only two, he had been her rock and her guide, and she would be adrift without him. She couldn't lose him – she *wouldn't*.

'Did you remember to lock the door?' Her mother's voice interrupted her thoughts.

Reminded of what she'd meant to tell her mother, Evangeline wiped her eyes and turned to her. 'Yeah, but that skinny white girl was there. The one he brought home the other week. Reckons she's been staying with him.'

Her mother didn't say anything, and her eyes gave nothing away so Evangeline didn't know if she was angry, or shocked, or even if she had known about the girl all along. But that soon changed when she added, 'She knows who did this.'

Now Claudine's head jerked up, and she demanded, 'Who?'

'She wouldn't tell me,' Evangeline admitted. 'But she was

terrified, and she told me to get out of there, because he'd kill me if he caught me.'

'Why you not tell me this when you come?' Claudine gave her a disapproving look, stood up and started walking towards the door.

'What you doing?'

'Tellin' the police.'

'*No!*' Evangeline squawked. 'Mommy, sit down, you're just going to make it worse.'

'What you mean?' Claudine stopped and frowned at her. 'How can dis get worse?'

'The girl wasn't just scared, she was *petrified*,' Evangeline whispered. 'This wasn't some random attack, Mommy. I think our Kel's involved in something, and we can't risk telling anyone until we know what's going on or we might get him in trouble.'

'And how we gon' find out?' Claudine came back to her seat.

'I don't know.' Evangeline gazed thoughtfully back at Kelvin. 'Wait till he wakes up and ask him.'

She didn't add *if he wakes up*, but that was what she was thinking, and the possibility that he might not brought fresh tears to her eyes.

31

Marnie was asleep when Yates got home after dropping Keith off, but she woke up with a start when the sound of the TV suddenly blared up from the living room below. Pissed off when she peeked at the clock and saw that it was only just gone eleven, she pulled on her dressing gown and marched down the stairs.

Yates was perched on the edge of the couch, flicking through the channels. 'What the hell are you playing at?' Marnie demanded. 'You stay out all night, then think you can waltz in here and start making noise?'

'Don't start,' he muttered.

'Are you having a laugh?' she squawked. 'I think you're forgetting whose house this is.'

'Here.' Yates reached into his pocket, pulled out a wad of money and threw it at her. 'Go buy something. That should keep you quiet for a few hours.'

Offended, Marnie pursed her lips and put her hands on her hips. 'Oh, so you think that's all I'm interested in, do you? *Money?*'

'Starting to seem like it, considering how much you've had off me in the last few weeks.'

'For your *baby*.'

'Yeah, right! And it needs all them handbags and shoes, does it?'

Marnie glowered at him. He was trying to twist things around and turn it into an argument about money, but she wasn't having it.

'Where were you last night?'

'At my flat, getting a bit of peace and quiet.'

'Liar! There's no way you were at yours, or you wouldn't be here so early. And you're still wearing the same clothes. You found her, didn't you? You've been with her all night. *Answer* me!'

'Have you finished?' Yates jerked his head around and stared up at her coldly.

'No, I fuckin' haven't,' Marnie snarled, her face white with rage. 'You've been with her, and now you think you can lie to my face like I'm some stupid little bit on the side. Well, I'm not having it!' She reached down, snatched the remote out of his hand and switched the TV off. 'Get out!'

'Put it back on,' Yates ordered, his eyes glinting a warning that Marnie was too angry to see.

'No, I will not! This is *my* house, and that's *my* TV, and if I want it off, it goes off!'

Yates leapt up and grabbed her by the throat. 'Turn it back on before you get hurt.'

Marnie was so shocked that she dropped the remote. When Yates let go of her and snatched it up, then sat back down and turned the TV back on as if nothing had happened, she clutched at her throat and stared down at him in disbelief. She'd never seen him like this before, and it scared her. Amy had once accused him of beating her up, but Marnie hadn't believed her. Now she wasn't so sure.

'I'm sorry,' Yates murmured after a moment. 'I shouldn't have done that. But it pisses me off when you keep going on about Amy.'

'What do you expect me to think?' Marnie asked warily. 'We were getting on fine till I saw that bloke coming out of hers yesterday, then you went all weird, like you were more interested in her than me.'

'She owes me money,' said Yates. 'And that's the only reason I'm interested in her. I've got you now – why would I want her back?'

'So if you weren't with her, where were you?'

'I went back to my place for a kip, then called round at Keith's. We had a few sniffs and played some cards, then I came here. And I stayed downstairs 'cos I didn't want to disturb you. That's all.'

It sounded plausible, and Marnie exhaled loudly to release the tension. Then, giving him an apologetic smile, she said, 'Sorry for jumping to conclusions. Want a brew?'

'I'd love one.' Yates smiled back, but the smile slipped as soon as Marnie left the room and he turned his attention back to the TV. It was too early for the police to have released any details yet, but he didn't want to miss it when they did, because he couldn't do anything until he knew if he was on the run or not.

'Amy . . . *Amy* . . . ?'

Evangeline had been dozing, but she sat bolt upright when she heard Kelvin's voice and grasped his hand.

'Kel, it's me – Evie. Are you awake?'

Kelvin swallowed dryly and opened his eyes. 'Where's Amy?'

'Never mind her,' Evangeline said dismissively. 'How do you feel?'

'Not too good,' said Kelvin, wincing when he tried to move his other hand and the drip feed dragged against his skin.

He gazed around, confused by the monitors. 'What happened? Why am I here?'

'You got shot coming out of work,' Evangeline told him quietly. 'Don't you remember?'

Kelvin shook his head. He could see blurry images of a scuffle in his mind's eye and guessed that Yates must have caught up with him, but he couldn't recall any of the details.

'I'll get the nurse.' Evangeline stood up.

'Wait!' Kelvin held on to her hand. 'I need to know if Amy's okay. Will you check on her for me?'

'No, I won't,' Evangeline told him firmly. 'I don't know what you've got yourself involved in, Kel, but I know it's got something to do with her, and she can rot in hell as far as I'm concerned.'

'It's not her fault,' Kelvin insisted, pain flaring in his eyes as he struggled to speak. 'There's a man—'

'I know, she said,' Evangeline interrupted. 'But she wouldn't tell me his name, so she's obviously covering for him. Shows how much she cares about you.'

'It's not like that. Please, Eve. For me.'

'Look, Mommy already wants to tell the police, so I don't think it's a very good idea for me to—'

'No!' Kelvin shook his head from side to side. 'Don't let her. It's too dangerous.'

'Don't worry, I sussed that something was going down and told her not to say anything,' Evangeline assured him. 'And I kicked your so-called friend out, so she won't be showing her face again any time soon. Now you just forget about her and concentrate on getting better, and then we'll talk. Okay?'

Kelvin sighed and closed his eyes. He knew his sister inside out and there was no point trying to persuade her to look for Amy now she'd convinced herself that this was Amy's fault. If he'd been able, he'd have got up and done it himself. But he wasn't, so he couldn't do a thing apart from pray that Amy was strong enough to look after herself until he got out of here.

Evangeline gazed down at her brother and, thinking that he'd gone back to sleep, kissed him on the cheek. Then, tiptoeing out of the room, she told the nurse that he'd come round. Then she called her mother to let her know the good news.

Over on the other side of Manchester, Amy had just been woken by the sound of children playing outside the derelict gatehouse of the park where she'd spent the night.

She had hidden in the takeaway yard for hours after her run-in with Kelvin's sister – and might still have been there if the rats hadn't come out to play. It was said that people were never more than a few feet away from a rat at any given time, but Amy had never believed it until she experienced it for herself. As soon as it had got dark the yard had seemed to come alive with them, and she'd been frozen with fear as the nasty hunchbacked creatures had scuttled around her. It had been terrifying to hear them fighting and scavenging in the bins, but when one of the filthy things brushed against her she'd been on her feet and out of there in a flash.

Cold and hungry, she peered out through the broken window to make sure that no one was nearby, then climbed out and, hood pulled low, set off for her mum and dad's house. It had been months since she had seen them, and she doubted she'd get a rapturous welcome because her mum had made it quite clear at the custody-court hearing that she blamed Amy for losing the kids. But if they realised that she was clean of the drugs now and desperate to make amends, they might find it in their hearts to help her.

Please God.

An alarm was going off in the distance when Amy turned the corner onto her parents' road, and she hesitated when she saw a police car parked across from their house. For a moment, she thought that Kelvin's sister had reported her for knowing who had shot Kelvin. But she reminded herself that, apart from Yates, none of the people she'd met since this nightmare began knew her maiden name, much less her mum and dad's address.

Reassured, she put her head down and walked quickly down the road. But just as she was passing the next-door neighbour's gate, the front door opened and Phil Nolan stepped out. He spotted her and said something to the policeman who was right behind him, and Amy squeezed her eyes shut when the copper called, 'Just a minute, miss. Can I have a word?'

Her first instinct was to run, but she knew she'd stand no chance of getting away. So she turned and gave him a questioning smile. 'Yes?'

'I believe this is your mum and dad's place?' the officer asked, nodding towards the house. 'Don't suppose you've got a key?'

Amy shook her head. 'No, sorry, I haven't lived here for years. Why, what's up?'

'That!' Phil pointed at the flashing alarm box on the wall. 'It's been going off all flaming morning, but this lot reckon it's got to have been going off for twenty-four hours before they can authorise entry.'

Amy stared at the box. She hadn't realised that the alarm was coming from her parents' house until now, and she felt her stomach flip with dread. 'What happened?' she asked. 'Where are they?'

'Oh, don't worry about them,' Phil said with a scathing edge to his voice. 'They're off on their jollies in Torquay, them. Won't be back till Wednesday.'

'Oh.' Amy's heart sank.

'Sorry.' The officer gave Phil an apologetic shrug. 'Nothing else I can do.'

'Yeah, I know.' Phil sighed. 'Thanks for coming, anyway, son.'

He waved the officer off, then turned back to Amy and gave her an exasperated look. 'I could bloody throttle your mam and dad. I've been trying to ring them all morning to see if they've left a spare key anywhere, but it keeps going to voicemail. It's driving me and Fran round the flaming bend.'

'Do you know what set it off?'

'Yeah, some little bastard tried to jemmy the back window this morning. I heard it and called the cops, but the bugger legged it when he heard the sirens. That's what you get for blabbing your business to all and sundry. I told your mam. I said, if you advertise that your house is going to be empty, you're asking to be burgled. But she just had to let everyone know they could afford a nice holiday.'

Amy couldn't argue with that. That was her mum all over: always showing off, always bragging.

'Oh, well.' Phil shrugged in a gesture of defeat. 'Nowt I can do about it, so I suppose I'll just have to keep the telly turned up to drown it out. Bye, love.'

Amy bit her lip when he turned to go back into his house. Then, blushing deeply, she called, 'Phil . . . you couldn't lend us a couple of quid, could you? My money hasn't gone in yet, and I've got an interview in town. I'm going to be late if I don't go now.'

Phil sighed, reached into his pocket and tossed her a fiver.

'Thanks,' she murmured shamefacedly. 'I'll drop it round later.'

'Forget it,' he said, pushing his door open. 'I'll get it off your dad when he comes back – along with compo for putting up with this flaming racket.'

When he'd gone inside, Amy shoved the money into her pocket and walked away quickly. Phil hadn't given her a description of the man he'd seen trying to break in, but she would bet her life that it was Yates. In which case, the police obviously hadn't connected him to Kelvin's shooting, and he was still free to hunt her down – so she was still in serious danger.

She stopped at a shop and bought an *Evening News*, some cigarettes and matches, and a couple of packets of crisps. Then, using her last fifty pence, she called the hospital. But they wouldn't tell her anything, so she went back to the gatehouse and scoured the paper for news of Kelvin.

There was no mention of the shooting at all, and she hoped that meant he was still alive. She wished she could see him, to thank him for everything he'd done – and apologise for the trouble she'd brought to his door. But she decided that the best thing she could do for him now was leave him well alone.

32

Too scared to go out into the open again, Amy hid in the gatehouse for the next three days. She had intended to stay there until Wednesday, and then sneak out and make a reverse-charge call to her mum and dad. But by Saturday she felt so weak and sick that she was afraid she might die if she didn't get out of there.

The crisps were long gone by then, and her stomach was growling continuously. There had been plenty of times in the past when she'd gone without food so the kids could eat, so she wasn't bothered about that. It was the lack of sleep she couldn't handle. And only one thing would help: heroin.

She tried to resist, but the craving took hold and before she knew it she had climbed out of the window and walked into town. Sick to her stomach at the thought of what she was about to do, she stood on the corner of a dark backstreet and waited. Less than ten minutes later a car pulled alongside her. A vision of Kelvin's smiling face flashed into her mind as she climbed into the passenger side and her heart wept, because she knew how disappointed he would be if he could see her. But she pushed the thought aside, telling herself that he couldn't see her – and never would again.

The punter drove her to a parking lot at the rear of a derelict factory on the outskirts of Ancoats. He switched off the engine, lowered his seat, unzipped his fly and lay back with his arms behind his head.

'Start with a hand job and a quick suck, then get on top. I'll give you fifty for the lot.'

Amy swallowed sickly. His penis was already erect, and it would be so easy to just do it and get it over with. But her hand refused to move. She'd done this a thousand times before, but never when she was straight, and never of her own free will.

'I'm sorry,' she cried, scrambling to open the door.

'What you playing at?' The punter jerked up in his seat.

'I can't do it,' Amy told him tearfully. 'I thought I could, but I can't. I'm really sorry. Please let me out.'

The man raised his hands into the air, and Amy winced, sure that he was going to hit her. But he just slapped his fists down on his thighs, and then zipped his fly back up before releasing the central locking.

'Get out. But don't let me see you out there again, or I won't be so fuckin' nice next time.'

Muttering, 'Don't worry, you won't,' Amy jumped out and ran.

Stopping when she reached town, she swiped at her tears and gazed at a tramp sitting in a doorway up ahead, swigging from a bottle of cider. There was a paper cup on the floor in front of him, and it gave her an idea. If she couldn't get money the other way, she would beg instead.

She walked further into town, to a street that was busy with nightclubs, and stood in the shadows of a doorway. Before too long, a couple came around the corner. They were sharing a bag of chips and her stomach growled when the scent of hot vinegar reached her.

'Excuse me . . .' She stepped out as they passed. 'You couldn't spare a bit of change, could you?'

'Fuck off!' The man glared at her with disgust in his eyes.

'Aw, don't be mean, she's only a kid,' the woman scolded, reaching into her jacket pocket. 'Here you go, sweetheart. Don't spend it all at once.'

Pride almost made Amy refuse the pound coin, but she took it and mumbled 'Thank you' before rushing away.

Absolutely mortified at having been forced to sink so low, she rushed around the corner. But her shame quickly turned to fear when a group of singing women stumbled out of a karaoke bar and started walking towards her arm in arm. The one in the middle stopped singing when their stares met, and then she stopped walking, too.

'Come on.' One of the others tugged on her arm. 'I need a kebab.'

'You go,' Marnie said quietly. 'I'll catch up with you in a minute.'

When her friends staggered away, she stuffed her hands into her pockets and gave Amy an uncertain smile. 'All right?'

Shaking like a leaf, her gaze flicking every which way in dread of Yates being close behind, Amy said, 'Yeah. You?'

'Not bad.' Marnie gave a little shrug.

Neither of them spoke again for a few seconds, and Marnie felt awkward. They had fallen out way before she stole Lenny off Amy, and she'd convinced herself that she had done nothing wrong. But now, face to face with the girl who had once been her closest friend, she couldn't help but feel a little guilty.

'You know I never meant to hurt you, don't you?' she said

quietly. 'Me and Lenny . . .' She paused and sighed before continuing. 'Well, you can't help who you fall in love with, can you?'

'*Love?*' Amy nearly choked on the word. 'You think he loves you?'

'I know it's been hard for you,' Marnie went on. 'But you've got to admit that you and Lenny weren't right for each other. It's different with me, we understand each other. And we're going to be a family now,' she added proudly, 'so I hope you can let it go and get on with your own life.'

Amy's gaze dropped to Marnie's stomach and she felt sick all over again when she saw the bump. 'Oh, God,' she moaned. 'Not with him . . . please not with him.'

'Oi, Marn, what's taking you?' one of the women from the group called out before Marnie could answer. 'We've got a cab!'

Marnie looked at Amy with pain in her eyes. Things had been pretty toxic between them towards the end, but that didn't mean she hated her or wished her ill.

'Oh, Amy, why are you doing this to yourself?' she asked. 'You look terrible.'

Amy's eyes immediately started to smart, but she determinedly held back the tears. She wanted to warn Marnie that Lenny was dangerous, and that one day he would hurt her just like he'd hurt Amy. But she'd tried that once before and Marnie hadn't believed her. So she raised her chin, and said, 'I'm fine – don't worry about me.'

Marnie didn't believe that for one second, but there wasn't much she could do or say. Lenny had already tried to help, only for Amy to throw his efforts right back in his face. She didn't want Amy to think that she was offering the hand of friendship and risk the girl turning up at the house and messing up her and Lenny's new life, but she couldn't walk away without doing *some*thing.

'Look, I know I probably shouldn't do this,' she blurted out. 'But here . . .' She pulled a twenty-pound note out of her pocket and shoved it into Amy's hand. 'Get yourself something to eat, you look half starved.'

'I don't want your money,' Amy protested, offering it back.

But Marnie stepped out of reach and scuttled away with her head down. Sighing, Amy pocketed the money and walked in the opposite direction.

A few streets on, she ran into another group of women. But this time they were street girls, and they weren't about to let her pass through their territory without a fight.

'Oi, Blondie, fuck off while you can still walk,' one of them warned, stepping in front of her and pushing her hard in the chest.

'I'm not working,' Amy told her, wincing when her head hit the wall. 'I'm just trying to go home.'

'Find another way,' spat the woman, pushing her again. 'This is our street, and we say who gets to walk on it. Now *do* one before I glass you.'

Terrified when the woman snatched an empty beer bottle up off a step and smashed it against the wall, Amy put her hands out in front of her and took a staggering step back.

'Please don't,' she cried. 'I'm going.'

'Put that fuckin' bottle down before I stuff it right up you!' another voice suddenly barked. 'She's me mate, and if anyone touches her they're dead.'

Amy almost fainted with relief when Ella pushed her way through the group and stood in front of her to shield her.

'Thanks,' she gasped when the girls backed away. 'I thought she was going to kill me.'

'Probably would have, knowing her,' said Ella, still eyeing the group. 'What you doing round here, anyhow? Thought you were too good to work the streets?'

'I needed some money,' Amy admitted.

'Rattling?' Ella gave her a knowing look.

Amy nodded and dipped her gaze, thoroughly ashamed of herself.

'Yeah, I can tell,' said Ella. 'You look fucked. How long since you had a fix?'

'A few weeks,' Amy told her miserably.

'Yeah, right.' Ella gave a disbelieving snort. 'Been locked up, have you?' she added, that being the only reason that *she* had ever gone without for any length of time.

'No, I stopped using,' Amy told her. 'But things haven't been going too well, so I thought I'd get a little bit to tide me over.' She paused and licked her lips. 'Don't suppose you've got any, have you? I've got money.' She held up the twenty-pound note that Marnie had given her.

'Not on me, no. But I can easy get some. Might take a bit of time to find my guy, though. Where you going? I'll drop it off.'

'Can't I come with you?' Amy asked. 'Only I'm not really staying anywhere just now.'

'What d'ya mean?' Ella frowned. 'You're not sleeping rough, are you?'

Amy nodded and wiped her nose on her sleeve. 'Look, can you get it for me, or not? Only I don't really want to be out in the open just now.'

'Yeah, course.' Ella snatched the money out of her hand. Then, pursing her lips thoughtfully, she said, 'Why don't you come back to my place? I've only got one bed, but you can kip on the couch.'

'Really?' Amy's eyes widened. It hadn't even occurred to her to ask, but it would be the perfect solution while she sorted herself out. 'God, that'd be great. I'll need to go and get my bag, but it'll only take twenty minutes.'

'Where is it?'

'In the old house in Alex Park,' Amy told her, relief loosening her tongue. 'I've been sleeping in there for the last few days.'

'Tell you what, you go and get it while I find my guy,' Ella suggested. 'I'll meet you at the back gate in half an hour and we can catch the bus on Prinny Parkway.'

Amy nodded. Then, lurching forward, she gave Ella an impulsive hug. 'Thank you so much!'

'Leave it out.' Ella shoved her off. 'I might have turned the odd trick with a bird in the past, but that don't mean I'm into pussy.'

Sure that she was joking, Amy grinned and walked away backwards, saying, 'Don't worry, I won't try and jump into bed with you. See you in a bit.'

Happier than she'd been in days, she turned and rushed off to pick up her stuff. Ella was the only friend she had in the world right now, and she couldn't believe her luck at having bumped into her.

Ella was thinking much the same thing as she watched Amy go. When Mani had decided to temporarily close *Hawaii* after Kelvin got shot, she'd had no choice but to start working the streets again, and she hated it with a passion. Hated being out in the cold, hated having to stand around for hours on end, and especially hated the freaky bastard punters, because they were a different breed from the soft touches who frequented *Hawaii*. Brothel punters asked for what they wanted rather than demanded it, because they were on the girls' territory with a security guard to keep them in line. But when a girl got into a punter's car she never knew if she was going to get out alive – or even if the freak would pay up when he'd had what he wanted.

Ella, like a lot of the girls, had a habit to feed, so she was forced to take the risk. But there were plenty of ways to earn cash if you had a bit of savvy about you – you just had to have the right merchandise to sell. And, as luck would have it, a valuable piece of merchandise had just landed right in her lap.

Smiling slyly now, she pulled her mobile phone out of her pocket and dialled a number.

'This is Ella from Mani's place,' she said when her call was answered. 'Remember that little chat we had when you came in a while back? Well, I've found what you're looking for. And if the price is right, I can tell you exactly where she's going right now . . .'

Amy was out of breath by the time she reached Alexandra Park fifteen minutes later. She was shaking all over, her legs were aching, and her head was pounding. But the thought of sleeping on Ella's couch, having a cup of tea and her first hit in weeks, gave her the strength to pull herself through the gatehouse's broken window and up the rickety stairs to the bedroom where she'd been sleeping.

She pulled her bag out of the cupboard where she'd stashed it, then looked around to make sure that she hadn't left anything before running back down the stairs. But just as she had climbed back out and was making her way to the gate to wait for Ella, a car turned onto the road, and her legs almost gave way when it screeched to a halt.

Unable to go forwards or backwards, Amy dived sideways

into a clump of bushes and watched in terror as Yates climbed out of the passenger side, followed by Keith when he got out from behind the wheel.

Ella! This was *her* doing. Nobody else knew where Amy had been staying, so the bitch must have got straight on the phone to Yates as soon as Amy left her. And, to add insult to injury, she'd taken Amy's money as well.

After climbing into the gatehouse, Yates stalked from room to room in search of his prey while Keith kept watch by the window.

'There's nothing here – she must have been and gone,' he said when he thundered back down the stairs after searching the upper floor. 'That's your fuckin' fault for dragging your feet.'

'I was having a crap,' Keith reminded him. 'What did you want me to do, suck it back up?'

'I should have just left you there and come by myself,' snapped Yates, climbing angrily back out of the window and dropping down onto the grass.

'Oh, yeah, great idea,' said Keith, dropping down beside him. 'Drive round coked out of your skull and get yourself nicked.'

'I already told you, I ain't gonna get nicked,' spat Yates. 'Any cunt gets in my way, they'll get what the black twat got.'

'Put that away!' Keith hissed when Yates pulled the gun out. 'You can't go waving it around in public, you mad bastard. And you deffo can't go shooting dibble, 'cos you won't just get nicked, you'll get fuckin' life.'

'It'll be worth it,' Yates grinned. 'One less cunt on the street.'

'Fuck that,' snapped Keith. 'You ain't taking me down with you.'

'Oh, yeah?' Yates prodded him in the stomach with the weapon's barrel. 'Think you're calling the shots now, do you? Think I won't take you out, an' all?'

'Go on, then.' Keith spread his arms. 'If you're gonna do it, do it.'

Yates stared him in the eye for several long moments, then kissed his teeth and slotted the gun into his waistband. 'Get back in the car,' he ordered, heading for the gate. 'She can't have got far, so it should be easy enough to spot her if we drive round.'

Still crouched in the bush, Amy bit down on her hand to keep herself from crying out. She'd heard every word, and knew with absolute certainty that Yates intended to kill her when he found her. And he *would* find her eventually, because she had nowhere left to hide. Ella had betrayed her, so she couldn't stay here. She also couldn't go back to her mum and dad's, because Yates would probably go there again at some point. Kelvin was still in hospital and would probably go to his mum's from there, so she couldn't go to him. And she'd lost touch with all her other friends after marrying Mark, so there was absolutely nobody left to turn to. She might as well be dead.

33

Layla kept adjusting her position in her seat, and Steve peered at her with concern. 'Are you sure you're all right? Do you want me to pull over for a minute?'

'No, I'm okay.' Layla forced a tight smile. 'Just hurry up and get me home.'

'You're not having pains again, are you?' Steve persisted. 'We're not far from the hospital. I can easily divert.'

'Baby, please stop fussing,' Layla said patiently. 'I've already made a fool of myself once today, and I've got no intention of doing it again. The nurse said it was Braxton Hicks, and she knows better than us, so just stop panicking and take me home. I just want a cup of tea, and the loo.'

'All right, have it your own way,' Steve conceded. 'But I still reckon it's worth getting a second opinion. That hospital was out in the middle of nowhere – they're probably twenty years behind.'

'The Lake District is hardly Mars,' Layla teased, reaching out and squeezing his hand. 'I'm sure the doctors get the same training as in every other hospital in the country. Anyway, it's not hurting, I'm just uncomfortable.'

Steve sighed and smiled at her. Layla smiled back, but a movement in the corner of her eye brought her head around with a snap and, when she saw a figure lurching off the pavement in front of them, she screamed.

Steve swerved just in time and slammed on his brakes. 'Are you all right?' He twisted around in his seat. 'Are you hurt?'

'I'm fine,' Layla gasped, clutching at her stomach where the seat belt had dug in. 'Go and see to the boy.'

Angry now, Steve unclipped his seat belt and threw the door open. 'What the bloody hell do you think you're playing at, you stupid idiot?' he yelled at the boy who was dragging himself up off the ground. 'Are you on crack, or something? My wife's eight months pregnant – you could have killed her!'

'I'm sorry,' the boy muttered.

'*Sorry?*' Steve repeated, marching over. 'You think sorry cuts it after what you just did?'

'Steve, stop shouting,' Layla called from the car. 'See if he's hurt.'

Steve turned and waved for her to stay put. Then, turning back, he was just about to – reluctantly – ask if the boy was hurt, but hesitated when he caught a glimpse of the face inside the hood.

'*Amy?*'

Amy glanced up when he spoke her name, but then her eyes rolled and she collapsed back down to the ground.

'Oh, Christ,' Steve squawked, squatting down and pushing the hood off her face. 'Amy, wake up.' He patted her cheek. '*Amy . . .*'

'What's wrong?' Layla called. 'Is he hurt?'

'It's not a him, it's Amy, Mark's ex,' Steve called back. 'I think she's fainted.'

'Oh, God!' Layla put her hand over her mouth and climbed out of the car. 'We didn't hit her, did we?'

'I don't think so. But she doesn't look too good.'

'Shall I call an ambulance?'

'Yeah.'

'*No!*' Amy croaked, coming round in time to hear this. 'Please don't. He'll find me.'

'Who?' Steve looked around. 'There's no one here. Was somebody chasing you? Is that why you jumped out in front of us?'

Amy covered her face with her arms and rocked her head from side to side.

As Steve stared down at her, a cold chill of realisation skittered down his spine. 'Oh, Christ, you did it on purpose. You were trying to get hit.'

'I've got to go,' Amy sobbed, hauling herself to her feet. 'I'm sorry, I'm really sorry.'

Steve ran his hands through his hair and watched as she staggered onto the pavement and limped away. But, as she made to go down an alley, he called, 'Amy, wait!' and ran after her.

'Just leave me,' Amy begged when he grabbed her by the arm. 'It's too dangerous.'

'Just tell me what's going on,' Steve insisted, holding on as she tried to wriggle free. 'I might be able to help.'

'You can't.' Amy shook her head. 'He'll kill you if he sees you talking to me. Just let me go and forget you saw me.'

'How can I?' Steve peered down at her with genuine concern in his eyes. 'We're mates, and you're in trouble.'

Layla had climbed out of the car by now, and she walked over to them and put her hand on Amy's arm. 'Listen, love, I don't know you, and I don't know what's going on, but I really need to go home or I'm going to wet myself. It's only round the corner. Why don't you come and have a cup of tea? It'll make you feel better.'

Amy shook her head again. 'No, you shouldn't get involved.'

'I know Steve, and he won't leave you here like this, so you've got no choice,' said Layla. 'If you still want to go after that, he can drop you off somewhere.'

Overwhelmed by the woman's kindness, Amy burst into tears again.

'Come on.' Layla put an arm around her shoulder and led her gently back to the car. 'Whatever's wrong, we'll soon sort it out.'

Steve's flat had been laddish and a bit stark, but the small mock-Georgian house he'd moved into since Amy had last seen him was furnished like a show home. There was stylish patterned paper on the walls, a plush carpet underfoot, comfortable-looking couches, and lamps instead of the harsh overhead light.

Steve saw her gazing around and grinned as he switched on the lamps and the fire. 'It's all Layla's doing. Not really my taste, but I suppose I'll get used to it – eventually.'

'Oh, be quiet, you love it,' Layla admonished him playfully. Then, looking at Amy as she slipped off her coat, she said, 'Sit down and make yourself comfortable while Steve puts the kettle on. If you're lucky, he might even stretch to a butty.'

'I'm not hungry,' Amy lied, perching on the couch.

'Well, I am,' said Layla, deciding not to mention the loud gurgles and groans she'd heard coming from Amy's stomach when they had been in the car. 'This little one demands food on the hour every hour, and I feel like a right greedy so-and-so eating by myself.'

'Okay,' Amy agreed. 'But I'll go after that.'

'Where to?' Layla asked, sitting beside her when Steve went off to make the teas.

'My mum's,' Amy lied.

'At this time of night? Won't they be in bed?'

'Probably, but it doesn't matter.'

'Look, why don't you stay here?' Layla suggested. 'We've already done the spare room up as a nursery, so there's only a cot in there. But you're welcome to sleep on the couch.'

Amy shook her head. She was already warming up, and the couch was very comfortable, so it was tempting. But if she stayed she would be putting them at risk, just like she had Kelvin.

Layla smiled an understanding smile and held out her hand. 'I don't think we've been properly introduced. My name's Layla, and I'm a busybody.'

A frown of confusion flickered across Amy's brow.

Steve had just walked in, and he chuckled softly as he placed their teas down on the coffee table. 'She means she's a bossy bitch, and she won't take no for an answer,' he explained.

'So, that's settled, then,' said Layla with finality. 'You're staying on the couch, and you and me are going to have a nice girly chat.'

'Tomorrow,' Steve said firmly. 'You can have your tea and your butty, but then you're going to bed – and no arguments. We've had a long drive, and you need some rest. And so does Amy, by the looks of her.'

Layla rolled her eyes at Amy. 'And he calls *me* bossy.'

Steve grinned and went off to make the sandwiches. Then, while the girls were eating, he busied himself finding a quilt, a pillow, and one of Layla's spare nighties.

When the couple had said goodnight and left her, Amy undressed quickly and lay down. She didn't think she would be able to get to sleep, but the combination of food in her stomach and the feeling of being safe for the first time since being parted from Kelvin did the trick.

Upstairs in bed, Steve pulled Layla into his arms and kissed the top of her head. 'Have I ever told you how amazing you are?'

'Lots of times,' she purred, cuddling up to him. 'But what have I done to deserve it this time?'

'Letting Amy stay, and that. Not many women would have done that for someone they don't know.'

'She's your friend, and she's in trouble. What was I going to do, tell her to get lost? Anyway, my instincts are good, and I reckon she's nice under all that dirt. Do you think we should have asked if she wanted to take a shower?'

'She does honk a bit, doesn't she?' Steve chuckled. 'But it might have seemed a bit rude when she'd only just walked in. I'll suggest it in the morning.'

'I bet she's really pretty when she's clean,' Layla mused. 'Damn sight prettier than that sour-faced little madam Mark's hooked up with now.'

'You're not wrong there,' Steve agreed. 'But you can't knock Jenny for the way she's stepped up to the mark with Cass and Bobby.'

'Maybe not, but I still don't like her. And I don't reckon Mark's as happy as he makes out, either.'

'Well, he definitely won't be happy when he finds out Amy's been here,' said Steve. 'It's funny, but I blamed him when they split. And I didn't really believe it when it all came out about her being on smack and going on the game, and that, 'cos she wasn't that kind of girl. But now I've seen her again, I'm not so sure.'

'Mmmm,' Layla murmured. Then, in a whisper, she asked, 'You don't think she's got any drugs on her now, do you?'

'Wouldn't have thought so,' Steve said, frowning in the dark. 'Judging by the way she wolfed that butty down, I doubt she's eaten in days, so I can't see her having the money to score.'

'That might be why she looked so desperate when we found her,' said Layla. ''Cos she's withdrawing. Oh, no!' she added when something occurred to her. 'I left my bag by the couch.'

Steve pulled his arm out from under her. 'I'll go and get it.'

'Knock before you go in,' Layla cautioned as he pulled his dressing gown on.

Steve nodded and tiptoed out. He crept down the stairs and was about to tap on the living-room door, but hesitated when he heard soft snores coming from the other side. Easing the door open, he checked that Amy was sleeping before picking up Layla's handbag from the side of the couch. Then, looking around to make sure there were no valuables or money lying around, he went back to bed.

'Spark out,' he told Layla.

She grimaced guiltily. 'I feel terrible now.'

'Don't,' said Steve. 'The old Amy would never steal off a mate, but I haven't seen her for ages so we can't take any chances. We'll see how she is in the morning, and if we get any bad vibes I'll tell her to go. But I think I'll set the alarm a bit earlier,' he added, reaching for his phone. 'Just in case.'

Amy slept right through to noon the next day. Refreshed when she woke, she stretched long and hard. But when she opened her eyes and saw the unfamiliar surroundings, she sat up in a panic.

'Morning.'

Amy snapped her head around when she heard the voice and gazed at the woman who was sitting on the other side of the room. It took several seconds for recognition to sink it, but when it did she smiled shyly.

'Sorry, I was dreaming about home. Didn't know where I was.'

'Oh, I do that all the time – it's a bugger, isn't it?' said Layla, pushing herself up off her seat. 'Steve's nipped out to do a bit of shopping, but he shouldn't be too long. Fancy a coffee?'

'Shall I do it?' Amy offered, feeling guilty as the other woman waddled towards the door.

'Thanks, but it's best I don't sit still for too long.' Layla rolled her eyes and rubbed her enormous stomach. 'The baby seems to be most comfortable when it's lying on my bladder, but I end up having to go to the loo every five minutes. Suppose I don't need to tell you, though, seeing as you've already been through it.'

'Yeah, twice,' Amy said quietly.

Layla saw the sadness in her eyes and wished she could bite her tongue off. 'I'm sorry,' she apologised. 'That was really insensitive.'

'No, it's fine,' Amy lied. 'It's been a long time and I'm used to it. How long have you got to go?' she asked now, following as Layla made her way to the kitchen.

'Five weeks, give or take, but we both reckon it'll come early,' Layla told her as she filled the kettle. 'We've just been to my mum and dad's cottage in the Lakes for the weekend, and weren't supposed to be coming back till later tonight, but I started getting pains so Steve dragged me off to hospital. It was only Braxton Hicks, and I felt like such a hypochondriac. But Steve's such a worrier, he insisted on bringing me home early.'

'It's hard to tell the difference,' said Amy. 'But you'll know about it when the real ones kick in.'

'That bad?' Layla gave her a *please-tell-me-it's-not* look.

'Sorry, but yeah.' Amy smiled apologetically. 'And I'm only telling you 'cos I wished someone had told me. But as soon as it's over, it's the most amazing feeling in the world,' she added wistfully.

'You must miss them,' Layla said softly as she spooned coffee into the cups.

'More than I ever thought possible.' Amy sighed. 'And it's been ten times worse since I came off the drugs. I'm guessing you and Steve know about that?'

'A bit.' Layla shrugged. 'None of my business.'

'I'm not proud of what I did,' Amy told her. 'And if I could turn back time . . .' She trailed off and stared down at her feet.

Layla saw her bite down on her lip and guessed that she was struggling to hold it together. 'Look, why don't you have your coffee, then get a shower?' she suggested. 'I put a wash on while you were sleeping, so your clothes are nice and fresh. And, when you feel like it, we can talk. But only if you want to.'

'Why are you being so kind? You don't even know me.'

'No, but Steve does, and I trust his judgement.'

A tear trickled down Amy's cheek and she quickly swiped it away. 'God, you're nice. No wonder he loves you so much.'

'Oh, don't worry, he knows how lucky he is.' Layla chuckled, handing one of the coffees to her.

Amy sipped it and looked at Layla over the rim of her cup. Her stomach was huge, and her ankles were bloated, but her face was beautiful, and Amy guessed that she was stunning without the baby weight. Gorgeous, genuinely lovely, and to cap it all she'd bagged herself a wonderful man who clearly worshipped the ground she walked on. Amy would have hated her if she didn't already envy and like her.

Layla gave a curious smile when she noticed Amy staring at her. 'Are you okay?'

'Yeah, fine.' Amy shook herself out of it. 'Sorry, I was miles away. Do you mind if I go and take that shower?'

'Help yourself,' said Layla. 'There's a clean towel on the rail. Oh, and try that shampoo on the shelf – it's to *die* for.'

When Steve came home a short time later, he paused in the living-room doorway and frowned when he saw Layla alone in there. 'Let me guess . . . she did a runner?' He peered around with narrowed eyes. 'What did she take?'

'Sshhh!' Layla put a finger to her lips, then pointed at the door. 'She had a shower, and now she's making a brew. Oh, and she wants to cook dinner tonight,' she added with a smile. 'To thank us for letting her stay.'

'Oh, right.' Steve looked suitably contrite as he put down the shopping bags and sat down. 'I just thought . . . Well, you know what I thought. How's she been?'

'Bit subdued. But it's to be expected, considering what she's been going through.'

'Why, what's she said?'

'You need to talk to her,' Layla said quietly. 'She only told me a bit, but her side of the story is nothing like Mark's version.'

They stopped talking when Amy walked in, and Steve smiled up at her. 'I believe we're going to have the pleasure of your cooking tonight?'

'It's been a while, so you might not think it's such a pleasure when you taste it,' said Amy, putting two cups of coffee down on the table. 'I heard you coming in, so I made you one. Hope you still take two sugars?'

'Yes, he does. And I'm sure whatever you make will be lovely,' said Layla, standing up. 'Now, if you'll excuse me, I need a wee.'

She touched Steve's shoulder as she walked past the couch, and gave a surreptitious nod in Amy's direction.

Steve grinned at Amy when she'd gone. 'Think that's her subtle way of saying we should talk.'

Amy smiled and twisted her wedding ring around on her finger. She felt shy all of a sudden, and that was weird because she'd known Steve for ever. But having spent a bit of time with his wife, she'd realised that she didn't really *know* him any more. It wasn't just the house that was new, his whole life seemed to have changed. He was a married man now, with a beautiful wife, and a baby on the way. But one thing definitely hadn't changed: he was still rock solid, reliable, honest and lovely.

Steve had been watching Amy closely as she sank into her thoughts, and it saddened him to see how troubled she looked. The Amy he knew had been feisty and bubbly, and more than capable of dealing with whatever life threw at her. Hell, she'd survived all the shit Mark had put her through during their ill-fated marriage when lesser women would have crumbled. But the light seemed to have been extinguished from her eyes and there was an air of hopelessness about her, as if she'd taken as much as she could take and was just waiting for the final blow.

'Want to tell me what's been going on?' he asked, his voice soft and low.

Amy gave a non-committal shrug and gazed down at her entwined hands. She'd already said too much to Layla, and she didn't want to drag Steve into the mess.

'At least tell me about last night,' Steve persisted, sensing that he was going to have to drag it out of her slowly and gently. 'You don't have to go into detail if you don't want to, but I can't get it out of my head that you tried to get yourself killed. Is it really that bad?'

Amy's eyes flooded with tears. Steve saw them and reached for her hand. 'Look, we're mates, so anything you say to me *stays* with me. I'm not an idiot. I know you're scared of something – or someone. Is it Mark? Has he been hassling you?'

'No.' Amy shook her head and swiped at a tear. 'I haven't spoken to him in months.'

'Well, is it your boyfriend, then?' Steve probed. 'Mark told me you were seeing someone. Has it finished? Is that what's up? 'Cos you know no man's worth trying to kill yourself over, don't you?'

'Oh, God,' Amy moaned. 'Stop being so nice to me, I don't deserve it.'

'Why?' Steve frowned. 'What have you done that's so bad? If you're talking about the drugs, we've all dabbled. That doesn't make you a bad person.'

'You don't know the half of it,' Amy said in a whisper.

'I know *you*,' said Steve. 'And I know you're not the kind of girl to do what you've done without a bloody good reason. You love your kids too much.'

The mention of the children broke the dam, and when the floodgates opened in earnest Steve pulled Amy into his arms and rocked her. 'Talk to me,' he urged. 'Let me help you.'

Amy hadn't told even Kelvin half of what came pouring out now. But Steve had always had the power to make her feel safe, and before she knew it she had told him everything, from Mark borrowing the money and running away, to Yates shifting the debt onto her and making her work the streets, to him getting her hooked on smack and setting her up in the brothel, to the fire and Kelvin getting shot.

'A girl I thought I could trust told Yates where I'd been staying last night,' she finished. 'And I knew he was never going to give up, so I decided to put an end to it before he caught up with me.'

'Why didn't you come to me?' Steve asked, his broad chest heaving with the rage he was struggling to contain.

'I didn't want to get you involved,' Amy told him. 'Anyway, I was too ashamed.'

'You had no reason to be ashamed. None of this was your fault. I could kill Mark.'

'It's not his fault. Not all of it. He didn't know what was happening after he left – I never told him.'

'He shouldn't have put you in that position in the first place,' said Steve angrily. 'And after what you've been through, there's no way you should be defending him. He took your kids off you and made everyone think it was your fault. Shit, even *I* thought they were better off with him. Some mate I am.'

Feeling stronger now that she'd got it all off her chest, Amy said, 'Don't feel guilty. Everyone else has turned on me, but you brought me home and gave me a bed for the night even though you thought all that stuff was true. And Layla doesn't even know me, but she's been brilliant. You both have.'

'I'm still sorry for taking Mark's word as gospel without even asking you,' said Steve. 'I should have known something was wrong. But now I do know, I'm going to make sure no one ever hurts you like that again.'

Amy sighed, and pulled herself out of his arms. 'That's what Kelvin said, and look what happened to him,' she murmured, wiping her eyes. 'I'd never forgive myself if you and Layla got hurt. It's best I just go.'

'You're going nowhere,' Layla said firmly, walking into the room just then and sitting on the other side of Amy. 'Sorry, I wasn't eavesdropping, but I heard some of what you were saying, and I'm with Steve . . . this isn't your fault.'

'It doesn't matter whose fault it is any more,' Amy said wearily. 'It's gone way past that. Yates thinks he owns me, and I got away, so now he wants me dead. I just thank God he doesn't know where Cassie is. But she'll be safe as long as the social services are involved, 'cos he won't go near the authorities.'

Steve and Layla exchanged a hooded glance. Amy saw it and frowned. 'What?'

'The social services have closed the case,' Steve told her. 'Now that Mark and Jenny have set the date, they reckoned they didn't need any more intervention. They said they'd reassess if you decided to get back in touch, but they're in the clear for now.'

'Oh, God,' Amy murmured, fear leaping into her eyes. 'They'll be in danger if Yates finds out. He'll get at Cassie to get to me.'

'I'm sure they'll be fine.' Layla patted Amy's hand reassuringly. 'Mark would never let any harm come to them.'

'Mark's terrified of Yates,' Amy reminded her. 'He won't be able to stop him. No one can. He's a maniac.'

'Sounds more like a bully to me,' Layla said dismissively. 'And bullies are only strong when they're threatening vulnerable people. The police would soon sort him out.'

'You don't know what he's like. He's not scared of anyone.'

'I'm sure if the police heard about the gun they'd soon pick him up.'

'No, Amy's right,' Steve interjected. 'Knowing the police, they'll go wading in and cock it up. Then he'll know they're onto him and he'll have nothing to lose. Probably best to try and sort it out ourselves.'

'How?' Layla gave him a worried look. '*You* can't go after him.'

'I'll think of something,' Steve said quietly. 'Till then, Amy stays here. And I'll have a word with Mark – warn him to keep a close eye on the kids.'

34

Mark had never been so bored. The wedding was still three weeks away, but Jenny had been like a woman possessed for months and it was seriously doing his head in. He wouldn't have minded so much if he actually *wanted* to get married again, but he just couldn't summon up any excitement, and the dread increased as the day drew ever nearer. He was sure he had an ulcer, because he seemed to have constant stomach ache. Then again, it was probably a reaction to all the ibuprofen he'd been taking to tackle the constant headaches.

It was said that getting married was one of the most stressful things you could do in life and, boy, was he finding that out the hard way. He didn't remember feeling half as stressed in the run-up to his and Amy's wedding, but he'd only been a kid that time and had treated it all like a big party, little knowing how bad things were going to get after the partying stopped. Now he knew *exactly* what to expect, and he was dreading it.

Jenny, however, seemed to have no such worries about the future, and she was going all out to make this wedding as spectacular as possible. Although why she was bothering, considering no one from her side was coming apart from two dorky old schoolmates and a couple of batty old aunts who hadn't even confirmed yet, Mark had no idea. His side wasn't exactly going to be packed out, either; just his mum, a handful of aunts, uncles and cousins, and some of his mates and their birds. But the way Jenny was going on, anyone would have thought they were catering for half of Manchester. Everything had to be just so, from the reception venue, to the choice of starters and mains, to the ridiculously expensive dress she'd set her heart on.

The dress was a real bone of contention for Mark. It was going to cost more than the rest of it put together, but every time he asked where the money was coming from Jenny fobbed him off and changed the subject. He had a horrible feeling she'd got herself another credit card behind his back, but he'd searched all the drawers for statements and hadn't found anything. Jenny kept telling him not to worry about it, but that just worried him even more, because he just knew it was all going to come crashing down around his ears once the day was done and reality set in.

'Mark!' Jenny's voice cut into his thoughts. '*Mark!* Are you listening to me?'

'Uh?' He looked up at her.

'I said, what do you think?'

'Of what?'

'Your daughter's dress.' Jenny pushed the child forward. 'You don't think it's too long?'

'It's fine,' Mark said with absolute lack of interest. The dressmaker had been here for two hours now, measuring and snipping and sewing, and he'd long ago switched off from it all.

'It hurts my neck,' Cassie mumbled tearfully.

'Oh, stop being such a mard.' Jenny tutted and turned the girl roughly back around. 'You're just sulking because you wanted pink and I chose peach. But this isn't about you, it's about me.'

'She said it hurts her neck,' Mark said protectively. 'She didn't mention the colour.'

'No, but that's what she meant,' Jenny countered, smiling as if she wasn't really annoyed about it. 'I know, 'cos I'm the one who's had to put up with her tantrums while you've been out having fun with your mates. But not to worry, she'll be happy on the day. Won't you, darling?'

When she smiled down at Cassie now, the little girl shivered and nodded.

'Good, that's sorted, then,' Mark said, standing up.

'Where are you going?' Jenny frowned when he picked up his jacket and slipped it on. 'Maggie needs to take your measurements.'

'No, she doesn't. I'm hiring that suit I looked at last week. See you in a bit.'

'Can I come, Daddy?' Cassie gave him an imploring look.

'Nah, best you stay here,' said Mark. 'Bobby will be awake in a bit, and he'll only cry if you're not here.'

Cassie's chin quivered, but she said no more.

Jenny followed Mark out into the hall and pulled the door shut. 'You promised to stay in today, so where are you going?'

'I need some fags,' Mark told her, trotting down the stairs. 'And I've got a headache, so I wanted to get a bit of air.'

'Can't it wait?'

'No, I'm gagging. Anyway, I thought I wasn't supposed to see the dress before the day.'

'No, but . . .'

'But nothing. Unless you *want* to jinx it?' Smiling when Jenny shook her head, Mark pulled the front door open. 'Won't be long.'

'You'd better not be,' Jenny warned. 'You've been out every

night this week, and I'm starting to think you only want me as a nanny.'

'Don't be stupid.' Mark frowned. 'Where's all this coming from? Are you due on, or something?'

'No, I'm just worried you're not taking this seriously,' Jenny said sulkily. 'You're treating me like you used to treat Amy, and I don't like it.'

'Am I hell,' Mark sneered, stepping out onto the path. 'Anyhow, hadn't you best get back to Widow Twanky before she messes about with your colour scheme?'

Jenny gritted her teeth and clenched her fists when he turned and walked away. She felt like slamming the door and kicking it, but pride refused to allow her to reveal that they weren't quite the perfect family she'd made them out to be. So she took a deep breath and reminded herself that Mark was probably just suffering last-minute nerves. His and Amy's wedding had been a farce, so it was understandable that he would be reluctant to get involved in the preparations of this one for fear of history repeating itself. He was only a man, after all, and everyone knew that women were the true force behind the marital throne. All she had to do was put her plans into place, and then lead him through the event by the metaphorical dog collar.

But woe betide that little bitch of a daughter of his if she dared to try and put the mockers on it. She never misbehaved when Mark was out, but the minute he was around she seemed to think she could act up and nothing would come of it. Well, if she thought she was getting away with today's little stunt, she was wrong. The dress hurt her neck, did it? Just wait till the dressmaker had gone . . . Jenny would give her something to make her forget all about that other little pain.

And the same would go for Bobby if he dared to wreck

his suit trousers on the day by soiling himself. Mark might keep excusing the little moron, but Jenny knew he was doing it on purpose, and if he carried on . . .

Well, he'd better not, that was all.

Mark had forgotten to take his mobile phone, and it was ringing when Jenny walked back into the front room. She picked it up and smiled at the dressmaker when she saw the name on the screen. 'It's Mark's friend. Won't be a minute.'

She walked back out into the hall to answer it, but it went to voicemail before she had a chance. Ordinarily, she'd have left it for Mark to pick up, but curiosity got the better of her as it occurred to her that it might be something to do with the stag party Steve was supposed to be organising. Mark had assured her that it would be just a few of the lads going out for a quiet drink, but she had a sneaking suspicion that his loutish friends might have lined up a stripper. And if Steve mentioned it now, there would be no stag – full stop.

'Mark, it's me,' Steve's message began. 'I've been talking to Amy and she's a bit worried about the kids. Give us a ring when you get this and I'll bring you up to speed. Till then, just keep an eye on them, yeah?'

Jenny's nostrils were flaring when the message finished, and her teeth were so tightly clenched it made her jaw ache. The bitch! How *dare* she think she could walk back into their lives after all this time. And right before the wedding, too. No, it wasn't happening. Jenny had to get rid of her before she threw a spanner into the works.

Chin raised, Jenny went back into the front room and put Mark's phone back where it had been before reaching for her own. 'Just need to make a quick call,' she told the dressmaker who was adjusting the straps on Cassie's dress. 'Then I'm all yours.'

35

Yates leaned forward in his seat and tipped a thick line of coke onto the coffee table. It was the first time he'd been back to his flat in days, and it reeked of stale smoke and sweat. It was cold, too, and a gang of flies kept dive-bombing him as if he'd intruded on their territory. He slammed his fist down on one that landed next to his line, and snorted the powder up through a rolled-tenner straw. His eyes immediately started to water, and he threw his head back to wait for the acrid burn in his nose and throat to ease.

He felt like he had a ticking bomb inside his head, and he needed it to explode so that he could think clearly again. The pressure had been building for weeks, but after missing Amy last night it had swelled to the extent that there was no room in his mind for anything else. The only thing that would relieve it was to get his hands on her, but he'd had Keith drive him around for ages last night only to find that she had vanished into thin air, and his rage had escalated to blind fury to think that she had escaped him again.

Forced to stop the hunt when a cop car started following them, he'd had Keith drop him off at Marnie's. But, too wired to sleep properly, he had tossed and turned all night and had woken in an even more foul mood this morning. Almost losing it when Marnie started nagging him for staying out so late again, he'd picked his car up and come back to the flat to get his head together. But several hours and numerous lines of coke later, he was no less angry.

Keith had been right when he'd accused him of having fallen for Amy. He'd denied it at the time, and had even tried to convince himself that it wasn't true. But it was, and it infuriated him that he'd been so weak. Blonde, blue-eyed and feisty, Amy was exactly the kind of girl he'd always fantasised about. Their courtship had been short, and it might have appeared at times as if he was being overly rough on her. But she ought to have known that it would have got better if she'd just stopped fighting him. He'd have given her the world, and maybe then it would have been *her* who was carrying his child now instead of that slapper Marnie.

But no . . .

Like every other pretty girl he'd tried to be nice to in the past, Amy had chucked his kindness back at him and spat in his face.

'*That's what you get for aiming too high, you spazzy little mutt.*'

'Fuck you!' Yates muttered, gritting his teeth when his mother's voice piped up in his head.

'*Fuck you back,*' she sneered. '*All you'll ever get is a mong what no one else wants. You'll be lucky if a prozzie opens her legs for ya, never mind a proper woman. You wanna go down the mental hospital and find yourself a retard, 'cos that's all you're fit for . . .*'

Yates leapt up from his seat and paced the room. He'd heard those words a million times throughout his childhood, and if anyone else had taunted him like that he'd have cut them to pieces. But she was his ma, so he'd taken his anger out on his schoolmates instead. And his teachers, and neighbours and coppers . . . Anyone, in fact, who got in his face and tried to make him feel as small as his ma had made him feel.

And now Amy had picked up the flaming stick that his ma had dropped when she died, and she'd been burning the fuck out of him with it ever since. Verbal abuse was water off a duck's back to a man like him, who didn't give a flying fuck what people thought of him. But when someone he'd been nice to looked at him the way Amy frequently had, it formed scars on his heart; scars that bled and wept and demanded vengeance.

He needed to hurt someone.

Since all this shit had been going on with Amy, Marnie and the baby, he'd been letting things slide, and a few of his debtors had obviously taken it as a sign that he wasn't arsed if they were late with their repayments. But he was done with being mugged off. It was time to show the fuckers what was what.

He'd switched his phone off after leaving Marnie's, but he yanked it out of his pocket now and switched it back on to ring Keith and tell him to get ready to do some business. There were ten missed calls, and several messages. Assuming them all to be from Marnie, Yates was about to dismiss them, but he hesitated when he saw that one of the missed calls was from somebody he hadn't expected to hear from. Eyes narrowed, he forgot all about Keith and rang the number back.

Ten minutes later, Jenny had just shown the dressmaker out and was making her way back up the stairs to punish Cassie for her disobedience when a knock came at the front door. Irritated to have been disturbed, she trotted back down the stairs, fully expecting it to be the dressmaker having forgotten something. Face paling when she saw who was standing on the step, she glanced nervously out at the road beyond.

'What are you doing here? Mark could be back any minute.'

'And?' said Yates, walking in uninvited.

'You can't come in,' Jenny protested as he started making his way up the stairs. 'Please, Uncle Lenny, you promised not to come round here again without calling first. If Mark finds out, he'll call off the wedding.'

'No, he won't,' Yates called back over his shoulder. 'Not if he knows what's good for him.'

He walked into the living room now, and smiled when he saw Cassie sitting as stiff as a board on the edge of the couch.

'There's my girl. Come and give your Uncle Lenny a kiss.'

Cassie gazed nervously up at Jenny who had just followed him in. Jenny nodded and flapped her hand, muttering, 'Hurry up before your dad gets back.'

Cassie reluctantly went to Yates. He'd called round a few times since they had been living here, always when her daddy was out, and Jenny had warned her in no uncertain terms what would happen if she ever mentioned his visits. He always made Cassie kiss him and sit on his knee, which she didn't like because he was ugly and his breath smelled horrible. And he made her feel funny inside – in a really, really bad way. But she was too scared to disobey, so she quickly kissed him now and then scuttled back to her seat.

'You've got to go,' Jenny insisted. 'Mark only went out for fags, and I don't know anything more than I've already told you.'

'You didn't tell me the address,' said Yates, sitting beside Cassie and patting his knee.

'I don't *know* it,' said Jenny, frowning when Cassie reluctantly moved onto his lap. 'He moved out of his flat a couple of months ago, and I haven't been invited to the new house yet. I'm sure you'll find him if you ask around, but you've got to go.'

'Not until I get what I came for,' said Yates. 'And if you can't tell me, I'll just wait and get it off your man instead.'

An icy hand gripped Jenny's stomach. 'You can't ask Mark. He'll know I told you.'

'Not my problem.' Yates shrugged. 'We had a deal, but it seems to me the only one who's benefitted so far is you. You said you'd find out where she is, but you ain't even bothered looking, have you?'

'No one's heard from her before today or I'd have told you,' Jenny argued. 'I rang as soon as I heard she'd been talking to Steve – what more could I do?' She bit her lip nervously now and glanced at the clock on the wall. 'Look, why don't you go home? As soon as Mark gets back, I'll get Steve's address off him and text it to you.'

Yates curled his lip and shook his head. 'Nah. I'll wait.'

'You'd better not hurt him,' Jenny said quietly. 'I mean it, Uncle Lenny. This is all I've ever wanted, and I won't let you ruin it.'

Yates laughed softly and turned his attention to the little girl on his knee. 'So, how's my little princess?' he crooned, stroking her long hair. 'Missed me, have you?'

Cassie flinched and gazed down at her hands. Jenny was nervous about her daddy coming home and finding Uncle Lenny here, and Cassie didn't want to get into trouble if she was caught sitting on his knee. She wished Bobby would wake up. Jenny hated having to look after him, so if he woke up she would send Cassie into the bedroom to keep him quiet. But he always slept for a long, long time when Jenny gave him his special medicine, so he probably wouldn't.

Yates spotted something on the back of Cassie's arm and narrowed his eyes. 'Did you do this?' he demanded, glaring up at his niece.

'What?' Jenny frowned. Then, blushing guiltily when she

saw the line of fingertip-sized bruises she'd left behind after dragging the child into the bedroom the previous night, she folded her arms defensively. 'I didn't do it on purpose, if that's what you mean. She was having a tantrum and I was trying to calm her down.'

'You'd best not be lying,' Yates warned quietly. 'If I find out you've been battering her . . .'

'Course I haven't,' Jenny lied. 'But what do you care, anyway? You messed about with me when I was her age, so why should she be any different? Or are you trying to say she's more special than me?'

A slow grin spread across Yates's face. 'You always was a jealous little fucker. Ain't changed much, have you?'

Annoyed that he was taking the piss out of her, Jenny's eyes flashed with anger. 'Look, you've got to go,' she repeated firmly. 'I'll talk to Mark when he gets home, but if he finds you've been here and finishes with me I'll never forgive you. And before you start threatening me, just remember that I know enough to get you put away for life.'

Caught in the middle when the adults locked stares above her head, Cassie held her breath as the animosity pressed down on her like a physical blanket. She was relieved when Yates broke the stare after several agonising moments and chuckled softly, but fear coursed through her when he put a tight arm around her waist and stood up.

'What are you doing?' Jenny gasped, bravado gone in a flash when he started walking towards the door. 'You can't take her. What will I tell Mark?'

'About what?' Mark asked, walking in just then. It had started raining while he was out, and he was too busy shaking his wet hair to see who Jenny was talking to when he first entered the room. But when he looked up and saw Yates, his face drained of colour. 'W-why are you here? I thought you said we were straight?'

'*Daddy!*' Cassie squealed, reaching out her arms for him to rescue her.

But Mark didn't move; he was too busy staring at Yates.

'Ask your woman.' Yates nodded towards Jenny as he tightened his grip on the struggling child.

'He just wants to know where Amy is,' Jenny spluttered, wringing her hands when Mark turned to her. 'Just tell him, then he'll go.'

'I don't know where she is,' Mark said truthfully. 'I haven't heard from her in months.'

'No, but your mate Steve has,' said Yates.

'He called while you were out,' Jenny explained, her cheeks flaming when Mark looked at her again. 'He said he'd been talking to Amy and wanted to speak to you about it.'

A deep frown of confusion drew Mark's eyebrows together. But when realisation suddenly flared in his eyes and he gave Jenny an accusing stare, Yates grinned, and said, 'Give the monkey a nut. Now, enough of the yadda-yadda. Give us your mate's address and I'll leave youse to it. Oh, and just in case you get any bright ideas about warning him I'm on my way, I'll be taking the little one along for the ride.'

Mark felt as if the wind had been kicked out of him, and the room went into a spin. 'You can't,' he croaked. 'She's only little. She'll be scared.'

'Oh, don't you worry, Cassie knows her Uncle Lenny will look after her – don't you, darlin'? We're good pals, me and you, aren't we?'

'I'll take you,' Mark blurted out, desperate to get his daughter away from the man. 'Just leave Cass here with Jenny.'

'Nah, I don't think so.' Yates shook his head. 'I'm sick of being given the runaround, but this should fetch her out of hiding.'

'Look, whatever's going on with you and Amy it's got nothing to do with me,' Mark argued. 'Anyhow, she hasn't bothered with the kids in months, so she's not gonna care about them now, is she?'

'We'll soon find out, won't we?' said Yates. 'Address?'

Mark's breath felt harsh in his chest. Cassie was crying hysterically by now, and he was ashamed of himself for being so weak. Inhaling deeply for courage, he said, 'I'm not telling you anything until you put Cassie down. You can do what you want to me, but I won't let you hurt her.'

Yates gave an amused snort. 'Bit late in the day to come the big man, don't you think?'

'That's the deal.' Mark stood his ground. 'Put her down, and I'll tell you where Steve lives.'

'How's about I *don't* put her down, and you tell me anyway,' said Yates, pulling the gun out of his pocket and pressing the tip of the barrel against Cassie's temple.

When she started screaming, a thudding sound came up through the floor, and the old man who lived below shouted: 'Stop all that noise or I'm calling the police! Do you hear me? I'm calling the police!'

'Uncle Lenny, just go,' Jenny implored. '*Please!* You're just going to get us all into trouble.'

Yates threw a hand over Cassie's mouth to silence her and looked at Mark. 'Right, I'm off. But she's coming with me, and if you want her back in one piece you'd best tell your mate to send Amy to me.'

'Where will you be?' Mark asked sickly.

'She'll know,' said Yates. 'And don't get any funny ideas

about coming with her, 'cos if you, your mate or the pigs come anywhere near, the kid gets it. You've been warned.'

He carried Cassie out of the room now and down the stairs. When the front door slammed shut behind him, Mark turned on Jenny.

'Why the fuck did you tell him about Steve's call?'

'I had to,' Jenny spluttered, clutching at his arm. 'Don't worry, he won't hurt Cass. He just wants to bring Amy out of hiding.'

'Get off!' Mark snatched his arm away. 'This is your fault!'

'Just ring Steve and tell him what Lenny wants,' said Jenny. 'Then he'll give Cassie back and we can go back to normal.'

'Are you mad?' Mark seized her by the shoulders and shook her roughly. 'He held a gun to my daughter's *head*!'

'Stop it, you're scaring me,' Jenny protested, tears springing into her eyes. 'I love you – I'd never let him hurt you.'

Her words pierced the haze of rage and confusion in Mark's mind, and he took a step back. She wasn't the slightest bit concerned about Cassie, all she was bothered about was him. And something else was niggling at him, too.

'You called him uncle,' he said as his jumbled thoughts began to slot into place. 'But back at the start, you said he was just a family friend and I wasn't to tell him you sent me to him. What's going on?'

'Nothing,' Jenny snivelled. 'It's not like we're close, or anything. He – he just helps me out every now and then. And he promised he wouldn't hurt you, as long as I kept you away from *her*.'

'Oh, my God!' Mark stared at her in disbelief and disgust. 'You must have had it planned all along. You sent me to him, *knowing* what he'd do if I messed up. I bet you even told him to beat the shit out of me so I'd leave Amy and move in with you.'

'Of course I didn't,' Jenny protested. 'I wasn't to know you'd mess up your repayments.'

'You'd have had a fair idea,' countered Mark. 'You knew I was a fuck-up where money was concerned, so it was only a matter of time. Jeezus, I can't believe I've been so stupid.'

'This isn't my fault,' Jenny cried, reaching for his hand. 'All I've ever done is try to help you. Amy was never right for you, and if you'd been with me in the first place, none of this would have happened. I've loved you all my life. We were meant to be together.'

'Get away from me, you freak!' Mark pushed her away roughly.

'I know you're angry,' said Jenny, desperately trying to calm things down. 'But it'll all blow over once he's seen Amy, I promise. And if you're worried about Cassie, I'll talk to him, make him bring her home. He'll listen to me.'

'If he touches one hair on her head, I'll kill you,' Mark said icily. Then, turning, he marched towards the door.

'Where are you going?' Jenny cried, running after him. 'You can't go to *her*! I won't let you.'

'Get out of my way before I do something I regret,' Mark warned when she positioned herself between him and the door to prevent him from leaving.

'What about Bobby?' said Jenny. 'You can't just go out and leave him.'

'He's asleep,' Mark reminded her. 'And considering what you've done, the least you can do is watch him till I get back. But I won't be stopping when I do,' he added coldly. 'So don't bother acting like everything's all right, 'cos it ain't.'

He threw her aside now, and stormed out.

36

Amy hadn't seen Mark since that awful day at the court months earlier when he'd been granted provisional custody of the kids, so when he walked into Steve and Layla's front room now her heart skipped several beats. He was as handsome as ever, but she could see from the dark shadows beneath his eyes that full-time parenting hadn't been a breeze. He had only been doing what she'd had to do on her own before he took them away from her, but she hoped it hadn't been as hard on the kids as it had apparently been on him.

'Got my message, then, did you?' Steve said, waving for him to sit down. 'Sorry it was so vague, but I didn't want to say too much in case Jenny picked it up.'

'She did,' said Mark, staying on his feet. 'And it's kicked off good style.'

'Sorry,' Amy murmured, misunderstanding him. 'I didn't mean to cause trouble between you, I just wanted to make sure the kids were okay. There's things going on that you don't—'

'He's got Cass,' Mark blurted out before she could finish. 'And he says he'll only give her back if you go to him.'

'What?' Amy gasped. '*No!* Please, God, no!'

'Jenny reckons he won't hurt her,' Mark went on. 'But he's got a gun, and I'm scared what he might do if he doesn't see you. You'll have to go to him. He says you'll know where to find him.'

'Let's go . . .' Steve was already pulling his jacket on. 'I'll drive.'

'No, she's got to go alone,' Mark told him. 'He said he'll kill Cass if anyone else goes near.'

'And he'll kill Amy if he gets his hands on her,' said Layla.

'No, he won't, he just wants to see her,' argued Mark. He turned to Amy now and gave her a pleading look. 'I don't know what's going on with you and him, and I don't really care, but you're the only one who can stop him.'

'No, you don't know what's been going on, do you?' Steve interjected angrily, unable to keep his thoughts to himself any longer. 'He's been beating the shit out of her and forcing her to sell herself, and now you want her to go and face him on her own?'

'I should never have left,' Amy murmured guiltily. 'He said he'd get Cassie if I did. This is all my fault.'

'Too right it is!' Mark turned on her angrily. 'You knew he'd do this, but you took off anyway? Christ, I knew you didn't give a shit about the kids, but that's low even for you.'

'Shut your mouth,' snapped Steve. 'It's not her fault, it's *yours*. You're the one who borrowed the fucking money and left her to pay it back. Did you think he was just going to forget about it and walk away?'

'She ain't the little innocent she's making out,' Mark shot back indignantly. 'She was shagging him before my side of the fucking bed was cold. It ain't *my* fault they've had a barney and he's pissed off with her.'

'Are you thick?' Steve roared. 'Haven't you listened to a word I've said? She wasn't sleeping with him 'cos she wanted to, he's been *raping* her.'

'Not according to Marnie and Gemma,' Mark yelled back. 'And they should know, seeing as they watched her sneaking him in over the back fence for months on end. Who does that if they've got nothing to hide?'

On the couch, her hands over her ears as the argument raged, Amy snapped and slammed her fists down on the cushions. 'Shut up, both of you! This is getting us nowhere.'

'Yeah, well, you shouldn't make out like I'm the bad one,' Mark muttered. '*They* might believe you, but they don't know what you're really like.'

'To be honest, I don't care what you think about me any more,' Amy told him wearily. 'I just want to find my daughter.'

'Can you think where he might have taken her?' Steve asked, swallowing the rage that had almost propelled him to smack his one-time best mate in the mouth.

'No.' Amy shook her head, her mind racing over various possibilities. 'I'm trying to remember where he's taken me in the last few months, but I was out of my head most of the time, so it's all hazy.'

'Well, you'd best hurry up and start thinking,' said Mark irritably. 'The longer he's got her, the more chance he'll have to hurt her.'

'Do you think I don't know that?' Amy glared at him. Then, standing, she marched towards the door.

'Where are you going?' Steve called after her. 'You're not going on your own – we're coming with you.'

'I just need the toilet,' she lied. 'I'll be back in a minute.'

Steve turned to Mark when she closed the door and shook his head. 'This is all your fault, this. You've got no fucking clue what you've done to that girl, have you?'

'What *I've* done to *her*?' Mark retorted indignantly. 'You saw the state of the kids when I took them.'

'What did you expect? You abandoned them! And now you've got the cheek to stand here and make out like—'

'Steve, she's going!' Layla interrupted, struggling to pull herself up out of her seat when she saw Amy running down the path. 'Quick, go after her!'

Aware that Steve and Mark would follow when they realised she had sneaked out, Amy ran down the road and hid in an alley until Steve's car had driven past. Then, zipping up Kelvin's freshly washed hoodie, she set off in the opposite direction. Yates had said that she would know where to find him, but she didn't have a clue. But she wasn't going to find him by standing there thinking about it.

As she walked, a cold feeling of finality began to settle over her. Mark had been her world since she was fourteen years of age, and even after everything that had happened because of him her heart had still ached at the sight of him. But he'd made it quite clear that he considered her responsible for all this, and that had killed off the last stupid bit of hope she'd been harbouring of them getting back together in the future. Whatever happened now – if she even managed to get out of this alive – there was no going back. Mark was as dead to her as she had obviously been to him for the last few months.

37

Cassie's tear-swollen eyes were stinging from the effort of trying to keep them open. Uncle Lenny had taken her to his flat after leaving Jenny's and they had stayed there for ages, which had been horrible because it smelled bad and there were flies everywhere.

He had been nice to her to start with, giving her a can of Coke and a packet of crisps, and putting the TV on so she could watch cartoons while he smoked his strange-smelling cigarettes and sniffed his medicine powder. But, after a few hours of constantly getting up to look out of the window, he'd started to pace up and down the room and talk to himself. And that had scared Cassie, so she had tried to shrink herself into the corner of his dirty couch in the hope that he might forget she was there.

But he hadn't forgotten, and when it started to get dark he'd taken her back down to the car and driven her here. Although she hadn't realised where *here* was until they reached the house, because he'd parked a few streets away and made her walk through the field before lifting her over the back fence. *Then* she'd known, and her heart had soared at the sight of Bobby's old bike sitting where he'd left it in the middle of the overgrown grass alongside her old skipping rope and headless Barbie doll. But the joy had quickly turned to sorrow when Yates opened the back door and pushed her inside.

In her dreams, Cassie always saw the house as it had been back when they were still a family. But the reality was shockingly different from those happy memories. It smelled even worse than Yates's flat and, as dark as it was, she could see heaps of rubbish everywhere she looked. And without electric or gas, there was no TV to watch, or heating to take the chill off. But, after telling her to lie on the sofa, Uncle Lenny had brought down the quilt off her mum's bed and covered her with it, so at least she was warm now.

As the faint, almost forgotten scent of her mother rose to her nostrils now, she lost the battle to stay awake and Yates, whose eyes had long ago adjusted to the dark, smiled to himself when he saw that she'd fallen asleep.

It wouldn't be long now.

He'd made a mistake going to his own flat, but he'd forgotten that Amy had never actually been there. Still, she'd find him now, he was sure, because mothers were like that. Where their children were concerned, they had an inbuilt radar. At least, *decent* mothers did. The alkie bitch *he*'d been cursed with wouldn't have spat on him if he'd been rolling on the floor in front of her with flames coming out of his eyes. But Amy loved her kids, so it wouldn't be long.

Amy's legs felt like jelly by the time she reached the house. She'd been walking around all day, and had just about given up on ever finding Yates.

After leaving Steve's place she'd gone to Levenshulme, to see if anyone at *Hawaii* had seen him or heard from him. It had been closed, so she had gone to Moss Side instead, to The Beehive pub where Mark had told her he'd first met Yates. Nobody there knew where he lived – or, at least, they weren't about to tell her if they did. So, from there, she'd

walked aimlessly around the streets of Moss Side in the hope
that Yates might drive past and see her. But he hadn't. So
now, finally, she had come home. Not because she expected
Yates to be here, but to ask Marnie if *she* knew where he
might be.

As she was walking past her own house en route to Marnie's,
a movement at her living-room window caught her eye and,
even though she couldn't see him, she instinctively knew that
it was Yates.

Heart in her mouth, she turned and walked up the path.

Yates opened the door before she reached it and stepped
aside to let her in before closing it again – quietly, so as not
to alert the neighbours that something was going on. Then,
turning to face her in the dark hall, he peered at her closely,
a mess of conflicting emotions raging through him.

He knew she was scared: he could feel it and smell it. But
there was a glimmer of defiance in her eyes, and her chin
was raised as if she was ready for a fight. It was as if the old
feistiness which had first attracted him to her had returned,
and that excited him.

But it didn't mean he was going to let her get away with
making a fool of him.

'So, the wanderer returns,' he said, grinning nastily as he
took a step towards her. 'What've you got to say for yourself?'

Amy forced herself not to flinch as his breath enveloped
her face. Her instincts, which had been dulled for so long,
were sparking back to life with a vengeance. She sensed
that he wanted to punish her for escaping him, but the
fact that he hadn't yet made a move made her wonder if
she might not be able to turn the situation around. It would
be tricky, because he wasn't stable at the best of times,

but even if he ended up killing her, she had to try – for Cassie's sake.

'I had to get away,' she told him quietly. 'My head was messed up, and I needed to sort it out.'

'Is that right?' Yates drawled. 'And you really thought I'd just let you walk out on me?'

'No, I knew you'd find me,' said Amy, keeping her voice even and calm. 'But I had to get straight, or I wouldn't have stood a chance.'

'A chance to what?' Yates narrowed his eyes. He'd been waiting for this moment for weeks, had dreamed of torturing her and making her beg for mercy. But she was acting as if she was here of her own free will, and that threw him.

'To sort this mess out,' said Amy, choosing her words carefully because she sensed that she was only going to get one shot at this. 'I've been doing a lot of thinking since I left, and I kind of understand why you got so mad at me. You were good to me after Mark left, and I was horrible to you. But you should have given me a bit more time.'

'For what?'

'I don't know.' Amy shrugged. 'To get to know you, I suppose. Mark's the only lad I'd ever been with before you, and I felt guilty.'

'He cheated on you,' Yates reminded her. She sounded sincere, but no one had ever been truly sincere towards him before, so he wasn't sure he could trust her.

'I know.' Amy sighed. 'But I don't care any more; I'm over him. So where do we go from here?'

'Are you fucking with me?' Yates was staring at her intently. ''Cos you know I don't like being fucked with, so if you are, you'd best quit while you're ahead.'

'I'm too tired for games,' Amy told him wearily. 'If you're

going to do something, just do it. I'm not going to fight you. I just want to see Cassie and make sure she's all right.'

'Course she's all right,' snapped Yates. 'What did you think I was gonna do to her?'

'I didn't mean it like that,' Amy replied quietly, annoyed with herself for upsetting the fragile balance she'd achieved. 'I just meant it's late, and she must be scared. She's not used to being away from her dad for so long.'

'Yeah, well, she's fine,' Yates muttered. 'Fast asleep.'

Amy licked her lips. 'Can – can I see her?'

Yates pursed his lips and carried on staring at her for several long moments. Then, jerking his chin towards the living-room door, he said, 'She's in there.'

'Thanks.' Amy gave him a tiny grateful smile.

Her eyes brimmed when she entered the room and saw her daughter's silhouetted shape beneath the quilt on the sofa. Treading carefully to avoid tripping on the rubbish that was strewn all around, she tiptoed across the floor and knelt beside her. It was the first time she'd seen her in months, and she couldn't believe how much she'd grown. This child and her brother owned Amy's heart, and she couldn't believe that she had put them at risk. But whatever happened next, she would make sure that no harm came to them. And if the price of keeping them safe was to offer herself to the devil body and soul, then that was what she would do.

Yates was standing over her. Turning her head, Amy gazed up at him with tears streaming down her cheeks and whispered, 'This is all I ever wanted, you know? That's why it didn't work out for us, 'cos it was killing me not to have them with me. But it's too late now,' she went on, regret thickening her voice. 'They belong with Mark now, not me.'

She turned and gazed down at Cassie again. Then, taking

a deep breath, she said, 'I'll come back, if that's what you want. And I promise I'll stay. But you've got to let her go home.'

'Why should I believe you?' Yates asked. 'What's to stop you from running off again the minute my back's turned?'

'What would be the point?' Amy asked. 'You'd only take her again.'

It was the wrong thing to say, and Yates switched in a flash.

'You don't really want to be with me at all,' he spat. 'You're only saying you'll stay to stop me from getting at *her*. I should have fucking known. You're all the same, you slags. Tell me what I want to hear, then shaft me the first chance you get. Well, fuck you if you think I'm falling for your lies.'

Amy realised that she'd messed up, but she had to try and rectify it before he went crazy. So, making a massive effort to keep the terror from her voice, she looked him in the eye and said, 'I'm not saying it's going to be easy, 'cos it isn't. You hurt me, and it'll take time for me to trust you again. If this is going to work, you've got to respect me. I don't want any more drugs, and I won't sleep with men for money again. If you want me, you've got to meet me halfway.'

The pressure was building in Yates's head again, and her words were bouncing around his brain like bullets. No woman had ever spoken to him like this before. Marnie never shut up, but everything she said was a lie designed to con money out of him. Amy was different. She always had been. That was why he'd had to break her the first time around: because she'd refused to give him a chance. But now she was offering what he'd wanted all along: the chance of a real relationship; just the two of them; no brats, and no lingering yearnings for her dickhead of an ex.

It could work.

'Dream on, you little mong . . . she hates you, just like the rest of 'em did . . . Just like I did . . . And if a ma can't love her own son, no one can!'

'Shut up,' Yates muttered, backing away from Amy. 'Just keep your fucking mouth shut and let me think.'

Amy nodded and turned back to Cassie, praying that he would say they could start over. It would be hell on Earth, but she owed it to the kids.

Behind her, Yates sat down and pulled his wrap of coke out of his pocket. Unable to wait, he tipped a heap onto the back of his hand and snorted it straight up his nostrils. It smashed into the back of his throat like a burning freight train, and he grimaced as the pain ripped through his head. But, seconds later, the fog cleared and he knew he was back in control.

'Get over here,' he ordered. 'And don't even think about saying no, or you know what'll happen.'

Amy squeezed her eyes shut as bile rose into her throat. Then, taking a deep breath, she said, 'Not here. Not in front of Cassie.'

Yates gritted his teeth and clenched his fists. But then, standing up, he said, 'All right, upstairs, then. And hurry up about it.'

38

In desperate need of a wee, Marnie paid the driver, hopped out of the cab and rushed inside the house.

She'd been pissed off when Lenny walked out on her that morning, and her mood had deepened as the day dragged on with no word from him. Karaoke always cheered her up, so she'd readily agreed when her sister had rung to ask if she wanted to go. But it hadn't cheered her up this time. If anything, it had made her feel worse.

She was barely even showing yet but she felt like a beached whale, and she was sick to death of feeling nauseous all the time. And she was obviously throwing off mumsy vibes already, because not one single bloke had given her the eye all night. Not even the pissed-up rugby players who had been groping everyone from her fat sister to the bog-eyed, buck-toothed barmaid. And, to cap it all, she hadn't even been able to have a proper drink, because her sister had gone all pregnancy-police on her.

After relieving herself, Marnie came back downstairs in search of alcohol to take the edge off her depression. But a faint sound when she walked into the living room stopped her in her tracks. Sure that it was coming from next door, she walked over to the wall that divided her house from Amy's and pressed her ear against it.

It sounded like a child crying, but how was that possible?

Amy hadn't been back to the house in weeks, and the kids had been living with Mark for the best part of a year.

But that was definitely a child she could hear. And it didn't seem like anyone was in any hurry to see what was wrong with it.

Curiosity getting the better of her, Marnie opened the door and tiptoed through the grass to take a peek through Amy's window. It was pitch dark in there, so she couldn't see anything. But she could hear the child even more clearly now.

She stepped over the small fence, walked up to Amy's door and knocked a couple of times. She got no answer, but the crying stopped abruptly, so she raised the letter-box flap and called: 'Amy . . . are you in there?'

When dead silence came back to her, she retreated back to her own house, wondering if she'd imagined it. Lenny talked to himself sometimes, as if he was having a conversation with someone invisible. Maybe it was a ghost?

Marnie tutted as the thought entered her head, and told herself to stop being so stupid. It was no ghost, it was definitely a real child she'd heard. And the only explanation she could think of was that Amy was back, and Mark must have let her have the kids for the night – and she'd gone back to her old tricks and left them on their own.

Angry now, she pulled her phone out of her bag and rang Amy's mobile. It was switched off, so she called Mark instead. It was possible that Amy was asleep and hadn't heard her knocking but, with her history, Marnie would rather be safe than sorry.

In a light sleep on Steve's couch, Mark was jolted awake by the sound of his phone ringing. They had hit a brick wall in their search for Amy earlier, and after several hours of driving around had decided to come back here and wait for Yates or Amy to contact them. Hoping that it was one of them now, he sat up and snatched his phone off the table.

'Mark, it's me,' Marnie said before he could speak. 'Sorry if I've disturbed you, and I hope you don't think I'm speaking out of turn, but I'm a bit worried.'

'Why, what's up?' Mark was wide awake now. 'Is it about Cassie? Have you seen her? Was Amy with her?'

'I haven't seen them,' said Marnie. 'But I've just heard Cass crying, and no one's answering the door. I'm not being funny, but if you've let Amy have her for the night, I think you'd best come and check on her.'

'What about Yates?' Mark asked, already pulling his jacket on. 'Have you seen him?'

'Why?' Suspicion leapt into Marnie's voice. 'What's he got to do with anything?'

'If Cassie's there, he is an' all,' said Mark, trotting up the stairs and tapping on Steve's bedroom door. He felt bad for disturbing them, because Layla had looked worn out when they got back. But if Marnie was right, he needed Steve to drive him over to the house.

Marnie had gone quiet, but Mark could hear the heaviness of her breathing as she digested what he'd just said.

'If you're saying what I think you're saying,' she said after a moment, 'I'll kill him!'

'Don't go round there!' Mark said sharply, guessing that that was exactly what she was about to do. 'Just stay out of this or Cassie might get hurt.'

Already at her door, Marnie hesitated. 'What you talking about?'

'He took Cassie earlier,' Mark explained, waving for Steve to follow him back down the stairs when his bleary-eyed friend came out of the bedroom. 'He said he'd let me have her back when he saw Amy. We thought she'd done a runner, but if they're in hers she must have found him. Just do me a favour and keep an eye on the house till I get there. Let me know if they leave.'

'Why should I?' Marnie protested. 'He's supposed to be with me now, so why shouldn't I go and kick the pair of their heads in?'

'Because he's got a gun!' Mark barked. 'And if you kick off, my daughter might get hurt. Just stay out of it until I've got Cassie out, then you can do what the fuck you want.'

Mark cut the call now and turned to Steve.

'They're at the old house. Get your keys.'

Marnie couldn't settle after talking to Mark. Her mind was reeling, and her stomach was so tightly clenched that she felt sicker than ever.

She was furious to think that Amy still had such a hold over Lenny, after everything he'd said to the contrary and everything Marnie had done to support him. But whatever she felt about Amy, she couldn't get Mark's words out of her head.

Lenny was about to be a father. How could he be so cruel as to snatch an innocent child and use it to force its mother to come back to him? That was disgusting.

And what if Mark was right about the gun? What if it went off and Cassie got hit?

Unable to bear the thought, Marnie reached for her phone.

Mark had told her not to interfere, but she would never forgive herself if something happened to that child and she'd done nothing to prevent it.

39

Tears trickled down Amy's cheeks and soaked the pillow below her head. Yates had banged away at her for ages but he hadn't been able to keep it up, so now he was pacing the bedroom floor, sucking angrily on a cigarette.

'This is your fault,' he said, kicking the bed as he passed and glaring at her in the dark. 'You've fucked everything up.'

'I didn't mean to,' Amy whimpered, desperate to get to her frightened child, who she'd heard crying a few minutes ago. 'I swear on the kids' lives I won't run away again.'

'That's what they all say, but they all run in the end. 'Cos you're a retard, and they can't stand the fuckin' sight of you . . .'

'Shut up!' Yates punched the side of his head in an effort to silence his mother's voice.

'Mongy little Lenny,' she sneered. *'Kissed the girls and made 'em cry, hung himself but wouldn't die . . .'*

'I'm warning you,' Yates hissed, his hand involuntarily going to his throat as the memory of the belt cutting into his flesh washed over him. 'Shut your mouth, or I'll kill you!'

'I didn't say anything,' Amy cried.

'I'm not talking to *you!*' Yates roared. 'Stay out of this – it's got nothing to do with you!'

Scared now, Amy eased herself up in the bed. 'Lenny, come and sit down,' she urged. 'There's no one here but us.'

'*She*'s here,' he snapped, his eyes glinting crazily as he turned and stared at her. 'She's *always* here. Don't pretend you can't hear her.'

'I'm ignoring her,' Amy said carefully, guessing that he had finally flipped. 'She doesn't matter. We're all that matters – you and me.'

Yates gave a sharp, bitter laugh. 'She won't let us be together. She's just gonna keep on pecking and pecking till there's nothing left, can't you see that?'

'We're stronger than her,' Amy said, wondering who the hell he was talking about. 'We can beat her if we stick together.'

'No, we can't,' Yates said defeatedly. 'I've tried, but you don't know her, you don't know what she's like. She's evil, and she won't stop till she destroys us.'

He paced the floor from wall to wall and back again. Then, turning back to Amy, he reached out and grabbed her by the wrist.

'What are you doing?' she squealed when he pulled her off the bed. 'Lenny, stop it! Talk to me!'

'Too late for talking,' he said through gritted teeth as he dragged her out onto the landing. 'There's only one way to get away from her. You want to be with me, don't you?'

'Yes, but not like this,' Amy protested, tripping as he hauled her down the stairs. 'You're going to frighten Cassie.'

'She's coming with us,' said Yates, pushing open the living-room door. 'Sorry I couldn't get the other one, but the three of us will be all right.'

Cassie was huddled on the couch, trying to stifle her sobs with the quilt. She took a fearful breath when Yates stalked into the room, but she stopped breathing altogether when she saw the hazy shape behind him.

'Sit with her and keep her quiet while I get things ready,'

Yates said, hurling Amy towards the couch. 'What do I need
. . . what do I need?'

Amy pulled Cassie into her arms and held her tight, her
gaze riveted on Yates as he walked in a circle, punching at
his head. She'd always known that he had a screw loose, but
this was real madness, and she was seriously scared.

'It's okay, baby, Mummy's here,' she whispered, her mouth
against Cassie's hair. 'I won't let him hurt you, I promise.'

Cassie was rigid in her arms, and the little girl's young
mind reeled. Her mummy was here: she could see her, hear
her, smell her. But her mummy hated her, so it couldn't be
real. It had to be a dream – a bad, bad dream.

40

'Whatever happens, just stay calm,' Steve cautioned when he had parked up around the corner from Amy's house.

'Easy for you to say,' said Mark, his legs shaking wildly as he climbed out of the car. 'It's not your kid in there with him. I could fucking kill Amy for taking off like that. Why didn't she ring to let me know she'd found them? She knew how worried I was.'

'He probably wouldn't let her,' Steve murmured, remembering what Amy had told him. 'And I wouldn't be too hard on her, 'cos it's been a nightmare for her, all this.'

'Whatever,' Mark muttered, setting off down the road. Steve might have fallen for Amy's sob story but Mark was having none of it. She'd had a row with Yates, but now they were back together she obviously thought she could keep Cassie and Mark would just roll over and accept it. Well, she was wrong. Mark had custody, and he wasn't leaving until he got his daughter back.

'What we gonna do?' Steve asked as they neared the house.

'Knock on the door and tell him I want Cassie back,' said Mark. 'He can't say no – he knows I've got the law on my side. Anyhow, he's got what he wanted.'

'Didn't you say Marnie said she'd already knocked and got no answer?'

'Even better if they're not there.' Mark shrugged. 'I've got my key. I'll just let myself in and take her.'

The house was in darkness when they reached it. Mark went up the path ahead of Steve and cautiously approached the front door. He could physically feel the tension coming from within as he knocked. He waited for a moment, then knocked again. Getting no response, he flashed Steve a nervous look and slotted his key into the lock.

41

Yates was huddled in the far corner of the room with his arms over his head. Still on the couch shielding Cassie, Amy could feel her heart racing with terror at the thought of what he might do when he got up again.

He'd paced the floor and argued with the phantom woman for a while after bringing Amy downstairs, and it seemed to have prevented him from getting his head together enough to carry out whatever crazy plan he'd dreamed up. Amy had a horrible feeling that he intended to kill them all, so the longer he stayed confused, the better chance she had of trying to talk him out of it. But, right now, she didn't dare make a sound for fear of tipping him even further over the edge.

Already on a knife's edge waiting for Yates to make his next move, she bit down hard on her lip to keep from crying out when the living-room door opened slowly. A wave of relief washed over her when she saw Mark's silhouetted figure, and Steve's taller, broader one immediately behind him. But it was a fleeting sensation, and when the fear returned it had intensified a thousandfold.

'*Go away . . .*' she mouthed, praying that Mark could see her as she surreptitiously shook her head. '*Don't come in.*'

But Mark was blinded by the darkness, and he walked slowly into the room while Steve crept upstairs to check the bedrooms.

'Len . . . are you here, mate? It's me – Mark . . . I've come for Cassie. You said I could have her back when you saw Amy, and it's past her bedtime.'

'Get out,' Yates said quietly from the corner. 'You don't belong here. This is holy ground.'

Mark stopped in his tracks and squinted into the gloom. The words were weird enough, but the way Yates had said them was even weirder. He caught a movement in the shadows out of the corner of his eye and jerked his head around. Amy was staring up at him from the couch.

'*Go . . .*' she hissed. '*Let me talk to him. It's me he wants.*'

'Not without Cassie,' said Mark. 'Hand her over, and I'm out of here.'

Steve came trotting down the stairs just then. 'There's no one up there,' he said, walking into the room, unaware that Mark had already found them. 'They must have gone before we—'

A shot rang out before he had a chance to finish what he was saying, and Amy squeezed her eyes shut and threw herself on top of Cassie as a body slumped heavily to the floor.

Still naked, having come downstairs straight from his unsuccessful attempt to have sex with Amy, Yates stood up and walked into the centre of the room with the gun held out in front of him.

'Filth,' he hissed. 'You've intruded on holy ground, so now you must die.'

'Mate, stop,' said Steve, backing away with his hands out in front of him. 'This has gone far enough. He was only trying to protect his kid – there was no need to shoot him. Just let me get them out of here, and no one will ever have to know it was you.'

'Death to the filth,' Yates replied, calmly aiming the gun at Steve now.

Amy cried out when another shot shattered the silence, and peeked out through her lashes. She could see the dark shapes of Mark lying in the middle of the floor and Steve slumped against the wall. Neither of them was moving, but one of them was moaning.

'Lenny, stop this,' she urged, thinking that, if she could just get him out of there, whichever of the men was still alive might be able to summon help. 'Let's just go. Just me and you. We can go away together, find somewhere to live where no one knows us.'

'We *are* going away,' said Yates, staring down at Mark. 'But not till I've made sure he can't follow us again.'

He squatted down beside Mark and placed the tip of the gun's barrel against his forehead.

Mark groaned and opened his eyes, and the last thing he ever saw was Yates's penis dangling limply between his legs.

Yates stood up and turned towards the couch. Under no illusion now that he might spare them, Amy sat up to shield her daughter. A cold calmness settling over her, she said, 'You're not hurting my child.'

'It won't hurt,' Yates assured her. 'I'll make it fast, I promise.'

Before Amy could reply, several police vehicles screeched to a halt outside. Blue flashing lights strobed through the curtains, and an amplified voice called: 'Armed police . . . You're surrounded, so drop your weapon and come out with your hands in the air . . .'

Yates flicked a glance at the window. Then, sighing, as if it was nothing but an irritation, he turned back to Amy and gestured with the gun for her to move away from Cassie.

'Hurry up – we haven't got much time. Best if I do her first, 'cos she'll only freak out if she has to watch you go.'

Amy leapt up off the couch and launched herself at him, screaming, 'CASSIE, *RUN!*' as she tore at his face with her nails and kicked and punched him with all her might. '*RUUUN . . . !*'

EPILOGUE

Amy put down her hairbrush when the bell rang and scrutinised her reflection in the mirror to check that nothing was out of place before she went to answer the door.

Ever since Yates had been sentenced to an indefinite term in Broadmoor, her life had been slowly but surely getting back on track.

Steve had been lucky. The bullet that Yates had fired at him had only skimmed his shoulder, and it had been the bang on the back of his head when he'd hit the wall that had felled him.

Mark hadn't been so lucky, and his funeral had been traumatic. Not so much for Bobby, who had been so doped up on the sleeping pills that Jenny had been feeding him that he'd been hard pushed to remember his own name at the time, never mind understand what was going on. But Cassie had been inconsolable. Which was only to be expected, considering what the poor mite had been through. But it had filled Amy with guilt to see her daughter breaking her little heart.

Jenny hadn't been invited to the funeral, and nobody had thought for one minute that she would dare to turn up since the truth had come out about the way she'd been mistreating the kids. When the police had gone round to tell her about Mark's death, she had demanded that they get Bobby out of her flat there and then, even though it had been the middle of the night. So when she had brazenly walked into the chapel in the middle of the service, weeping and wailing like a grieving widow, Amy had had to be physically restrained from attacking her.

The kids were living with Amy's mum and dad at the moment, and Amy had moved back home for a while, too. But it had torn her apart to watch her children accepting affection from her parents while shunning her own attempts to get close. Cassie had been the hardest to get through to. No matter how many times Amy told her that she had never stopped loving her, for some reason the child was convinced that Amy hated her.

'You left her, so she's bound to think you didn't want her,' Amy's mum had reasoned when Amy had sobbed her fears to her one night. 'She'll get over it in time. You've got to stop just saying that you love her and prove it instead.'

It was hard to take a back seat when all she wanted to do was hold her children in her arms, but Amy had agreed that it was probably best if she moved out to give the kids space to come to terms with everything in their own time. So when the council had offered her this flat, she'd taken it without hesitation.

It was her birthday today, and she'd decided to use it as a double celebration, a kind of birthday party plus house-warming. Nothing spectacular; just a few close friends, her mum and dad, and, most important of all, the kids.

She opened the door now, and smiled when she saw Marnie.

'Sorry I'm late,' Marnie apologised, pushing the pram over the step and into the hall. 'Mister Greedy wouldn't let me get ready.'

'Don't worry, you're the first,' Amy assured her, leaning over to peek at the baby boy who was snuggled in the pram. 'God, he looks more like his dad every time I see him,' she said, reaching in to stroke the child's silky jet-black hair. 'Majid must be proud.'

'Oh, he is.' Marnie smiled. 'He's been great. Gets up in the middle of the night to do the nappies, and everything.'

'I'm glad,' Amy said quietly. 'Could have been a lot worse.'

'Don't remind me.' Marnie shuddered. She didn't know how she'd managed to get her dates mixed up between sleeping with Majid and Lenny, but she would be eternally grateful for the way things had turned out.

The doorbell rang again. Telling Marnie to go into the living room, Amy answered it.

'Please take this child away from me,' Layla begged, thrusting the beautiful little girl she was carrying into Amy's arms. 'Steve's parking up, and I'm about to wet myself.'

'Toilet's back there.' Amy pointed the way. Then, chuckling softly as Steve's pregnant wife waddled off down the hall, she kissed the little girl on the nose, and purred, 'Hello, Isabella Rockerfella. Come to see Auntie Amy's new flat, have you?'

Steve walked in just then, and grinned when he saw his daughter giggling at Amy. 'How do you do that?' he asked, giving Amy a peck on the cheek. 'She was crying all the way here.'

'I've got the magic touch,' said Amy, handing the child over. 'Go and make yourself comfortable while I get the drinks out. Beer or wine?'

'Tea,' said Steve, rolling his eyes. 'Under orders from her majesty.' He nodded towards Layla who was coming back from the bathroom. 'Apparently, if *she*'s not allowed to drink, neither am I.'

'Too right,' said Layla, pushing him playfully. 'You're the one who wanted to have another baby without pausing for breath, so you can damn well suffer with me.'

Amused, Amy went into the kitchen to take the cling film off the plates of sandwiches and sausage rolls she'd prepared. When the doorbell rang again Steve answered it, and when she heard her father's voice Amy wiped her hands on her jeans and rushed out into the hall to see the kids. Not wanting to make them feel awkward, she resisted the urge to leap on them and smiled down at them instead.

'Don't you look smart,' she said to Bobby. 'And that dress is beautiful,' she added to Cassie. 'And I *love* that hairband.'

'What do you say?' Their grandmother gave them each a little prod in the shoulder.

'Happy birthday!' yelled Bobby, rushing forward and wrapping his arms around Amy's legs. Then, losing interest when he heard the sound of a baby in the living room, he ran off to investigate.

'Happy birthday,' said Cassie, giving Amy a shy little smile before handing over the gift-wrapped box she was holding. 'Nana and Grandad paid for it, but me and Bobbsy picked it. Hope you like it.'

'Thank you.' Amy squatted down and took the present from her. 'I'm sure it'll be absolutely perfect.'

Cassie suddenly jerked her head forward and planted a kiss on Amy's cheek. Then she turned and ran after her brother.

Tears glistening in her eyes, Amy looked up at her mother.

'Told you they'd come round in time,' Sonia said quietly. 'Just let them come to you – that's the trick.'

Amy nodded and stood up. Laughing when her dad said, 'Where's me beer? Thought you'd have been waiting with it at the door,' she went into the kitchen to get a can out of the fridge.

Sonia followed and looked at the food on the ledge with disapproval as she slipped off her coat.

'Is that it? That's nowhere near enough. And where are your serviettes? You can't expect people to drop crumbs on themselves.'

'I've got it all under control,' Amy assured her, pushing her gently towards the door. 'There's a kitchen roll and plates on the table in the front room, and I've got an extra loaf so I can make more butties if we run out. And there's another tray of sausage rolls in the oven.'

'What about the cake?' Sonia asked, resisting as Amy tried to push her out. 'You can't have a party without cake.'

'*Mum . . .*' Amy gave her a mock-weary look.

The doorbell rang again. Glancing past her mother when Steve came out of the living room to answer it, Amy felt the heat rise to her cheeks when she saw who it was.

'Mum,' she said, her voice suddenly shy. 'This is the friend I told you about. Kelvin . . . this is my mum.'

Kelvin limped up the hall. Then, moving his walking stick to his other side, he held out his hand. 'Really pleased to meet you. Amy's told me all about you.'

Amy held her breath and waited for her mum's reaction. She knew she wouldn't be rude, but her eyes would give her away if she didn't approve.

Sonia shook his hand, and said, 'Very nice to meet you, too.' Then, turning to Amy, she raised an eyebrow, and mouthed, '*Ooh, he's lovely,*' before leaving them alone.

'Did I pass the test?' Kelvin whispered.

'I'd say so,' Amy whispered back. 'But that was the easy bit. You've still got to meet the kids yet.'

'Can't wait,' said Kelvin, pulling her towards him with his free arm and kissing her softly on the lips.